Praise for Catherine Bybee

Wife by Wednesday

"A fun and sizzling romance, great characters that trade verbal spars like fist punches, and the dream of your own royal wedding!"

—Sizzling Hot Book Reviews (5 stars)

"A good holiday, fireside or bedtime story."

—Manic Reviews (4½ stars)

"A great story that I hope is the start of a new series."

—The Romance Studio (4½ hearts)

Married by Monday

"If I hadn't already added Ms. Catherine Bybee to my list of favorite authors, after reading this book I would have been compelled to. This is a book *nobody* should miss, because the magic it contains is awesome."

—Booked Up Reviews (5 stars)

"Ms. Bybee writes authentic situations and expresses the good and the bad in such an equal way . . . Keeps the reader on the edge of her seat."

—Reading Between the Wines (5 stars)

"*Married by Monday* was a refreshing read and one I couldn't possibly put down."

—The Romance Studio (4½ hearts)

Fiancé by Friday

"Bybee knows exactly how to keep readers happy . . . A thrilling pursuit and enough passion to stuff in your back pocket to last for the next few lifetimes . . . The hero and heroine come to life with each flip of the page and will linger long after readers cross the finish line."

—*RT Book Reviews* (4½ stars, top pick [hot])

"A tale full of danger and sexual tension . . . the intriguing characters add emotional depth, ensuring readers will race to the perfectly fitting finish."

—*Publishers Weekly*

"Suspense, survival, and chemistry mix in this scintillating read."

—*Booklist*

"Hot romance, a mystery assassin, British royalty, and an alpha Marine . . . this story has it all!"

—*Harlequin Junkie*

Single by Saturday

"Captures readers' hearts and keeps them glued to the pages until the fascinating finish . . . romance lovers will feel the sparks fly . . . almost instantaneously."

—*RT Book Reviews* (4½ stars, top pick)

"[A] wonderfully exciting plot, lots of desire, and some sassy attitude thrown in for good measure!"

—*Harlequin Junkie*

Taken by Tuesday

"[Bybee] knows exactly how to get bookworms sucked into the perfect storyline; then she casts her spell upon them so they don't escape until they reach the 'Holy Cow!' ending."

—*RT Book Reviews* (4½ stars, top pick)

Seduced by Sunday

"You simply can't miss [this novel]. It contains everything a romance reader loves—clever dialogue, three-dimensional characters, and just the right amount of steam to go with that heartwarming love story."

—Brenda Novak, *New York Times* bestselling author

"Bybee hits the mark . . . providing readers with a smart, sophisticated romance between a spirited heroine and a prim hero . . . Passionate and intelligent characters [are] at the heart of this entertaining read."

—*Publishers Weekly*

Treasured by Thursday

"The Weekday Brides never disappoint and this final installment is by far Bybee's best work to date."

—*RT Book Reviews* (4½ stars, top pick)

"An exquisitely written and complex story brimming with pride, passion, and pulse-pounding danger . . . Readers will gladly make time to savor this winning finale to a wonderful series."

—*Publishers Weekly* (starred review)

"Bybee concludes her popular *Weekday Brides* series in a gratifying way with a passionate, troubled couple who may find a happy future if they can just survive and then learn to trust each other. A compelling and entertaining mix of sexy, complicated romance and menacing suspense."

—*Kirkus Reviews*

Not Quite Dating

"It's refreshing to read about a man who isn't afraid to fall in love . . . [Jack and Jessie] fit together as a couple and as a family."

—*RT Book Reviews* (3 stars [hot])

"*Not Quite Dating* offers a sweet and satisfying Cinderella fantasy that will keep you smiling long after you've finished reading."

—Kathy Altman, *USA Today*, *Happy Ever After* blog

"The perfect rags to riches romance . . . The dialogue is inventive and witty, the characters are well drawn out. The storyline is superb and really shines . . . I highly recommend this standout romance! Catherine Bybee is an automatic buy for me."

—*Harlequin Junkie* (4½ hearts)

Not Quite Enough

"Bybee's gift for creating unforgettable romances cannot be ignored. The third book in the Not Quite series will sweep readers away to a paradise, and they will be intrigued by the thrilling story that accompanies their literary vacation."

—*RT Book Reviews* (4½ stars, top pick)

Not Quite Forever

"Full of classic Bybee humor, steamy romance, and enough plot twists and turns to keep readers entertained all the way to the very last page."

—Tracy Brogan, bestselling author of the Bell Harbor series

"Magnetic . . . The love scenes are sizzling and the multi-dimensional characters make this a page-turner. Readers will look for earlier installments and eagerly anticipate new ones."

—*Publishers Weekly*

Not Quite Perfect

"This novel flows extremely well and readers will find themselves consuming the witty dialogue and strong imagery in one sitting."

—*RT Book Reviews*

"Don't let the title fool you. *Not Quite Perfect* [is] actually the perfect story to sweep you away and take you on a pleasant adventure. So sit back, relax, maybe pour a glass of wine, and let Catherine Bybee entertain you with Glen and Mary's playful East Coast–West Coast romance. You won't regret it for a moment."

—*Harlequin Junkie* (4½ stars)

Not Quite Crazy

"This fast-paced story features credible characters whose appealing relationship is built upon friendship, mutual respect, and sizzling chemistry."

—*Publishers Weekly*

"The plot is filled with twists and turns, but instead of feeling like a never-ending roller coaster, the story maintains a quiet flow. The slow buildup of a romance allows readers to get to know the main characters as individuals and makes the romantic element more organic."

—*RT Book Reviews*

Doing It Over

"The romance between fiercely independent Melanie and charming Wyatt heats up even as outsiders threaten to derail their newfound happiness. This novel will hook readers with its warm, inviting characters and the promise for similar future installments."

—*Publishers Weekly*

"This brand-new trilogy, Most Likely To, based on yearbook superlatives, kicks off with a novel that will encourage you to root for the incredibly likable Melanie. Her friends are hilarious and readers will swoon over Wyatt, who is charming and strong. Even Melanie's daughter, Hope, is a hoot! This romance is jam-packed with animated characters, and Bybee displays her creative writing talent wonderfully."

—*RT Book Reviews* (4 stars)

"With a dialogue full of energy and depth, and a twisting storyline that captured my attention, I would say that *Doing It Over* was a great way to start off a new series. (And look at that gorgeous book cover!) I can't wait to visit River Bend again and see who else gets to find their HEA."

—*Harlequin Junkie* (4½ stars)

Staying For Good

"Bybee's skillfully crafted second Most Likely To contemporary (after *Doing It Over*) brings together former sweethearts who have not forgotten each other in the eleven years since high school. A cast of multidimensional characters brings the story to life and promises enticing future installments."

—*Publishers Weekly*

"Romance fans will be sure to cheer on former high school sweethearts Zoe and Luke right away in *Staying For Good*. Just wait until you see what passion, laughter, reconciliations, and mischief (can you say Vegas?) awaits readers this time around. Highly recommended."

—*Harlequin Junkie* (4½ stars)

Making It Right

"Intense suspense heightens the scorching romance at the heart of Bybee's outstanding third Most Likely To contemporary (after *Staying For Good*). Sizzling sensual scenes are coupled with scary suspense in this winning novel."

—*Publishers Weekly* (starred review)

Fool Me Once

"A marvelous portrait of friendship among women who have been bonded by fire."

—*Library Journal* (best of the year 2017)

"Bybee still delivers a story that her die-hard readers will enjoy."

—*Publishers Weekly*

Half Empty

"Wade and Trina here in *Half Empty* just might be one of my favorite couples Catherine Bybee has gifted us fans with so far. Captivating, engaging, lively and dreamy, I simply could not get enough of this book."

—*Harlequin Junkie* (5 stars)

"Part rock star romance, part romantic thriller, I really enjoyed this book."

—*Romance Reader*

Faking Forever

"A charming contemporary with surprising depth . . . Bybee perfectly portrays a woman trying to hold out for Mr. Right despite the pressures of time. A pitch-perfect plot and a cast of sympathetic and lovable supporting characters make this book one to add to the keeper shelf."

—*Publishers Weekly*

"Catherine Bybee can do no wrong as far as I'm concerned . . . Passionate, sultry, and filled with genuine emotions that ran the gamut, *Faking Forever* was a journey of self-discovery and of a love that was truly meant to be. Highly recommended."

—*Harlequin Junkie*

Say It Again

"Steamy, fast-paced, and consistently surprising, with a large cast of feisty supporting characters, this suspenseful roller-coaster ride will keep both series fans and new readers on the edge of their seats."

—*Publishers Weekly*

My Way to You

"A fascinating novel that aptly balances disastrous circumstances."

—*Kirkus Reviews*

"*My Way to You* is an unforgettable book fueled by Catherine Bybee's own life, along with the dynamic cast she created that will capture your heart."

—*Harlequin Junkie*

Home to Me

"Bybee skillfully avoids both melodrama and melancholy by grounding her characters in genuine emotion . . . This is Bybee in top form."

—*Publishers Weekly* (starred review)

Everything Changes

"This sweet, sexy book is just the escapism many people are looking for right now."

—*Kirkus Reviews*

The Whole Time

"Adorable. Sweet. Sparky. Sexy. Full of good food and wine and family and friends and all the things! I so need to see this series on TV one day! *The Whole Time* was such an adorable + fun + sweet + sparky + just beautiful romance—I loved it! Run to your nearest book dealer for your own Ryan—this one is mine!"

—*BJ's Book Blog*

Maybe One Day

OTHER TITLES BY CATHERINE BYBEE

Contemporary Romance

Weekday Brides Series

Wife by Wednesday
Married by Monday
Fiancé by Friday
Single by Saturday
Taken by Tuesday
Seduced by Sunday
Treasured by Thursday

Not Quite Series

Not Quite Dating
Not Quite Mine
Not Quite Enough
Not Quite Forever
Not Quite Perfect
Not Quite Crazy

Most Likely To Series

Doing It Over
Staying For Good
Making It Right

First Wives Series

Fool Me Once

Half Empty

Chasing Shadows

Faking Forever

Say It Again

Creek Canyon Series

My Way to You

Home to Me

Everything Changes

Richter Series

Changing the Rules

A Thin Disguise

An Unexpected Distraction

The D'Angelos Series

When It Falls Apart

Be Your Everything

Beginning of Forever

The Whole Time

The Heirs Series

All Our Tomorrows

The Forgotten One

No More Yesterdays

Paranormal Romance

MacCoinnich Time Travels

Binding Vows

Silent Vows

Redeeming Vows

Highland Shifter

Highland Protector

The Ritter Werewolves Series

Before the Moon Rises

Embracing the Wolf

Novellas

Soul Mate

Possessive

Erotica

Kilt Worthy

Kilt-A-Licious

Maybe One Day

CATHERINE BYBEE

This is a work of fiction. Names, characters, organizations, places, events, and incidents are either products of the author's imagination or are used fictitiously. Otherwise, any resemblance to actual persons, living or dead, is purely coincidental.

Published by Montlake, Seattle

www.apub.com

EU product safety contact:
Amazon Media EU S. à r.l.
38, avenue John F. Kennedy, L-1855 Luxembourg
amazonpublishing-gpsr@amazon.com

ISBN-13: 9781662517204 (paperback)
ISBN-13: 9781662517211 (digital)

Cover design by Caroline Teagle Johnson
Cover image: © Jacobs Stock Photography Ltd, © jomphon penvijit, © Kirk Fisher / Getty

Printed in the United States of America

To my readers.
The ones who encourage me to write another book in a series even after I think I'm done.

CHAPTER ONE

"Mama! I told you I was cooking tonight."

Mari cocked her head to the side and motioned toward the plate filled with caprese salad.

"Cooking? This isn't cooking. This is slicing and stacking. No oven or stove was involved." She picked up the platter with both hands and headed up the stairs toward the voices of her family.

Luca, her oldest son, clicked his tongue and followed her. The scent of his baked ziti lofted from his hands.

One step onto the balcony, and Dante relieved her of the platter, winked, and turned toward the long table that already overflowed with food.

"Gio," Luca called over to his brother. "Give Mama a glass of wine to keep her hands busy."

Mari lifted both of her hands in the air in full Italian animation and said, "What?"

Gio slid to her side and placed a glass of something red in her palm.

"Mari. Let our children do the work. We deserve to rest." Rosa, her closest friend, patted the seat beside her on the outdoor couch and scooted to the side.

Mari smiled and conceded.

This was her favorite day of the month.

Sundays, as a rule, had always been a family day. Now with her family completely filled out, she needed to share those Sundays more often than not.

But this first Sunday of the month was hers.

Luca and his wife, Brooke, lived on the floor above hers. Franny and Leo, her precious grandchildren, were the constant joy in Mari's daily life.

Giovanni, or Gio as they all called him, poured the wine and helped his older brother, Luca, with the food on the table. Gio's wife, Emma, sat across from Mari with her feet up and five months' worth of growing babies weighing her down.

Mari took the first sip of her wine and imagined what the twins would look like when they were born. According to the doctors, a perfectly matched set of boys would join their family in four months.

"How are my grandsons treating you?" Mari asked Emma.

She patted her stomach with a grin. "My bladder is a trampoline and sleep is something I did in my twenties."

Mari placed a hand to her chest. "I wish I could do something."

"They will be worth it."

"You'll have lots of help when they're born," Gio said from across the patio.

"I will remind you of that," Emma retorted.

Chloe, Mari's daughter, held Leo on her hip and danced around to the music playing in the background.

Rosa leaned closer to Mari. "Anything from them yet?"

Chloe and Dante had been married for nearly two years, and as far as Mari and Rosa were concerned, that was too long to wait for a grandchild.

Mari, at least, had others to occupy her time and sate her thirst for grandbabies. Rosa, on the other hand, had none.

Mari shook her head, and Rosa grumbled.

The rapid footfalls tumbling toward her could come from only one source . . .

Franny.

At ten years old and rapidly reaching eleven, Franny had yet to completely slow down when family was close by.

Luca caught his daughter and whispered something in her ear.

Franny turned back toward the stairs and disappeared.

Brooke passed Luca, only to be caught in his arm, and they shared a brief kiss. A touch to the cheek and a smile.

Mari's heart was full.

"Everything is on autopilot at the restaurant," Salena announced when she walked through the door.

Salena was Mari's honorary daughter, and family by default. She also worked as a part-time manager of the family restaurant on the bottom floor of the building.

"Where is my brother?" Emma asked.

Salena had married Ryan, Emma's brother, the previous year. "There's traffic getting off the Point. He'll be here." Salena turned to Gio. "Where's my wine?"

Gio laughed but was quick to take care of her request.

"Is this yours?" she asked.

"Yes."

Gio and Emma had a vineyard in Temecula and had completed their third harvest the previous fall.

The lifelong dream of Mari's sommelier son was to own his own label, have a wife and a dozen children. Though from the looks of poor Emma pregnant with twins, Gio might have to settle for half a dozen.

"Not bad," Salena teased.

Gio wagged a finger in Salena's direction, but smiled. "Better than 'not bad,'" he said.

Salena nudged her shoulder against his with a grin.

Brooke took a seat across from Emma.

Mari felt a hand against hers and looked away from her children. "Seems like only yesterday that was us," Rosa said.

"What do you mean?"

"Young, in love . . . just starting our lives."

Mari sighed. "We're not so old."

"Easy for you to say."

"You're two years older than me."

Brooke began laughing. "You're both younger than you act," she said.

Mari and Rosa both scoffed at the same time.

"Seriously," Brooke said. "My friend Carmen's mom just turned fifty-five. She and a group of friends take two trips a year, one cruise and one random trip abroad. About half the women are single, the others happily married . . . or unhappily married, it's hard to tell. Carmen and I joined them on a five-day trip, and let me tell you . . . these ladies partied like women in college."

"That sounds exhausting," Mari said.

"It might not if you took a little more time for yourself," Emma suggested.

"I have a restaurant to run."

Brooke pinned her with a stare. "Chloe . . . help me out here."

Chloe tore her gaze away from her nephew and glanced at Mari. "I'm with Brooke. You turn fifty-five next month, Mama. You're not old. And the restaurant runs without you."

"Why does it feel as if you're turning me out to pasture at the same time you're telling me I'm not old?"

"That's not what I'm saying, Mama, and you know it. When was the last time you left San Diego?" Chloe asked. "It was before Papa passed."

Just the mention of her late husband put a soft smile to Mari's face. Her life with Paulo felt like a lifetime ago. "I had a family to take care of. Frivolous time away wasn't possible."

"Mama, I was seventeen. Gio was just twenty and Luca twenty-three. We weren't exactly children."

"It's been almost ten years, right?" Brooke asked. "Since Paulo passed?"

"Ten years next month," Mari said without missing a beat. "He held on until my birthday." She felt a familiar ache that always accompanied his memory. But time had done what time does and softened the pain until it was nothing more than a passing memory.

"A forty-five-year-old widow. So young," Emma said.

Mari met her daughter-in-law's eyes. "We lived a lifetime. We were children when we met. Nineteen when we married. I had twenty-five wonderful years with Paulo. I'm thankful every day we met when we did or we would have missed out on so much."

Chloe handed Leo to Brooke and moved to sit on the arm of the outdoor couch by Mari.

Leo took that moment to mumble "Nonna" as his little arms reached toward her.

Mari sat her wineglass down and lifted her arms toward her grandson.

Brooke reached across the table and handed him over.

Leo instantly placed his hand on Mari's face, his tiny fingers slipping into her mouth.

"Papa would have wanted you to go out and live a little," Chloe told her.

"I live every day." Mari smiled at Leo and bounced her knee. "Don't I?"

"I think your daughter has a point," Rosa said. "Maybe we should find a group of women our age to travel with."

"And go where?" Mari asked, somewhat tired of the conversation.

"Anywhere. We've raised our children, sacrificed for them." Rosa sipped her wine and looked off as if already on a vacation.

"Dinner is ready," Luca called from the table.

Mari placed a finger on Leo's nose. "Saved by your papa."

They migrated to the table, where Mari took her place at one end while Luca took the other.

Before she knew it, plates were passed, and everyone seemed to be talking at once.

God, she loved her family. Every loud one of them.

Her voice grew hoarse, and her cheeks hurt with the muscles it took to smile so much. With full bellies and heads warm with wine, they talked until the space heaters on the terrace had stopped doing their jobs and the night air became too much.

One by one, everyone made their way back home. The only exception was Gio and Emma. They had the longest drive and decided to stay in the fourth-floor apartment above Luca and Brooke's.

The layout of the family home above the restaurant had worked since before Mari and Paulo had taken over the building.

The stairway connecting the apartments was closed off to the restaurant with only a door. The arrangement was both a blessing and a curse. Though Mari never really thought about it that way until she started pulling away from the daily responsibilities of the restaurant. It was so easy to turn a day off into a workday. Even on Sundays. It simply wasn't possible, as the owner of D'Angelo's, to walk past a staff member with an issue without being pulled aside with an "I have a quick question."

After making sure her kitchen was spotless, Mari made her way into the heart of D'Angelo's, where a half a dozen tables were still occupied by customers and some of the staff was being flexed off.

Sergio, the long-time bartender, was on deck to close, allowing Mari, Luca, and Salena to turn in early.

"*Buonasera*," Mari greeted her friend.

Sergio smiled with a wink. "What are you doing? Shouldn't you be upstairs watching a late show?"

"I'm going." Mari looked around the room. "Smooth night?" she asked.

"Only had to call the police twice," he teased.

She took the hint, said her good nights, and made her way upstairs.

While the entire stairwell may have had a rudimentary shape, there were windows on every landing, and it had been given a warm coat of paint, decorative moldings, and family photos.

The lights on the stairs were left on, but Mari turned off the ones in her apartment and made her way to bed.

Not much had changed in her bedroom since Paulo had passed. The thought jumped into her head faster than she could stop it.

Even though the conversation had moved on from her and Rosa flying off to God-knew-where, that didn't mean Mari had stopped thinking about it. Paulo had entered her thoughts several times throughout the evening, which somewhat surprised her.

Of late, when she was alone with her thoughts, she wondered how her life would be different if Paulo was still with her.

The two extra bedrooms in her apartment had been vacant for a few years now. Almost all of her children's things had been removed, leaving only empty beds and echoes of memories.

Luca and his family had defaulted to this building as their residence. But did they stay there because of her? Someday they might want a home with a yard. A place for a dog that Franny had been begging for since she saw her first puppy. And shouldn't she have that? Shouldn't Luca have the choice?

Chloe was right. The restaurant did run without her. At least the cooking portion. Luca managed the kitchen. Took many of the shifts. Mari only filled in on the occasion of a sick employee or someone wanting time off. Ironically, something Mari hadn't done in over ten years.

And Salena ran the rest of the staff. Though that was limited. Newly married with her own business building, it was only a matter of time before Salena moved on.

Piece by piece, Mari dusted her hands of the daily responsibility of the restaurant. Her father had been younger than her when he passed the establishment over to her and Paulo to return to Italy. They'd been so young, so full of energy to take on the restaurant and make it theirs.

Mari wondered, if her husband was still alive, would they have done the same to Luca? Would they be staring down at retirement in ten years and walk away then?

But Paulo wasn't there.

And what would Mari do if not for her business keeping her busy?

As these random thoughts and memories swam in her head, Mari changed into her pajamas and brushed her teeth.

On her way to bed, she grabbed a photo album and snuggled with the covers up to her waist before she began flipping through the familiar images.

She ran a finger over a high school image of her. Two years before she met Paulo.

The faded color photograph had been taken by the San Diego Harbor. The city skyline was much less developed and barely recognizable from what stood there now.

This, Mari mused, was why she felt so old.

So much had changed in Little Italy in the life she'd lived there. Which was all of it.

Her parents had opened the restaurant back when Little Italy was twice the size it was today.

According to her father, what was once a fishermen's village with Italian roots thrived when he'd first come to America to start a new life. Then, around the time of Mari's birth, San Diego expanded, and construction of the 5 freeway split Little Italy in half.

The photograph she was looking at had been taken after many people in the community had sold and fled to the suburbs. Those that were left struggled.

Thankfully, Mari's parents had built their living quarters on top of the restaurant, and they stuck it out.

Mari flipped the page of the photo album, knowing what came next.

"Look how young I was." Just a baby.

She imagined Franny walking down the aisle in nine short years and shook her head. No wonder her parents had put up such a fight when she and Paulo pleaded their undying love.

But things had worked out for them when so many young married couples didn't stand the test of time.

Rosa was a prime example of that.

Her husband felt forced into their marriage and regretted it from the beginning. Eventually, he'd gone on a "business trip" to Italy and never came home.

It had only been a year since Rosa's divorce had been finalized, even though she'd been alone for some time now.

And Rosa was itchy.

Something had taken hold of her between Chloe and Dante's marriage and Rosa's divorce.

The cozy conversations about easing into the next thirty years of their lives with grandchildren and family dinners didn't seem to be enough for her.

Probably because Rosa wasn't blessed with grandbabies . . . yet.

The evening conversation about age and next chapters might have been recently brought up by her family, but Mari had been listening to Rosa carry on for months.

Damn if Rosa hadn't planted a tiny seed.

One that had Mari pulling out old photographs and trying to remember what life was like before she was left on her own with her children.

Before Paulo got sick.

"You're too young to live your life alone, bella.*" Paulo's hand rested on Mari's cheek just days before his last hospitalization.*

They both knew his time was limited.

He'd lived longer than predicted, desperate to see that his family was going to be okay once he was gone.

"I have our children. I will never be alone," Mari told him softly.

"And they will have families of their own. Franny will have brothers and sisters . . . cousins, with our children tucking them in at night. But who will tuck you in, cara?*"*

Paulo's frail hand looked thirty years older than it was with his body decaying from the inside. He gripped her hand and placed his dry lips to her fingertips. "Promise me."

"Promise you what?"

"That you'll look for love again."

The thought of another man gutted her. "You can't ask that of me."

"I can and I am. You're too young and too full of life. This cancer has robbed us of laughter for so long. I want to leave knowing you'll dance again."

She placed a finger over his lips. Telling him she would look again someday was a lie. Denying his last request was cruel.

Mari gave him the only thing she could.

"Maybe one day. Many years from now."

That seemed to sate the tension behind his eyes and allowed his breathing to slow.

Mari remembered the bone-tired agony of those days.

She'd spent every moment possible beside him. Forcing herself to stay up and capture every second she could when he was awake.

Her forty-fifth birthday had come, and within three days, Paulo was gone.

With him went her promise of "Maybe one day."

Mari pressed her lips to her fingers and touched the photograph from their wedding day before closing the book and setting it aside.

She turned the light off and rolled to her side.

Her hand reached for the pillow on the other side of the bed. She tried to remember the way he looked lying beside her. Or the sound of his soft snores, or loud ones on days he worked too hard.

His touch . . . it was almost impossible to remember the way he held her. The feeling of safety was all she recalled. And when his body weakened, that feeling was gone and replaced with dread.

As much as Mari had tried to toss aside everything negative about those days, the dread of being left without her husband had lingered like nothing before or since.

Not when her parents had returned to Italy.

Not when her mother had died soon after.

Not when Luca's first marriage had fallen apart.

The uncontrollable fear of living her life without Paulo was only tolerable with her children at her side.

She'd kept it together for them.

And wept when she was alone.

Those tears were gone now.

She didn't love Paulo any less.

Mari simply didn't let grief take hold any longer.

CHAPTER TWO

"We're going to bunco."

Mari looked up from her desk to see Rosa standing in the doorway. "We're going to what?"

"Bunco." Rosa pushed past the door and dropped her purse on the desk before folding into a chair.

"What's a bunco?"

"It's a game."

"Like football?"

Rosa rolled her eyes. A new habit she'd picked up somewhere between filing for divorce and signing the final papers.

"No, not like football. It's a game with dice."

"I have zero interest in going to Vegas." Mari returned her attention to the inventory order she was in the process of filling out.

"Bunco isn't a game you play in Vegas. It's played with twelve people, three tables, and three sets of dice. It's easy."

Mari stopped writing and glanced at her friend. "And why are we doing this?"

"It's called fun, Mari. Remember fun?" Rosa asked.

Mari returned Rosa's roll of her eyes and went back to the restaurant's inventory list. "I have to work."

"I haven't even told you when it is yet."

"Doesn't matter, I have to work. Inventory orders don't create themselves."

Salena's voice from the doorway had Mari and Rosa looking at her. "Actually, they do."

Salena stepped into the office and placed a digital order form in front of Mari to review. "The new program we're using is saving man-hours for more important things."

"Like playing bunco!" Rosa announced.

"That sounds fun. When are you guys doing that?" Salena asked.

"Tonight. Seven o'clock."

"Is it close by, or do you need a ride?"

Mari squeezed her brows together while Rosa and Salena discussed the evening's activities as if it were a foregone conclusion that it was happening. "Why would we need a ride?" Mari asked.

Salena shrugged. "The nickname for bunco is drunko. I substituted twice for a group where I used to work. Halfway into the second round, they were pretty ripped."

"I don't get *ripped*," Mari reminded her.

"There's always a first time."

Rosa stood, picked up her purse, and hiked it high on her shoulder. "I'll be here at six thirty. We'll grab an Uber."

"I didn't—"

Rosa patted Salena on the shoulder and said, "Make sure she's not in her pajamas."

"You got it."

Mari loved Salena like her own daughter . . . but sometimes . . . "My evening just got hijacked."

"You'll have fun, trust me."

Mari released a long-suffering breath and glanced down at her order sheet. The numbers on her handwritten form were identical to Salena's new digital system that she and Luca had insisted on.

With the restaurant fully staffed and the kitchen manned by her son, apparently, she was going to learn a new game and possibly overdrink.

~

Pinching the bridge of his nose, James squeezed his eyes shut and listened to the fast-paced, overly loud voice of his daughter.

"I can't find my cleats! I have to have them."

Sitting behind his desk with his phone on speaker, there wasn't a whole heck of a lot he could do about helping Ellie with her current tragedy. "Have you looked in the garage?"

"They're not there."

"The laundry room?"

"Nope."

"What about under the mound of crap on the side of your bed?"

"They're not there, Dad," she yelled. The sound of a door slamming through the phone suggested Ellie was franticly rummaging through the house, leaving chaos along her path.

James sighed. "Did you leave them at your mom's?"

"I had them yesterday."

And since it was his week, the missing cleats had to be in the house . . . somewhere.

"Maybe your sister knows?"

Ellie didn't miss a breath before she yelled her sister's name at the top of her lungs. "Maddie!"

James winced, let loose his nose, and stared at the monitor on his desk.

"Did you check the trunk of your car?"

His question landed on deaf ears.

Ellie's out-of-breath voice lowered a smidge. "Have you seen my cleats?"

"No. And I haven't smelled them either."

James grinned, knowing full well the scent Madison spoke of.

Ellie made a noise between a growl and a moan. "I'm starting to freak. I'm going to be late for practice." Softball was Ellie's life. She'd taken the sport and made it her religion since she was old enough to catch a ball and hit it with a bat.

And she was good.

So much so that she was likely going to have her pick of DI colleges to choose from in only a few short months.

"Did you check the trunk of your car?" James asked again.

"Of course I did."

"Check again."

An exasperated sigh escaped his daughter's lips.

He heard the screen on the side door of the house clap against its frame, indicating Ellie was walking out to the driveway. "I'm telling you, they're not here."

James held his tongue when he imagined the dumpster-fire mess in her car that matched her bedroom.

"Coach Gusmann is going to be . . ."

Ellie's words trailed off.

James smiled.

"Found them."

"You know if you kept things cleaner, you'd—"

"Gotta go. Thanks, Dad."

Ellie hung up.

"You'd keep my hair from falling out," James said to the disconnected line.

He glanced from the screen of his phone that faded to black to the picture of his daughters standing beside each other, their heads close together as they stared into the camera.

They were not identical twins, but they did look a whole lot alike. Dusty blonde hair that Ellie wore shorter than Madison. Same blue eyes and determined jaws.

Madison's face was rounded like her mother's, while Ellie's took on more of James's.

Ellie had a tiny scar on the side of her eye from a slide into third base in her freshman year of high school.

Personality-wise, Ellie and Madison couldn't be more different.

Ellie lived her life on fire. Frantically spinning like a stockbroker in a bear market.

Madison had moments of that enthusiasm, but she was more of a flame from a match and not a wildfire. Madison was all books and AP classes.

Instead of a DI college, she had her eyes set on Caltech.

While James was equally proud of his daughters and their drive and determination to follow their passions, he knew that Madison would leave college with the skills to obtain a job.

Ellie seemed to think that she was destined to play professional softball, and the liberal arts degree she had down as her desired major was her means to get there.

Even though James suffered an aching head on many of the days his daughters were with him, he did his best to relish them. His nest would be empty a mere seven months from now.

James's secretary, AJ, stuck his head around the door. "Mr. Colton is here."

James stood and buttoned his jacket before sliding around his desk.

Now that Ellie's cleat dilemma was behind him, it was time to do the job that would afford his daughters a college education.

~

They were on threes during their first round of bunco, and Mari and Rosa had been there for well over an hour.

Apparently, eating and drinking were the more favored parts of the game.

Which was a practice Mari knew very well.

Ten new faces of women ranging in age from thirty-five to sixty-one welcomed her like they'd known her for years.

Rosa had met Summer, a name Mari remembered only because of its uniqueness, at a singles meet-and-greet event the previous week. An event Mari had managed to dodge, unlike bunco night.

Despite going in with a *not all that interested* attitude, Mari found herself utterly amused.

Their hostess, Leandra . . . or Leanda, Mari didn't quite catch the right name, had kicked her husband and son out of the house to entertain for the evening.

Mari had asked, "Your husband is okay with that?"

Leandra/Leanda replied, "I only do this once a year, he better be."

Hosting bunco rotated every month, spreading the "entertaining burden" around.

A term Mari couldn't identify with.

Especially how this group of women worked.

Everyone brought a dish, or in her and Rosa's case, wine.

Guilt scratched at Mari's spine when she realized bunco was a potluck. She never missed an opportunity to feed people.

Not that she needed to worry herself about anyone going hungry.

Aside from dinner, there were dishes of candy on each table.

Mari rolled the dice, didn't come up with any threes, and passed the dice to the player on her left.

"Do you have kids?" Summer, her current partner, asked from across the table.

"Three. And two grandbabies, with two more on the way."

The woman on her left rolled one three, picked up the dice, and rolled again. "How old are your kids?"

Mari rattled off their ages and was met with surprise.

"You don't look old enough to have a son in his thirties."

"I was a young bride," Mari said.

Summer rolled the dice, got two threes, which Mari tallied on her sheet. "I would imagine grandkids keep you and your husband busy."

Mari shook her head. "No, I'm a . . . widow."

Summer hesitated with the dice in the palm of her hand. "I'm so sorry."

"It's okay. It's been nearly ten years."

"You're kidding," the woman on her right said.

"Cancer," Mari replied matter-of-factly.

"That's awful."

"How did you survive that?" Summer asked.

"One day at a time."

The dice shifted to the left and were tossed onto the table.

"Ten years is a long time. Are you dating?"

Mari glanced down at the paper the woman on her right was using as a score sheet to try and see her name.

Susan.

"No . . . no. I don't. No."

"Never?" Susan asked.

Mari shrugged and picked up the dice to roll. "I loved my husband."

"But—"

"And was raising my children."

"But ten years?"

No threes were thrown, and Susan picked up the dice.

"Bunco!" one of the women yelled out from another table, halting that round.

Susan and her partner had the higher score, which meant Summer and Mari needed to move to another table.

Mari was once again partnered with Rosa.

"Mari just told us she hasn't dated for ten years," Summer announced before Mari could sip from her wine.

"I lost my husband, we didn't divorce. Dating hasn't entered my mind."

"Not even once?" the woman Mari had yet to talk to asked.

"I've encouraged her," Rosa said.

"I wouldn't even know how."

"What's to know? You meet an available man, he's not an asshole, you go out," Summer instructed.

Rosa started to laugh. "Where do you find him?"

"The *available man* or the *not an asshole*?"

Mari felt a genuine smile on her lips.

"Both," Rosa said.

"Not in the same place." Summer picked up the dice.

"I thought the event you two met at was a place for singles," Mari said.

"It is," Summer said. "There are new people every time I go. But it's pretty easy to figure out why the men are single."

"That's the problem with dating in your fifties," Susan said from the other table. "Red flags are easier to spot than when you're young and dumb."

"That never stops you," Leandra/Leanda teased.

"You can't call what I do dating, Leann."

Well, crap. I had her name wrong completely.

"What do you call it?" Rosa asked.

"Playing."

Everyone laughed.

"What about sex?" Leann asked.

It took Mari two full breaths before she realized the question was pointed at her.

Heat reached her cheeks. Was she really going to talk about sex with a group of women she didn't even know?

"I think I've forgotten how."

Even though her words were sincere, the women busted out in laughter.

"I know I have," Rosa said.

"So, what's your story?"

What started out as three tables with three different conversations shifted to Mari and Rosa holding the spotlight on female celibacy.

At least now Rosa took much of the conversation in the direction of her having a desire to date and discover her new single life.

Eventually that morphed into Susan talking about her two failed attempts at marriage and her embracing her single status, promising never to let it go. The single part, but not the no-sex part.

When they took a break between rounds, Summer came over to Mari and Rosa's side.

"Are you having fun?"

The wine had found its way to Mari's head, much like Salena had told her.

"Yes."

"Good. Good. We only do this once a month, you should consider joining us full time."

"I think that's a great idea," Rosa blew out before Mari could take a breath. "Don't you think?"

Mari blinked several times. "Well . . ." Words dried up in her mouth. There wasn't a reason to say no, and the truth was, she was enjoying herself more than she thought she would. It had been a long time since she'd met anyone new. Outside of her daughters-in-law and their families. "I don't see why not."

Summer leaned closer and lowered her voice. "Don't worry, we won't put either of you on the list of hostesses for a few months."

Mari accepted that with a smile.

"Listen," Summer began. "I know this is kinda last minute, but I'm on a committee for our singles group, and we're going on a cruise in two weeks. Do you have passports?"

Rosa's eyes were already filled with excitement.

Mari felt her head starting to shake. "Yes, but—"

"One of the rooms opened up last week, and we're trying to fill it. You two would have a blast."

"I don't know—"

"Yes," Rosa interrupted.

Mari looked at her friend.

"The restaurant," she started.

"I don't want to hear about the restaurant. That has been your excuse for years."

"Not an excuse. A reason. There is a difference."

Rosa shot out an expletive in Italian, a word Summer clearly didn't understand. Not that Mari expected her to. None of the women playing bunco were Italian or indicated that they spoke the language.

"A singles group?" Mari asked for clarification.

"Primarily."

"I'm not looking for a man," Mari said.

"It's mainly women," Summer pointed out. "And the cruise isn't only for singles. It just happens that our singles group wanted to do this, and the cruise line invites singles groups twice a year. The discounts were too good to pass up. It's probably going to be a lot like tonight. Laughing, drinks . . . no responsibilities. Let the staff on the ship do all the work."

Rosa's pleading eyes put some serious Catholic guilt on Mari's soul.

"I'll think about it."

"Great."

Rosa was already grinning.

"I'll *think* about it."

"Where are *we* going?" Rosa asked.

"The Caribbean."

Rosa sighed as if she were already there. "I've always wanted to see the islands."

Summer beamed. "Now is your chance. I'll send you an email with all the details."

Mari pressed her lips together until Summer turned her attention to one of the other ladies. That's when she tugged on Rosa's arm and pulled her away from the ears of others.

"One game night is now once a month *and* a cruise?"

"We need to go shopping."

Was she even listening? "Rosa!"

"I need a swimsuit. And a summer dress. And—"

"Rosa?"

"What?"

"I didn't say yes." Mari's words were a rushed whisper.

You didn't say no, Rosa fired back in Italian.

They both looked over their shoulders to the women gathered around the open kitchen island, filling their wineglasses and chatting.

Speaking in Italian while in the company of people that didn't understand the language was on a level of rude that Mari chided her children for doing from day one.

Yet as she opened her mouth, she found herself breaking her own rules. *If you want to go so bad, you go. I don't have to travel with you.*

Rosa plastered on a mirrored smile that Mari wore. *If you wanted this, I'd go with you. You're a sister to me.*

Still speaking in Italian, Mari replied, *Are you trying to make me feel guilty?*

Instead of answering the question, Rosa spelled out the facts that Mari knew quite well. *Half of my life I've been married to a man who walked away to live with another woman and start another family in Italy. I remained here, doing the right thing. Following the rules. Raising my children and bringing lasagna to the church socials . . . and for what?*

"Happy children," Mari reverted to English.

"Who are living their own lives. Happy lives. It's my turn . . . our turn, Mari. I feel like I've been an old woman since I was thirty. I'm staring down sixty, and even though I love my children, I no longer live for them. There is no telling if Dante and Chloe will stay in San Diego forever. If they will have children that they raise here. Anna and Jackie don't come around often. I've been alone, Mari. Lonely."

Mari felt her resolve start to crack.

"I made a bad choice with Joseph. I want my friend . . . my best friend, the woman who knows me better than Joseph ever did, to help me find the right man."

Mari opened her mouth to speak.

Rosa didn't let her. "He never loved me. I didn't have what you and Paulo did. Is it so much to ask that I have that at least once in my life?"

Anything Mari wanted to say died in her throat.

She felt her bags were already packed.

CHAPTER THREE

"We need to talk."

As he sat in the stands, staring down at the softball field, Cindy's "we have a problem" voice sent alarm signals in James's brain.

When he glanced to his right, his ex-wife's expression made his instincts kick in. "Oh no . . . what's going on?"

Cindy sucked in a breath . . . then slowly blew it out. "When was the last time you went on a date?"

Of all the things to come out of his ex-wife's mouth, this, James wasn't expecting.

"What?"

"A date, James. With a woman?"

He dropped his hands to his lap and cocked his head to the side. "Why is my ex-wife asking about my love life?"

"Because you don't have one."

"You don't know that."

It was Cindy's turn to cock an eyebrow and her head. "What's her name?"

There wasn't a her.

Or a name.

James turned his attention back to the field.

"I heard the girls talking . . . arguing."

"That's not new," James said, unsure what this had to do with his lack of a love life.

"Don't you want to know what they were arguing about?"

Not particularly, but he knew from experience that Cindy's question was going to get answered without his input if he was silent long enough.

He took a breath.

"You. About which one of them was going to pick a college close to home to make sure you aren't alone."

Ellie's teammate smashed the ball into left field, where it was caught by the opposing team. Even though the play registered in James's vision, his mind was wrapping around what Cindy had just said.

"What do you mean?"

"Exactly what I said. Madison wants Caltech, right?"

"That's all I've heard of since the seventh-grade science fair."

"And Ellie has her heart on—"

"U of A," James said before Cindy could. Ellie had backups to the University of Arizona, but Arizona was the top pick.

"Caltech isn't next door, and the University of Arizona is always an airplane away. Neither of them have a San Diego college in their top three."

"She can drive from Arizona. And they both applied to San Diego State."

Cindy met his gaze. "Oh, they both applied, but it's not in their top three."

"But they said—"

"Doesn't matter what they said to our face."

Something happened on the field, drawing both his and Cindy's attention to the game.

The teams were switching places.

James noticed Ellie running to third base.

"When they got home from school yesterday, I heard them barking at each other. Like a good parent, I listened from the hall. What happens if they both get into their number one pick? Which one is going to sacrifice and take San Diego State? Then they started accusing the other of not putting as much effort into the application process to get accepted into SDSU."

"Are you sure you heard this right?"

"To be honest, I wasn't sure. Sooo, like a good mom, I checked for myself."

"What do you mean?"

"I checked their applications."

"How did you—"

James stopped himself from finishing his question. Cindy worked in cybersecurity, and if there was anyone who knew how to hack anyone's computer anything, it was someone who was paid to keep people out.

"What did you find?" James changed his question.

"Both of them did in fact apply. And both of them left out parts of their educational history that would help them stand out. Ellie's letter of recommendation from her Spanish teacher was conveniently not attached. Madison's letter from her English teacher. Both of their essays had spelling errors, incomplete thoughts and sentences. I could go on, but you see the point."

"But—"

"I considered that could be a completely innocent mistake, so I pulled up their chosen schools' applications, and guess what I found?"

James stared absently at the field. "Perfection."

"Every *i* dotted and every *t* crossed," Cindy confirmed.

Why?

"They both applied to SDSU because of my relationship status?" he asked.

"*Single* you. *Not dating* you . . . *Doesn't even have a dog at home to keep you company* you."

It was utterly ridiculous. "They don't have to worry about me. I'll tell them I'm okay."

"Yeah, sure. That will work, James. Our strong-willed, independent thinkers that we've raised to not accept anyone's word for anything and only watch their actions are going to lie down and accept you 'telling them' that you're okay."

What was Cindy suggesting? "I'm not going to let them piss away their own dreams because they're worried about their dad. I'll sit them down next week, tell them I'm onto them and—"

"The hell you will. They'll know exactly who dug up their college applications. You're not throwing me under the bus."

She had a point.

"Then we'll do something more subtle."

"We? No . . . you. I remarried. They're not debating my happiness."

The crowd around them jumped to their feet and started to cheer.

James and Cindy clapped before either of them realized what happened on the field.

"I'm happy."

"Prove it to them."

He stared at the hard eyes of his ex. "How do you propose I do that?"

"Date. Take a vacation and tell them you're looking for the next Mrs."

"Lie to them," James said, deadpan.

"We've been lying to them since the tooth fairy, James. If they think you're at least considering a relationship, they'd feel less obliged to live their lives close by to take care of you. That's going to happen in time anyway if we both live long enough. They shouldn't be burdened with the task now."

Cindy wasn't wrong.

Which was annoying.

"I can't just pull a woman out of a hat."

Cindy's lips eased up slowly on each end.

"What?"

"Remember Summer?"

James started shaking his head. "No."

"She's single."

"No!"

Cindy tossed her head back with a laugh. "Don't worry, she wouldn't date you for all the money in the world."

Suddenly the hypothetical rejection of Cindy's long-term friend slapped him in the face. "What's wrong with me?"

Cindy full-on laughed then. "You're my ex."

That makes sense. "Then why bring her up?"

"She's involved with a singles group that is going on a cruise in two weeks. They're out of the normal staterooms, but they do have a couple of suites still available."

Cindy sounded like she'd already booked a room. "Back up. I'm not going on a cruise in two weeks."

"You are."

Shit . . . did she book a room? "You can boss Clayton around, but . . ."

"A perk of you being my ex-husband is me no longer placating you. Acceptance letters will start rolling out as soon as next month. Ellie and Madison need to see you reaching toward stability without them."

"As if I'm not stable."

Cindy slapped at his arm.

"Hey!"

"Tell them you're going on a singles cruise. You don't have to come back with anyone. Just show them you're looking. That should be enough so that when the acceptance letters arrive, they both pick the schools they truly want to attend, and you can go back to your hermit life."

James screwed up his face, staring Cindy down. "Were you always this demanding?"

"It's part of the appeal," she joked. "It's why you love me."

And he did.

Not in an "in love" kind of way. But a "great friend" kind of way. A "mother of his children" kind of way.

Unlike every other divorced couple they knew, their split wasn't filled with hate and venom. They simply fell out of love. If they were ever truly in it to begin with.

When the twins were born, they kept up the ruse of a happy family, until Cindy met Clayton.

The girls were just going into first grade when they called it quits.

In reality, James was relieved.

It would have been easy to blame Cindy since she was the one who found herself attracted to someone else. But that didn't happen.

James was actually happy for her.

And Clayton was a good guy, despite his misguided Yankee-fan state of mind. He was a great stepdad to the twins and adored the ground Cindy walked on.

Even divorced, James had spent many holidays with them, to the surprise of their extended families.

His sister had asked him once if he was in some kind of polyamorous relationship. Although he denied her allegations, there wasn't a holiday that went by without her giving James the side-eye.

James had dated in those early years. But nothing stuck.

He'd promised himself that he wasn't going to bring anyone into his daughters' lives that wasn't going to stick around. He would be damned if his girls would suffer instability in their childhood despite the fact that their parents were divorced.

As time went on, the women he dated were like him, divorced with their own children. Many of them latching on for the wrong reasons.

Eventually, James shifted his focus to his work and his girls.

He had a lover a time or two . . . but nothing more than that.

James pushed away the thoughts of his dating—or in his case, nondating—life and released a sigh.

"Where is this cruise going?"

Cindy smiled like the Joker himself.

~

"I'm not wearing that." Mari took the low-cut blouse Chloe had taken off the rack at the department store and put it back.

"Why not?"

Mari looked beyond her daughter and removed a button-up white shirt from a pile on a nearby table. "This is more like it."

"That looks like something you'd wear to work."

"Which makes it more sensible to buy for the cruise. I'll wear it later."

Chloe pulled the blouse out of Mari's hands and shoved the low-cut variety back at her. "You don't wear work clothes on a cruise, Mama."

"How many cruise ships have you been on?"

"Just because I haven't been on one doesn't mean I don't know how to dress for one. If you walk around looking like you work on the thing, you'll be directing traffic or telling the kitchen staff how to do their jobs within a day."

Chloe pivoted and pulled several shirts randomly from a pile. "You need color, and short sleeves, and thin fabric. And linen . . . something nice for the day trips and warm evening strolls on the upper decks." She kept moving around, tossing articles of clothing over her arm as she spoke. A sundress draped over her arm . . . a skirt. "Shorts . . ." Chloe moved to a table stacked with shorts and shirts that complemented them.

"I almost never wear shorts."

"The Caribbean is hot."

Before Mari could stop Chloe from stacking more items in her arms, an employee approached. "Can I get a room started for you?"

Chloe handed the ever-growing pile over. "Yes, please."

"I don't need all of that," Mari said once the attendant walked away.

Her daughter ignored her. "When was the last time you bought clothing for yourself?"

Mari paused, opened her mouth, then shut it again. "I don't remember."

"Then you need it." Chloe removed a lightweight beige shirt that was displayed on the manikin as a jacket. She held it up just below Mari's chin, then put it back on the rack. The same shirt in a bright orange was looked at next, and a new pile started to form.

"I'm doing this for Rosa. She's the one looking for romance."

"I know that." Not that it stopped Chloe from blazing through the store on her hell-bent mission. "But here's the thing. Women dress for other women. Not men." Chloe flipped through a rack with linen pants as she spoke. "When you're chatting away with the other women at your table, feeling and looking your best, you'll thank me when you get home."

"Clothes don't change a person," Mari said.

"Lies."

"Chloe!"

She marched to a section of the store where swimming suits lived and dignity was shelved elsewhere. "You wear something like this . . ." Chloe played with the string of a bikini. "It changes you."

"I'm *not* wearing that, young lady."

Her daughter didn't dare push the bikini button.

She did, however, remove two one-piece suits before walking to the back of the store to the dressing rooms.

"Humor me, Mama. Try it all on."

Mari felt a bit like an insubordinate child when she tugged the swimming suits from her daughter's hands. Since Chloe received her stubborn streak from Mari's side of the gene pool, she knew that leaving the mall without a swimsuit wouldn't come without a fight.

A fight Mari had no desire to have.

Besides, that's what receipts and leaving the tags on clothing were for.

Outside of the dressing room, Chloe chatted while Mari slipped out of her clothes and into her daughter's choices.

"I have wanted to change your wardrobe for years," Chloe said.

"There is nothing wrong with my clothes."

"Debatable."

Mari pulled on the linen pants and matching shirt. Turning to the side, she smiled back at the mirror.

The lightweight fabric felt like butter on her skin.

She could see how clothing like this would be welcome in the warm tropical sun.

"I wanna see."

Mari pulled back the curtain.

Her daughter's eyes widened, and a slow smile crept over her lips. "Now *that* is what I'm talking about."

"I'm glad you're happy." Mari closed the curtain and moved on to the next outfit.

"Immensely," Chloe called out with a giggle.

By the time Mari put a stop to the purging of her bank account, both Chloe and herself were overburdened with bags. More clothing than Mari could possibly wear for one vacation. New sandals and sneakers, makeup, and yes . . . a swimsuit.

The only stop she put to her daughter's need to overhaul everything Mari put on her body was lingerie.

"There is no need for that," she told Chloe.

"What if you meet—"

"Stop that right there. If you want to buy fancy underwear for anyone, let it be Rosa. She's the one destined for the confessional when we return. Not me."

Chloe didn't push.

CHAPTER FOUR

"No parties."

Madison rolled her eyes.

Ellie scoffed.

The fact that neither of them made a verbal comment wasn't lost on him.

"You're the one that will be doing the partying, Dad," Madison said.

"Is that right?" James glanced at his phone to see how far out his Uber driver was. "When was the last time you saw me party?"

Ellie narrowed her eyes. "The Halloween where you dressed up as Captain Jack Sparrow."

"You were twelve," he reminded her. And while he had been dressed up as a drunk pirate, he'd kept the rum out of his soda since the party Ellie spoke of was for nothing but twelve-year-olds.

Ellie and Madison exchanged glances.

"Send us pics," Madison told him.

"And don't turn off your tracker."

"Isn't that my line, Ellie?" The caveat to the girls having cell phones was that their whereabouts were tracked every minute of every day. "Besides, I doubt it will work in the middle of the ocean."

"He's right," Madison said.

According to his phone, his ride was one minute out.

"Which reminds me . . . watch out for each other." Not that he needed to worry. Cindy was fifteen minutes away. While they could have mandated that the girls spend the time James was away on the cruise at their mother's, the adults in the situation realized Ellie and Madison were two months away from their eighteenth birthdays . . . and were leaving for college in August. It was time to cut the cord.

"We will."

James opened the front door.

The morning sky was still sleepy.

"And no boys over."

The driver pulled up to the curb.

"Yes, Dad."

Leaving the girls sent a strange wave of panic through him.

Misplaced panic, since he'd been turning on and off the parenting button since his divorce, but anxiety nonetheless. "Remember, don't add to the population, don't subtract from the population. Don't end up in the hospital, the newspapers, or jail."

Madison and Ellie both laughed and finished his weekend speech for him. "And if we do end up in jail, establish dominance early."

God, he loved his girls.

James opened his arms, and they both stepped close.

One arm around each of them, he kissed the top of their heads. "Love you both."

"Love you, too, Dad," Madison cooed.

"Do crazy shit and have a good time," Ellie encouraged.

James stepped out of the house.

"Love you," Ellie said.

He looked back and winked. "No parties, no boys."

Both the girls muttered as he made his way down the steps and into the driveway.

Once he settled in the back of the beat-up Toyota that smelled a little like cigarettes and regret, the driver asked him what airline he was flying.

"United."

The driver pulled away from the house, looked in his rearview mirror. "Going on vacation?"

James almost said yes . . . Instead he shook his head. "Business."

There was no way he was telling a stranger that he was leaving his home for an extended amount of time.

Especially with the most important people in his life being left behind.

As that thought circled in his head, he removed his phone from his pocket and pulled up the group chat between his daughters and him. Don't forget to set the house alarm when you leave.

Madison responded with a thumbs-up.

James tapped his finger on his knee.

And when you're in for the night.

Ellie sent a wide-eyed emoji followed by one rolling their eyes.

Don't tell your friends I'm gone.

James knew that last one was a stretch . . . but he had to try.

A few seconds passed before Ellie responded.

Get here at eight. Dad's gone for ten days, Trevor is bringing the beer.

James read the text twice.

Before he could wrap his brain around the words, Ellie texted again. Oops, that wasn't meant for you.

A grin swept over his lips.

She's kidding, Dad, Madison texted.

James laughed and put his phone away.

Dorm rooms didn't have security alarms, and boys were down the hall.

How had that happened?

Eighteen years gone . . . just like that.

~

The chartered yacht Mari's daughter and son-in-law owned was the closest thing she'd ever come to a cruise ship.

It was nothing close.

The singles group from San Diego poured in like a wave. Summer had given Mari and Rosa matching T-shirts with the words *San Diego Singles* along with the cruise line's logo. The lime-green color singled their group out of the crowd.

And what a crowd.

The special T-shirts weren't an original idea. There were several singles groups huddled together as they walked onto the ship.

Employees with smart uniforms and pleasant smiles greeted and directed them toward the general area of their rooms.

"Room 6521 is starboard, midship." The employee pointed toward the stairwell. "Up two levels. Your luggage should arrive at your stateroom within the hour. In the meantime, feel free to join the bon voyage party on the Lido deck. The buffet is open."

Rosa thanked the woman enthusiastically. "This is going to be great."

While Mari had been a reluctant participant, the sheer number of people and smiles had her changing her mind.

"Let's find our room, then join the party."

"Lead the way," Mari said, following her friend.

Map in hand, the two of them took the stairs.

Navigating the narrow halls and other passengers finding their rooms led them to theirs.

Mari's first impression when Rosa opened the door was instant. "Looks much smaller than the pictures."

Rosa moved straight to the window and looked outside. "At least we have a view. Besides, we won't be in here other than to sleep."

Mari peeked into the bathroom. It was on par with what she found on the airplane. A bit larger because of the shower. It had all you needed.

Two beds, a TV . . . a small desk. "It will work."

Near the TV sat a piece of paper, which addressed their group.

Mari read it out loud.

"'Welcome aboard, San Diego Singles. Join us on the main pool deck, or Lido deck, for the bon voyage party and group photo. Please wear your T-shirts. There will be music, dancing, and of course . . . cocktails. We are all seated in the same general area of the main dining room and encourage you to move around to meet other members of our group. Each day, along with the ship's itinerary, we have our own supplement. Group games, competitions, and costume parties, to name a few. Join as many or as few of the activities as you like. Though we really did work hard to make this a vacation you'll never forget and hope to see you often. Enjoy your first afternoon and evening on board.'"

It was signed *San Diego Cruise Crew*.

Rosa tossed her purse on one of the beds. "Let's find the party."

Without their luggage to unpack, there wasn't a reason to stay in the room.

Mari glanced at her purse. "Do we need to carry our purses around?"

Rosa shook her head. "Our room key pays for everything."

"Maybe put our passports and wallets in the safe."

Rosa agreed.

After locking the room safe and stashing their purses in one of the drawers in the room, they made their way to the upper deck and followed the sound of the party.

The loud thump of music overtook the noise of the people.

Already, the pool was overflowing with bodies. Obviously, seasoned cruisers knew to pack their swimsuits in whatever they walked onto the ship with, and they wasted no time in making themselves at home.

Mari and Rosa stood on the fringes, taking it all in.

Two bars, one on each side of the pool, were three people deep. Every chair was taken. And kids ran past with plates of food in their hands.

Mari knew, without a doubt, that she was staring at what would be the main theme of her life the entire time they were on this ship. Like happy hour at her restaurant during the holiday season. A nonstop party.

~

James stood on the balcony of his suite looking out over the port of Fort Lauderdale, kicking himself for packing his computer in his suitcase.

The group T-shirt that could be seen from a mile away sat on the bed along with Summer's itinerary.

There was no way he was going to wear an advertisement for his single status.

A lack of a wedding ring should be enough. Although James knew the moment the thought entered his head that missing a ring had very little to do with missing a wife.

He turned back to his room and looked around the space.

It was two and a half times the size of a normal stateroom, complete with a living space, separate bedroom, kitchenette, and bathroom that included a bathtub. It was total overkill. But unlike the other guests on board, James planned on working and therefore spending plenty of time in his room.

That was, once his luggage arrived.

He glanced at his watch and considered his options.

He might as well grab a bite to eat and explore the ship instead of staring out the window.

He didn't have far to go before he found the long line into the buffet.

Yeah, he wasn't that hungry.

Music led him to the pool, where everyone who wasn't eating seemed to be gathered.

James weaved in and out of people . . . a lot of them wearing matching T-shirts. Not just the lime green Summer came up with, but people in bright yellow, soft blues, orange, and reds.

All the shirts had similar themes.

Sassy Singles from Seattle.

Right Swipe from Richmond.

Always a Bridesmaid, Never the Bride.

The girls wearing the pink shirts had the bridesmaid logo, and they all looked like they were only a couple of years older than his daughters.

There was even a group from The Villages, a retirement community that lived an hour outside of Orlando. Their logo said *The Real Village People.*

As the music faded, a man's voice, in a distinct British accent, called out over the PA system.

"Good afternoon. And welcome aboard. I am your cruise director, Percy, and these beautiful people you see beside me will be guiding you through all the fantastic adventures you'll be experiencing over the next ten days. Are you excited?" His question ended in a yell.

The crowd on deck clapped, and a few cheered.

"Oh, c'mon, friends, that was weak. I asked, are you excited?"

This time, the applause, whistles, and cheers were loud enough to wake the dead.

"As you can see by the matching attire, we have several groups joining us. Our biannual single and mingle sail always brings out some of our favorite guests. For our married couples and families, don't fear . . . you're not on the wrong ship. We have daily events set aside for you as well."

James inched his way to the bar while Percy continued to work the crowd.

"Before we continue the music, we're going to organize a few group photos, starting with Always a Bridesmaid."

Percy directed the squealing girls to one side of the deck, where a photographer stood at the ready.

James edged his way up to the bar and waited until he could catch the eye of one of the three bartenders running their asses off.

Tropical and fruity seemed to be the drink of the day. According to the sign, it was the cruise ship's rendition of a mai tai.

Two women in the obnoxious green shirts, the same one that sat in James's room, stood to the side of the bar, their heads close together in conversation. The sound of the cruise director wasn't as loud on this corner of the deck, allowing the conversations around him to filter in.

"Best idea ever."

Two men, no older than thirty, sat at the bar, their backs to the booze, their eyes stuck on the women walking by.

"I couldn't think of a better way to celebrate my divorce finalizing."

"Wouldn't have happened as quickly if you'd had kids," the bulkier of the two men said.

The bartender tapped the space in front of James. "What can I get you, boss?"

He kept it simple, asked for a beer.

His beer came, and the bartender walked away with his room card.

"No, man. I'm not going there. I want my women a little bit older on this trip," James heard the newly divorced man say to his friend.

As the words registered in James's brain, he noticed the two guys take in the lime-green San Diego Singles duo, only a few feet away.

The side view of the ladies in green not only said older, but it also suggested a different energy. Neither was holding a drink or bopping around to the music.

Versus the guys on the hunt, who already had one empty cup in front of them and another full one in hand.

The heavy guy nudged the divorced dude. "Cougar hunting starts now."

Divorced Guy grabbed his drink, slid off the barstool, and squared his shoulders.

The bartender took that moment to ask for James's signature and return his room card.

By the time James turned back around, Divorced Guy stood about a foot away from the two women, who were seemingly taking in the cruise director moving groups around for pictures.

"Hello, ladies."

Divorced Guy, charm dancing from his smile, stepped closer to the slightly shorter and thinner of the two women.

The woman said something that James didn't hear.

Either Divorced Guy didn't hear her either, or he wanted an excuse to move closer.

James banked on the latter of the two scenarios.

Both women nodded.

The taller of them pulled on her shirt and pointed to the graphic. "From San Diego," James heard her say.

Fascinated by the fact that a thirty-year-old was actively trying to pick up a woman some twenty years older than him, James took a step closer, his eyes stuck to the dance floor. Though in his periphery, he focused on hearing the voices of the three of them.

"It's our first cruise."

"My second," Divorced Guy said. "You're in for a good time. Plenty of dance partners."

The woman standing closest to Divorced Guy looked him up and down.

Her profile matched her straight shoulders and less-than-relaxed stance. Her jaw was set, a pleasant yet not-so-welcoming smile on her lips.

But her eyes . . . they spoke volumes.

Dark, piercing, brown, with knowledge beyond the depths that said this kid was barking up the wrong cougar. Yet there was something in how she held herself that suggested she didn't realize he was trying to pick her up.

Those eyes kept pulling in, just a tad, as Divorced Guy kept talking.

"I've never been to San Diego."

"We love our city," the taller woman replied.

"Are the men there all blind?"

James wanted to laugh. He finished the pickup line in his head.

"Why would you ask?" Finally, the smaller woman spoke.

James detected an accent. Spanish, Portuguese . . . Italian? San Diego had a significant population of all three of those nationalities.

"The men would have to be blind to let two beautiful women like you resort to a singles cruise to find a dance partner."

That was painful to hear. James actually winced.

"Can I buy you ladies a drink?"

Poor kid lost his game during his marriage. That is to say, if he ever had game to begin with.

The taller woman snickered.

The woman with soul-filled eyes turned her frame toward the kid. She looked him dead in the eyes. "I have children older than you."

"Are they here?" Divorced Guy asked. His eyes filled with hope.

"No," the second woman stated.

"Then let me buy you a drink. They'll never know."

The shorter woman turned to her friend. Whatever she said next was completely lost on James. It was heated, loud, and not in English.

Italian.

James held in his laughter, but there was no mistaking his smile.

"Another time," the taller woman said.

The woman Divorced Guy was hitting on rolled her eyes and turned her attention back to the cruise director, completely ignoring the man-child at her side.

"Can't blame a man for trying," he said as he turned. "You're a beautiful woman."

Divorced Guy moved back to his barstool.

"Hit and miss," his friend teased.

"I'm just warming up."

James walked around the women now that the interplay was over. He took a good look.

The kid had one thing right. You couldn't blame him for trying. The hot-blooded Italian was beautiful.

If she wore makeup, there wasn't much of it.

Olive skin, dark hair, though there were a few highlights . . . or maybe that was age coming through. If she had children older than the man who had just hit on her, she must have been young when she had them. Guessing a woman's age was never James's strong point. If anyone should have hit on her, it wasn't the kid fresh out of his teenage-crush divorce.

"Okay, San Diego Singles, it's your turn."

With the cruise director's encouragement, the two women left their perch and walked toward the photographer.

James held back and watched their departure.

Seemed the majority of the group from San Diego was exactly what he expected. Twenty-five- to thirty-five-year-olds that would likely need headache medication on the daily to ward off the hangovers that were absolutely coming.

He noticed Summer doing what Summer did best. Bossing people around.

James made sure he was behind enough heads that she didn't see him and rope him into the photograph. He'd rather keep his "I'm single from San Diego" status on the down low.

At least for now.

CHAPTER FIVE

Weaving their way down the stairs and through the narrow corridors of the ship, Mari and Rosa found their room. Both of their suitcases sat outside the cabin door, much like others in the hall.

"They leave it in the hall?" Rosa asked.

Mari waved her room key by the electronic lock and heard a click. "If they had problems, they'd do it another way."

Rosa shrugged.

Mari pushed the door open with her shoulder and dragged her luggage inside.

The ship had already left port.

The party on the pool deck was still going strong when they decided to return to their room.

Their group had the early dinner in the main dining room, and they both wanted to decompress before joining the San Diego Singles.

Mari wanted to get out of the T-shirt.

"How old do you think that boy at the bar was?" Rosa asked.

Mari placed her suitcase on her bed and opened it. "Chloe's age . . . maybe."

"He was hitting on you."

"He asked to buy us drinks."

"Same thing." Rosa giggled.

"I don't think so."

Sandwiched between the mesh holding her underwear and her clothes, a red-tissue-wrapped gift, complete with a ribbon, stared at her.

The tiny note put there by Chloe said not to open it until they were on the ship. Mari noticed it when they arrived at the hotel the day before for their one night in Florida.

As much as Mari wanted to know what her daughter gifted her, she'd put it aside and waited for this moment.

"You don't think so because it's been so long since either of us have had the interest of a man, we've forgotten how it's done," Rosa said.

"He was a child. Not a man," Mari told her.

"Ehhh."

Mari sat on the edge of her bed and untied the ribbon. It was evident it was an article of clothing since the gift wasn't in a box.

The dark red tissue paper unveiled a black nightgown. Silk, or at least a fabric that felt like silk. It had cap sleeves and a V-neck and fell just below her knees.

"How sweet." Mari pulled the fabric to her cheek.

Rosa glanced up from the pile of clothes in her hand. "You like it?"

"What's not to like?"

Rosa grinned like a woman with a secret.

"What?" Mari asked.

"I was with her when she bought it."

Mari folded the nightgown back in the tissue paper and stood to put it in a drawer.

"Then you knew I'd like it."

Rosa narrowed her eyes. "It's a negligee."

"It's a nightgown."

"To be worn in the company of a man."

Mari looked back to the nightgown. "No."

"Yes."

"Chloe knows I'm not—"

"Not what?" Rosa interrupted. "A single woman on a cruise designed to help you meet a man?"

Mari lifted an accusing finger in the direction of her friend. "You're the one looking for male companionship. Not me."

Rosa laughed. "Chloe would like to see it otherwise."

"So gift me a nightgown? That's a jump, even for my willful daughter."

"Well-intending daughter," Rosa corrected. "I suggested she have you wait to open it until we were on board. I was afraid you'd *accidentally* leave it at the hotel."

"I wouldn't have done that." *Well . . . maybe.* "She'll be sad to hear that the only one who will see me in that is you."

"That's what I told her, but she insisted." Rosa moved to the small closet.

Mari continued to stack her clothes into the drawer. "Even if we did find someone interesting here . . . a nightgown? Chloe should know me better than that."

"What can she know? She didn't know you before Paulo."

"*I* barely knew me before Paulo," Mari scoffed.

"I'm sure you dated other men."

"Be serious, Rosa. I went to school dances with *boys*. The occasional movie. That was a lifetime ago. I'm a completely different person."

"I'm just suggesting that maybe it's time to enter the nightgown phase."

Mari felt heat fill her cheeks. "Do we need to have a flag on our cabin door so I know when not to come in?"

Rosa opened her mouth, closed it again without saying a word. "Maybe."

Mari choked on a laugh.

After tucking the now-empty suitcases in the closet, Rosa sat back on the bed and let out a long breath. "What if I did meet someone?"

"You deserve to."

Rosa sat opposite her friend.

"If I did . . . would you judge me?"

Mari reached over and grabbed her friend's hand. "How long have we been friends?"

"Over twenty years."

"And have I ever judged you?"

"I don't believe I've given you reason to." Rosa's eyes softened.

"You're a grown woman who has the freedom to do whatever you want. Now, if you meet someone that I think is going to hurt you, I will say something. And not as judgment, more as a caution. Otherwise, you'll get no pushback from me. If you want to find a husband and need to kiss a few frogs along the way, I'm here to support you."

Rosa squeezed her hand. "And if I don't want a husband?"

"You said you wanted that last week."

"Last week I did. And maybe I still do."

Indecision was written all over Rosa's face.

Who could blame her after what she'd been through? "Still not my place to judge."

A half smile split Rosa's lips. "Not a word to anyone when we get home? You know . . . if anything happens."

Mari sat up tall, removed her hands from Rosa's. "We tell everyone we had a wonderful time and met a ton of people. That's all anyone needs to know."

"And if they want specifics?"

Mari repeated herself with a grin. "We had a wonderful time and met a ton of people."

Rosa sighed. "I love you, my friend. Thank you for doing this for me."

"You're welcome."

They both laughed while Mari slid off the bed and pulled the T-shirt from her shoulders. "I need to get out of this if I'm going to be your wingman."

"My what?"

"Wingman. That's what Chloe suggested I am. Help you find a date but keep you safe doing it."

Rosa bounced off the bed like a woman half her age. "*Andiamo.*"

~

The main dining room was beautifully appointed, with tablecloths and perfectly matched place settings. It opened to the deck above, where another mass of tables with chattering guests filled the room with noise.

Once Mari and Rosa told the hostess which group they were with, the two of them were ushered to the tables set aside for them.

A couple of familiar faces smiled and waved them over.

"Hello again," Mari said as they took a seat.

"Hello. I'm sorry, you're going to have to remind me of your names," the brunette said.

"I'm Mari, and this is Rosa."

The brunette pointed to her chest. "Amanda and Jill."

"Amanda and Jill," Mari repeated aloud, then to herself several times, hoping the information would stick.

"Have you been to the singles events at home?" Amanda asked.

"I have once," Rosa announced.

Mari shook her head.

"Newly single?" Amanda asked.

"Yes and no," Rosa answered. "Newly divorced. But my ex left many years ago."

"That sounds complicated," Jill said.

"It was."

"And you?" Amanda turned her attention to Mari.

"My husband passed ten years ago." Mari had stopped using the term *widow*. Without an immediate explanation, the quick response from everyone was sorrow. The decade of time pulled some of that weight aside.

"That sucks," Amanda said. "You're just now getting out there?"

"No. I'm here for Rosa."

Rosa nudged her arm. "Keep me out of trouble."

It was comical hearing Rosa talk that way. Even more entertaining was the excitement on her face as she said it.

"Where is the fun in that?" Amanda asked.

"What about you two?"

"I have a thirteen- and fifteen-year-old at home. Their dad is an ass. Shows up every other weekend when it's convenient."

"It's never convenient," Jill added.

"We've been divorced for four years."

"I'm sorry," Mari said.

"Don't be. Did I mention he was an ass?"

They laughed.

"I've never been married," Jill told them. "Got close a couple of times. Have one engagement ring to show for it."

"What happened there?" Rosa asked.

"He didn't quite understand that marriage meant monogamy."

Rosa huffed. "At least you learned that before you married. Some of us weren't as lucky."

"If someone had told me that I'd reach forty and not have a husband or kids, I would have said they were crazy. But here I am."

Mari felt her heart sink for the woman. "You wanted kids?"

"I always thought I would have them. Now it's too late."

"You can still—"

"Please. No."

"I don't know what I'd do without my children," Mari said. "Or my grandchildren."

"You're a grandmother?" Amanda asked, eyes wide.

"Two," Mari said with pride. "Two more on the way. Twins."

"How old are you?" Jill burst out.

"Fifty-four."

As words of surprise escaped their lips, other guests arrived at their table. All of them women.

Eventually, the waiter came around, and a mix of conversations ensued.

The other four women at their table were part of the younger group. Even though they were likely close to Chloe and Dante's age, they seemed so much younger. Mari instantly wanted to warn the young women against drinking too much. Which was already too late since they spoke nonstop about their time at the pool and the men buying them drinks.

In the end, it wasn't Mari that gave them advice . . . it was Amanda.

"You girls watch out for each other. No disappearing with someone without the others knowing where you went."

"We have a plan," one of them said.

Mari gave up on memorizing their names from the minute they sat down.

"Pictures of their driver's license and the number of their stateroom."

"And preapproval from us."

The girls thought that was hysterical and went on to talk about not letting a man's accent sway them to get naked.

"Words should never take you to a man's bed," Mari said a little louder than she wanted. "Only his actions."

"That's what I was saying," one of the girls announced.

Any more advice would have fallen on deaf ears.

These girls were determined to have a story to tell by the end of the cruise. She couldn't help but wonder if her own children acted this way when they were among their friends.

She wasn't naive enough to think that halos hovered over their heads.

Her sons alone had reputations that leaked into conversations. They used their accents to turn heads. That was before they married. It didn't make her love or think of them any less. And Chloe . . . well, her daughter was . . .

Mari took a closer look at the girls as they chatted away.

It didn't matter. Chloe and Dante were happily married, and whatever was before . . . wasn't any longer.

The waiter arrived and collected the last of their dishes.

"What's next?" Amanda asked as they stood to leave the dining room.

"The dating game starts at eight," Rosa announced.

"That gives us an hour."

The younger women said their goodbyes while Mari, Rosa, Amanda, and Jill stayed together.

The ship was a floating city. It had everything anyone could possibly want or need and several of each.

Bars were everywhere. As an owner of a restaurant, Mari was well acquainted with the profit margin of alcohol sales. There were cozy piano lounge bars. Bars with live music. Dance clubs with bars. Bars in all the entertainment venues and casino.

The ship was making a killing on booze.

Plenty of space was set aside for children. They had an arcade, laser tag, and kid club space where parents dropped the kids off so they could have some adult time.

And restaurants.

The main dining room and buffet were included, but that didn't stop the ship from offering everything from sushi to steak and, of course, Italian cuisine.

Mari held out hope that the Italian food in the specialty location wouldn't disappoint, considering the international diversity of the staff. She knew taking the main dining room's offering of pasta was a quick and decisive "no."

Buffet-style lasagna never hit the spot.

She had to admit that the thought of seeing the kitchens aboard the ship gave the chef in her a little kick. Maybe a behind-the-scenes tour was in order.

While the four of them explored the floating city they would call home for the better part of two weeks, they passed an Irish pub where several women from their group sat drinking shots with other ladies their age.

The scene wasn't surprising, but the age of the women who had the emptiest shot glasses in front of them was.

The women north of sixty-five were reliving their twenties.

"Join us," one of them said as Mari's group walked by.

"We're on our way to the dating game," Amanda told them.

"Maybe we'll see you there," Rosa said.

The lounge where the singles gathered was a mix of all ages. Much more diverse than what Mari witnessed by the pool earlier that day.

And for Rosa's sake, there were many more men floating around the room than expected.

The room was packed, and seats were filling in fast.

They found a small table to the left of the stage with space for the four of them if they didn't mind sitting close together.

The low ceiling seemed to muffle some of the sound of the people, but the sheer number made it hard to hear what the person next to you was saying.

"This is nuts," Jill pointed out.

The three of them agreed.

The stage had an arch constructed with pink and white heart-shaped balloons. On it were the words *Breaking the Ice*.

Percy took the stage and jumped behind the microphone. "Welcome. Everyone, make yourselves comfortable. We will be starting in a few minutes. I hope you're ready to have a great time."

Several groups of people clapped and yelled their approval.

Jill looked around and behind them. "It's going to take a while for bar service."

There were at least a dozen servers running around. And they were running.

"Do either of you know what to expect?" Mari asked their new friends.

"Other than asking for volunteers, I have no idea," Amanda said.

Mari pointed at Rosa. "You dragged me on this boat. I'll drag you on that stage."

Rosa's eyes widened. "You wouldn't."

"*Calciando e urlando!*" Kicking and screaming, she said in Italian.

Rosa laughed with genuine excitement in her eyes.

Mari stood. "I'll get us something from the bar."

"I'll go with you," Jill said.

Mari shook her head. "I'll make two trips if I have to. Just make sure this one raises her hand. She needs a reason to lie to our children when we get home."

Weaving in and out of people, Mari found the end of what looked like a line.

"I wonder if OSHA would approve of this many people in the room."

An older gentleman standing behind Mari asked the question to anyone listening.

"I doubt it," Mari replied.

The man looked directly at her and smiled.

"The main ports of these ships never reside in a country with laws as strict as ours," he told her.

"I'm sure the ocean has its own set of rules."

Mari inched forward.

The older man smelled a little bit like a minty arthritis cream. "Looks like it's going to be fun."

Mari smiled, not sure what to say to that but not willing to ignore him. "Yes."

"Have you . . . before?"

The people in the room upped the volume, causing Mari to miss half of the man's question.

"I'm sorry, what was that?"

"I said . . . have you been on a cruise before?"

She shook her head. "My first."

"I come all . . ."

The last of his words were lost on her. She assumed what he said and simply nodded with a smile. "That's nice."

"My late wife loved . . ."

Mari leaned forward. "What?"

"She loved to cruise!" This time, he yelled.

The man moved closer, causing her to take a step back. "That's lovely."

Mari's gaze drifted to where Rosa and the other women sat.

More of the cruise director's staff started to arrive on the stage, and the noise just kept elevating.

"It's awfully loud in here. Can I convince you to skip this and find a quiet place for a drink?"

Mari's smile dropped, her eyes snapped back to the man old enough to be her father, and her jaw slacked.

She swore she heard someone nearby chuckle.

"No . . . that, ah . . ." What? She needed to shut this down quickly. "I'm not . . ."

"Single?"

"Yes. I'm . . ." *Single* sounded like something Rosa would say. *Widowed* invited more explanation and conversation. "I'm not interested in . . ." *You! A quiet bar.* When had she forgotten how to speak?

The man lifted his chin, his smile forgotten. "Well, you don't have to be rude."

Mari opened her mouth to reply but didn't get a chance.

The stranger turned on his heel and headed for the door leading out of the room.

"What just happened?" It was her turn to talk to no one.

The chuckle she thought she heard earlier returned.

Mari rotated her head to the side to find the amused smile of a man who was close enough to hear her question. "Did you see that?" she asked.

"I did."

"Was I rude?" The Italian in her said no. She didn't raise her voice once. Except to be heard. A necessity in the room.

"Some men can't take rejection," her observer said.

"I didn't think he was . . . he couldn't be serious. My father is younger than him."

"Age doesn't seem to matter on this ship."

No truer words had been said. First the boy at the pool, now this. "I'm not cut out for this," she said.

The bar line moved, putting Mari up next.

"If you don't want to get hit on, you might avoid the singles parties."

The man talking with her . . . and maybe even laughing at her, let mischief dance in his smile.

"I don't get hit on. This is not my . . ." She seriously needed to remember how to speak.

He chuckled again.

When she glared at him, he tried hard to stop.

Channeling Chloe, Mari rolled her eyes and smiled as she turned to the bartender.

"What can I get you?"

Good question. "Wine, what are your reds?"

Instead of answering, the bartender turned, picked up two bottles, and showed her the labels.

She winced. Her sommelier son would remind her that wine behind a bar at a club was good for only one thing. A headache.

"How about a martini?"

"Apple, lemon drop . . . dirty?"

Another chuckle from the stranger.

Without looking, she lifted a hand to her side in the man's general direction. "Enough from you."

He laughed harder.

The bartender glanced between them.

"Lemon, and two of them, please."

He left to make the drinks. Mari stood tall and waited.

Out of the corner of her eye, the observer acted as if he wasn't watching her. "Lemon was safe."

She bit her lip so she wouldn't smile. "No, you can't buy them for me."

"I wouldn't dream of asking."

"Good."

"Good."

The cruise director took the spotlight and started warming up the crowd.

People who weren't sitting found a seat, except for those in the line at the bar.

Mari looked over the heads of all the people and noticed a waitress talking with Rosa and the others. Thankfully, it looked like they were ordering.

Her martinis showed up, she gave the man her room key with a quick signature, and she lifted the drinks to return to her seat.

Mari faced her unnamed observer, lifted her chin.

"Be careful out there," he said.

"I don't think it's me that has to be careful. It's them." In addition to finding her voice, Mari had learned the game. If she was going to be accused of being rude, it wouldn't be for no reason at all.

"I hope I'm around to witness the wreckage."

Was that a wink?

No.

No.

Ignoring the strange stirring in her chest, Mari nodded to her stranger and returned to her seat.

"We need four female volunteers," Percy announced.

The room erupted in shouts of women offering up themselves or their friends.

Mari hung back long enough to not get roped into going onstage.

As requested, Amanda and Jill both grabbed Rosa's hands and yelled for Percy to pick her friend.

Percy singled out two young women, picked a third slightly older lady, and then zeroed in on Rosa.

Mari sipped her drink as she took her seat right as Rosa was stepping under the lights of the stage.

Her friend was blushing already.

"Now for the men."

Again, yells and calls were shouted out.

Percy turned toward the women. "Ladies' choice. Pick wisely. It will be up to you and your partner to work together to win this competition."

Rosa stared over Mari's way.

Mari lifted her cocktail in the air as if to say . . . "This is what you wanted."

One by one, the women before Rosa singled out a stranger in the room to partner up with.

When it was her turn, the room grew even louder, knowing it was their last chance to take part.

Mari took in Rosa's options. There were several men close to their age to pick from, but the most noise came from men slightly younger.

Finally, she made her choice.

Close in age, maybe a bit younger. Thin hair on top with a huge grin on his face.

He jumped onstage and took his place to Rosa's side.

Percy walked in front of the participants, asking their names and where they were from.

Julio from Spain spoke perfect English and quickly linked his arm with Rosa's.

Mari leaned over to Amanda.

"Please take a couple of pictures."

She didn't have to be asked twice.

"Here are the rules. We have three relays. Whichever team completes them first wins. Simple, right?"

The participants agreed.

"First relay we call Pucker Up." Percy stood back as his crew brought out four tall, narrow benches, then proceeded to place four tennis balls on individual pedestals. On the far end of that same table was the canister the tennis balls fit in. "You and your partner need to place the tennis balls into the container using only your lips."

Laughter erupted.

Two members of the crew demonstrated. With hands behind their backs and facing each other, they leaned over and pressed their lips against the ball, one on each side. They lifted the ball together and quickly, yet carefully, shuffled down the table, hovered the ball over the tube, and let it loose.

Basically, it looked like two people were kissing with a tennis ball between them.

"If you drop a ball, you have to start over. Next, you move on to the hula hoops. Holding hands, you must pass the hula hoop from one person to the other."

A crew member stood in the center of one hula hoop while holding hands with their partner. The crew member then kicked at the hula hoop until they brought it up to their waist, catching it with their elbow but not their hands. Wiggling their bodies and contorting their limbs, eventually, the hula hoop passed from one person to the next until it hit the floor around the feet of their partner.

Rosa's mouth opened wider and wider as the examples played out.

"Last but not least . . . we have Push the Box. You and your partner both put this on like so." Percy tied a strap around his waist. The strap extended down to the floor, and on the end was a long plastic eggplant.

By now, the crowd had clued in, and everyone was laughing.

Percy moved in front of a small box and shifted his hips until the eggplant hit the box and moved it to the other end of the stage, where the other partner would be waiting to push it back to the other side.

"This is fantastic," Jill said, laughing.

Mari almost felt sorry for her friend.

Almost.

While the contestants moved around onstage to get ready to go, Mari lifted her drink to her lips and felt her neck tingling.

Glancing over her shoulder, she saw laughing eyes smiling her way.

From across the room, her observer met her gaze.

He lifted his drink in the air before turning his attention back to the show.

Mari swallowed hard and stiffened her spine.

Her drink went down quickly.

The whistle blew, and Rosa and Julio, complete strangers, were working together, kissing a tennis ball and shuffling down a bench.

What was happening?

Less than twenty-four hours on the ship, and Mari hardly recognized the laughter coming out of her lungs, or the feeling in the pit of her stomach.

CHAPTER SIX

James met the day surprisingly rested.

He wasn't sure if the sway of the ship contributed to that, or the fact that he'd gone to bed late and didn't have an alarm clock pulling him out of bed before the sun rose.

Either way, he rolled out of bed and pulled open the drapes of his stateroom to find nothing but the vast blue sea and a sky dotted with clouds.

He pulled on the sliding glass door and was met with wind.

The first day on this cruise was at sea. Nothing but whatever the ship had on offer to entertain the passengers. And from what he'd witnessed the night before, that offering was expansive.

The PG-13-rated dating game had been a riot to watch. Something he'd expect from a bunch of college kids, only without alcohol shots at the end of each round.

That thought instantly had him envisioning his girls and realizing that they would be facing weekends filled with nights like what he'd just experienced before the year played out. Alcohol, boys . . . party games. Yes, laughter, fun, and excitement, but that wasn't the part that concerned him. It was the boys and alcohol.

Boys trying to pick them up.

Sneak them off to a quiet place.

Like the Italian spitfire he'd run into twice now.

The image of her put a smile on James's lips.

She was something. Funny, without trying to be, and completely taken aback by the interaction with the old guy trying to pick her up. It was as if she hadn't been hit on before.

The part that struck James the most about her was the fact that she wore every thought as a different expression on her face. From being formally polite, to confused, to dumbfounded, appalled, angry, daring, bossy, and last but most importantly, bewildered.

It was that last adjective that had James smiling as the morning salt air kissed his skin.

He would bet money her double take on him wasn't planned. Once she'd taken her seat with her friends and then looked back at him, the wonderous puzzlement that crossed her eyes had him kicking himself for not catching her name.

"Ah well," he said to himself. Meeting a woman wasn't his goal.

Convincing his daughters they were free to live their lives and placating his ex-wife with this forced vacation was.

He moved back inside, picked up the phone in the room, and ordered a carafe of coffee with a light breakfast from room service. Then jumped in the shower.

Wearing shorts and a casual shirt, he set up in the living room portion of his suite to tackle his workday. It was too early at home to expect any interaction with his staff, but at least he could work on a couple of bids for upcoming contracts.

Just as he was settling in, a knock on the door announced his meal.

James answered the knock, expecting to see Koi, his steward . . . and instead found Summer.

"There you are."

"Good morning," James said to Cindy's friend.

"I was starting to think you didn't get on the ship yesterday."

James stood back and motioned for her to come in.

"I've been here the whole time."

Summer was in full get-shit-done mode.

Around her neck was a lanyard holding God knew what. In her hand she held a clipboard. Sunglasses were holding her hair back like a headband, and the tennis shoes suggested she planned on running all day.

It reminded him of the days when the elementary school carnival was run by the PTA . . . aka Summer, Cindy, and all their friends.

James had never been so happy to be Cindy's ex at that point. Poor Clayton was roped into doing all kinds of chores for the women.

James had no problem being the fun guy, hanging with the kids, and spoiling them rotten.

"You weren't at the kickoff party."

"Yesterday at the pool?" he asked, playing dumb.

"Yeah."

"I was there."

"I didn't see you."

"Among the other five hundred people, I'm not surprised."

Summer cocked her head to the side. "We gathered for a photo."

"I forgot my shirt," he lied.

She rolled her eyes and turned to look at the room. "Leave it to you to book a suite."

James let that go. "What can I do for you, Summer?"

"And what's this?" She pointed to his computer.

"Work."

"You're on a cruise," she exclaimed.

"I am?" James turned around and shrugged his shoulders.

"Oh my God. I promised Cindy that you'd have a good time."

Someone knocked at the door.

"Hold on."

Koi, the Vietnamese steward, offered a toothy smile. "Good morning, Mr. Russell. I have your breakfast."

James stood back, giving the man room. "Perfect."

"Room service?" Summer questioned.

"On the dining table is fine," James directed.

Koi glanced at Summer, smiled, and said good morning.

Out came a tablecloth. A small vase with a tiny flower. A full set of silverware, glass of water, coffee, juice, and a covered plate.

James and Summer watched as Koi worked.

"Do you need another cup for the coffee?" he asked.

"No," Summer answered before James could. "Thank you."

"Anything else, just let me know."

And Koi was gone.

"Room service," Summer said a second time. "You do realize there are three dining rooms and a buffet you can catch, right?"

"And free room service." Well . . . not free. It came with the room, and the room wasn't exactly cheap.

"I completely understand why Cindy divorced you."

"I'm glad to have cleared up any confusion," he told her.

Summer huffed and shook her head. "You know I can't let you stay in the room all day. As nice as it is, there is a whole world happening out there."

He needed to throw the woman a bone so he could eat his breakfast while it was hot.

"I have some work to do. I'll get out. I explored the ship last night. I'm not a complete hermit."

Doubt crossed her eyes. "Oh yeah . . . what did you do?"

"I saw strangers kissing tennis balls."

"The dating game?"

"Yeah."

"I didn't see you there."

"I didn't see you either," he said.

It looked like she didn't believe him. "Did you meet anyone?"

James thought of the Italian. "I did."

"What was her name?"

"Did I say it was a her?" James reached for the coffee.

"James!"

It was like having a second ex-wife.

Though maybe he could get some information if he played this right. "I think you might know her. I believe she was wearing that green shirt earlier."

Summer's eyes lit up. "Who?"

"I didn't get her name. We chatted at the bar. I think she was Italian."

Summer's brow knitted together, then lifted. "Rosa?"

"Maybe."

"Or Mari? Wait, was she the one that got onstage?"

"No. I think that was her friend."

Summer lifted her hand to reach a tad shorter than her. "Yea tall, hair about here." She moved that hand to her shoulder. "Accent?"

James nodded. "Dark eyes, petite. Attractive."

"Yeah, that's Mari."

Mari. She looked like a Mari.

Not that James had ever met a Mari.

"She's kind of quiet."

James shrugged. "She had a lot to say last night."

"Huh!" Summer stared him down, and that computer brain of hers spun and spun.

"Satisfied?" he asked.

"I don't know."

James looked to the door of his room. "If you don't mind. My breakfast is getting cold. And if I'm going to get my work done so I can join all the frat boys playing drinking games at the pool later, I need to get started."

Summer drummed her fingers on her clipboard, huffed again, and turned toward the door.

"Don't make me drag you out of this room, James."

"Goodbye, Summer."

She let herself out while he stared at the closed door.

Her name was Mari.

~

Mari had no idea where Rosa was storing her energy.

The night before didn't land them in bed until after eleven. Which wasn't that bad, but considering they hadn't slept much since getting on the airplane, Mari had met her edge.

Rosa bounced out by six while Mari rolled over to catch more shut-eye.

"Enjoy the buffet without me," Mari had encouraged.

She stumbled out of bed just before eight and was in the shower when Rosa returned from breakfast.

"You wouldn't believe the amount of people who stopped me to tell me how much fun they had watching us last night."

"You're an overnight celebrity."

Rosa laughed. "That was so much fun."

While Mari brushed out her hair, Rosa held both the ship's daily itinerary and Summer's edition of things to do.

"There is more where that came from, I'm sure."

Rosa dropped her hands to her lap. "What do you want to do today? Ping-Pong tournament? Sexiest man on board? Salsa lessons?"

"Those are the choices?"

"That and twenty other options."

Mari turned toward her friend, offered a smile. "How about we find a sunny spot on deck that isn't completely overrun. I can read, and you can dance around from one activity to another."

"I can work with that."

An hour later, Mari and Rosa perched themselves on the deck above the pool, shielding them slightly from the party happening below but giving them a bird's-eye view should Rosa decide to jump in to join the fun.

The sun in the middle of the ocean was intense.

Happy in a pair of cotton shorts and a sleeveless shirt, Mari ducked under a wide-brim hat and smothered her skin that was exposed to the sun with sunblock.

So far, Chloe's clothing choices were working beautifully.

Aside from the lingerie.

That piece of clothing was going to require a conversation.

And scolding.

Her children were never beyond an age in which a good reprimand would remind them who their mother was. Though her words had much less of a punch these days.

Thinking of home had her wondering what they were doing.

It was half past seven in the morning there.

Luca and Brooke would be getting Franny off to school. Maybe take Leo to the park before the day busied up.

"What are you thinking about?" Rosa asked from the lounge chair next to Mari.

"Nothing."

Rosa lowered her chin and lifted a brow.

Mari sighed. "Home," she confessed.

"Mari!"

"Cosa?"

"Don't 'what' me. Home is exactly as it was last week. And the week before, and the week before."

Mari opened her mouth.

Rosa jumped up and cut her off. "You need a distraction."

"This ship is a distraction."

"Bloody Mary or a mimosa?" Rosa asked.

Mari's eyes widened. "It's not even noon."

"You pick, or I will."

"I am not—"

"Fine." With one word, Rosa marched away.

Neither spiked tomato juice nor orange juice–filled champagne ended up being the drink of choice. Instead, Rosa returned with the ship's drink of the day. A peach-vodka something that the ship had a silly name for.

Mari gave up arguing.

The book she'd opened up was finally catching her attention and helping her tune out the party that grew around her.

The clouds floated overhead just enough to keep her from getting overheated but not enough to make her want to seek another spot to read.

Down at the pool, Percy had arrived and started working the guests up for the "Hottest Man on Board" contest.

Just as the night before, the crew used the audience for grabbing volunteers or let friends push friends to the front of the crowd.

Mari was content watching from her perch, but Rosa wanted to get into the mix.

"Go. Please," Mari insisted.

Thankfully, Rosa didn't need to be told twice.

Once her friend was out of sight, Mari covered her face with her hands and sighed.

This was going to be a long vacation.

"It looks like you've been abandoned."

She spread her fingers and looked through them at the man behind the words.

It was him.

The man from the lounge.

"You."

"Hi," he said with a smile.

"Hello." Mari sat a little taller, feeling a little strange lying on a lounge chair with a man leaning against the railing of the ship looking down at her.

"Your friend likes the party."

"Apparently. I've honestly never seen this side of her."

Another smile. "I didn't catch your name last night. I'm James."

Should she stand? Shake his hand?

"Mari," she said without doing either of those things.

James waved a hand at the empty chair to her side. "Mind if I sit?"

"That depends."

He lifted a brow. "On?"

"If you don't offer me a drink or suggest we go somewhere else."

"Deal."

Mari pushed the hat she wore a little farther back on her head.

"You're not interested in the party down there?"

Mari glanced over the railing at the crazy going on at the pool. "I have no need to rate the men on this ship."

"Not out loud."

"Not at all," Mari insisted.

James narrowed his eyes. "Fascinating," he muttered.

"What is fascinating?"

James sat back on the chair and crossed his arms over his chest. "A single woman on a singles cruise with a singles group who isn't searching out the single men."

Mari's jaw opened, then closed. "I'm . . . How do you know I'm with a singles group?"

"The T-shirt yesterday."

"You saw me?"

A knowing smile crept onto his face. "I might have overheard you scolding the kid at the pool."

"He was ridiculous."

"Ballsy."

"My son is older than him."

James smiled. "How many children do you have?"

"Three. All married. Two grandchildren with two more on the way," she said. "What about you?"

"Two daughters. Both going off to college later this year."

"Both?"

"They're twins."

Mari sat taller. "My daughter-in-law is pregnant with twins."

"Really?"

"We were shocked. Twins don't run in the family. My Gio couldn't be happier. He's always wanted a dozen children."

"I don't think I know anyone with more than three. A dozen sounds like a made-for-TV movie."

A cheer from the pool rose, capturing Mari's attention. "Maybe two babies at once will quell his ambitious desires. Emma may take some convincing after this."

"Emma is your daughter-in-law?"

"Yes."

James nodded a couple of times. "Cindy wasn't interested in trying again. We do have twins in the family, and she was worried it would happen again."

Mari glanced at James's left hand. "Cindy . . ."

"My ex-wife," he said with a smile and long breath. "We split when the girls were young."

"I'm sorry to hear that."

"Don't be. We're good friends. Her new husband is perfect for her. Great to the girls. Bitterness after a failed marriage only poisons the kids." James smiled. "We didn't want that for Madison and Ellie."

The tone in James's voice softened when he spoke of his daughters.

"You didn't love your wife?"

"Of course I did." He paused. "But not in the way Clayton does. We knew that if we'd stayed together for the girls, we would have ended up hating each other."

Mari thought of Rosa and her hatred for Joseph. A man who married her because she got pregnant, stuck around long enough to have two children, and then up and left one day, never to return.

"I suppose that's admirable of you. Both of you."

James cocked his head to the side. "What about you? What happened with you and your ex?"

Mari hummed and smiled. "Paulo is not my ex."

The look on James's face froze.

"I lost him ten years ago to cancer."

He released a sigh. "Oh my God. I'm so sorry."

Instead of saying he needn't be, Mari responded, "Thank you. It feels like a lifetime ago. He was a good man. Loving. Hardworking. A wonderful father." Mari tried to envision his face and found it hard.

"You never remarried?"

"Lord, no. I still loved my husband. I was busy raising my children. Keeping the restaurant going. The thought of another man never entered my head." *Not even as a passing thought.*

"But that has changed."

It wasn't a question. Though Mari answered it as if it were. "No . . . well, yes. My children are grown. The restaurant practically runs itself."

James kept his eyes on hers. "But you're here. On *this* cruise with *these* people."

It dawned on Mari, then, what James was alluding to. "*Allora.* I'm . . . No. I'm here for Rosa. She wanted this." Mari lifted a hand to the surrounding ship and people. "She wants a second chance at love. Or perhaps to discover herself. I'm here to support her."

Mari wasn't sure if there was disappointment in his eyes or concern.

"You're a good friend."

"I certainly don't want to mislead anyone." She looked up at him and smiled. "Not the older gentleman last night or the . . . child yesterday. And not you," she tacked on the end.

"Oh?"

Mari placed a hand on her chest, felt heat in her cheeks. "You're much too nice of a man to waste your time with me."

"Is that what I'm doing?"

She paused. "Isn't it?" Maybe she read that wrong. Read him wrong. Maybe he was just being polite and wasn't seeing if she was receptive to his attention. *Oh, God. What am I doing?* "You said it yourself. This is a singles cruise. You're single." Her words were coming in a rush.

James looked away, hiding a grin. "I'm here under duress myself."

"Oh?"

Mari watched as James looked around. "I told you, my daughters are going off to college."

"Okay."

"Apparently, they've been discussing which one of them needs to pick a school close by so they can take care of me."

Mari's heart melted. "That's so sweet."

"Cindy didn't think so. She believes the only way I'm going to convince our girls that I'm all right is to start dating. Or at least make it look like I'm trying. We told the girls I was going on this vacation to do just that."

"Date?"

"Or make them think I am. Once they're settled at school, they'll forget about me and my love life, or lack of, and things can go back to normal. Cindy talked to Summer, and here I am." He shrugged his shoulders.

"Summer? You're from San Diego?" Mari had assumed he was from somewhere else.

"I am. Didn't I say that?"

"No. You didn't." She would have remembered that. "I haven't seen you with the group."

He shook his head. "This was a Cindy and Summer thing. Like you, I'm not here looking for romance."

"Right."

He turned, swept his feet from the lounge chair, and faced her. "You know . . . maybe we could help each other out."

"*Cosa?*" Mari shook her head, realized she'd spoken in Italian. "What? How?"

"Well, men keep approaching you. Like last night. I can't imagine that is going to change for the duration of this vacation. You are an attractive woman, Mari."

She swallowed, and her face heated. It had been a very long time since she'd heard a man say those simple words.

"I'm a grandmother."

"That's not a deterrent. Anyway, my point. When Rosa is busy rating the men on the ship or playing games, perhaps I can keep you company. Maybe the curious men will leave you alone."

Mari wasn't buying it. "I'm capable of turning men away."

James let out a deflated sigh. "I guess that's true."

The look on his face was comical.

"What is it that I could do for you?"

He slowly let a smile creep on his face. "Take a couple of pictures with me? On a beach or in the casino? To show my girls that I'm trying. Pictures will help my cause."

"Oh, well. That makes sense. I can't imagine that would hurt." Smiling for a camera wasn't asking a lot.

James lifted a brow. "You'll help me out?"

"I don't see why not," she said.

"Perfect. Thank you."

"I haven't done anything yet."

"That's not true." He relaxed back into his chair. "I was planning on spending most of my days in my stateroom."

"Why?"

He lifted his hand, palm up. "I mean . . . I'm a good-looking man. I don't need women hitting on me."

Mari laughed. "Humble, too."

He laughed with her. "Not today."

It felt good to smile.

CHAPTER SEVEN

James peered out into the crowd in front of the tour bus, hoping he hadn't screwed this up.

The first port of call was in the Dominican Republic. The ship pulled up right along a dock surrounded by the bluest ocean he'd ever seen.

Tour guides held pamphlets and attempted to pull people into a conversation as they passed, even though it was obvious they were already on a tour and simply waiting for everyone to show up.

James had stood in front of the activity desk, trying to figure out which activities his new friend would likely go on.

The three main excursions were waterfall trekking; zip-lining and ATV adventure; or a party boat out on the water, which included snorkeling.

Considering Mari had sat by the pool the previous day and the fact that she'd refused free drinks, he ruled out the party boat. Zip-lining and ATVs? Yeah, James didn't see that one happening for her either.

That left the waterfalls.

He'd booked his ticket with the ship the previous night and now stood with a small sack that held a change of shorts and a towel.

There were three massive tour buses in line to pick up the tourists and ship them off to the jungles of the island to explore.

And James was looking for Mari.

Shortly after they'd struck their bargain, her friend Rosa showed up to pull Mari away to play Ping-Pong.

James had returned to his stateroom to do the work he promised himself he'd do. Only he found himself staring at his computer, then glancing out the open sliding doors of his stateroom at the vast blue sea that stretched out in every direction and asking himself, "What the hell am I doing in this room?"

Sure, he hadn't planned on meeting a woman on the cruise.

But . . .

Mari was beautiful and funny. She acted unaffected by everything going on around her but kept side-eyeing the fun with a tap of her fingers. James couldn't help but think that with the smallest of nudges, Mari would be on the dance floor, laughing it up with the rest of them.

And when was the last time he was that guy on the dance floor?

It had been a while.

And probably for the same reasons Mari sat on the sidelines.

Kids that had dominated her life, now she had grandchildren. Which blew his mind.

She'd gone on the cruise to play wingman to her best friend.

And James had come to appease his kids.

But why not have as much fun as possible?

And why not do that with someone as engaging as Mari?

Here he stood, attempting to execute that engagement, with a ticket in his hand for an excursion he assumed Mari and Rosa were on.

Since the person he'd booked the tour through asked which singles group he belonged to, James hoped that meant he would be on Mari's bus. James found the bus he was assigned and climbed inside. He passed several rows of unknown faces before finding an empty seat.

No Mari.

As the bus filled, he started to wonder if he'd made a mistake.

His heart skipped at a familiar face. Only it wasn't the one he wanted to see.

Clipboard in hand, Summer stood in front of everyone, counting people.

When she noticed him, she gave a little wave and continued counting.

James watched as Summer said something to the driver and then looked at her watch.

The driver started the bus.

Damn it. He'd made the wrong call.

Then James saw Summer duck her head and point.

James followed her gaze and smiled.

Mari and Rosa climbed onto the bus while James patted himself on the back.

James studied his lap, hoping she didn't see him watching.

"James," Mari called.

He looked up. "What a surprise."

Rosa took a seat close to the window directly across the aisle from his. Mari joined her friend.

Talking over the empty seat beside him, Mari asked, "What happened to getting your work done?"

"I'll have time for that later. When will I be in the Dominican Republic again?"

"You planned on working?" Rosa asked over her friend.

More than one head turned his way from the other passengers.

"Well—"

Four more people walked between the seats, cutting off their conversation.

Following them came Summer. "I see you found Mari," Summer said loud enough for everyone to hear.

Shit.

Mari turned up one eyebrow.

"Yesterday, actually," he said. James swallowed and attempted to keep a smile while glaring at Summer.

"Good." Summer dropped her clipboard on the seat beside him. "Mind if I sit here?"

"Uhm." *Kinda.*

"Thanks." And she was gone, back to the front of the bus while the driver pulled away from the curb.

"You know Summer?" Rosa asked.

He nodded.

"Okay, ladies and gentlemen . . ." The tour director spoke over the intercom, pulling everyone's attention to him.

While the tour guide introduced himself, Summer slowly made her way back to the seat beside James.

"We have about an hour's drive to our first stop . . ." the tour director continued.

Summer leaned close and said in a hushed whisper, "Did your computer break?"

"No."

She stifled a laugh and glanced at Mari from the corner of her eye.

James pretended not to notice and stared at the guide as if he was riveted by his instructions.

"She's a widow," Summer whispered again.

Without looking over, he clenched his jaw and uttered, "I know."

"I don't think she's dated—"

"If I needed a wingman, I'd ask," he cut her off.

The bus started to move.

Summer chuckled.

Thankfully, she stopped talking until the guide was finished telling them about what to expect on the tour.

Conversations among the passengers started up, filling the quiet space.

Summer leaned across the aisle. "I heard you had quite a night, Rosa. Everyone has been talking about it."

James let out a sigh.

"Who was your partner?"

"Julio."

"Have you seen him since?" Summer asked.

"No." Rosa sounded disappointed.

Summer scooted forward in her seat. "When we get back home, I have some ideas on how to bring more people into our group. I think you'd be great at leading some of the activities."

James shook his head. He'd heard Summer's pitch to gather volunteers so many times, he could recite her script verbatim.

"You think so?" Rosa asked.

"Yeah." Summer shifted again. "Uhm, Mari . . . would you mind switching seats? I need to save my voice, and this bus is loud."

"Of course," Mari said.

Summer leaned in, grabbed her clipboard, and whispered, "You owe me."

James cleared his throat, wanting to strangle hers.

But he didn't have time to do anything but smile when Mari and Summer switched seats.

"Hello," Mari said.

"Hi. Did you two have fun last night?"

"We did. We turned in entirely too late."

"I think that's the expectation on this cruise," he said.

"What about you? Did you get out?"

He shrugged. "I thought it was best to put in a couple of hours last night since I booked this tour today."

"Then you're sticking with the 'working while you're on vacation' plan?"

He shrugged. "A few hours here and there won't hurt."

Mari fixed him with a stare. "You never mentioned what you did for a living?"

James felt his shoulders relaxing as he stepped into familiar territory. "I own a rental company."

"Homes?"

He shook his head. "Equipment. Heavy machinery. Cranes, mostly."

Mari's brow knitted together.

"Whenever a skyscraper is under construction, you'll see massive cranes moving material around. My company supplies projects with the equipment and operators," James explained.

"Really? How did you fall into that?" Mari's smile and dark eyes felt genuinely interested.

"I went to trade school straight out of high school and eventually became an operator. It didn't take me long to realize the real money was in owning the equipment and renting it out. I didn't want to work for someone else my entire life, so I took night classes to figure out the business part. I came up with a plan and talked my way into a loan to buy my first two pieces of equipment."

"Two?"

He nodded. "One to lease out and one that I could operate. They weren't the kind for skyscrapers. Much smaller scale. Every year, I brought in more. With it came employees, operators, and maintenance workers. I went from renting yard space to store machinery to buying my own property and office building."

"That's impressive. All while raising your girls?"

"Like I said, Cindy and I co-parent well." He didn't like bringing his ex-wife into their conversation, but he couldn't take all the parenting credit. "Did you say something about a restaurant? I meant to ask you about that yesterday."

"D'Angelo's, in Little Italy," she told him with a smile.

He tried to picture the area. "I think I know where that is. I can't say if I've ever eaten there."

Her smile fell slightly, she gave a small toss of her hand and a roll of an eye. "Then you haven't sampled the best Italian food in San Diego."

"Is that right?" he teased.

"Paulo and I took it over when my parents returned to Italy. It's one of the oldest restaurants in the neighborhood." Pride spread over her features.

"You're the chef?"

She hummed. "Some days. Not as often anymore. Luca, my oldest, runs the kitchen staff. I jump in when needed."

"Running a business is just as hard as working in it."

Mari nodded. "I have help for that these days. Which is why I'm on this cruise, I suppose."

"You've done the right thing if your business can run without you," he said.

Her sideways glance and tiny smirk saw right through him. "This from the man who brought his computer and planned on working the entire time."

James hung his head in mock shame. "Guilty. Maybe you can give me some pointers on how to get others to do my job so I can vacation work-free."

"Unless your daughters are interested in taking over, I don't have any other suggestions."

James laughed. "God, no. Ellie thinks she's going to play professional softball, and Madison wants to be a rocket scientist."

Mari winced. "That won't work, then."

"No. It won't. At best, I can hope to have someone else running my company for me by the time I want to retire. Or maybe I'll sell." That thought had only crossed his mind a couple of times.

"You would sell what you've worked so hard to build?" Mari sounded shocked.

He sighed. "I honestly don't know. It depends. If one of my girls marries someone who wants to take it over . . . or maybe a grandchild. But that's a long way off. I wouldn't be surprised if Ellie stayed single, and something tells me Madison will find a man more interested in inventing machines than running a company that uses them."

His words seemed to soak into Mari's head.

"Life has a way of working out."

The bus jolted as they turned off the main road and onto one that hadn't been repaved in who knew how long.

"That's tomorrow's problem," James said. "Today I'm trekking to waterfalls." *With a beautiful woman.* But he left that part out.

CHAPTER EIGHT

"He's flirting with you," Rosa whispered in Mari's ear.

"He's being nice."

Rosa switched to Italian and spoke louder. *Nice* and *flirting.*

Mari cleared her throat. *It's rude to talk about someone in another language when they're standing right in front of you.* Sadly, she chided Rosa in Italian, breaking her own rules.

Would you like me to say it again in English?

"No." Mari glanced over her shoulder and found James talking to Summer a few paces behind them.

The entire drive to the first waterfall was filled with laughter and conversation.

The man was easy to talk to, especially with them having so much in common. "He's a new friend, that is all," Mari told her friend.

Rosa switched back to English. "It's okay, you know. If he is *flirting.*" To Rosa's credit, she said *flirting* an octave lower than the rest of her sentence. But that didn't stop Mari from feeling heat rush to her cheeks.

"He's not." Even as the words left her lips, they tasted a little off. Like sauce made from tomatoes that were past their prime.

Rosa lifted her hands in the air as if in surrender.

A few seconds later, Rosa said, "He's attractive."

"Shhh!"

Their guide brought them to a meeting point where, according to Rosa, they would be putting on a life jacket and water shoes to get closer to the falls themselves.

Five minutes into the tour guide's instructions, Mari realized that looking at waterfalls and taking a few pictures was not what they were in for.

"We have lockers for you to leave your dry clothes and valuables behind. As a preferred guide for your cruise line, we can assure you everything will be safe. If you've brought a waterproof pouch for your phone, fantastic, otherwise we suggest you leave it behind. It will get wet. There is about a forty-minute hike uphill, where we will get into the stream and make our way back down."

"Did he say 'into the stream'?" Mari asked to anyone listening.

No one answered her.

"Once everyone has changed, see one of us for a life jacket, helmet, and water shoes if you didn't bring your own."

Mari grasped Rosa's arm. "I thought you said we were going to the waterfalls, not *in* them."

"I asked if you looked at our options. You said you did."

"Sightseeing waterfalls is what you told me."

Rosa pulled on Mari's arm. "Don't look at me like that. I read the fine print."

"Divertimento."

Mari should have known something was amiss when Rosa insisted she pack her swimsuit.

The open changing room where women pulled clothing off to squeeze into their suits was something Mari hadn't seen since she was in high school.

She glanced around while simultaneously attempting to avert her eyes to the bare flesh of women everywhere.

Rosa opened an empty locker and pushed her bag inside.

Before Mari could protest, Rosa's shirt was off her back and she was unhooking her bra.

A bit shell-shocked, Mari followed her friend's lead. "You would think they'd have individual stalls for this," she muttered.

"Who cares, Mari. No one is looking and no one cares."

With her bag tucked away and her swimsuit at the ready, Mari slipped out of her clothes as quickly as she could and into the suit. She started to put her shorts back on over the suit when Rosa stopped her. "If you do that, you'll be wearing wet clothes all the way back to the ship. The seats on the bus are cloth."

Mari tsked and tossed the shorts into the locker.

Thank God for Mari's good sense to not buy the two-piece suit Chloe had attempted to talk her into. Walking out of the locker room and into the jungles of the Dominican Republic in a one-piece was nerve-racking enough.

Without lingering, Mari marched directly to the guide handing out life preservers and quickly put one over her head. Next came the shoes and then the helmet, which she held.

Even with all that, she still felt air brushing the back of her thighs. Air never played there in public.

"Are you ready for this?"

James's voice came from behind.

Her back stiffened. "I don't know what 'this' is."

"You didn't read the description?" he asked.

She glanced over, realized he wasn't wearing a shirt or a life preserver, and forced her eyes to stay on his face. "A mistake I won't make twice," she told him.

He laughed.

"You can swim, right?"

"Of course."

"Then you'll be fine. Just a few waterslides and—"

"Water *what*?"

"Slides. Down rocks."

"What?" *He did not just say* rocks.

"Natural waterslides, Mari. Don't worry." Rosa stood close, a smile way too big over her face.

Mari turned to glare at her friend. "How far are the drops?" The image of sliding off a rocky mountain, down a waterfall, and into a pool of crashing water clouded her vision.

"From what I read, they're not big."

Mari felt a hand on her shoulder. "I won't let you get hurt," James told her.

"What? Are you going to catch me?" The question came with a little fire in its delivery.

He smiled. "If I have to."

Behind them, Rosa laughed.

Mari turned, pointed a finger at her friend, and snapped. "Enough from you."

Rosa tried to hide her smile and cleared her throat. "I'm going to find Summer. Keep her safe, James. And mind her temper. She has one for all of us."

Just like that, Rosa abandoned her.

Mari muttered an expletive in Italian under her breath.

James chuckled. "I have a feeling that wasn't meant for children's ears."

"You'd be right."

"C'mon. There're kids here, it can't be that bad."

"If I break anything or come up bleeding, I'll make you eat those words."

James pinched his lips together, but the sparkle in his eyes said he was laughing. "A little blood might be worth seeing what that looks like."

She pulled her thoughts in and reluctantly followed James.

The good news was, she'd completely forgotten that her butt was on display in a bathing suit she hadn't worked up the nerve to even wear by the pool.

They entered the water by a vertical wooden ladder.

Below, crystal-clear blue water was surrounded by a tall, rocky landscape.

Rosa and Summer were already in the river, along with half of their group.

"I'll go first," James said.

Once James cleared the ladder and the water directly below, the guide encouraged Mari to take her turn.

She slowly descended the ladder, doing her best to ignore the shudder in her knees.

It wasn't that the climb was all that far, it was the fact that Mari couldn't remember the last time she'd been on anything but a stepladder in the stockroom at the restaurant since the time her children were little.

As soon as her feet touched the water, relief rushed through her veins.

"See, that wasn't bad," James said.

Mari took a deep breath and nodded.

They walked, waist-deep, to where one of their guides waited.

Mari looked up. "It's beautiful."

"Yes," James agreed. "And not something you can really appreciate from above."

A few meters from where they entered the water, Mari's foot slid on a rock, causing her to lurch to one side.

James caught her arm before she could correct herself. "Oh, boy."

He squeezed her arm. "You got it?"

"I see how this is going to go," she told him.

He lifted his shoulders. "I don't mind."

Maybe Rosa was right about James flirting.

Or maybe her friend had planted that seed, and now Mari was looking for any evidence to prove he was or wasn't.

Mari inched a little closer to the side of the canyon to use nature's walls to help steady her steps. "This is better," she told him, giving him a reason to step back.

Only he stayed within arm's reach.

"Have you ever done anything like this?" Mari asked.

He nodded. "In Cancun with my girls. Only the river ran both above- and underground."

"Under?" she questioned.

"It was beautiful. Swimming in a cave is an experience. The girls loved it."

They continued to talk as they maneuvered in the water. At times, the river was swirling around their knees, at other times, their waists.

It wasn't long before the guides directed them out of the river and pointed to a twenty-foot drop. "You have the option of jumping in, or there is a footpath where you can join us on the other side of this waterfall."

Mari took one look at the twenty-foot drop, and the twenty-year-olds jumping in, and shook her head. "No, thank you."

A woman behind her laughed. "I'm with you," she said.

Mari looked at James. "Are you going to jump?"

He glanced over the edge. "I think so."

"You're crazy. I'll watch." With that, Mari followed the less adventurous to the stairs.

"Mari!"

She turned to see Rosa yelling her name from her perch on the jumping spot.

Mari's smile fell. "What are you . . ."

Her words dropped off as Rosa hurled herself into the water.

Her head bobbed up almost as quickly as it had disappeared below.

Mari continued to walk, her hand tight on the railing.

Rosa swam over once Mari was back in the water. "That was fantastic."

"Who are you, and what did you do with my quiet, reserved neighbor down the street?"

Rosa just laughed. "I forgot how fun life is."

Mari thought she heard her name again and looked up.

James lifted his hand in the air and jumped.

"Oh, boy."

A few yards away, their first natural waterslide waited.

Like before, she watched others before taking her turn. Not that she had a choice. There wasn't an option to walk around.

Mari lay down, her arms over her chest, and let the water take her to the next level of the river.

Aside from her bathing suit riding up her butt, nothing bad happened. Her head didn't even go all the way in the water.

James waited for her, and they both swam until they felt the ground.

The second waterslide was a much bigger drop. Like the first, the worry of what could happen was gone as soon as she came out of the water.

Then came an unavoidable jump. There was no way to walk around and no turning back.

Mari looked down. "I can't do this."

James took her hand. "Yes, you can."

"I—"

James placed a hand on her cheek. "The last slide was a longer drop."

"I can't."

"You raised three kids and ran a restaurant by yourself. You can jump ten feet."

Two people from their group moved around them.

"Want to go in front of me?" James asked.

She nodded and shook her head at the same time.

James laughed.

And that spiked the skin on her neck. "Fine."

She moved to the edge. The guide standing there looked bored and held out a hand to stop her.

Once the person in the water swam out of the way, he dropped his hand. "Go."

The thudding of her heart whooshed in her ears.

"You got this," a complete stranger said from behind.

"Jump out," the guide said.

"Okay." She looked down. "Okay . . . okay."

Clenching the bridge of her nose with one hand and fisting the other . . . she jumped.

Water rushed around her face, her ears did that popping thing, and Mari sputtered to the surface.

I did it.

I didn't die.

Someone was clapping.

James smiled from above. "You made it look easy."

Mari smiled, swam out of his way, and watched him follow her in.

From then on, everything was easy. One of the slides was definitely going to leave a bruise on her hip, and two of the jumps pushed water up her nose. But the rush that came from overcoming her fears was the greatest reward of the day.

Once their waterfall hike concluded, they returned to where they began, changed clothes, and had lunch. James sat across from her, sipping a rum-laced drink and smiling.

And flirting.

Something she'd forgotten how to do.

~

Before Mari and James made it back on the bus, Summer and Rosa had resumed the seats they'd taken en route earlier.

Any awkwardness in being pushed together had passed as Mari eased back in her seat.

Eventually, their quiet conversation and the movement of the bus had Mari's eyes drifting closed. "I'm not great company on the way back," she said apologetically.

"Don't stay awake on my account."

She smiled and closed her eyes, only to be woken up what felt like a few minutes later.

The bus was pulling into the parking lot, and James was patting her arm. "We're back."

She yawned and stretched to bring life back into her limbs. "I was out."

"You and half the bus."

Back on the ship, James walked with her and Rosa until they reached their deck. "Thanks for hanging out with me today. It wouldn't have been nearly enough fun without you ladies."

Rosa patted her chest. "Ahh, you're welcome. Maybe we'll see you at dinner."

"I don't think I can eat anything more today," Mari moaned.

"We have an hour to get ready."

She turned to Rosa. "You go ahead. I'm going to sleep off that rum."

Her friend laughed. "Speaking of, we're doing the rum and food tour tomorrow, are you signed up for that?" she asked James.

He blinked a couple of times, looked between the two of them. "I'll see if they still have room."

"Great," Rosa said.

Mari met his gaze. "I guess we'll see you then."

"Tomorrow," he replied before continuing his way up the stairs.

Before Mari and Rosa turned to the long corridor to their stateroom, Rosa nudged her. "Huh."

"Hush." Mari took the lead.

"I didn't say anything."

"You didn't have to." Mari knew exactly what Rosa's "Huh" said. It said James was flirting and was interested . . . and Mari wasn't sure what to feel about that.

CHAPTER NINE

Rum and food were popular. So much so that the tour Mari was going on was completely sold out. James cursed his luck. At the same time, he acknowledged that jumping into daily involvement with a woman who had told him that she wasn't interested in a relationship was a bad idea.

That didn't mean he wanted her to think he was standing her up. And assuring that happened required a conversation with Summer.

Or at least a text message or two.

Instead of intercepting Summer in the dining room, he sent a message, hoping she had her phone on her.

Hey.

What a lame way to start a conversation.

James watched the screen on his phone for nearly a minute before three dots appeared.

Hello Mr. I'm not interested in finding a date.

Fine. He had to own that. About that . . . Do you know which room Mari and Rosa are in?

He could practically see Summer's Cheshire-cat smile.

Mari and Rosa?

Yes.

Three dots lingered, and he could almost taste the sarcasm that was bound to come next.

I don't think Mari plays that way, James. She seems too reserved for that.

Pitch and hit.

James rolled his eyes.

Ha ha. Do you have the room number or not?

An emoji of Summer laughing flashed and then four digits.

Thank you.

James moved to the edge of his bed and picked up the phone in his room. The second the phone rang, he remembered that Mari was going to try and get some rest.

Damn.

Too late now.

Thankfully, Mari didn't sound asleep when she answered the call. "Hello?"

"Hello, Mari. I didn't wake you, did I?"

"James?"

He smiled, felt an extra beat in his chest that she knew it was him. Good God, how old was he? "Yeah."

"No, I, ah . . . I thought I'd be able to sleep. I think I just needed some alone time."

James toed his shoes off and sat against the headboard of the bed. "I understand that. It's hard to get that on this ship unless you're in your own room."

"Having a roommate as energetic as Rosa has been making it difficult."

James wanted to keep her on the phone but also be sensitive to her need for solitude. "I bet. Listen, I wanted to let you know that I couldn't get tickets for tomorrow."

"Oh?"

"They're sold out."

"That's unfortunate. You sounded excited about it."

James couldn't determine if there was disappointment in her voice or if it was just his wishful thinking. "Maybe I'll see you after? Singles night in the casino?"

There was definitely a little giggle from her end of the line. "Do you gamble?"

James eased back against the bed and made himself comfortable. "I played poker in college. Mainly because girls were involved, and clothing was optional."

He heard her soft chuckle. "College indiscretions aside?"

"If tossing a few dollars on red is gambling, then yes. Blowing my mortgage payment on black . . . then no." He sighed. "I've never been in a California casino, and I've only been to Vegas twice. Once at twenty-one because . . . turning twenty-one. And again, for a friend's bachelor party."

"Oh . . . That can be dangerous."

"A bachelor party?"

"Yes."

"You've been to a bachelor party?"

"No," she said with amusement. "Luca, my oldest, and Brooke had a bachelor-bachelorette weekend in Vegas. All the kids jumped on a plane to celebrate, and when they got home, Chloe and Dante were married."

"Wait . . . what?"

"You heard me. Dante flew in from Italy for Luca's wedding and ended up marrying my daughter at some cheesy chapel on the Vegas Strip."

James had heard of that kind of thing in the movies, but in real life . . . no.

"Were they dating?"

"Not at all. Dante had been living in Positano for quite some time. I knew Chloe had a crush on him growing up, but after he moved away, Rosa and I scrubbed the idea of them getting together."

"Oh, that's right, Dante is Rosa's son." James was starting to piece together Mari's family in his head. A family she always talked about.

"Yes."

"You showed me pictures of Chloe and Dante at their wedding. Did they get married twice?"

"Yes . . . well . . . They didn't tell anyone about Vegas. They'd been drinking—"

"Ohhh," he interrupted.

"Hangovers with unexpected wedding rings are not a great combination."

That made him laugh.

Mari was laughing, too.

"Chloe and Dante kept the entire Vegas debacle to themselves. When they came home, they were set on getting an annulment before anyone found out what they'd done."

"That makes sense. After their annulment, they married again," James concluded.

"No," Mari said. "They never got to that point. When they decided they wanted to stay married, I made them go to the church. My only daughter was not going to miss out on a proper wedding because of a few too many with her childhood crush."

James let that soak in for a second. "That's quite a Vegas bachelor party story."

"It took a while for Luca and Gio to accept what happened. Especially when Chloe and Dante were working out if they wanted to stay married. It was touch and go there."

"They didn't approve?" James asked.

Mari hesitated. "I don't think they saw Dante beyond their days of clothing-optional poker. Dante is an attractive young man and certainly commanded the attention of women."

James laughed. "That was a very elegant way of saying he was a player."

"Ehh . . . he was young. They all were at one point. Once the fists were thrown and everyone calmed down, it all worked out."

"Fists?" James asked.

"Gio was protecting Chloe's virtue. I don't condone violence, but sometimes . . ."

That, James understood. "I have daughters. I get it."

"They're all inseparable again. Like I said, it all worked out."

"You know, Mari . . . I don't consider myself a romantic. Hard to be when I haven't dated in years, but that's one hell of a romantic story."

James heard her sigh and imagined the smile she had on her face.

"It is," she said.

"I should let you go. You were looking for a quiet evening, and here I am keeping you on the phone."

"It's okay."

"What do you say? Casino night? I promise not to give you one too many and find a chaplain."

Mari coughed. "How thoughtful of you. Considering I don't know your last name, a chaplain shouldn't register in your head when thinking of me."

"I'm teasing. And it's Russell. I'll see you at the casino."

"Did I say yes?" she asked.

"You didn't say no." James waited long enough to give her time to say no . . .

She didn't.

"Enjoy your day tomorrow."

"I will. Good night."

When was the last time a woman said those words to him? "Good night, Mari."

James stared at the phone receiver and nodded.

Maybe he had some game after all.

~

"Is someone sitting here?"

Mari glanced up at a man standing over her. A drink in his hand, a smile on his face.

"Yes, actually. There is." She pointed toward the bar. "He just went to get us a drink."

The stranger tilted his head to the side, then said, "Lucky guy." And turned and walked away.

James had talked her into the nickel slot machines. "How much damage can you do with a nickel slot?" he'd asked.

Twenty minutes into playing, she was up twenty dollars and decided to accept James's offer of a drink. Avoiding one too many was the agenda.

There was a chapel on the ship, which Mari noted on her way to meet James at the casino. Recalling their conversation put a perpetual smile on her face. She'd truly forgotten what it felt like for a man to flirt with her.

There was a tiny voice way in the back of her head asking if she should be allowing it. Paulo may have been gone for a decade, but he was still a part of her.

"You're not dishonoring Paulo," Rosa had told her.

Which Mari knew was true.

So, here she was, in a casino, waiting for James to return with their drinks.

She put another nickel into the slot and pressed the button.

"That took a while," James announced when he returned.

Mari accepted the martini and pointed at the screen. "I won another ten."

"Next round is on you."

"We both have the alcohol package. The drinks are free."

"Oh, that's right," he teased.

James resumed his spot, set his drink down. "Where did Rosa run off to?"

"She said roulette, but I don't see her standing over there."

James glanced over Mari's shoulder. "Oh, well."

"She mentioned a dance party in the observation lounge." Rosa truly was making up for lost time.

"I'm guessing her divorce is recent," James said.

"Why do you think that?"

He pressed a button on the slot machine and had the bells ringing. "Because she's bouncing from one thing to the next, trying to see where she fits."

"You think so?"

"Yeah. I've seen it in both my male friends and my female friends after their divorces."

Mari lost twenty cents and pressed the button again. "Is that what you did?"

"Not really. I knew who I was before I got married."

Another twenty cents down. "In my culture, it's normal for women to marry young and start a family. Seems young people today are more interested in their careers."

"They have to be," he said. "It's expensive to have children."

"Not if family is close enough to help raise them."

"Did you have help?"

"When the children were small, yes. Not always family, but a community that helped. And I'm there for Luca and Brooke. It helps that we live above the restaurant."

"You do?"

"I thought I mentioned that."

He shook his head.

She shrugged. "My apartment is on the second floor. Luca and Brooke are on the third, and there's a guest flat on the fourth, along with a terrace."

"Does that ever feel crowded?"

"No. I would rather feel my family crawling all around me than so far away I have to fly to see them."

"I'm sure there is something in between those extremes."

"Eh." She threw up her hands. "It's all I've ever known."

James's slot machine started to flash, and bells rang.

They both looked at the display.

"Four thousand nickels."

"Two hundred dollars. We should quit while we're ahead," Mari said.

"Let's finish our drinks first."

She turned back to her game. "Suit yourself. Don't blame me if you lose it all."

An hour later, they cashed in their tickets. Mari stopped when her original hundred dollars was back in her pot.

James kept twenty out of his original hundred.

Losing all he'd won.

They found Rosa at the dance party, where she'd joined a group from the San Diego Singles. It wasn't completely clear if she was dancing with a man or a group of women . . . or maybe a group of men and women.

Summer jumped up from where she sat and waved them over.

"Where have you two been?" she asked once they were at her side.

James gave her a side-eye, and Mari responded, "The casino."

"Win anything?"

"It isn't about winning, it's about having fun," James said.

"That means you lost."

"I broke even," Mari said before pointing at James. "This one should have quit while he was ahead."

"Advice I'm sure you gave, and he ignored."

"Yes."

Summer shook her head. "Listen to the women in your life, James. It's good for your health."

Mari and James found empty seats that likely belonged to the people on the dance floor.

"Does Rosa ever stop?" Summer asked. "She's running circles around the twenty-year-olds."

"I'm not sure she's the person I left San Diego with. I'm glad she's having a great time. She deserves it."

The woman in question currently had her hands in the air as she danced to music that didn't have words. It reminded Mari of the music that came out of the clubs in the Gaslamp District. All electronic and bass. The kids loved it.

Mari didn't see the point.

"Would either of you ladies like a drink?" James asked.

"Vodka tonic," Summer requested.

He looked at Mari.

"I'd love an ice water."

He stood, winked, and walked away. "Coming right up."

Mari found herself watching him walk away. *One too many,* she mused.

Summer slid into the seat he'd just vacated. "How are things going with the two of you?"

"There is no 'two of us,'" she insisted.

"Are you sure about that? Every time I turn around, you two are together."

"He's here alone, and my roommate has abandoned me for the party crowd." And Mari wasn't about to put a label on their flirtation.

Summer picked up what remained of her drink and swirled around the melting ice. "His ex-wife is a good friend of mine."

"He told me."

"He hasn't dated much since the divorce."

"He told me that, too."

"Did he tell you about his business?"

Mari nodded. "He's made quite a life for himself and his girls."

"He told you about Ellie and Madison, too, huh?"

"What is your point?"

Summer glanced into the cup and shrugged. "You sure do know a lot about a man you just met."

"He's easy to converse with," Mari said.

"He's actually pretty reserved. But apparently not with you."

That felt at odds with what Mari had witnessed from the man.

The beat of the music changed, and Rosa drifted over. She sank into a chair and fanned herself with her hand. "I didn't dance this much at our children's weddings."

"Even Chloe and Dante had better taste in music."

"True." She leaned forward. "But I'm having more fun with this. I think Dante would be embarrassed if he saw me now."

Mari shook her head. "Your son wants you happy."

Rosa twisted in her chair and pointed across the dance floor. "See that man? In the black shirt?"

The man in question was currently dancing with several women, occasionally taking a hand and spinning them around. And he was young. "The one that could have gone to school with my Luca?"

"That's him." Rosa beamed.

"What about him?"

"He asked me to leave with him."

Mari's jaw dropped.

Summer spat out a laugh. "What did you say?"

Rosa just laughed. "I didn't say anything."

"You can't possibly be considering it," Mari said.

"Why not?" Summer asked.

Because Dante wouldn't want his mother *that happy*.

As that thought danced around to the beat of the music, Mari kept it to herself.

Who was she to question or to judge?

She looked at the man again. Midthirties . . . maybe late thirties. Attractive.

Rosa was beaming.

"What happens at sea, stays at sea," Summer suggested.

"Be careful," Mari said.

And before Rosa could reply, Mari knew what she was going to say.

"I've been careful my whole life." With that, Rosa stood and went back to the dance floor.

James returned with the drinks. "What did I miss?"

Summer pointed to Rosa. "That."

Mr. Let's Leave Together had his arm on Rosa's waist and was whispering something in her ear.

"I'm guessing that's a surprise," James said.

"More of a shock."

"People think nothing of an older man with a younger woman. Why should there be such a double standard in the twenty-first century?" Summer asked.

Mari took a long drink from the water, her eyes glued to her friend.

"Summer, would you mind taking a picture of us?" James asked, interrupting Mari's thoughts.

Mari shifted her attention to him.

"For the girls," he told her.

"Oh . . . right." She smiled. "Sure."

Summer took the phone James offered, her eyes narrowing as she looked at Mari.

"His daughters need to believe he's going to be okay when they go to college," Mari explained.

"Ah-huh." Summer's smile was way too big.

"It's not—"

"Why don't you stand up?" Summer asked.

Mari put her glass down.

James stepped in behind her.

"A little closer."

Mari moved.

James leaned in.

Summer looked over the phone. "Put your arm around her waist, James."

Mari looked up at him. "She's enjoying this too much."

James laughed, forcing a smile on Mari's face. "Maybe she was the wrong person to ask."

Mari felt James's hand touch the small of her back. She shivered.

For a moment, he stilled, and they both stared at each other.

"Do you guys want to look at the camera?" Summer asked.

Mari released the breath she was holding and turned for the photo.

James's fingertips tightened when Summer said, "Cheese."

CHAPTER TEN

Mari wasn't a stranger to early mornings.

It was the late nights that were taking their toll.

Much as she wanted to shake off the mother gene, the one that kept her up long after she retired to the stateroom . . . the one that wondered when Rosa was going to return . . . the one that wanted to ask where she was, what she was doing, and who with . . . Mari couldn't.

Her eyes had finally closed sometime after midnight.

The sound of Rosa bumbling around the room woke her around two in the morning. Mari decided to pretend to be fast asleep, banking on the fact that the two of them would be spending the majority of the next day on a beach relaxing. And likely discussing Rosa's evening.

Mari stayed relatively quiet until she heard the first moans coming from her friend.

"Someone was out late," Mari said once she was positive Rosa was awake.

Rosa moaned again. "I think I'm dead."

Mari chuckled. "I assure you, that isn't the case."

"What time is it?" Her voice sounded rough around the edges.

"Just past seven." Mari pushed off the bed and opened the blinds.

Rosa pulled the covers over her head. "Please, no. I feel awful."

"Dancing and drinking all night might be the cause." And whatever else Rosa had been up to.

"I feel like a vampire, Mari."

She glanced at her friend, who peeked over the edge of the covers. Her face was pale, her skin looked clammy.

Taking mercy, Mari darkened the room. "I think it's safe to say that you're hungover."

"I'm too old for this."

"No breakfast this morning?"

Rosa rolled to her side. "Don't mention food."

Mari moved closer and placed a hand on Rosa's forehead. "You're warm."

"It's cold in here."

"It's not."

Rosa looked up. "Would you hate me if I abandoned you today? I don't think I can muster the strength to even sit on the beach, much less kayak or snorkel."

James had suggested they meet at nine thirty so they could find their spot on the cruise line's private island to spend the day.

From the look of her friend, Rosa wasn't going anywhere.

"I won't hate you."

"Good."

"But I'll remind you of this tonight."

Rosa curled up in a ball. "Let me die in peace."

After a quick shower, Mari gave Rosa the solitude she needed.

Mari took her coffee and plate of food from the buffet outside to stare out at the water.

A couple of familiar faces waved as they walked by.

There hadn't been too many quiet moments since she'd arrived on the ship. No real time to reflect. Which was exactly what she found herself doing.

Before going on this trip, Mari would have sworn she wasn't in need of a vacation, or new experiences. She didn't have a desire to foster new friendships and certainly never thought she'd be looking forward to a man's company later that morning.

Yet that was exactly what she was doing.

Even though Mari had made it perfectly clear that romance was off the table, that didn't stop James from seeking out her company.

It was nice.

Probably more than nice.

It was then Mari realized that she hadn't thought of Paulo much at all. Yes, when James had asked questions about her life, but not at other times. Like when James stared a little too long, or placed an innocent hand on her arm or shoulder. Or moved close for a picture.

Perhaps she should feel something, guilt, unease . . . anything about starting a friendship with a man who wasn't a neighbor, family member, or otherwise attached. And maybe that guilt would come.

In this environment, the cruise, the islands, the lack of family close by or responsibilities of life, it was easy to live without guilt.

Paulo would be chiding her if he were alive. "You should only be guilty for having a full life and not living it. My life has been short, but I lived it fully. Live yours, *cara*."

Death has a way of making you wise, even when you're young. Perhaps especially when you're young.

Rosa had certainly embraced that mantra.

Slowly, Mari felt herself doing the same.

Paulo would be proud of her for going on this cruise and taking risks. He'd tell her it's about time she did.

Mari finished her coffee, gave up on most of the food, and made her way back to her room to get what she needed for the day.

Wearing a wide-brim hat, sunglasses, and a swimsuit under her outfit, Mari made her way to the departing deck.

James was already there.

"Where's Rosa?" he asked after they said their hellos.

"Hungover and sleeping."

He smiled. "This doesn't surprise me."

"Me either."

James cocked his head to the side. "Are you okay with it just being me today?"

"On a beach filled with hundreds of other people? I think I'll be all right."

James offered her an elbow. "Let's do this."

Mari put her arm through his and let him lead her down the bridge connecting the ship to the pier.

"Have you ever snorkeled before?" he asked.

"No." *But how hard can it be?*

"Kayak?"

"At least twenty years ago."

They stepped onto the dock and left the ship behind.

"This should be fun."

~

James reminded himself that karma was real and, at the very same time, mentally thanked the universe for Rosa's hangover.

He and Mari found a spot on the beach far away from the singles party crowd and the family groups with screaming children.

Because the cruise line owned the island, the food and drinks were included. And the equipment rentals were easily obtained.

They found an empty palapa that offered plenty of shade and thick cushions to relax on.

"Have you ever seen water so blue?" Mari asked once they set their things down.

"Yes," James said. "Yesterday."

She laughed and shook her head.

James pulled his shirt from his shoulders and stretched out.

Mari stretched out, too. Only she wasn't as quick to shed the cover-up. What was it with women hiding behind a thin mesh fabric? The woman was beautiful.

"I hope you're not bored with my company today," she said. "I have a feeling I'll doze off at some point."

"If you're comfortable enough around me to fall asleep, I'll consider that a win."

She diverted her attention away from him, but not before he caught her smile.

"Have you talked to your girls?"

"I sent them both text messages this morning."

"No phone calls?"

James huffed. "Teenagers don't realize the device in their pocket makes phone calls. My kids respond to text messages. Leaving a voice mail is like screaming for help in the middle of the ocean. They'll never hear it. I'm convinced Ellie doesn't even know how to retrieve her voice messages."

"Chloe was like that. Until I threatened to take her phone away."

"My girls know that would only be a threat. Their phones are more for my peace of mind than their social life," James said.

"Little Italy is a small community. When I took Chloe's phone away, there was always someone close by so I could reach her."

"Torn between two homes makes that hard," he explained.

"I can't imagine," she said. "Remember life before cell phones?"

The image of the house phone flashed in his memory. "We had one landline with a very long cord."

"That stretched all the way to the bathroom, where you could get some privacy," Mari finished for him.

"Exactly. And long-distance calls always happened at night since they were cheaper."

Mari nodded. "And we'd make a collect call to let our parents know we arrived somewhere safe. But they wouldn't accept the charges."

James placed a hand on his head. "I forgot about that. I bet the operators hated those calls."

"Do they even have operators anymore?" Mari asked.

"Naw. I think that was on the way out before the first car phone. Everything was automated by then."

Mari crossed her legs and sat up. "I used to think that my grandparents had lived through the most innovative time in history. From wars to ease of travel. The telephone, film, and music. But when I look back on my own life, I think we've seen just as much, only different. Life before cell phones and the internet. Paying for anything with a swipe of our phones. You couldn't convince me that this was how we'd be living our lives."

"It makes me excited to see what the next forty years is going to do."

"Your Madison will be on the ground floor of our future innovations. She's the one that wants to be the rocket scientist, right?"

"You remembered."

"And Ellie wants to play professional softball."

James groaned. "I wish her head wasn't in the clouds."

Mari paused, tilted her head to the side. "If you can't pursue your dreams when you're young, when can you?"

"I suppose."

"Did you ever wish you'd tried something and regret that you didn't?" she asked.

"Of course. Marriage, children, a mortgage . . . these things have a way of forcing you into reality."

"Then your Ellie needs to try before any of those things come along. No one wants to live a life of what-ifs. Besides, you never know what will happen. You said she's good."

James felt pride in his chest. "She is."

"Then you support the softball. And encourage a second major in something practical she can fall back on. Even star athletes get hurt or retire young from their sport."

Mari held a sparkle in her dark brown eyes when she spoke of something with passion.

"I think I need to take your advice."

"No thinking about it. You absolutely do."

If he smiled any wider, his cheeks were going to cramp up.

"Chloe studied yoga." Mari stopped, rolled her eyes, and focused on him again. "Yoga. She started an online studio a couple of years ago. She'll never get rich, but she's happy. And when babies come, she can continue to work and be home with her children."

James chewed on that for a minute. "I don't want my girls to be dependent on a man."

Mari didn't miss a beat. "They will always have their father, and they can depend on you if the wrong man comes around."

"And if I'm not here?" As soon as the words left his lips, James regretted them. Hadn't that been Mari's life after losing her husband?

He didn't need to worry, Mari had an answer to that, too. "You said it yourself. Your business is worth something, and if, God forbid, your life was cut short, your girls would be provided for."

She made it sound so easy. "Are you always the voice of reason?" he asked.

"I am the matriarch of my family. When my children stop listening to me, it's time for me to hand over my wand. But until then . . ."

"Pay for the cleats and the DI school."

Mari nodded. "Exactly. Let the world disappoint her. That isn't your job. Keep her safe, guide her, be there to pick up the pieces when she needs you. *That* is your job."

James stared into Mari's eyes, a soft smile on his face. "Your children are lucky."

She didn't agree or deny it. Mari simply smiled and turned to look out over the ocean.

Like on the ship, a waiter walked around the beach, offering drinks.

Mari waved them off, stating she'd drunk enough to last her half the year since arriving on the ship.

Other than wine.

Apparently, Italians didn't really consider wine alcohol.

James made a mental note to find a decent bottle to share with her before the cruise ended. Preferably with a dinner for two.

They found a taco bar for lunch. Opted out of the kayak but donned snorkel masks and waded into the crystal-blue water to look at the fish willing to swim close to the rocks that divided up the beach.

Mari had tucked her hair into a short ponytail but lost the binding the first time she pulled her mask off. From that moment on, every time she removed her head from the water, her hair spilled around her mask.

Twice James brushed it away.

Twice Mari let him.

They stayed out of the sun more than in it. The palapa made it easy to avoid a sunburn.

After their short stint of looking at what lived under the sea, Mari wrapped her shoulders in her cover-up and reapplied the sunblock lotion everywhere else.

James considered asking if she needed help with the sunscreen in places she couldn't reach but held back.

As much as he wanted to know if her skin was as soft as he imagined it would be, he wasn't about to push knowing for certain.

The day went by entirely too fast, but eventually, it was time to work their way back to the ship.

"This was the perfect day," he started.

"It was. Quiet and relaxing. Just what I needed after all the go, go, go since we boarded in Florida."

"You made it perfect."

She blinked twice and hesitated.

"Do those words scare you?"

He could see that they did . . . on some level.

"They shouldn't. I know they're not meant to."

They kept walking.

James let her process whatever was going on in her head.

"I wouldn't have enjoyed today nearly as much sitting there alone. But I know that isn't what you mean," she finally said.

"Not just anyone makes a day perfect."

"I know," she said, looking away. "You made today special, too. Can we leave it at that . . . for now?"

James wanted to fist-bump the sky. "Absolutely."

The bridge to board the ship was much busier than it was when they left.

They approached the person scanning their badges, but when Mari's ID was checked, a yellow light instead of a green one lit up.

The attendant looked at her ID again. "Mrs. D'Angelo?"

"Yes? Is there a problem?"

"No. Not at all." But instead of waving her along, the attendant used a radio and said something James didn't quite catch into it. "Can you wait here a moment?"

James moved closer to her side. "Is there something wrong?"

The person behind Mari scanned their badge and was waved through.

"Our concierge would like to speak with you."

"Concierge? About what?" she asked.

Another guest scanned and walked past.

Before James could ask any more questions, the employee in question approached with a wide smile on her face. "Mrs. D'Angelo. Thank you for waiting. I'm Astrid."

"What is this about?" Mari asked before James could.

"Please, if I can have a moment of your time?"

James didn't think "No" would be an accepted answer.

Astrid directed them both from the entrance of the ship to a corridor away from the other passengers.

Mari took a quick glance over her shoulder at him, her eyes wide.

Was there a problem at home?

An emergency?

James brushed his fingers against Mari's arm.

She immediately took hold of them and squeezed.

Taking that as permission, he kept her hand in his as Astrid opened a door to an employee-only room.

As soon as the door closed, Mari's question came out in a rush. "Did my family call? Is something wrong?"

"I'm sorry to worry you. No. Nothing like that." Astrid pointed to a sofa. "Do you want to sit?"

"We want to know what's going on," James said with less patience than he expected.

Astrid smiled. "It's your roommate."

"Rosa?"

Mari squeezed James's hand tighter.

He placed his other hand on her shoulder.

"She alerted our staff that she wasn't feeling well."

"She drank a little too much last night. Was out late."

"Exactly what she said. She assumed a hangover was the cause of her discomfort. But then she developed a fever."

James waited for something bigger than a fever to drop.

"A fever?" Mari asked. Her voice sounded as confused as his thoughts.

"Yes. That, along with a stomach illness, is something we need to quickly isolate on board. If an outbreak occurs . . . well, I'm sure you've heard the news in worst-case scenarios."

"Is Rosa okay?" Mari asked.

"She's resting in her room. Please, what I'm about to tell you, I need you to keep to yourselves. Panic is the second thing we fear as cruise staff."

"We can stay silent," Mari said for both of them.

Astrid's smile wasn't as big now. "We have about a dozen passengers with Rosa's symptoms. Our infirmary isn't designed to keep that many. We've asked Rosa to isolate in your stateroom. Our doctor and his staff will treat her there."

"But she's okay?" Mari asked again.

"She's resting. I've seen these situations many times in my years. Most cases turn out to be nothing that would require much more than fever reducers, hydration, and sleep for a few days. But if you've had children, you know how much this kind of thing can spread. And with a ship this full . . ."

"You can't take those chances," James said.

"We can't. Which is why we've singled you out before you return to your room. With your permission, the doctor would like to see you before you rejoin the rest of the passengers." It was then that Astrid looked directly at James. "Your name is?" she asked.

"James Russell."

She looked between the two of them. "You've spent the day together?"

"Yes."

Astrid squinted her eyes with a tight smile. "We'll want to test you as well."

James let out a long breath. "Of course. I feel fine, though."

"I'm not sick either," Mari said. "But I'm okay with your doctor making sure."

"Thank you," Astrid said with a sigh. "If you can just wait here."

Astrid left them alone in the room.

Mari released James's hand and sat in one of the chairs. "I thought for sure she was going to tell me something was wrong at home."

James sat beside her. "That's where my thoughts went."

"Poor Rosa. I thought she was just hungover."

"It might be a combination of both a stomach bug and too much tequila."

Mari lowered her chin to her chest. "I need to remind my friend that we're not as young as we once were."

The door to the room opened, and a short man wearing an officer uniform followed Astrid inside.

The Greek doctor made an introduction and quickly pulled out what he needed to take their vital signs and ask them several questions.

With nothing but good health and maybe a bit of excessive sun exposure, he deemed both of them healthy enough to avoid quarantine.

"However, if it is possible for you to avoid any large crowds this evening, we would appreciate your efforts. We'll make a dinner reservation at one of the specialty restaurants for you both, on us. They are a bit quieter. Nothing like the buffet or main dining room."

"That would be fine," Mari said.

James nodded his approval.

"Now, about your stateroom . . ." Astrid started.

"She can't go back in there," James said. Mari was bound to get ill and spend the rest of the cruise stuck in her room.

"That does pose a bit of a problem. We did have a few rooms that weren't filled but now are with the other guests that roomed with the sick passengers. Are you traveling with anyone else? Someone who you can stay with?"

Mari started to talk.

James stopped her.

"She can stay with me."

Mari quickly turned her head. "I can't do—"

"I'm in a suite, Mari. The bedroom is separate from the living room." James looked at Astrid. "The sofa turns into a bed, correct?"

"It does. That would be perfect."

Mari put a resistant hand in the air. "I can't put you out like that."

"You're not putting me out. I basically have three of your staterooms all to myself. You can take the bed. I'll sleep on the sofa. It's not a big deal." In James's head, the problem was solved.

"But—"

"If the shoe was on the other foot, would you suggest I sleep on the sofa in your room?"

Mari shook her head as if what he was saying was ridiculous. "Of course. I mean . . ." Her words trailed off. Her shoulders relaxed. "Of course."

"Wonderful," Astrid said. "We'll have your things removed from the room. We're happy to launder any clothing for you."

"That won't be necessary," Mari said.

"We insist."

In other words, hand over your crap so we can bleach the hell out of it so the entire ship doesn't go on lockdown and get quarantined ten miles offshore for weeks on end.

He could see an argument boil in Mari's expression.

"Do you have clothing Mari can wear while you're decontaminating her belongings?" James asked.

"We'll have something delivered to your room," Astrid said.

"Thank you," the doctor said. "Any symptoms at all. Please alert the staff right away."

"We will," James answered for them both.

The doctor left while Astrid lingered. "Do you have a preference on where to dine tonight?"

"Italian," Mari said quickly. "Wait. Is the chef Italian?"

"From Rome, I believe."

"*Bene.* I need comfort food," Mari told James.

James smiled. "And a good bottle of wine."

"Red," Mari added.

"Consider it done. And thank you again for your cooperation in keeping this quiet."

James narrowed his eyes, turned to Astrid. "You said panic was the second thing you feared breaking out on board. What is the first?"

"A stomach virus."

CHAPTER ELEVEN

"I'm sorry to do this to you."

From the sound of Rosa's voice over the phone and the sheer exhaustion in every sigh and pause, Mari knew it was the right thing to stay clear of her friend.

"Stop. You've done nothing."

"I've been going like I'm thirty," Rosa said.

"Which explains a hangover, not a stomach flu. Have they been feeding you?"

Rosa moaned. "I'm not hungry."

"You still need to eat." Mari's solution to most things in life was food. It pained her to not be able to provide for her friend this way.

"They've sent fluids. Broth, Jell-O . . . almost as if I'm in a hospital."

Mari sat in a chair looking out over James's balcony, watching the ship pull away from the island they'd spent the day on.

"Are you able to keep that down?"

"Not really."

"It's best, then. I'll see what the chef in the Italian restaurant has on offer for tomorrow. Maybe I can convince him to lend me his kitchen so I can prepare something for you." Mari's mind whirled with possible combinations that would settle Rosa's stomach.

"At least tomorrow is a day at sea. My only hope is that we have good weather. I don't need this boat rocking."

Mari chuckled. "Write down the room number I'm in. If you need me, call."

"Did they put you in a suite?" Rosa asked after Mari gave her the cabin number.

"Yes and no." Mari glanced over her shoulder and listened for the water running in the shower. James was rinsing off first since the promised clothing had yet to arrive from guest services. Hearing water still dripping, Mari returned to her conversation with Rosa. "The ship is out of extra rooms. James is in a suite, and he volunteered to accommodate me."

For the first time since the call started, Rosa's voice lifted an octave. "Is that right?"

"It was a nice thing to do."

"A *very* nice thing."

Mari found herself reaching for excuses. "They put him on the spot."

"You mean to say he didn't want to help out?"

"Of course not. He's a decent man. You and I would've likely done the same thing," Mari said.

"Ah-huh."

"There's a separate bedroom and living room. It's almost the same as two separate staterooms."

"Ah-huh."

"Rosa!"

"What? I said nothing."

"Ah-huh," Mari tossed back to her friend.

The shower turned off, and Mari wrapped up the call. "You should be resting. Call me in the morning. I don't want to wake you."

"I'll do that. Enjoy your evening, my friend."

"Get better."

A knock on the stateroom door pulled her out of her thoughts.

Still in the clothes she wore on the beach all day, Mari pulled the cover-up tight across her chest as she opened the door.

A porter on the other side held a garment bag in one hand and had her wheeled suitcase at his side. "Mrs. D'Angelo?"

"Yes."

The man handed her the garment bag. "This is from our onboard clothing store. Take whichever you like, I'll pick up the others when I'm back with your clothing."

Mari stood aside for the porter to enter the room. "Isn't that my clothes?" she asked, looking at her suitcase.

"Shoes, toiletries. Everything has been cleaned. The rest is still being seen to," he told her.

"Oh."

After placing her suitcase in the room, the porter left.

Mari moved to the sofa and unzipped the bag.

"Was that the door?" James asked as he walked into the living room wearing only a pair of pants and holding a towel that he used to brush against his wet hair.

Even though Mari had been with a shirtless James all day, there was something far more intimate in being in a room alone with him half naked and fresh from a shower.

She diverted her eyes and focused on the bag in her hands. "They brought something for me to wear."

There were three dresses in the bag. Two of them black, and one in a cream color.

The cream was something Chloe would wear and look fantastic in. Straight, spaghetti string, a dress one didn't wear with a bra.

Mari had had three children.

Braless wasn't an option.

One of the black dresses was similar, with straps for sleeves but a plunging neckline.

The third had cap sleeves, a modest neckline, and a slender but not tight fit on the bottom.

The final dress would have to do.

Chloe would approve.

"Looks like I need to up my game tonight," James said from behind her.

Mari nearly forgot he was standing there. "You don't have to."

"If a woman puts in the effort to put on a dress like that, the least I can do is find a dress shirt and tie."

Mari found herself smiling. If she hadn't expressly taught both of her boys that very etiquette, she might have pressed the issue. Instead, she placed the dress on the sofa and opened her suitcase to see if the shoes she'd need to wear with the dress were in there.

They were. Black, simple, with a small heel.

"Are you done in there?" she asked James.

"Let me grab a couple of things and I'll get out of your way."

A few minutes later, she stood behind the closed door of the bedroom.

The bag she'd brought with her on the beach had a change of clothes, basically shorts and a shirt with clean undergarments that she'd never changed into. And that was a blessing. Otherwise, they'd be having room service, and she'd be eating dinner in a wet bathing suit or one of the ship's bathrobes. There was no way Mari would leave the room without a bra.

James's bathroom was huge in comparison to the one she'd shared with Rosa.

The shower actually had room to turn around, which Mari enjoyed to the fullest. Removing the salt and sand from her body was just as refreshing as the sea had been the first time she'd gotten in.

Taking her time, she dried her hair completely and considered putting it up. But she'd worn her hair on top of her head nearly every day and, with that, found tension building as the days went on.

She'd wear it down, put in a simple curl to help it brush from her face.

A little powder evened out her complexion, a small amount of mascara and lip gloss was all she was willing to use. "The basics," Chloe had told her.

Truth be told, Mari was happy with her daughter's intervention and insistence on a few cosmetics.

James had seen her without makeup all day. Every day, now that she thought about it. But this dinner and this night were intentionally just for them.

A forced first date.

The moment the word *date* popped into her head, Mari turned to the reflection in the mirror. "I'm going on a date."

Nerves in her stomach began to flutter.

Looking down at herself in only a bra and panties had her evaluating what she saw. What a man would see.

Outside of pregnancies, she'd never been heavy. She also wouldn't win a fitness award anytime soon. Her Italian heritage gave her a slight advantage in skin tone, but her age did nothing to help the elasticity of said skin.

And why was she standing in a misty bathroom, considering what her body would look like to a man when she had no intention of letting him see it?

Pushing the thoughts aside, Mari moved into the bedroom and pulled the borrowed dress over her head. For what felt like ten minutes, she struggled with the zipper in the back until perspiration threatened to undo what the shower had accomplished.

She did not want to ask James to help with the zipper.

And why the hell was she worried about that? "A woman in her fifties should not be this shy," she chided herself.

Mari slipped on her shoes and checked her appearance in the mirror one last time. Happy with what stared back, she opened the door connecting to the living room and entered it talking. "I'm having a terrible time with this zipper."

James was standing at the sliding door.

His lips were slightly open, his eyes wide.

No words came.

Mari looked down at herself, hoping she hadn't missed something wrong with the dress. "Is it okay?"

"You-you're stunning."

Heat filled her cheeks. "Please, James, you don't have to—"

"Stunning, Mari. The most beautiful woman on this ship by miles."

How did she follow up that?

She took in what James wore. Black pants, a dark gray shirt, black tie, and dress coat. His clean-cut hair was away from his eyes, and he had a fresh shave. "As my kids would say, you clean up well yourself."

James took a few steps toward her, his smile wide across his lips. "Let me see that zipper."

Feeling on display, Mari pulled her hair aside and turned her back to him.

His fingers brushed her shoulder as he tugged at the zipper.

For a moment, James's hands lingered on her before pulling away. "There."

Mari let loose her hair and turned around. "Thank you."

"My pleasure."

"I'm convinced men design dresses that make it difficult for us, so we need to ask for help."

James smiled. "Remind me to thank the designer if I ever meet them."

Mari ran a nervous hand over her stomach. "Are we ready?"

"I am if you are," he said.

She nodded, and James led her to the door and opened it.

They only had two flights of stairs to reach the deck where the restaurant holding their reservation was located.

Twice, Mari felt James's hand on the small of her back as they maneuvered in and around the other passengers going in every direction. Both times, a flow of warmth washed over her with that simple touch.

She missed it, she realized. That possessive hand, the one that said, *I'm with her. Don't bother looking.* Perhaps that was too strong a statement for such a simple act. But it was how she felt.

And she liked it.

At the restaurant, people were waiting in groups of two and four. Virtually no families.

The scent of home lofted from inside.

Already, Mari's nerves were calmed.

The hostess greeted them with a smile. *"Buonasera."*

"*Buonasera,*" Mari replied back.

James stepped forward. "We have reservations. It's either under James Russell or Mari D'Angelo."

The hostess looked at her list. "Ah yes, Mr. Russell. *Va bene,* please follow me."

Again, James took a step beside Mari, his hand on her back, as they were led to their seat.

The inside of the restaurant was a page out of Italy. Tuscan walls crafted to look like the aged facade of an old city. Plants draped over window boxes under painted-on fake windows. The lights were low, and ambient music gifted from Italy was coming from the speakers in the room.

An unexpected twinge of homesickness poked at Mari's soul.

Tucked in one of the farthest seats, in a booth meant for three people at the most, Mari slid in and folded her hands in her lap.

The hostess assured them their waiter would be right over and left.

"I feel guilty passing all of those people waiting," Mari said once they were alone.

"I'm sure that is all by design. As well as this seat."

They could see a table set for two in front of them, the booth to the side was occupied, but there was space between them for even more privacy.

Before they could say more, the waiter arrived. He, like the hostess, started with a greeting in Italian, followed by an introduction in English. "*Buonasera.* My name is Lorenzo. I'll be serving you tonight."

His accent was thick, and his English was flawless.

He handed them both menus and gave James the wine list.

"Good evening," James said.

"*Buonasera,*" Mari added.

Lorenzo's eyes widened. "*Parlo Italiano?*"

"I do," Mari said in English.

"*Perfetto.* I'll give you time to settle in and look at the menu. I in no way want you to rush." Lorenzo looked to the booth closest and then leaned in and lowered his voice. When he spoke again, he did so in Italian. *Our reservations are normally set for two hours. Under the circumstances, we welcome you to stay as long as you like.*

As much as Mari disapproved of speaking Italian when the person she was with didn't, she understood why the waiter had decided to tell her about their special treatment in the other language.

She placed a hand on top of James's as if asking forgiveness for being so rude before responding to Lorenzo's instructions. *Thank you for letting us know. Neither of us feel ill in any way. I'm sure this is all a precaution.*

Lorenzo thanked her and said he'd be back momentarily.

"What did he say?" James asked as soon as they were alone.

Mari leaned closer, her voice just above a whisper. "Their reservations are set at two hours, but we're encouraged to stay longer. I don't think they want us out mingling."

James whispered back. "Let's not tell them that we didn't really want to."

She realized her hand still covered James's.

Slowly, she slipped it away. "I apologize for speaking in Italian. I don't think it could have been avoided."

"Why are you apologizing?"

"Because it's rude."

"I think it's fantastic. I can mutter my way through a little construction Spanish, but being able to speak another language fluently . . . I'm envious," he said.

"When someone switches languages midconversation, it's often mistaken that whoever is speaking is gossiping about someone that doesn't understand them. I have a hard-and-fast rule in my home. Group conversations are in English if someone there doesn't speak Italian. Except for Sundays."

"Why Sundays?"

"We have family dinners on Sundays. Franny, my granddaughter, is encouraged to only speak Italian on Sundays. It is our way to ensure she is fluent in the language. My two daughters-in-law don't speak Italian, so that rule has some wiggle room these days. Both Brooke and Emma are slowly learning, with Franny as their prudent teacher."

"That's great. I have never understood why families who have a second language in their home don't make sure their children are fluent."

"That's because many families who immigrated here want their children to assimilate as quickly as possible. To them, that means leaving the old language behind."

James shook his head. "They think being an American means they can't speak a second language?"

"Most Americans don't. Thankfully, my parents didn't think this way, neither did I. Now my grandchildren will grow up learning two languages and understand when it is appropriate and inappropriate to speak them."

James smiled. "Like talking in code at a table in a restaurant?"

"Correct. Unless the staff didn't speak English, then conversations need to be translated. Sometimes it helps to slip in and out of Italian for those who don't speak fluent English. But that is completely different than isolating those that don't speak both."

"You've put a lot of thought into this," James said.

"I have. My family is loud and loveable. Add our language to that mix, and it can sound as if we're arguing."

"You don't argue?"

Mari lifted both hands in the air. "Sometimes we argue. Sometimes we need to be louder to be heard. But it's always with love."

"That sounds like my home when the girls are there."

Mari wondered what his home was like when his daughters weren't there. She assumed it was quiet.

Too quiet.

She loved the chaos of her family. If the noise suddenly stopped, she wouldn't know what to do with herself. Not for long periods of time, that is.

Lorenzo returned with a bottle of sparkling and clear water and asked if they'd taken a look at the menu.

They passed on a cocktail, and James handed her the wine menu, deeming her the expert.

Mari passed that on to the waiter.

Lorenzo then passed that on to the sommelier.

In the end, they settled on a Montepulciano from the Abruzzo region of Italy and waited on the chef-recommended appetizer that paired with the wine.

"Tell me about your girls." Mari sipped her wine and sat back to enjoy what was destined to be a wonderful meal. "Do they have boyfriends?"

From the hard stare James delivered, Mari knew she'd hit a sore subject.

"Madison likes her books more than boys. Ellie, on the other hand . . ."

"I wish you could see the look on your face."

"His name is Trevor, and I don't like him. He rides a motorcycle."

"Gio had a motorcycle. Ryan, Salena's husband and Emma's brother . . . he drives a motorcycle."

"I'm not suggesting motorcycles make the person, but this is Trevor."

"Is that the dad in you talking? The one that would shield his daughters from boys all their lives?" she asked.

He narrowed his gaze. "I'm going to say something and please don't hold it against me."

"Okay."

"You sound like Cindy. My ex." James put his wineglass to his lips.

Mari wasn't offended. "You mean like a mother?"

"Maybe."

Since James easily brought up his ex-wife, Mari felt at liberty to mention Paulo.

"When Chloe was finishing high school, Paulo was sick. That didn't stop him from having an opinion on the subject of boys. Having her brothers act on Paulo's behalf made Chloe crazy."

"I wish I had a son to help out."

"Did you want more kids?" Mari asked.

He shrugged. "I would have been open to it. Cindy was happy with two, and since we weren't batshit crazy about each other, I didn't see a need to push it. After the divorce, it never crossed my mind."

"Until the girls started to date."

James pointed the wineglass in her direction. "Exactly."

The waiter returned with two pieces of bruschetta that they didn't order. "Compliments of our chef. He understands you own a restaurant and would love your opinion."

"That's lovely."

"This is something he's working on. Bruschetta, of course, with the garlic in the bread and a hint of truffle oil. Enjoy."

James reached for the Italian classic and winked. "I see how this is going to go tonight."

"In restaurants like this, I'm happy to tell the chef who I am. Italian chefs love to share their creations. If you're lucky, they'll tell you their secret ingredients."

They took a bite.

The truffle, which was often overdone, gave the bruschetta a rich, smoky flavor that put weight on the otherwise light appetizer.

Mari approved. "*Deliziosa.*"

In addition to the appetizer they'd ordered, the chef sent out samples of three others.

Mari happily reported what she liked and shared what she did with her versions of the same dish.

When their main arrived, the tables around them had turned over.

Their conversation shifted to Giovanni and Emma and the winery they ran in Temecula. She shared how they had met and fell in love while touring wineries in Italy.

Simply recalling those days and watching her children find their forever love reminded her of how lucky she was.

How full her life had been.

As their dinner plates were whisked away, the chef made an appearance.

The look of him immediately reminded Mari of her father. A little round in the middle, thinned hair on top, and not exactly vertically gifted.

He introduced himself as Chef Matteo. "You are my testers this evening," he said with a huge smile.

James placed a hand over his stomach. "You stuffed us."

"But you left room for dessert, yes?"

Mari laughed at the look on James's face.

"Maybe a cappuccino," James suggested.

Matteo's smile fell.

Mari placed a hand on James's. "No, no, no. We don't . . . How about two American coffees."

Matteo shrugged. "And my tiramisu."

Mari knew better than to argue.

Matteo signaled Lorenzo over and spoke in a rapid-fire Italian. *Two American coffees, tiramisu, oh, and a dish of panna cotta with berries . . . and biscotti. For two.*

"He's ordering more than a couple of coffees, isn't he?" James asked in a whisper.

"Yes," she said. "I'm going to ask him in Italian for something special for Rosa."

James nodded his understanding.

When Matteo turned his attention back to them, Mari switched languages. *You've been so generous to us tonight, and I hate to ask.*

Anything, Matteo responded.

I know you're not open until the evening, but is it possible for some pastina *to be delivered tomorrow to my friend who isn't feeling well?*

Matteo placed both hands on his head, then pulled them away. *Of course. I should have thought of that. Do you think she'd like it tonight?*

Tomorrow will likely be better, Mari said. A bland broth with small bits of pasta always hit the spot when you finally kept food down.

I will prepare some first thing in the morning. If you think of anything else.

I'll let you know.

Lorenzo arrived with coffee. Behind him was another server with the sweets neither she nor James had room for.

"I'll leave you to it," Chef Matteo said, this time in English.

"If you're ever in San Diego, you must come see me," Mari told him.

"I will, I will."

"Thank you again. Everything was delicious," James said.

Matteo placed a hand on his chest. "*Grazia.*"

Once the chef walked away, Lorenzo stepped up to the table. "I'll bring out takeaway containers when you're ready."

Mari eyed the tiramisu with a sigh and picked up a fork.

James reached for the coffee. "I thought Italians loved cappuccino."

Mari dipped her fork into the dessert. "We do. Just not after noon. This simply isn't done."

"Why?" James asked.

Mari looked at him, paused. "It just isn't."

James started to laugh.

"I think you just told me the equivalent of 'because I said so.'"

The fork hovered in front of Mari's lips. "Because all Italians everywhere said so."

The tiramisu was just this side of heaven.

"All Italians?"

Mari pointed her now-empty fork at James. "If an Italian chef suggests a cappuccino with his or her desserts, run. American coffee is accepted, espresso is preferred."

James picked up a fork. "Okay. I'll put that on the Italian 101 page, right next to not breaking dry spaghetti in half before tossing it into a pot."

Mari's smile fell, her fork hit the table. "*Cazzo*. I would run you out of my kitchen so fast . . ."

James kept laughing. "You should see the look on your face."

"You're messing with me."

"Even I know not to break spaghetti." James went in for dessert. "But you have to admit, ketchup makes a decent sauce when you're in a pinch."

Mari broke all her rules with the stream of unpleasant Italian words that escaped her lips. Both hands were in the air, her body turned toward James in heated disapproval.

James couldn't stop laughing.

CHAPTER TWELVE

James felt like a teenage kid counting the number of times he'd touched his high school crush on a date.

Seven.

Once walking out of the room and into the hall. Twice as they found their table in the restaurant. Twice she'd placed her hand over his while talking during their meal. Once more as they were leaving the restaurant . . . and one more time when they found a quiet deck to stroll after all the food they'd consumed.

James was pretty sure there was one more, but he couldn't quite place when it was.

Counting the contact wasn't so much the goal, but the lack of Mari's uncontrollable flinch from his hand that gradually faded.

Maybe it was the wine.

Maybe it was time and trust.

Or maybe, just maybe, Mari was desiring the contact as much as he was.

God, he hoped it was the latter.

Because, yeah . . . Mari D'Angelo was an unexpected gift he didn't know he needed.

There were times on the ship when it felt like the captain was racing to a finish line. Tonight, it drifted as if their next location was in sight, but they didn't have a parking space before the morning.

"I think that might have been the best Italian meal I've ever experienced," James announced as they walked along the covered deck.

"Mmm, it was good," Mari said. "But you haven't tasted mine."

He wasn't really talking about food, but James went with her lead anyway. "Is that an invitation?"

"I can't imagine we'd return to San Diego and never see each other again."

He liked where this was going.

"Seeing you and an invitation for dinner are two very different things."

"They are?" She genuinely looked confused.

"They're not?"

"I own a restaurant, James. You can't come by without me feeding you."

"I can't?"

She looked at him like he was crazy. "It isn't done."

"Like cappuccino after noon?"

Mari smiled. "You're a quick learner. I like that."

The breeze picked up, and Mari covered her bare arms with her hands.

James shrugged out of his jacket. "May I?"

She offered a nod, and he placed his jacket around her shoulders.

That's eight.

He cursed his own idiocy for counting.

Mari pulled the edges of his coat around her. "Thank you."

"Did you always want to be a chef?"

She chewed on that for a moment before answering. "I always knew I'd be a chef. It came with being the daughter of a restaurateur. I don't think I even considered anything else."

"No regrets?" James asked.

"No. Regret is a waste of time and energy. If there is something you wish to have, reach for it. At the same time, know you can't change the past. But every day you live in a life you don't want, it's a choice you're making. If I regretted being a chef my whole life and still chose to walk into the kitchen at my age . . . well, that's just stupid. Saying you regret it while still doing it is like, I don't know . . . standing in the snow with bare feet, regretting it, but still doing it. That's not regret, that's whining."

"I don't think I'll look at the word *regret* again without that colorful explanation."

"Don't you agree?"

"I do. That's the beauty of getting older, isn't it? The wisdom that comes only with age."

She sighed. "I like being older. I hear people complain about it. This hurts, that aches. Birthdays are a privilege that not everyone gets."

"Like your Paulo?"

That soft smile Mari wore when she mentioned her late husband lofted at the edges of her lips. "Thank you for saying it like that."

"What do you mean?"

They stopped and leaned against the railing as they talked.

"*My* Paulo. It must be strange for you."

"What do you mean?"

She swallowed. "This."

James said nothing and let the confused look on his face do all the talking.

Mari lifted her chin, a move James was coming to recognize as her way of gearing up to say something with passion. That passion could be anger, frustration, demanding, or simply explosive. Like whatever she'd said after his joke about ketchup.

Either way, she lifted her chin and quickly said, "Much as I'd like to convince myself that this isn't a date, it is a date. I'm on a date for the first time in . . . well, since I was a teenager." She quickly muttered something in Italian before she continued. "It must be strange for you to be dating someone who still has love for another man."

James slowly smiled and waited for Mari's eyes to find his before he spoke. "First of all, I'm glad you said all of that out loud. Yes, this is a date. I think it's a surprise to me as much as I think it is a surprise to you."

"It is."

James reached forward and pulled his coat tighter around her shoulders. Mari was shivering, but he thought that was more nerves than cold.

It wasn't cold.

"Second, how I feel about you still caring for Paulo can't possibly hold a candle to what being on a first date after him is to you."

"It's strange."

"I bet."

She shook her head. "I haven't thought about him nearly as much as I thought I would."

James did his best to contain the smile.

"I'm not sure that will last, James."

"This is new for both of us. Talk to me. I've never dated a widow. I have zero expectations. I just know I like spending time with you and want to continue doing so."

Mari looked at the ground and shuffled her feet.

James reached out, placed a finger under her chin, and directed her gaze to his.

They just stared at each other for several seconds. Neither of them talking.

He really couldn't imagine what she was thinking.

He did know that women needed to feel safe. And he was going to do everything in his power to prove that in his arms, she would be safe with him.

Proving that started now.

James took a chance and stepped close and slowly gathered her into his embrace.

There was no attempt at a kiss, there was nothing suggestive about his touch. He simply wanted to hold her and remind her what it felt like to be held.

An awkward moment passed before Mari's arms circled around his waist.

James guided her head to his shoulder and heard her sigh.

That sigh was heaven to his ears.

He wasn't sure how long they stood there, saying nothing, yet everything in that silence. He scolded his body to behave, knowing this was the extent of the contact they'd have at this point. Mari had to set the pace here. Or the trust he was building would shatter.

He liked this woman too much to risk that.

Eventually, they pulled apart, with both of them smiling.

They arrived back in his stateroom, where the cabin steward had pulled out and made up the sofa bed in the living room, as well as doing a turndown service, complete with a mint on the pillows and an animal designed out of bath towels on the beds.

Mari looked around the room with a huff. "My clothes aren't here yet."

"My guess is they'll be ready in the morning," James said.

Mari removed his jacket from her shoulders and draped it over a chair. "I can't exactly sleep in this," she said, pulling at the bodice of her dress.

James crossed behind her and opened one of the drawers in the bedroom. "How about one of my T-shirts?"

When she hesitated, James added, "Or you can sleep naked."

One look over his shoulder and he knew what she thought of that suggestion.

"One lucky T-shirt it is."

"James," she scolded.

He laughed and handed her the team shirt he wore at Ellie's softball games.

It sported the black and red colors of her team, with *Russell* written on the back of it. Under *Russell*, in smaller letters, was the word *Dad*.

"Thank you."

"And there's a bathrobe in the closet. No need for you to feel exposed in any way."

"That's very thoughtful."

He stared at her for a moment and knew he'd never be able to wear that shirt again without picturing her in it.

"Let me get a few things." He collected what he needed for the night, including his toothbrush from the attached bathroom, and moved into the living room.

Mari stood holding his shirt and watching him walk around the room.

Eventually, he stopped and smiled.

She opened her mouth, closed it, and opened it again. "I had a great evening."

"So did I," he replied.

"And thank you again for doing all this." She lifted her hand holding the shirt.

James removed some of the space between them and started to brush her hair over her shoulder, only to stop himself as he played with the strands between his fingers.

"To be perfectly clear . . . I want to kiss you."

Mari pulled in a tiny, sharp breath.

"I'm not going to. Offering my room to you wasn't about that."

Her shoulders relaxed.

"James . . ."

"Even if you wanted me to kiss you." He shook his head. "I'd have to say no."

That had her blushing like a woman half her age.

"I'd be happy to try that tomorrow."

She laughed softly, and James released her hair.

His fingers lingered, and the heat in the pit of his belly started to swell.

"Good night, James."

"Sweet dreams."

She started to turn, and stopped.

Maybe she wanted that kiss.

"I forgot." She turned her back to him. "The zipper."

That was it! The missing time he'd touched her that night and didn't count.

Reaching for the clasp, he carefully slid the zipper down, revealing her skin underneath. He wanted to kiss that spot between her shoulder blades more than he wanted to take his next breath.

He settled for ending his torture and letting go. But not before he placed a kiss on the top of her head.

Was that her leaning in?

Or was his imagination getting the best of him?

"That doesn't count," he whispered.

Mari stepped away and moved to close the door.

Their eyes met.

"See you in the morning."

"In the morning."

Once she closed the door, James heard her mutter something in Italian.

He needed to download an app.

~

Mari leaned her back against the closed door. What was happening? How was it that her stomach was filled with butterflies? She didn't do butterflies.

James was equally as charming as he was wise and funny. And thoughtful. So very thoughtful.

When he'd held her on the deck, a dormant spark broke free of the cage it had sat in for a decade. Just the act of being held by a man who wasn't family. She couldn't help but think of Paulo and his long, loving hugs. "I miss that," she said to Paulo as if he were standing right there.

A sense of comfort and warmth, a feeling so visceral she could reach out and touch it, drifted in the air around her.

"Promise me you'll try and love again."

How many times had he said that to her in his final days?

Was that what she was doing?

She'd convinced herself that she didn't need this.

Didn't need a man's arms around her. Or a soft touch or brush of his hand against her hair, or his breath on her shoulder . . . and yes, even a kiss on her head.

But God, it had felt so nice to feel that again.

A single tear broke free and ran down her cheek.

CHAPTER THIRTEEN

Mari lingered in bed longer than she normally would, not wanting to roam around the stateroom in a bathrobe.

The sound of James coming to life behind the door was enough to make her acutely aware of what had happened the night before. The dinner, the laughter, the conversation, the man.

The clarity of the morning had her second-guessing her involvement with James.

She was a mother. A grandmother. Happily living her life with a thriving business and a family that was growing by the year.

Her life was full.

Not one spot missing a puzzle piece.

But if that were true, then why had the sound of James behind the closed door put a smile on her face and skip in her heart?

Why had the feeling of his arms around her lingered long past the time he let go?

And why . . . why had Paulo's last request of her repeated in her head even while she dreamed?

"Are you telling me something, my love?" she whispered to the room.

Oh, how she wished Paulo could answer her question.

A knock on the door was followed by James talking to someone.

Mari took the distraction as a sign to get out of bed. It was time to face the day, and the man, instead of hiding in her room. Or his room, as it stood.

She went into the bathroom and splashed a little water on her face.

Putting on the bathrobe, she opened the door between the rooms.

James had his back to her.

Sitting on a table were two large clear bags filled with her clothing.

"Good morning," she said.

James turned around and smiled. "Good morning. How did you sleep?"

"Didn't wake up once. How about you? Is the fold-out bed comfortable?"

"I wouldn't have had it any other way," he told her.

"That was the most nonanswer I've ever heard in my life." But she appreciated his effort in ensuring she wouldn't feel bad about him being on a bed that was notorious for being awful.

"They brought your clothes."

"Good thing. I don't want to be in a bathing suit all day today." She moved to pick up the bags and was intercepted by James.

"I got it," he said.

Mari moved aside for him to pass into the bedroom.

He placed the bags on the bed, and Mari dug into them.

"Should we order room service or hit the buffet?" James asked.

"Didn't the doctor say they were coming by to check on us this morning?"

"Oh, that's right. I forgot why we're in this roommate arrangement."

Mari pulled a pile of clothing from the bag and glanced at James in disbelief.

"What? I did."

Mari came just short of rolling her eyes at the man.

On the inside, she was smiling.

Turning her attention back to her clothes, she dug into the pile, searching out the black shirt she wanted to wear. But instead of the shirt, she uncovered the negligee Chloe had slipped into her suitcase.

The moment she realized what she was holding, she dropped her arms and glanced at James.

His eyes went from the nightie to her. "Hmmm," was all he said.

Mari dropped it and continued to search for the shirt. "That's all Chloe," she told him.

"Ah-huh."

"She put it in my suitcase as a gift."

"Ah-huh."

"She wanted me to have something should . . . if . . ." Mari sucked in a breath. "Chloe wants me to date. Or at least she hints at it."

"I think I like Chloe," James said.

"My sons don't," she said quickly. Luca and Gio wouldn't be pleased with her roommate situation at the moment.

"They don't want you happy?"

"I am happy." She found the shirt and started to sort the other clothes.

"Happier?" James asked.

"I'm their mother. Not a woman."

James huffed a single laugh. "You know how ridiculous that sounds, right?"

"Ridiculous or not, Luca and Gio have never once suggested I entertain the idea of another relationship. And since it hasn't crossed my mind, I never needed to test how they would respond."

"Are you?" James asked.

Mari stopped sorting her clothes and looked at him.

"Am I what?"

"Entertaining the idea of a relationship?"

And there it was. The question she didn't even want to ask herself.

She thought for a moment and then said, "If you'd asked me that question a week ago, I would have told you you're crazy."

A slow smile crept on James's face.

"You look entirely too pleased with yourself," she said.

"I am."

She smiled back and then sat on the edge of the bed. "I don't know how to do this. I don't know the rules."

"There aren't any rules," he said.

"There has to be." She liked rules. They made sense and were easy to follow to determine outcomes. Without them, it was nothing but chaos. "If we wanted to see each other when we're home—"

"I already know I do," James interrupted.

Yeah, she knew that. "No one can know."

James hesitated. "I'm listening."

"I need to be comfortable with this before I even consider telling my children I've met someone."

"I do like hearing the 'I've met someone' part."

"I'm serious, James. My sons are very protective."

"Good thing I'm not a threat," he said.

"To them, you will be."

"Maybe you're underestimating their understanding of the human condition."

"The human condition?" she asked.

James nodded, pushed her clothes aside, and sat beside her on the bed. "We're not meant to be on this roller coaster of life alone."

To suggest she was alone was laughable. "I have my family. I'm not alone."

"Without a partner, then."

"Considering you've been single longer than I've been a widow, that's a surprise to hear you say," Mari said.

"Single, yes. But that doesn't mean I've not dated on occasion. Nothing that went anywhere, obviously."

She knew that. "I haven't. I'm not going to upset my children with any of this until I am comfortable with it myself. And I think you should do the same."

"Not tell Madison and Ellie?"

"Or anyone. Or at least anyone that would get word to your daughters. They want you to find someone and would be disappointed if things didn't work out."

"You want to date me in secret?"

Why did the word *date* sound like she was in high school?

"Yes. For now." It's the only way she could deal with her emotions and not invite those of her kids.

"Deal," James said.

"Good." She pushed off the bed. "I'm fine with a croissant and coffee for breakfast."

"That was a quick change of subject," he said.

"I've made a decision that I'm not sure I will keep if we continue to discuss it."

James stood, smiling. "A croissant and coffee it is. I'll call room service."

Once James left the room and closed the door behind him, Mari sat back down on the bed, and her hand landed on the nightgown. Too bad Chloe was too old to ground.

~

Rosa was feeling slightly better, but not nearly enough for Mari to return to her stateroom.

After the ship's medical personnel cleared them for a day roaming the ship, Mari and James went in search of activities to entertain them for a day at sea.

They avoided the main pool deck, deciding the ten-in-the-morning drinking crowd wasn't where they wanted to be.

They passed the ship's casino, which was packed with enough cigarette smoke lofting from it to set off a household smoke detector. That was a pass.

They sat in on one round of bingo before moving on.

Eventually, they found an open Ping-Pong table and set in for some healthy competition.

"I haven't played in years," James told her.

"Then I'll have the advantage," she warned.

"Do you play a lot?"

"When my children were little. There's an upper terrace at my home where we rolled out a table on Sundays."

James picked up his paddle and tapped the end of it on the table. "If your kids were kids when you last played, then how is it that you have the advantage?"

Mari lifted her chin and stared. "Because I'm good." And she loved a healthy competition.

"Is that right?"

She pulled a ball from where several were stored. "You've been warned."

James centered himself and lifted his paddle in the air. "You won't go easy on me?"

"For the first few rounds. Unless you're keeping up."

He laughed.

And Mari served.

The ball bounced where she intended it before hitting the deck.

James frowned. "I wasn't ready," he said, picking up the ball before it rolled away.

Mari hid her smile. "Then you serve."

"Why do I get the feeling that I'm in trouble here?"

Because he was smart like that. "Are we playing for money?"

"No."

"Then the only thing that can be bruised here is your ego. And if your ego is that sensitive, we won't have to worry about our children finding out that we're dating because we won't be."

"Well, shit. Sounds like we have more on the line than a few dollars."

"I have no time for delicate men."

"Good thing I've spent a lot of time in steel-toe boots."

James lifted the ball and served.

Mari softly hit the ball to give James a chance at hitting it.

"I find that . . ."

The ball came back to her.

". . . men in boots have the easiest egos to bruise."

James missed and once again chased after the ball.

"And how did you determine that?"

"There is no better place to learn behavior patterns than behind a bar serving drinks."

James stood poised and ready to serve again. He looked her in the eye. "But you're the chef."

"I'm the owner. Therefore, I do everything from washing dishes to signing checks. Waitstaff and bartenders are not always the most dedicated employees."

James served again. This time with a little more punch.

Still, Mari kept her return soft.

They volleyed four times before James hit the ball high in the air, where it missed the table altogether.

It was Mari's turn to retrieve the wayward plastic ball.

"You have a lot of boot-wearing men at the bar?"

"Mainly tourists or military sit at the bar."

"How do you know they're military? They're not there in uniform, are they?"

Mari shook her head. "It's the haircut. The occasional attempt at being served when they're eighteen. Which, if you ask me, is an absolute shame. You can die for our country and not even have a glass of wine with a meal." She tsked.

"I've never understood that myself."

She tossed the ball for James to start.

"How do you know when a man's ego has taken a hit?"

Mari met James's gaze. "When their smile falls and anger peeks out from under their overt charm."

"I don't think I've ever heard someone use the words *overt* and *charm* next to each other. Describe to me what that looks like."

She paused. "You see three men walk in. Friends. They grab a seat at the bar. They come in talking about something unpleasant. A breakup. An unhappy relationship, married or otherwise. Work. The scores of the latest game where their team lost. The why doesn't matter. They're drinking away their bad day, and a woman shows up. A lone woman. Likely single."

"How do you know she's single?" James asked.

"How many married women have you met that sit at a bar to drink when there is a perfectly good bottle of chardonnay at home? Not to mention children and a husband."

"You have a point."

"Men feel justified to stop at a bar on the way home from work, married or otherwise. It's not the same for a woman." Mari waved her hand in the air. "Anyway. This man who has done nothing but curse the air since sitting down is now all smiles and *charm* to grab the attention of this fictional woman. Having seen this play out more times than most, I can bet money this woman is going to turn this man down."

"How can you tell that? She might find him attractive. And maybe she's there because she is looking for the same thing," James said.

"She's not. If a single woman sits at the bar and orders food, she isn't looking for attention. She wants a meal. And she's not intimidated by dining alone. If a group of women shows up, then maybe this guy has a chance. Not the lone woman ordering one glass of wine with her dinner. When this man is turned down, one of three things will happen. He will try harder." Mari lifted one finger in the air. "He will say something respectful and leave her alone." She lifted a second finger. "Or Mr. Ego will let his charm fall and something nasty will be said." A third finger waved. "If this cycle happens a second or third time in one night, this guy doesn't even try to lay on the charm. He's just an ass."

James stood there holding his paddle. "And what does the man without the ego do?"

"I already told you. He says something respectful and leaves her alone. He might try again, but he isn't a jerk about it. And chances are . . . he isn't wearing boots."

"I'm still not sure why boots play a role in this."

"I can only go by what I see on a daily basis. Maybe if I owned a restaurant in the middle of a big city and not on one of the busiest tourist streets in San Diego, I'd have a different experience." Mari shrugged, but she didn't think she was wrong.

"I need to pay more attention the next time I take a crew out for happy hour."

Mari looked from James's face to the ball he held in his hand. "You do that. Now, are we playing this game or not?"

James tossed the ball back to her. "I think I'm warmed up now."

"You sure?"

"Yup."

She grinned, stood back, and served without holding back.

CHAPTER FOURTEEN

Mari didn't expect to have such a good time.

Maybe it was the sea air. Or the fact no one was around to judge her on any level. Not her children. Not her friend. Not neighbors that quietly watched what everyone on the street was doing and went on to tell anyone who would listen about what they saw.

James caught on to Ping-Pong but really didn't stand a chance.

Mari forgot how competitive she was. As a mother, she often let her children win. That is, until they were adults. Learning that life wasn't always a win started with family games.

Gio mastered Monopoly. Chloe had trivia down pat. And Luca excelled at anything physical. From Ping-Pong to basketball. Not that a lot of basketball was played when you lived in apartments above a restaurant.

The fact that James lost with humor said a lot about him.

"It isn't how you win that shows your character but how you lose," she'd told her children. "Never let someone win when you first meet them. How they react will tell you if you want to continue getting to know them."

James passed.

When they put away the paddles, James told her that he never anticipated going on a cruise and coming away with a new sport.

He had every intention of buying a table so he could give her a run for the money.

That only sparked her intention of practicing with Luca when she returned home.

They spent an hour playing bingo, where James won twenty dollars.

In one of the lounges, two parties of people were playing a musical trivia game. Mari and James answered among themselves. Proving that they'd both grown up in the '80s.

Mari had more pop hits in her memories, whereas James apparently listened to heavy metal.

"If we were on the same team, we'd be winning the grand prize," she said.

"Next time."

Mari smiled at him as he placed a hand on her back to lead her away from the lounge.

That simple hand put a smile on her face and a tiny skip in her chest.

They found the onboard mini-golf on a top deck. But by then, the seas were becoming increasingly choppy, and hitting a small ball into a small hole wasn't a game either of them wanted to play.

Late in the afternoon, they returned to his stateroom to change for dinner.

Mari called Rosa to learn that the toss of the boat on the water had increased the previous evening's nausea.

"I'm so sorry," Rosa pleaded.

"Don't be. Just get better," Mari encouraged.

Mari disconnected the call and looked at James. "Looks like you have me for another night."

Amusement met his eyes long before his slow smile spread.

"My friend is sick," she told him. Attempting to put the situation into focus.

James dropped his smile. "And that's awful."

Mari attempted a glare.

Only his smile had her lips lifting.

"You shouldn't look so pleased."

He blinked a couple of times as if he were trying to find the right response. "Sad for her. Pleased for me."

Mari clicked her tongue and quickly turned away before he could see her blush.

~

"Are you having a good time?"

James made a call home while Mari took a shower to get ready for the night.

Madison was better at answering her phone than Ellie, so he tried her cell first.

"I am. There is a lot to do on this ship."

"You're calling from the boat?" she asked.

"In the middle of the ocean."

"Must be a satellite," Madison said.

"No idea. Is our house still standing?" he asked, teasing.

Madison laughed but didn't answer the question. "Have you met anyone?"

Wow, he wasn't expecting that right off the bat. "I've met all kinds of people."

"That's not what I mean."

The sound of the shower stopped, directing his attention to the door between him and Mari.

"Do you really want to hear about your dad's love life?"

Madison hesitated. "Yeah, actually. I do."

He smirked. "Have you heard from any of the colleges?"

"Nice change of subject, Dad."

"Well?"

"No. Nothing yet. I did ace my Physics test."

"Of course you did."

"Nothing 'of course' about it. That stuff was hard," she told him.

"You make it look easy."

"Thanks, Dad."

He smiled. "Is your sister around?"

"No. She stayed after practice. I think Trevor is going to ask her to prom."

James lost his smile. He didn't like Trevor or his motorcycle. "Ugh."

"He's not that bad, Dad."

"He's not that good either."

"You say that about every guy."

James stared out the window at the waves. "Boys want one thing."

"Not all of them," Madison argued.

"Yes, all of them. I know. I was one."

Madison laughed like she always did when this subject came up. "What are you going to do when we're away at college?"

"You're both getting chastity belts."

He heard a noise behind him and turned to see Mari standing in the doorway.

She'd changed into a fresh linen pantsuit, a hairbrush in her hand.

"Yeah, yeah," Madison said.

"Tell your sister I said no Trevor at the house when I'm not there."

"You've already said that."

"Tell her again," James insisted.

"She has a phone."

Mari was smiling.

James lost his train of thought.

"You can tell her."

"Tell her what?" he asked.

"Ellie and Trevor?"

Watching Mari brush her hair had a kind of intimacy that he missed.

"What about them?"

"Dad! Are you okay?"

"I hear static. I should let you go."

"I hear you loud and clear."

Mari shook her head.

"I'll call you later," he said.

"Fine. Love you."

"Love you, too."

He hung up and turned his full attention to the woman standing in his room.

"Chastity belts?" she asked.

"It's better than locking them in a tower."

She ran the brush through her hair as she talked. "You're protective. It's a good quality in a father."

"Like Paulo and your sons?"

Mari waved the brush in the air. "The way Chloe put up a fight. Their arguments could be heard over the noise in the restaurant. If my sons didn't approve of the boy, he didn't stand a chance."

"Did they approve of any?"

Mari looked at the ceiling as if it held the answer. "No. And remember, they didn't even approve of their best friend . . . until they did."

James grumbled, "Can't we skip the Trevors?"

Mari set her brush down. "You should have had a son."

"Ugh."

~

Sometime during the night, Rosa's health started to improve.

The morning call to Rosa before James and Mari set off for a day in Saint Thomas suggested that Mari would be able to return to her stateroom by nightfall.

As they stepped off the ship, James took her hand and said, "I have you to myself until dinner."

They walked in and out of shops on the island. They found tourist trinkets that Mari picked up for her grandchildren, and James took advantage of the discounted jewelry prices to find graduation presents for his girls.

"Ellie's favorite color is blue, Madison's is green," he told her when they walked into the first store.

"What are you thinking?"

James stood over a brightly lit case with plenty of glitter displayed beneath the glass.

"I don't know. What do you think is appropriate?" he asked her.

Mari skipped past the cases with large chunks of diamonds and several carats of gemstones and over to a much more understated display. "What about something like these?" She pointed to several pendants on simple chains. Everything from circle shapes to hearts. Three stones increasing in size in a simple line.

"These are pretty small."

"Your girls are seventeen."

"So?"

A shop attendant walked over and asked if they wanted to see anything.

"These," Mari pointed out.

While the attendant removed the necklaces from the case, Mari turned to James. "There will be plenty of time to spoil your girls. Graduations. Weddings. Grandchildren."

In the end, James picked an emerald necklace for Madison and a duplicate in sapphires for Ellie.

"What about you?" James asked.

"What about me?"

He lifted a finger to her ear, where a simple silver hoop dangled.

"I don't wear a lot of jewelry."

"You don't like to, or . . ."

"Rings and bracelets get in the way of cooking."

"What about when you're not in the kitchen?"

Mari waved a hand in front of him. "I don't need a lot of glitter."

They walked along the street, stopping in front of windows. "Did Paulo buy you jewelry?" James asked.

"We didn't have money for things like this. About the time we had extra, the doctor bills started rolling in." She turned to him and shook a finger in the air. "And no."

"No what?"

"We hardly know each other. You're not buying me jewelry."

James stopped walking and pointed at a display in a storefront window. "Not even a little something?" he asked.

She tugged on his arm. "You're ridiculous."

"But gift giving is my love language."

Mari burst out laughing. "And barking orders is mine. No!"

The fact she was barking at him put a grin on his face. "Do you have a favorite color?"

"No."

"Everyone has a favorite color."

"Not while we're walking around this island, I don't."

He wasn't serious about buying her anything. She was right in that they hardly knew each other. But it was fun watching her march them away from the stores and bark at him.

"Not even a small pair of earrings? They don't get caught up in pasta making."

She narrowed her eyes before turning to the next display and pointing. "Those."

His gaze drifted to a pair of god-awful skull earrings the size of quarters. They were filled with black and white diamonds, with red stones as eyes. They were the kind of thing James was happy his girls never got into.

"I didn't see you being into goth."

"You should see my costumes for Halloween."

For a second, he stared. Not one hundred percent sure she was kidding. The woman had a stellar poker face.

Another few seconds passed before Mari rolled her eyes and tugged on his arm again. "I'm hungry. I'll let you buy me lunch."

"Okay. But if we see skulls in yellow diamonds . . ."

~

In the grand scheme of things, two nights and three solid days isn't a significant amount of time. And yet while Mari packed up the things she'd spread around James's space, she felt a strange kind of loss.

Leaning against the doorframe, James watched as she shoved her clothes into her suitcase.

"Did Rosa say if she was up for dinner in the dining room?" he asked.

"She didn't mention food. Whatever she decides, I really should spend the rest of my time with her. This entire cruise was her brainchild, and she hasn't been able to enjoy it."

"She enjoyed it plenty before she got sick."

"That's true. But still . . ."

James pushed away from the door. "I know. I have to share you now."

Mari stopped what she was doing and looked at him. "I didn't realize I was yours to share."

"You didn't?" he asked with a smirk.

Mari would be fooling herself to suggest she felt any different. Her alone time with James and getting to know him wouldn't have been nearly as fun with an audience. Even if that crowd was only Rosa. Just packing her bag, Mari felt her guard slowly going up. She knew that would only grow when they walked off that ship for the last time.

"It won't be long before we're back on the West Coast," she reminded him. Back to reality.

"I'm not ready to think about that yet," he said. "Are you planning on going to the farewell costume party?"

"If Rosa is up to it. Not that I have a costume."

"It's a '50s theme. A skirt and bobby socks with sneakers are all you need."

"I forgot my poodle skirt." She laughed.

"A pair of rolled-up jeans will work."

"You like costume parties, I assume."

James shrugged. "It's fun being someone else for a few hours."

Wasn't that what she'd been doing for the past few days? Being someone else? Or an earlier . . . younger version of herself? "Considering the depth of fashion for men hasn't changed much over the years, you can get away with jeans and a white shirt that you have with you. I'm fresh out of '50s-style clothing."

"What about Rosa? Did she bring anything?"

"Yes," Mari replied. "She was excited about all the events."

James moved toward the bed where Mari was attempting to close her stuffed suitcase. "Then I'll see you at the dance party, dressed up or not."

She stood back and let James wrangle the zipper into place before placing the case on its wheels.

"Did you double-check the bathroom?" he asked.

Mari poked her head into the space and looked around. "I got everything."

When she turned back around, James had taken a couple of steps closer.

Her pulse quickened.

"I'm going to miss you in my room, Mari."

"The bed has to be more comfortable than one you pull from a sofa."

He took another step closer. "I'll miss you, not the sleeping arrangement."

A part of her realized she felt the same way, but saying so out loud felt like a confession. One she wasn't sure she was ready for. "I'm not sure how to respond to that."

"That's okay," he said as he reached out and pushed a strand of her hair behind her shoulder. "There is this one thing I want to do before you leave."

One more step and James was close enough that she could feel his breath on her skin.

He moved his hand to the side of her face, one finger ran along her jaw.

Mari's gaze darted to his lips.

Oh, God.

He was going to kiss her. A moment she knew would come. Was she ready? Could she?

She hadn't been kissed in . . . "I—"

"Shhh. Don't think."

She felt herself leaning in.

James pressed his fingers to the nape of her neck and lowered his lips to hers.

Mari literally jolted. Her body stiff. Her mind racing.

Until it wasn't.

Until her brain took James's advice and washed away any thoughts that were there before the feel of his kiss penetrated everything.

He was soft, and careful. And he gave her plenty of room to back away.

To Mari's surprise, she didn't. She tilted her head back and encouraged James to lean in closer.

His free hand met her hip, and she placed hers on his chest.

Everything fluttered. The vibration inside her stomach, the hum that started somewhere in the back of her throat without her permission, and James's lips moved over hers.

He tilted his head, parted her lips with his as hot air exchanged between them.

The slight sweep of his tongue pulled her back into her body.

James must have felt her unease, and he ended their moment.

Mari stood there, eyes closed, her breath heavy.

"Are you okay?" James whispered.

"Ah-huh."

"You sure?"

"Yup." She swallowed and nodded a couple of times. Her fingers resting on his chest dug into him as she opened her eyes.

She was okay.

The smile in James's gaze matched the one she felt developing inside of her.

"That was the first . . ."

"I know," he said without her needing to finish her statement.

He moved the palm of his hand on her face.

She leaned into it.

"You set the pace, Mari."

She shook her head. "I feel like a virginal teenager."

"You look like a woman rediscovering herself."

"Yes. That's exactly right." And for the first time since James pulled her into his arms, she thought of Paulo.

"Promise me you'll try and love again."

"Let me walk you home," James said.

Mari nodded and pulled away.

They navigated the small hallways of the ship, down the elevator and to her shared stateroom.

Mari opened the door to see Rosa fully clothed and sitting up in bed watching the TV.

"You look better."

"I feel alive again," Rosa responded. She gave a little wave to James. "Hello."

"Glad you're among the living again."

"I'm sorry to put you out."

Mari noticed the mirth in Rosa's eyes that didn't match her words.

"No trouble at all," James said, his voice low in his chest.

Mari felt her heart kick.

She turned and reached out to take her suitcase. "Thank you again."

He let his hand linger on the handle of the suitcase, one finger slid along the side of her hand before he let go. "I'll see you at the costume party, if not before."

Mari lifted her chin, determined to not let the turmoil he set off simply by looking at her lips show.

"I'll be the one *not* wearing a costume."

He smiled and then waved a hand at Rosa. "I'll see you ladies later."

James turned on his heel and let the door close behind him.

The sheer weight of his presence left with him.

"Oh my . . . that looked very—"

"Nothing happened," Mari barked.

"Then why are you blushing?"

Mari turned to her friend and placed a hand on her cheek. There was no point in lying to her best friend. "Oh, Rosa. I have no idea what I'm doing."

Rosa swung her legs off the bed and patted the space beside her.

"This I need to hear."

CHAPTER FIFTEEN

The entire day after James had kissed Mari for the first time, he didn't see her once. Which completely bummed him out. He kept telling himself that Rosa needed her best friend.

But damn it, James needed her, too.

He sent an occasional text and made sure he said good night and good morning the next day.

The farewell party was his only promised date. And he was determined to make the most of it.

As promised, James donned a pair of jeans that he rolled up at the cuff, shoved a box resembling cigarettes in the sleeve of a simple white T-shirt, and then slicked his hair back. In the perfect we-want-to-get-more-money-out-of-you style, the shops brought out several racks of clothing items to be bought for those that didn't bring their own costumes.

James thought back on Mari's conviction that she wouldn't be in costume and decided he'd pick her up an accessory that could be worn with whatever she showed up in.

The lounge was transformed into a '50s-style diner. The staff had placed black and white stickers over the dance floor. Balloons surrounded the entry, and time-appropriate music filled the room.

At least half of the patrons were dressed in full costumes, complete with wigs and makeup. The others either didn't try at all or blended in with attempts at costumes much like his.

James scanned the room, searching out Mari.

He found her surrounded by the San Diego group, most of whom were dressed for the occasion.

Rosa wore tight capri pants and a sweater with a scarf tied around her neck.

From the look of the heavy makeup on Mari's face, James guessed that Rosa had insisted on something.

She also wore her hair in a high ponytail with a scarf billowing from the tie.

Mari must have felt his stare.

Even in a packed room and surrounded by people talking and music blaring, she suddenly looked up and saw him.

James liked the way her smile slowly curved over her lips and heat rushed to her cheeks when she looked at him.

After he'd kissed her, a kiss that she definitely returned, James was a little concerned that she'd have some kind of regret.

That wasn't what he saw in her eyes now.

Relief washed over him.

He stepped into the circle of women and said hello.

"There you are," Rosa said. "We looked all over for you earlier today."

"You did?" James glanced at Mari.

"Not all over," Mari said.

"You have my cell number."

"It wasn't urgent."

A beat of silence stretched.

"You remember Jill and Amanda?" Mari turned to the two women standing there.

"From the waterfalls," he said.

Jill nodded and fluffed the poodle skirt she wore. "I wouldn't expect you to recognize me like this."

Truth was, James wasn't interested in remembering any of the other women on the cruise.

Only one.

Mari looked at the package James held in his hand. "What's that?"

He extended it to her. "You said you didn't bring anything to wear for the party."

She narrowed her eyes.

The three other women gave them all their attention.

Mari took the package and looked inside.

She smiled and shook her head as she pulled out a bright pink jacket with black letters that said *Pink Ladies*.

"It was either that or black leather. I thought the leather would be too hot to wear."

"Where did you get this?" she asked.

"The gift store. I looked for one with skulls, but they were fresh out."

Mari tossed her head back with a laugh.

"Skulls?" Rosa asked.

James shook his head. "You had to be there."

Mari handed him back the bag before sliding her arms into the jacket.

Now she fit in with everyone around them.

"Looks great," Rosa said.

"Thank you," Mari said.

The music changed, and James extended a hand. "C'mon."

Mari started to protest.

James handed Rosa the bag and didn't give Mari the opportunity to say no. "I'll bring her back," he said as he pulled Mari onto the dance floor.

The rockabilly beat had James attempting to dance like he knew how.

Holding Mari's hands, he pulled her in and pushed her away before bringing her in again to swing her over the dance floor. Several other couples were hopping around the same way.

James snaked a hand around her waist and pulled her close as they swayed to the music. "How did we go from dancing like this to shuffling our feet a foot apart?" he asked.

"I have no idea."

He kept her on her feet for three songs before Mari tapped out. "I need water."

James directed her to the water station.

"Do you want something stronger?" he asked.

"No. But go ahead."

He tilted his cup back and refilled it. "I'm good."

He tossed the empty paper cup in the trash and moved closer to give the person beside him room to pass.

Mari looked him up and down. "What are these?" she asked, pointing to the box he had rolled up in his shirt.

"A small deck of cards I found in the gift shop."

"Inventive."

He looked over her shoulder. "Do you want to find Rosa?"

Mari glanced in the direction he was looking. "That's okay. If we find her, she's only going to ask you questions."

"Oh?"

"She's the only person I can talk to about . . ."

He waited a beat. "Us?"

Mari looked away.

Shy didn't suit her.

James ducked until he met her eyes before standing tall again. "Us."

"Yes."

Another person pressed into their space, searching out a glass of water.

James wrapped his arm around Mari's shoulders and moved them away from the heavy traffic of people.

He kept his arm where he placed it, his hand dangling as if he'd been in this position a million times. Leaning close to her ear, he asked, "What did you tell her?"

Mari glanced at his hand, then at him. "You know, just because this looks like a high school dance doesn't mean we're kids."

"I have two daughters, Mari. Both of whom are in high school. Whenever they have sleepovers with their besties, they're always talking about boys." He shrugged. "So, if the shoe fits."

Mari rolled her eyes but didn't pull away.

They found the dance floor, and the shy evaporated from Mari's body within seconds.

They moved like they knew what they were doing, bumping into people who laughed just as loud as them.

When a slow song finally played, James took full advantage and wrapped Mari in his arms.

"Should we sign up for another week?" he asked.

"And leave Ellie at home with Trevor?"

"Ouch."

She laughed.

"I'm sure Cindy is keeping an eye on them."

"But an empty house . . ."

James urged her head to fall on his shoulder. "Shh, don't ruin my trip."

Mari relaxed, and James savored the moment.

The slow song didn't last long enough.

James caught a breath alone when Mari went to the restroom.

As soon as she stepped away, Summer slid up next to him.

"That looks cozy."

That's because it is.

"Not a word to my girls," he told her.

"Excuse me?"

"I'm serious, Summer."

"Why? Are you embarrassed or something?"

James looked at her as if she was crazy. "It's not me. It's Mari. She's been a widow for a decade and hasn't dated once."

"So, she wants to keep this a secret?"

"*Secret* sounds deceptive," he said.

"Because it is," Summer said.

He turned to face her. "We don't want the interference of anyone else's thoughts or feelings about us. Not until we can label them."

"Okay . . . okay. I can buy that. But don't expect me to keep this from Cindy."

He expected nothing less. "Just make sure she keeps her trap shut."

"I'm not in charge of what other people do."

James saw Mari emerge from the bathroom.

"What happens on this ship stays on this ship. Now, if you'll excuse me."

He walked away with Summer laughing behind him.

"Ready for more?" James swayed to one side, then the other.

Mari pulled her shirt away from her body. "What I need is some fresh air."

James took her hand. "Your wish is my command."

They had to traverse the dance floor to get to the exit. James took advantage and swung her around twice before leading her out the door.

They stumbled into the corridor, laughing.

"I don't remember the last time I danced this much," Mari confessed.

James headed straight to the doors leading out to an abandoned deck.

A blast of air hit them both. "I say we take swing lessons when we get home."

Mari laughed.

"I'm serious . . . kinda."

"Don't you have a business to run?"

"The clock stops after five." He lifted her hand in the air and ducked under it before pulling her close.

He was getting entirely too comfortable listening to her laugh.

"You're crazy."

She reached out for the railing of the ship, and James leaned against it to look at her.

Mari placed a hand on his arm. "What are you staring at?"

"You."

She cocked her head to the side and started to lower her eyes.

"No. Don't do that."

"Do what?"

"Look away whenever you're feeling something."

She squared her shoulders and stared right back, almost in defiance.

"There you are," he said. "There's the woman who told the twentysomething to go to his room and take a nap the first day on this ship."

She laughed. "I did no such thing."

"You might as well have."

Her laughter faded, and James saw her fight the urge to disconnect.

God, she was beautiful. Warm and flush from the dancing.

The sea air blowing the strands of hair that came loose from the ponytail.

His body stirred when her eyes shifted to his lips.

James wasn't sure who moved first. Him or her.

One second, he was thinking, the next, he was dragging her lips to his.

Unlike their first kiss, this held so much more promise.

If she had to think about their first kiss, she wasn't thinking about it now.

He moved to press her back against the railing, his hands on both sides of her face.

Her small hands moved over his back, her fingers kneading his skin.

He urged her lips open.

Mari's sigh sounded like a surrender.

The power of the music, dancing . . . and flirting balled up and into their kiss.

There was something raw in how she touched him. The feisty, barking Italian in her, if he had to guess.

His body took on some serious heat, the kind that made him want to press his hips to hers. There would be no denying what he wanted if he did.

Mari shifted slightly, her lips stilled, but then she came back for more.

He kissed her for as long as she let him.

He wanted to touch more of her, learn what she liked and what she didn't.

But the door leading out to the deck was right behind them, and anyone could walk out.

He held too much respect for Mari to place her in that kind of compromising position. Even if his body was screaming.

He no sooner thought of the glass doors before the sound of people walking out of them had them both freezing in place.

James broke their kiss but held Mari close.

With her face buried into his shoulder, he felt her starting to laugh.

Voices, at least three of them, drifted as the people that walked out moved farther away.

Together, James and Mari silently laughed while holding each other.

When that laughter faded, James caught Mari's eyes. No remorse . . . only amusement. "C'mon." He draped his hand over her shoulder and turned back to the door leading inside. "We should get back to the party before I forget that I'm a gentleman."

~

Mari felt like a completely different person leaving the ship than she had when getting on.

James met her and Rosa at their door and pushed along with them in the mass of people as they disembarked.

Back on the dock, buses waited to take passengers to either the city or the airport.

Mari stood beside James while the driver placed her bags under the bus.

When the driver reached for his, James waved him off.

"You're not going to the airport?" Mari asked.

"I scheduled a meeting with a possible vendor. My flight isn't until tonight."

"Oh. Did you tell me that?"

"No. I don't think so. We were too busy for mundane work conversations," he teased.

She started to look away, then reminded herself of who she really was. A mother, a grandmother, the matriarch of her family . . . a business owner. Not a shy girl blushing every time a man looked her way.

Only James made her feel like that girl. The one that hadn't experienced the world and was excited to see what came next.

She'd relived that second kiss all night long.

Something was waking inside of her. Emotions long dormant and thought lost forever.

"This is goodbye, then," she said.

"No." He shook his head. "This is until we're both back home."

"Allora."

James glanced up at the bus, then back to her. "I'm glad Rosa bullied you to go on this trip."

"I am, too."

The driver started to close the door where the luggage was stored.

James stepped into her personal space. "Text me when you land so I know you're home safe."

"I can do that."

He kissed her, briefly, and stood back. "Safe flight."

Mari turned toward the bus, fingertips to her lips, and climbed inside.

Rosa was humming the tune to the '80s television show *The Love Boat*.

Mari shoved her friend's shoulder with a shush.

As the bus moved away from the curb, Mari glanced out the window to where James stood, one hand in the air with a wave.

"Oh, boy."

~

Between the wait time at the airport and the five-and-a-half-hour flight back home, it was after seven in the evening before Mari turned off the airplane mode on her phone to find two messages from James.

The first one said, Do you miss me yet?

The second . . . Text when you land.

Rosa looked over her shoulder. "It's him, isn't it?"

"I'm convinced he's twenty and lying about his age." *Do you miss me yet?* Mari rolled her eyes but couldn't stop her smile.

By now, James was on another flight on his way home.

We landed safely, she replied.

A message from Chloe followed James's.

Text me when you land, and I'll leave to pick you up. I can't wait to hear all about your trip.

Mari shot a message to her daughter, letting her know they were there but still needed to gather their luggage.

With the San Diego airport under construction, there was no reason for her daughter to try and meet them at the baggage claim.

"I can't wait to sleep in my own bed," Rosa said as they got off the plane.

"I agree."

Mari's phone buzzed in her purse.

She reached for it, expecting to see a text from Chloe.

It was James.

But do you miss me?

Yes, but she wasn't about to admit it. Are you texting from the plane?

I am. And the guy beside me snores like a trucker.

I didn't know you can text from the air.

Mari looked up from her phone as the other passengers all jumped from their seats the moment the plane was parked at the gate.

She was seated over the wing and saw no need to crowd into the aisle.

Depends on the airline, but yes. You can.

Do you pay for that? she asked.

Sometimes.

Rosa leaned over. "Is Chloe asking questions?"

"No. It's James."

Rosa tried to read his messages.

"Is he still in Florida?"

"No. He's talking from his flight."

"You can do that?" Rosa asked.

Mari shrugged. "I'm glad I'm not the only one in the dark about travel."

Passengers started to move.

I'm getting off the plane. Let me know when you're home.

She opened her purse to drop her phone in.

James sent a final text.

Ahh, she does miss me.

With a shake of her head, she left it at that.

The chilled air outside the terminal was a far cry from the heat and humidity Mari and Rosa left behind.

Chloe pulled up to the curb, and Rosa and Mari scrambled to get their luggage in the trunk before people started honking.

"I missed you both," she said, hugging each of them as they wrangled their bags.

Rosa slid into the back seat. Mari took the passenger side.

"Well? Did you guys have fun?" Chloe asked, pulling into traffic.

"It was great," Rosa said.

"Until Rosa got sick."

Chloe twisted in her seat to look back. "You got sick?"

"She ended up seeing the doctor on board and everything," Mari said.

"That's awful. It wasn't the whole time, was it?"

"Only a few days," Rosa said.

Chloe inched the car forward. "You didn't catch anything?" she asked.

Mari snuck a peek at Rosa. "I was fine."

"That's a blessing. Did you meet anyone?"

Another peek at Rosa. Then the practiced words came out. "We met a lot of people."

"And had a great time," Rosa finished.

Chloe looked disappointed. "I mean men."

Even to Mari's ears, her laugh sounded forced.

"A thirty-year-old hit on your mama before the ship left port," Rosa said.

"What?" Chloe's question was nearly a scream with a laugh. "I need you to spill the tea on that."

Mari nodded to Rosa, thanking her in a way for keeping her promise to leave James out of the conversation.

"He was a child. His mother should have taught him better."

Chloe laughed all the way back to Little Italy.

CHAPTER SIXTEEN

"Nonna!" Franny's voice woke Mari from a dead sleep.

It took a moment for her brain to register that she was no longer swaying on a ship. Her bedroom came slowly into focus.

Her return home was met with hugs, kisses . . . a good meal and an early bedtime. Because Luca was busy in the kitchen and Brooke had put Leo down by the time Mari was back in her apartments, the family reunion would have to wait.

"Nonna?"

"In here, *tesoro*," Mari called out.

Franny bounced through the bedroom door, stopped when she saw that Mari wasn't out of bed. "Are you sick?"

Mari sat up and patted the space beside her. "They call it jet lag." And since she'd woken up at two in the morning to toss and turn until she could fall back to sleep, it wasn't a surprise the clock was glowing a time of eight a.m.

Franny crawled up onto the bed. "Mama said not to bug you, but I knew you'd be awake."

Brooke was right, but Mari wasn't about to correct Franny.

Mari yawned and tried to blink the sleep from her eyes. "Did I miss anything while I was away?"

Franny chewed on the question for a minute, then opened the floodgates. "You know my friend Leah from school?"

Mari only knew the name, not the girl. "Yes."

"She cheated on her math test, and Mrs. Rosen caught her. She was sent to the office and her parents were called. They sent her home early. Which I don't get. Don't you think if you get in trouble cheating, you should spend more time in school and not less?"

Mari didn't have the chance to answer.

"Leah said she went home and watched TV the rest of the day. Her mom was mad cuz she had to leave work. And Leah had to take the test again, only with Mrs. Rosen standing over her the whole time. And now she has to sit in the front of the class, and Mrs. Rosen takes her phone away from her every day."

"None of you need a cell phone at school," Mari said.

"Yes we do. Sometimes the tablets don't work right, and the teachers let us look things up on our phones."

"But Leah can't do that."

"Which sucks."

Mari lifted a brow. "Excuse me."

"Well, it does."

"Leah made that bed by trying to shortcut her education by cheating. I hope you can learn a lesson from your friend and never try and do that yourself."

Franny rolled her eyes. "Math is easy. Mrs. Rosen thinks I will be able to get into an algebra class when I go to middle school next year. Most kids don't do that until their second year."

Mari brushed a finger over Franny's cheek. "I'm proud of you."

Her grandbaby wasn't really a baby anymore. Before long she'd be a teenager and her worries would be about which boy would be asking her to a dance.

Mari instantly thought of James and his girls. She wondered if Trevor had asked Ellie to prom. And if he did, how James handled it.

"Franny?"

Brooke's voice called from Mari's living room.

"In here."

"You didn't wake up your *nonna*, did you?" Brooke asked the question as her voice drew closer.

"No."

Mari chuckled and pushed the blankets away to get out of bed.

Brooke looked beyond the open bedroom door. "Franny! I'm sorry, Mari. I told her not to come in if she didn't hear you moving around."

Mari stood and grabbed her bathrobe that sat on the chair beside her bed. "You never have to worry about bothering me. Pretty soon Franny won't want to share her morning with me."

"Still . . ."

"Nonsense. Where is my grandson?"

"Luca is in charge this morning. I'm taking this one to school. And we're going to be late, so go grab your backpack and your lunch from the fridge."

"Yes, Mama."

Mari smiled as Franny left the room. Hearing her granddaughter refer to Brooke as her mama was always a blessing. Luca's first wife, and Franny's biological mother, was not a part of Franny's life. And for the brief amount of time she was, all she did was cause chaos and pain.

Brooke was the blessing Mari truly thought Paulo helped with from wherever he was now. She showed up at the perfect moment in her oldest son's life and never left.

"You look like you got some sun," Brooke told her.

"Hard not to when it's hot and you're surrounded by the ocean."

She stumbled into the kitchen and headed straight to the coffee maker.

"Did you meet anyone new?"

The image of James swam in her head. "We met a lot of people and had a great time. I didn't realize how much I needed a change from my routine."

"Do you think you'll do it again?"

"Maybe."

Franny's footsteps came in fast. "Ready."

Brooke headed to the door, then stopped. "I have an online conference call today at one. If Luca can't get away, can you—"

"Yes. And stop asking. You know the answer is yes. I haven't seen my grandson in ten days. You're going to have to pry him away from me."

Brooke smiled. "Thanks, Mari."

"Now go. And don't get any ideas from that friend Leah."

"I won't," Franny said. "Bye."

"See you after school."

And just like that, they were gone.

Mari dropped her head to her chest. She could really use another hour of sleep.

One glance at the coffeepot, and Mari diverted to her bathroom to wake up in the shower.

~

James didn't bother trying to go back to sleep when his eyes popped open at four thirty in the morning.

He took advantage of the fact that his girls were at their mother's until after school. He caught up on the local news on his phone, drank a half a pot of coffee, and headed to the office.

Sitting behind his desk before any of his employees arrived gave him the quiet he needed to catch up on his emails.

Emails he intended to take care of while he was on his vacation.

But then Mari came along.

A very welcome distraction.

He'd thought twice about texting her when he'd first gotten out of bed. But he wasn't sure if she kept her notifications off on her phone when she slept and didn't want to wake her.

Even though there was only a three-hour time difference from where they'd been on the ship, those three hours often messed with your sleep for a couple of days.

He fully expected his body to crash early.

But for now, it was coffee and willpower.

At a quarter to eight, he heard AJ outside his office door.

"You're back?"

"I'm pretty sure I put that on the calendar."

"I thought for sure you'd wait until midday."

"I didn't do nearly enough while I was away to sleep in."

AJ walked completely into the office. "Vacations are known to do that."

James nodded his agreement. "Anything happen?"

AJ took a seat across from him.

"The Mission Valley project caught a snag. Our guys were down for three days, but everything is back up and running now."

"What happened?"

"A hydraulic line sprung a leak."

"Oh shit."

"Ken caught it. Took a few days to get it replaced."

"It couldn't be overnighted?" James asked.

"That was overnight."

They were having problems with their parts vendor, and this just added to them. "That's unacceptable."

James spent the morning chasing issues and filled the afternoon with on-site meetings.

He left the office at eleven thirty and seriously considered stopping by Little Italy before his Mission Valley meeting. Even though Little Italy was beyond the Mission Valley project.

Instead, he settled for a phone call.

In his car, James set off and dialed Mari's number.

She answered on the second ring. "Hi."

"Good morning." Hearing her voice put a smile on his face.

"Almost noon," she corrected him.

"How did you sleep?"

"I woke up in the middle of the night, fell back asleep, and found my granddaughter at my door, calling my name."

"Ahh, she missed you."

Mari sighed. "She did. It's good to be home."

"Nothing like your own bed."

There was noise in the background James couldn't identify. "Where are you?"

"In my office."

"Is someone yelling?" He thought for sure he heard a man hollering.

"One of the chefs," she said like it was a daily occurrence.

"Is there a problem?"

Mari paused.

The yelling grew. Not that he understood what was being said. Whoever was making the noise was speaking Italian.

"He's unhappy with the tomatoes."

James couldn't help but laugh. "Tomatoes?"

"It's a restaurant. Our sauce is fresh. If the tomatoes are bad, the food is bad."

"Can your customers hear that?"

Mari laughed. "Most of the time. If it's too much, Luca or I will calm things down. Otherwise, it adds to the experience. Chefs yelling to perfect their meals only benefits the customer."

James pulled out of the parking lot and onto the road. "I'll try and remember that."

The sound of something hard hitting the phone, or perhaps the phone hitting something hard, stopped their conversation.

"Mari?"

She didn't respond. He did hear her voice but only fragments of her conversation.

James recognized the name Luca from whoever was talking. Then something about basil. After that, whoever was talking switched to Italian, and he didn't catch a thing.

Mari fired off something fast before the sound over the call became clear.

"I have to call you back," she told him.

"No hurry. I have meetings all afternoon. I'll call you tonight."

"You don't . . . Okay," she stuttered.

She hung up before he could say goodbye.

He imagined her marching into the kitchen, her small frame getting into the space of a chef twice her size, and her reminding him who was boss.

James could hardly wait to see that in person.

~

"You didn't meet anyone?"

"There were thousands of people on the ship. I met plenty of people."

Ellie looked down her nose at him. "Weak, Dad."

"Sooo basic," Madison added.

"What did you expect? That I eloped and brought you home a step-mommy?"

"Ewhhh, cringe."

James laughed at his daughters. "Getting out was a start, okay. I probably should have done it sooner."

"You think?" Ellie's sarcasm screamed at him. "I mean, you're getting old."

"Ouch."

"Are you going to book another cruise?" Madison asked.

"I haven't even unpacked from this one. No."

"What about a dating app? They have them for seniors."

"I'm *not* a senior." He couldn't believe he was having this conversation over a store-bought rotisserie chicken, a salad, and mashed potatoes that came out of a box.

"Well, you can't go on Tinder," Ellie said. "My friends will see you."

"You have friends on Tinder?" He didn't like the sound of that.

"Yeah."

"You're not on it." He didn't phrase it as a question but waited for her answer anyway.

"Gross." Ellie made a gagging noise.

"She doesn't need Tinder, she has Trevor," Madison teased.

"I don't *have* Trevor."

It was James's turn to gag.

"You should ask Maddie if she's on Tinder," Ellie tossed out.

James snapped his attention to Madison.

"She's lying. I don't even want to date."

That made him feel better.

"Everyone wants to go to prom. And for that, you need a date," Ellie said.

All James could do was sit back and watch his girls argue.

"I don't need a date date. I can take a lavender date."

James felt a headache coming on. "What the hell is a lavender date?"

Ellie looked at him as if he were an idiot. "It's when you take your gay friend. Or a friend who is your bestie but not your date."

"Oh." He liked the sound of that.

Those kinds of dates didn't end up in hotel rooms with condoms.

"What are you doing if Trevor doesn't ask you?" Madison asked.

"I'll ask him."

"No," James barked.

"Dad, it's 2025. Women ask men out all the time."

He pointed his fork at Ellie. "If Trevor isn't man enough to ask you out, he doesn't deserve you."

"Dad . . . 'man enough'? Really?"

He shook his head. "I know. I'm not being PC, or this century, or whatever you kids call it. I don't care. You don't lower the bar. If Trevor wants to take you to prom, he needs to ask. And he needs to show up at this door and shake my hand."

"Why?" Ellie asked.

So that I can squeeze the fuck out of it and remind the punk that it's my daughter he is with, and if he does anything I don't approve of, he'll have hell to pay. In short, so James could intimidate him. "Because that's how it's done."

"But—"

"But nothing. Besides, when I was in high school, plenty of girls went together."

"Cringe," both girls said at the same time.

"I was just on a cruise where there were more women on the dance floors dancing with each other than with men. And they were having a great time."

"Did you get out there?" Madison asked.

He instantly remembered Mari laughing as he spun her around. "A few times."

His girls went silent.

James shoveled up more potatoes. "And I did the asking."

For the next half hour, James was lectured on how things were different now.

And by the time dinner was over, his girls reminded him no less than a dozen times that he was old and completely out of touch.

~

"I miss you."

Mari pushed aside the laundry she was folding and sat on her sofa with her phone tucked close to her ear. "You saw me yesterday."

"Entirely too long ago."

"Don't be ridiculous, James."

"You know what made it worse?" he asked.

"No. But I have a feeling you're going to tell me."

"I couldn't talk about you. When the girls drilled me on who I met, I had to blow off their questions and pretend that nothing and no one special came out of the trip."

Oddly, Mari felt the same way. "It's for the best. We hardly know each other."

"That was changing by the hour."

Mari made a humming noise in the back of her throat. "Thank you for keeping your promise."

"I will never do anything to lose your trust."

"That's a big promise. And hard to keep when you don't know what would make me distrust you."

James huffed. "Lying to you would destroy your trust."

"True."

"Walking into your restaurant today and kissing you would blow your trust."

Her eyes widened as that image passed through her brain. "That would be a big mistake."

"Exactly. Seeing me walk down the street holding another woman. Or even hearing that I was seeing someone else would destroy your trust."

True, but . . . "Just because I haven't seen anyone since Paulo doesn't mean I'm naive to the dating world. I have no hold on you. We haven't promised to not see other people." And by *we*, Mari meant him.

James hesitated. "Do you want to see other men?"

She laughed. "Of course. A new man on Friday, another on Saturday . . . maybe I can squeeze you in on Tuesdays when the girls are at school."

James's laugh was entirely too confident. "What did your late husband do with your sass?"

Mari smiled into the memory of Paulo placating her. "He would call me *cara*, pat my hand or whatever he could touch, and then go on like I said nothing."

"And did that work?"

"Yes." Every time.

"Great. Thanks for the tip," he said. "I'm not a kid, Mari. I have no intention of dating other women. If you see me with someone, I promise you it isn't romantic."

His assurance was comforting. It was strange enough to enter into this . . . whatever *this* was they were doing. To think of him measuring her against different women was an image she didn't want to entertain.

"Are you still there?" he asked.

"I am. Thank you."

A moment passed. "This is where you tell me I'm your Mr. Saturday."

She sighed. "Sorry, James. Leo is my Mr. Saturday. And he sleeps in my bed."

He laughed. "I can't compete with a grandchild."

"No. You can't."

"If that's my only competition, I'll take it."

"I'm unsure how you and I work. The last thing I would do is invite anyone else into my life," she assured him.

"I'll give you a few days to settle in. After that, expect me to start pestering you for a few hours of your time," he warned.

"That's fair," she said.

"Good. Now, I have one more question before I let you go," he said.

"I'm listening."

"What does *cara* mean?" James asked.

"It's an Italian endearment. Like *dear* or *hon*."

"All right. I suppose I'll learn Italian one word at a time."

She laughed. "You'll be fluent in no time."

A moment passed. "Good night, Mari."

"Good night."

Mari held the phone in her hands, looking into it as if James sat inside.

Cara.

Paulo had always called her *cara*.

Thinking of the word in her head sent a familiar vibration through her soul. A ripple of her husband's presence.

A whisper of his voice in her ear.

The months following his passing, Mari literally saw him in every corner of her life. In the apartment she sat in now. The restaurant. At the market, or in the square.

Like the smell of him, eventually, those images faded.

Physically, his presence was moved along.

From removing his clothing to throwing away his favorite chair when the cushions were beyond repair, Paulo evaporated.

Only now, she felt him. Or at least she thought she did. A scent that was his . . . but different. His voice . . . only a note too low to match him perfectly.

Logically, she knew dating James wasn't a betrayal of her marriage.

Then why was there a sense of guilt? Misguided guilt, but guilt nonetheless.

Mari pushed off her sofa, disregarding the laundry that needed folding.

She was tired and needed sleep to wash away her conflicting emotions.

Perhaps seeing James was the closure she needed. He was a good man, and if something about them didn't fit, Mari would have at least made good on her husband's dying wish.

She would try.

She owed Paulo that.

CHAPTER SEVENTEEN

The first opportunity for Mari to meet James since the cruise came the following Friday for lunch.

He pressed for dinner but settled for lunch.

"As strange as it sounds, I don't leave my home in the evenings without my family unless Rosa has made plans for me. And that only started happening since her divorce was final."

"Never?"

"Never! Anything that needs doing can be done during the day. And Fridays are busy at the restaurant. Since Gio moved to Temecula, I'm gone more . . . but that's with my family."

James didn't push.

He'd take lunch.

Lunch that had to be far outside of Little Italy or anywhere Mari could be seen by anyone she knew.

James made reservations at a restaurant in La Jolla close to the ocean, where they could walk afterward.

Nothing fancy was Mari's request. "If I leave in anything other than comfortable shoes, questions will be asked."

"In my neighborhood, lunch, and casual . . . anything else?" he asked.

With his walking orders in hand, he gave himself three hours for his lunch date and arrived at the restaurant twenty minutes early.

Her outfit was understated, her makeup barely there, but the shine in her eyes lit up the room when their gaze met.

The hostess walked away before Mari had been led completely to the table.

James stood and greeted her with a familiar kiss on her cheek. "Hello, beautiful," he whispered in her ear.

"You spoil me with your compliments," she said.

He held out her chair and waited for her to sit.

Once seated across from her, James reached a hand across the table. "It's been a long week."

Mari grazed her fingers against his and smiled. "I have spent more time on the phone with you between texting and calls this week than I have with all my family combined in the past month."

"That's a win for me."

Mari took her hand away and rested it in her lap. She glanced around the outside patio that sat on a second story of a building. "What made you choose this place?"

"They have a fabulous Reuben."

"Is that what they're known for?"

He shrugged. "I have no idea. I'm the kind of person that chooses the restaurant based on what I want to eat. I've only ever had the Reuben here."

"You've never tried anything else?"

He shook his head.

"Where would you go for steak?"

"Steak is the one thing I do well on the grill. But if I do go out, I like Eddies."

"Fish?"

James rattled off the names of three places he moved between.

Her eyes narrowed. "Italian?"

He opened his mouth, then closed it. "Why do I feel this is a trap?"

She leaned forward. "If you say Olive Garden, I'm going to have to leave."

The longer he was silent, the more serious her expression became.

"You have to admit, their breadsticks are on point."

Mari scooted her chair back.

She made him laugh.

"Kidding," he said to stop her. Though he knew she was bluffing.

"I'll give you a pass on that one."

The waiter stepped up to the table and asked if they wanted to start with anything other than water.

Mari asked for sparkling water with lemon, then asked to hear their specials. Once the waiter finished describing both a fresh fish and a soup of the day, Mari quizzed the man on what was recommended as well as what was most popular.

Nowhere was the Reuben stated.

The waiter walked away, promising to return shortly.

Mari looked over the menu again before putting it down.

"How do you judge a restaurant? I would imagine owning one your whole life either gives you an advantage or makes it difficult to eat out."

She glanced around. "Cleanliness."

"Of course."

"No, I'm not talking about the tables or the dishes. I look at the floors and light fixtures. The restrooms. If there is a special, that means the chef is testing something out to determine if it should be on the menu . . . or the ingredients are in season. This is always a plus for me. I'm not sure you can consider my scale of judgment an advantage. It certainly limits my desire to eat out."

"Even when you have to cook for other people every day?"

"I'm not in the downstairs kitchen as much as I once was. Besides, you eat every day, don't you? You must cook."

"My girls would argue with you."

"You don't cook?"

James rubbed his hands together. "I'm more of a warmer-upper."

"I don't think I should ask what it is you warm up."

His lips pressed in a straight line. "Probably not."

She clicked her tongue. "Did your girls learn to cook from their mother?"

"They learned to microwave from their father."

Mari unwrapped her silverware from the napkin and placed the cloth on her lap. "I suppose I shouldn't judge. I tried with Chloe, but that girl . . ."

"Really?" James asked.

"Let's just say it's a good thing she and Dante don't live far away."

The waiter returned. Mari ordered the daily soup and a simple salad. James went with his favorite sandwich.

Their conversation flowed through lunch without any awkward pauses or moments of "what do I say next."

They followed their meal with a walk that led them down to the cliffs of La Jolla.

Tourists and locals alike spread out over the picturesque landscape, giving them little privacy.

When he saw Mari glance at her watch, James knew it was time to walk her to her car.

"What are your weekend plans?" he asked.

"We're going to Gio and Emma's for dinner on Sunday. A birthday celebration."

"Whose birthday?" he asked.

"Mine."

He bent down slightly. "Your birthday is Sunday?"

"No. It was yesterday."

"Your birthday was yesterday?" he asked.

"Yes."

"And you didn't tell me."

"It's a birthday, James. We have them every year."

He shifted from one foot to another. "If I had known, I would have done better than a Reuben sandwich." He'd have come with a gift and chocolates or something.

"It's not a big deal. I'll have another birthday next year."

"Don't think I won't write it down and remember it."

Mari looked away. "You have Ellie's game tomorrow, right?"

Mari had a great way of changing the subject off her. "With an early start time, I'd complain, but I know I'm going to miss these when she's away at college."

Mari turned and rested her back against the railing separating the park from the ocean. "Any more talk of them picking a local college because of your single status?"

He shook his head. "No. But they are adamant that I get on a dating app so they can help me look for a date."

Mari's smile fell slightly. "I hope they stay away from those things. They're not safe."

"Have you—"

"God no. But Chloe . . ."

"Chloe what?"

"It's a long story. The short version is . . . Chloe attracted the wrong sort of man."

James placed a hand on Mari's arm. "He hurt her?"

Mari nodded.

"Was she okay?"

"Ultimately. Dante says she still has nightmares on occasion."

James wanted to know more and didn't at the same time. "I'm not ready for my girls to leave."

"I'm sorry. I shouldn't have told you any of that."

"Of course you should have. Burying my head in the sand and not preparing my girls for the world is the fastest way to get them hurt."

"You can do all that, and still bad things happen. We can't stop our children from living their lives. Nor would we want to. But you can warn your girls of the sins of dating apps."

James leaned a hip against the railing. "They won't listen to me. They think I'm old and out of touch."

"Do they listen to their mother?"

"Cindy knows less on the subject than I do. I doubt she'd have any luck either."

"That doesn't mean you don't try," Mari said.

James glanced over Mari's shoulder as the call of a sea lion sparked the others sunbathing on rocks to join the choir.

Mari followed his attention and turned to watch the mammals.

"I really should let you go," James told her.

"Probably."

James nudged closer, their shoulders touching. "This is where I want to ask if I can plan something better than a meal when I see you again."

"Dance lessons?"

He knew she was teasing, but he ran with it anyway. "Don't threaten me. I'll have us booked in the next beginner class."

"I wonder what my family would say about that."

Was she really considering his offer? "It would be a great way for me to show you how amazing I am."

"You're so humble, James. You deserve a trophy."

He put a hand to his chest. "I'm date-worthy."

"Isn't that what we're doing now?"

"You know what I mean."

She grinned and looked away.

James lifted his hand to her chin and made her look at him. "I'll take what you're willing to give. And push for more later."

"You're a patient man."

"Remember that when later comes." He inched closer and tilted her head up. "And it will come."

Before giving her a reason to back up, he pressed his lips to hers for much too brief of a moment.

He wanted more. And from the smile on her face, she did, too.

That was enough for James to know that "later" would come sooner than, well . . . later.

~

Mari pulled Rosa away from the family for a private conversation once their Sunday meal was finishing up.

Giovanni and Emma's home set on a vineyard was a picture right out of the hills of Tuscany. Gio's slice of sommelier heaven.

Mari loved visiting.

She could hardly wait for the twins to come to have the excuse to stay over for several days at a time. At least in the beginning, when Emma would welcome the help. Though overstaying her welcome was always a risk. Mari never wanted to be that mother-in-law. She knew her son loved her, and Emma as well. But no one encouraged a hovering grandmother expressing how she did it. How she raised her children and how her way was the only way.

"James has suggested dance classes so we can see each other," Mari told Rosa once they were well outside of being overheard.

Rosa laughed. "That's not out of character at all."

"It might not be so awkward if we did them together."

"We? As in you and me?"

"You did convince me to join bunco as well as the cruise."

"Only I'm not interested in dance lessons," Rosa said.

"I didn't say you should take lessons . . . just pretend—"

"Lie." Rosa's smile was laughing at her.

"Pretend for a night or two. Then you can say you lost interest, and I was enjoying myself and stayed on."

"Ridicola."

Mari grumbled. "It's not ridiculous."

"You like James. There's nothing wrong with that. It's been ten years."

"Exactly ten years tomorrow. I know." They kept walking through the rows of budding grapevines. "I need more time alone in this. I'm not ready for the kids to know. I could practically hear Paulo's voice in our apartment when I returned."

"And what did you hear him say?"

"Not like that. More of a memory. A presence. I woke up yesterday swearing I felt the bed dip beside me."

Rosa stopped walking. "You're considering that with another man. There is bound to be some trepidation."

"I haven't gotten used to kissing the man, I can't even consider sleeping with him."

They both started walking again.

"Why not?" Rosa asked. "We're not as old as our children believe us to be."

"Paulo and I were married."

"Are you saying you *didn't* before you were married?"

"Well . . ."

Rosa laughed again and kept the pace. "I won't tell you to have sex with James. I won't tell you not to. But I will suggest that at fifty-five, you're old enough to take a lover if you want one."

"That sounds so strange."

"You're old enough to know what you're doing." Rosa gestured toward the house. "Maybe they'll surprise you."

Mari was certain they wouldn't surprise her. That Luca and Gio would protest or think differently about her. Chloe . . . maybe not. Even Franny might be confused to learn her *nonna* was dating.

"I'd be more nervous about the act and not about who knew I was doing it," Rosa said.

"What do you mean?"

Rosa looked down at her body. "The only one that has seen this in years is my doctor. And even then, I have a piece of paper tossed over my shoulders."

Mari ran a hand over her face. "Oh, God. I didn't even think of that."

"Really?"

"I am now."

Rosa tucked her arm through Mari's. "The good news is . . . James is the same age."

"He didn't have three children."

"But he had a wife who had twins. I think when the time comes, worrying about where your breasts are on your chest will be the last thing you're thinking about."

Mari squeezed her eyes shut and saw exactly where her breasts were.

Rosa laughed and tugged on her arm. "I will lie to the kids for you. But you're paying for my lessons that I'm only going to a couple of times."

"Thank you."

"On second thought, I'll make James pay."

CHAPTER EIGHTEEN

The first dance lesson was starting on the first of the following month. In the weeks up to the start of their classes, Mari and James met around the appointments they both had to manage.

Arguably, Mari's schedule should be easier to manipulate, but she quickly realized just how busy her family kept her.

At least once a week, in the evenings, she had both of her grandchildren staying with her. Luca and Brooke took their alone time, or "date night," as they labeled it.

Mari stepped in for baby duty when Brooke needed to concentrate or deal with conference calls.

All the managerial work defaulted to her when Salena wasn't on. Most of which was on autopilot thanks to Salena's efforts. Automated inventory, updated POS reports, and batching out at the end of the day. Even scheduling the employees had been streamlined. Salena had suggested the staff set their own schedules and then authorized a "comanager" for the waiters and the bar staff. The kitchen was Luca's, and Mari only found herself jumping in when mutual agreements couldn't be met among the employees.

Salena's system worked. And for the most part, employee retention was at the highest it had been since 2020.

In short, Mari found herself with plenty of time.

Where she once joined her neighbors for an afternoon coffee or walk down to the embarcadero, late breakfasts or lunches with James filled her time.

On the day of her now "regular" bunco date, Mari sat in the chair with her hairdresser.

Peering at herself in the mirror, a plastic cape buttoned around her neck, Mari stared back at herself.

"Are you ready for something different?" Her hairdresser, Deanna, was in her midthirties and had been cutting Mari's hair for five years. Slowly, the need to "cover her age" became more frequent. With the darkness of her Italian roots, literally, Mari had kept it simple. Color and trim. Nothing fancy.

Deanna ran her hands through Mari's hair and then let it fall.

"Oh, I don't know. The same, I guess," she told her.

"That didn't sound convincing."

Mari caught her eyes through the mirror. "I don't like change."

Deanna hummed. "What about a few highlights and maybe a little bit shorter? Nothing dramatic. The highlights will help you see past any gray peeking out between appointments. And the shorter style will feel breezier."

"I don't like short hair either." Mari never understood the need for women to cut off their hair at a certain age.

Deanna pulled her hair up to demonstrate the length she was suggesting. "Then, with a few passes with a curling iron, you'll feel ten years younger. Let's try it, Mari. If you hate the color, we can fix it. And at the rate your hair grows, it will look just like this in a few months."

Eventually, Mari agreed.

Then, as every hairdresser seemed to double as a therapist, Mari told her about the cruise.

She kept James's name out of it. Skimmed over the details regarding Rosa's sickness.

An hour and a half later, Mari twisted her head from side to side and smiled.

"So this is the fountain of youth," she stated.

"Do you like it?" Deanna asked.

"Do you?"

"I love it. I've been wanting to do this for years. Maybe even a few more highlights the next time."

What will James think?

"I like it."

After settling with Deanna, Mari walked home and entered through the front of the restaurant.

Salena saw her first. "Oh, wow."

"What?"

Salena circled a finger in the air. "This. I love it."

"Deanna thought it was time for a change."

"It's fabulous. You look like you're ready for a night on the town," Salena said.

Mari clicked her tongue. "If by 'night on the town' you mean bunco with Rosa and our new friends, then I guess I am."

Salena wrinkled her nose. "That's unfortunate. But maybe when you start those dance lessons you'll have the opportunity for a nightlife."

Again, James popped into her head. "If nothing else, I could use the exercise. I'm not getting any younger." Mari started to walk past.

"You wouldn't know that by looking at you, Mama D'Angelo."

"You're sweet."

She stepped into her office and settled behind her desk.

Her phone buzzed.

Even before looking, she knew who was texting.

Hi, Beautiful.

Good afternoon.

Have you spoken to Summer since the cruise? he asked.

I'll see her tonight at bunco. Why?

Three dots flashed on the screen for a few seconds before he replied with a picture.

The two of them stood in the middle of the dance floor on the last night of the cruise. Channeling a little Danny Zuko and Sandy vibes, James had his arm casually over her shoulder. Mari's head was tossed back, laughing, and James was whispering something in her ear.

She smiled into the memory of that moment.

Summer sent me this today. I thought you might want a copy.

That was a memorable night.

"Mari, can you—"

Mari all but dropped her phone on her desk and shot her attention to her office door.

Salena jolted and stopped talking. "Am I interrupting something?" she asked.

"No." Mari turned her phone screen-side down on her desk. "What can I do for you?"

The phone buzzed. The vibration tapped on the wood like a toddler demanding attention.

Salena glanced at the desk.

The phone buzzed again.

Cazzo!

"I can wait."

Mari placed a hand over the phone, willing James to hold off on the next message. "What is it?"

"I, ah . . . wanted to remind you to sign the payroll checks. I know you're leaving early."

"Right. Yes. I'll leave them here for you to distribute tonight."

"Great."

The phone buzzed again.

She placed the phone in her lap. "Anything else?"

Salena glanced at Mari's lap, then shook her head. "Nope."

Once Salena had walked out of view, Mari read James's message.

In more ways than one. Which was quickly followed by Mari?

After reading back to remind herself what she and James were talking about, she remembered how the rest of that night went. The way he'd kissed her when no one else was watching.

Yes, in more ways than one.

~

Chloe and Salena had their bimonthly nail salon appointment.

Over the course of the last couple of years, their lives had changed. They had both acquired husbands. Chloe helped Dante run their chartered yacht business and had also started a multilanguage online yoga class. And Salena, in addition to helping manage the restaurant, had opened up a physical pole-dancing studio.

A forced appointment, even one to have their nails done, was keeping them both in close contact. A promise they gave each other.

With feet soaking in warm, soapy water and a technician trimming their fingernails, they caught up.

"Have you told Mama that you want to leave yet?"

Salena had been putting off finding her replacement for months.

"I can't do that right now. When Emma has the babies, your mama is going to want to be in Temecula more than at the restaurant."

"And when that happens, then maybe Brooke gets pregnant. Then what? You put it off for another nine months?" Chloe wasn't about to put herself in the possible motherhood category. She and Dante weren't ready. Though Chloe had been thinking about babies a little more every month.

"I feel guilty."

"Mama knows you don't need the income. I wouldn't be surprised if she's shocked that you're still there."

"Did she say anything to you?" Salena asked.

"No. But I can talk to her. Let her know you're itchy."

"Don't. I can hang in there for a bit longer. Your mama has been filling up her social calendar. Bunco, the cruise . . . and have you seen her new haircut?"

Chloe shook her head.

"She has highlights."

"My mom?" Chloe pointed to her chest.

"Yeah, and get this . . . I walked in the office the other day. She dropped her phone like it was coming out of a frying pan. One minute she was smiling, the next, all Mrs. Business and 'what can I do for you?'"

"Was she talking on the phone?"

Salena shook her head. "Texting."

This sounded off. "You're sure she was texting?"

"The phone kept buzzing. And she refused to look at it while I was in the room."

"That sounds like something I did when I was hiding something."

"Right? Exactly what I thought." Salena sat up a little taller. "And since when does your mama leave the restaurant in the middle of the day for hours to 'run errands.'" Salena made air quotes with her free hand. "Takes her car and returns with nothing."

"Mama almost never takes the car. Unless she needs to do a Costco run or something." The nice thing about Little Italy was the fact that they could walk to nearly all their needs.

"Nothing, Chloe. Not even a T-shirt."

"How often has she done that?"

"A handful since she returned from the cruise. And you heard about the dance classes . . ."

"Yeah, that's weird. Rosa said it was her suggestion. Dante thinks his mother is having a midlife crisis. Ever since the divorce, she's been purging the house, meeting new people. She doesn't even sound like the same woman sometimes. I told Dante I thought she'd been in a low-level depression for years. Now she's waking up and realizing how much time she'd lost being married to his useless father."

"You called Joseph useless?"

"Dante says much worse. He believes Joseph will cut off the alimony payments long before the judgment date."

The technician had Chloe switch her hands.

"Ohhh, what will Rosa do then?" Salena asked.

"The house is free and clear. The taxes are nothing in comparison to the norm. She says she has savings. How much, we don't know." Chloe knew that when it all boiled down, she and Dante would make sure Rosa had what she needed. Worrying about her financial situation was one of the reasons she and Dante were putting off kids. They couldn't afford both.

"Has she ever worked?"

"Thirty years ago," Chloe said.

"I can't imagine having to figure it all out again in my fifties."

"Hopefully we'll never have to. In the meantime, my mama is hiding something, and Dante's appears to be living her best life."

They both sat with that thought bouncing around.

"Are you coming for Sunday dinner this weekend?" Salena asked.

"Yeah. It's low-key. Dante has a charter. Gio and Emma are staying home." Family dinners were a mixed bag at this point. But they were never missed, if possible.

"Tell you what. I'm going to staff up and invite myself. Can you get Rosa to come?"

Chloe hummed; a smile started to spread over her face. "You thinking what I'm thinking?"

"If your mama is hiding something, there is one person that would know what that is. Between the two of them, someone's bound to slip."

Chloe switched hands again, her mind racing.

Then, from nowhere, the technician said, "It's a man."

"I don't know. Rosa? Maybe. But my mama . . ."

Chloe's and Salena's gazes met.

"I think she's right," she said. "What else could it possibly be?"

Chloe blinked . . . twice.

A tiny spark of hope flared in her chest. "We need a plan."

CHAPTER NINETEEN

Ellie burst through the door as if the devil was on her heels. "I'm going to prom!"

Her voice carried all through the house, her excitement palpable.

James mustered up a smile. "Let me guess . . ."

She dropped her softball bag just inside the door and kicked off her shoes.

Madison ran down the stairs. "How did he ask?"

"He asked at practice."

"But how?"

James had been walking through the foyer with a pile of mail in his hand when Ellie had shouted her way into the house. Now the three of them stood staring at each other.

"He just asked."

Madison's shoulders fell. "What do you mean?"

"He was waiting for me at my car when practice let out, and he asked."

"No flowers?"

Good call, James thought.

"Flowers aren't my thing."

"A big sign with hearts?"

Okay, another good idea.

James looked at Ellie.

She didn't reply.

"Chocolate? A stuffed animal?" Madison continued.

Still no response from Ellie.

"A cute note?"

Ellie shook her head.

"Nothing?"

"He just asked!" Ellie's voice rose an octave.

James was slightly impressed at the depths to which Madison could roll her eyes. "Weak AF."

Now Ellie was frowning. "You're just jealous."

Madison turned and headed toward the kitchen. "Olivia's boyfriend serenaded her outside fifth period. He had a portable microphone and everything."

Ellie followed her sister.

James stayed a few steps behind.

"Olivia's boyfriend is in a band. Trevor doesn't sing."

"Still lame. He knew you'd say yes, so he didn't put any effort into it."

James could see Ellie's joy fading.

And as much as he didn't like Trevor, he didn't want to see his girl brought down because of the dating expectations of her sister.

"When I was in high school, most guys just asked. It's not a big deal, Maddie."

"Dad's right," Ellie said.

"He better make it up by taking you somewhere nice before."

Ellie lifted her chin. "He will."

"All I ask is he meets you at this door." James wanted to demand more.

"He will."

"And no motorcycle. It's a car or you're not—"

"We'll be dressed up, Dad. We can take my car if he needs to."

Chastity belts and ivory towers.

"Have you told Mom yet?" Madison asked from the other side of the kitchen island.

"I'm going over there after dinner."

Both girls looked at him at Ellie's mention of dinner.

"How about pizza?" he asked.

Ellie drew her phone from her back pocket. "Fine, but it's my turn to pick."

James tapped the mail in his hand on the counter and looked at the time. "Save me a couple of pieces."

"Where are you going?" Madison asked.

"I signed up for a dance class," he said without pause.

Both girls stopped what they were doing and gaped at him.

"What?" Madison asked.

"Dance class!" Ellie exclaimed.

James turned his attention to the mail. "I thought I told you."

"Ahh . . . no. You didn't."

They were both still staring as if he'd suddenly grown horns. "I had a good time on the ship. Your old dad has some great moves."

"Cringe, Dad."

He winked at Ellie. "Women love a man who dances. Maybe I'll meet someone." *Whose name is Mari that owns a restaurant and makes me smile like a teenage girl that has just been asked to prom.*

"Slightly less cringe," Ellie amended.

"What is it . . . like ballroom dancing or something?"

He shook his head. "We signed up for swing. I don't waltz."

James poked his finger between the edges of the envelope that looked like junk and started to rip.

"When will you be home?"

"No idea. Before you're in bed." He turned to leave the room. "Use Uber. We still have credit on that account," he said.

Both the girls said okay, and James walked away.

He needed a shower and a shave.

And Mari to spin around the dance floor.

It was going to be a great night.

~

Ellie and Madison linked eyes.

That knowing twin sixth-sense thing buzzed between them.

"You heard that, right?" Ellie asked.

"He said *we*."

"I knew he was acting weird."

Madison waved a hand at Ellie. "You order the pizza, I'm calling Mom. She'll know something."

~

The dance studio was situated in a town north of Mari and south of James. Eleven people, thirteen if you counted the instructors, stood around a large, open studio. Two entire walls were floor to ceiling mirrors, and the space was large enough to host five times the number of people than was there. The perimeter of the room had chairs lining the walls.

Turned out, Mari and James were one of three couples, the other two married and half their age. The other four people were closer to their age. Rosa, of course, plus two other women and one man.

"I'm a third wheel," Rosa whispered as the instructors rounded everyone up.

"It's only for a few lessons."

Their instructors, Leticia and Bayani, were somewhere in their midthirties. Both enthusiastically greeted each of them before going around the room and asking about their experience with formal dance lessons. One of the couples confessed to taking salsa lessons while the rest of them claimed this was a first-time experience.

"Those of you that are without partners, don't worry. That is why Bayani and I are here. In addition, we switch up your partners throughout the class."

"See," Mari whispered to Rosa.

"Tonight will be the easiest, yet the most fundamental, introduction to West Coast swing that you'll have. If you understand the concept of who is leading and where you're headed on the dance floor, the rest quickly makes sense."

For the following hour and a half, Mari counted to six more times than she had since she was a toddler learning her numbers. "One, two, three and four, five and six."

James virtually stood in one spot, stepping to the same six count, while he passed Mari from one side of him to the next. If his hand moved up, she passed with a spin. All of which felt a lot like what they'd done on the dance floor on the cruise. Only this was much more organized. Not that it didn't come with its own stepped-on toes.

Rosa was passed from Bayani to the lone male student who seemed to be struggling with how to lead.

For the most part, James and Mari danced exclusively with each other.

James pulled her in, passed her to the other side. Pulled in, *one, two* . . . spun her around, *three and four* . . . anchored her in place, *five and six.*

Repeat.

Repeat.

Repeat.

Several times, Mari felt herself looking over at Rosa. Her fake smile was easy to see.

"She's having a miserable time," Mari quietly told James.

"It's temporary."

"But . . ."

James pulled her in again. Turn, *three and four.* Shuffle her feet, *five and six.*

"Or we can tell our families that we're dating."

Pull in, *one, two* . . . "I'm getting there," she assured him. Since the return from the cruise, she'd been watching for red flags. The things Chloe spoke of relentlessly when she was dating.

Of course, Mari's red-flag barometer and her daughter's were entirely different. Okay, maybe not entirely. The man needed to be employed, age appropriate, and financially secure. In Mari's case, that meant he needed to own his own home. And while she'd not considered what a man needed to date her . . . since she never thought she'd be in this position . . . the man needed to be a father. Because without that element, how could he ever understand about family?

They needed to have similar interests.

Mari couldn't tell you what those interests were before meeting James. Aside from taking care of her family. Spending time with her grandchildren. Yet here they were, exploring professional dance lessons as a way to see each other without suspicion.

And she liked it.

More than bunco, but she supposed that had a place in her life. That new group of friends was how she'd met James, and for that, she was grateful.

Ninety minutes felt like ten.

On the way out the door, the instructors encouraged them to practice, if possible . . . and to consider buying shoes that made it a little easier to turn on the dance floor.

Sneakers weren't ideal for either party.

The sun had set while they were in class, leaving Mari and James to say good night in the dark parking lot.

Rosa waited in the car while James and Mari stole a few seconds alone.

Each time he gathered her in his arms, she anticipated his kiss before it happened. And as silly as it sounded, she felt like a young woman each time.

"I don't want to wait a week to see you again," he told her.

"But you have a business trip, and my weekend is full. Next Tuesday will have to do."

James looked over her shoulder as another couple from the class passed by.

Mari was keenly aware of how they looked.

Two adults talking in the dark, James's hand on her hip, their bodies close enough to feel the heat of the other.

"Dance classes was a genius idea," James said. "Not only do I have a weekly date, I get to touch you." His free hand ran down her arm.

She shivered.

"And you're cold." He pushed away from the car and pulled her close. "Just a little bit more."

He brought his lips to hers for more than a breath or two. But didn't linger, which Mari was grateful for because someone might be watching. Yet his short kisses were starting to feel incomplete. It seemed all they'd had since the cruise was short moments of intimacy. Always because there were people around. Outside of restaurants, by a car . . . in a park. Two grown adults stealing a touch.

Mari was starting to see the idiocy of that.

And she wanted more.

Her body wanted more.

Her heart wanted more.

James lifted his lips and stared. "This is getting harder and harder," he said.

"I agree." And she did.

He made a growling noise before turning her around and walking her to her car.

Rosa rolled down the window and leaned outside. "Are you kids done?"

Mari chuckled.

James opened the car door. "I have her back before curfew."

Mari felt James's hand on her hip tap as she slid into the passenger seat. "Call me when you're home."

"I'll get her there in one piece, James. Don't worry."

Mari waved Rosa's words away. "Good night."

Once she was settled, James closed the door and started back to his car.

From the dark interior of the car, Rosa's mirth could be felt. "You looked like teenagers out there."

"I know."

Rosa put the car in reverse and backed out of the parking space.

Mari glanced in the side mirror and saw the taillights of James's car glow.

"What is it you're waiting for?" Rosa asked. "Why keep this a secret?"

"Fear," she said without pause.

"Fear of what? James? The kids?"

They pulled out onto the street.

Mari stared at the passing lights as they drove along.

"Yes, the kids. I don't want this to touch them—"

"If it doesn't work out," Rosa interrupted. "Clearly, it's working out, Mari. And how can you truly tell if this is right if the two of you can't be alone? Don't you want sex?"

Yes. Yes, she did. But not just sex, she wanted James. "I know you're right."

They were silent for a moment.

"Is this about Paulo?"

She wanted to say no. "Less and less each day."

"Good," Rosa shot out. "Good."

CHAPTER TWENTY

"I'm not sure about this," Madison told Ellie while she was waking up their father's computer.

"We're only looking at pictures." And maybe his search engine.

Shortly after their father had arrived home from his cruise, he'd flashed a few pictures to prove that he'd had fun. Nothing in the photographs suggested a relationship.

And their mom was clueless. Or at least hid any knowledge well.

That was the problem when your divorced parents got along, they weren't easily persuaded to give away the indiscretions of the other.

"Maybe we should just ask him."

Ellie sat in her father's desk chair and clicked around his main screen before opening up his photographs.

"If we get caught, we tell him that I was looking for a picture he took of me at one of my games. It's not a big deal." It was a huge deal. They were invading their father's privacy, but . . . okay, no buts. Ellie knew this was wrong, but she couldn't stop herself.

When their father had announced that he had a business trip and suggested they stay with their mom, they seized the opportunity to snoop.

His photographs popped up, and Ellie started to scroll.

She spun past work pictures.

Cranes and hoses. Construction sites and screenshots of parts.

In short, not what they were looking for.

They jumped to blue waters and bright lights.

A few pictures of the ship and inside his cabin. He'd shown them those.

Then there was one at a casino.

Ellie was pretty sure that she'd seen that one.

A petite woman, olive skin, dark hair.

Another one with the same petite woman, this time with a taller woman.

"Didn't he show us something at a waterfall?"

Ellie found it. He was standing on what looked like a cliff in one frame, then coming up out of the water in the next.

Once again, he had his picture taken with a few more women. "Are these the same women as these?" Ellie asked her sister.

Madison screwed up her face. "Maybe. Hard to tell at that angle."

She kept going.

They recognized Summer.

Another group photo.

And another one.

"Dad's gone for ten days and took, like, twenty pictures. How is that possible?"

Madison stood back.

Ellie kept scrolling. Flipping back and forth, impatience nipped at her fingertips.

Her eyes drifted to the green thought bubble where his text messages lived.

"We can look at his texts. If there is anyone . . ."

Madison cringed. "We will be so dead if he finds out."

"How will he find out?"

"I don't know."

Ellie hovered the pointer over the icon.

Her heart raced in her chest, and her foot tapped on the floor.

Should I?

Shouldn't I?

She clicked and said, "Oops. My finger slipped."

Despite her sister's resistance, Madison leaned in.

Every person their father had sent a message to in the past few days was there.

One name stuck out.

"Who is Mari?" And there was a picture beside the name, but the thumbnail was too small to see any detail.

"We've already gotten this far . . ." Madison said.

When Mari's text message thread opened up, both of them were glued to the exchange like they were reading the final book in a six-book series. Only they read from the last page to the first.

Mari: Safe flight.

Dad: I'll call you tonight.

Mari: You'll survive.

Dad: I can't believe I have to wait until Tuesday to see you.

Dad: You did. Okay, I need to go, we're about to take off.

Mari: I warned you.

Dad: Someone kept me up late talking last night.

Mari: Give yourself more time.

Dad: It's not bad, but I had to hustle to my gate. Traffic was heavier than normal.

Mari: Leo woke me up. Thirty minutes isn't bad. Good morning.

Dad: I hope I didn't wake you. I just realized how early it is.

Dad: Since when is this airport lined up out the door? It took me thirty minutes with precheck.

Mari: Good night.

Dad: Okay, I'm going. Good night, beautiful.

Mari: Get some sleep. You have an early flight tomorrow.

Ellie stopped reading and turned to look at her sister. "Holy shit."

"He called her beautiful."

"Scroll down and see if they sent any pictures to each other."

"Good idea."

Their messages back and forth went on and on until . . .

"What the . . ."

Their dad was hanging on to a woman in a bright pink jacket, their father wore a white T-shirt, and the people around them were dressed up like it was the 1950s.

Madison pointed at the screen. "That's the same woman from the casino."

Ellie pulled up the photos again, found the image in question, and compared. "It is."

She started to copy the image to send it to herself.

Madison screamed, "Stop! He will see that."

Ellie dropped the mouse, startled. "Shit."

Madison took a picture of the screen with her phone.

Ellie slowly backed her way out of the computer and shut it down. "Dad has a girlfriend."

They were both smiling. "Why didn't he tell us?" Madison asked.

"No idea."

They were quiet for a minute. Ellie kicked around various reasons for the secrecy.

"Wait . . . what if she's married?"

Madison's jaw dropped. "No. He wouldn't . . ."

"Why the secret, then? We wanted Dad to date. I think he would brag about that." Ellie clicked the mouse to wake up the computer again.

It didn't.

"Shit. I logged out," Ellie said.

"Do you think he'll notice?"

Ellie shrugged. "We'll say the power blipped."

"He's going to find out."

Madison was the nervous one. Always playing by the rules. "If Dad is having an affair with a married woman, we need to stop him."

"There is no way. If she's married, how can she be talking to him late at night?"

Ellie stood and left the office. "I don't know. Maybe the husband works late. Didn't she say something about a Leo?" She'd skimmed the text so fast she didn't remember all the details.

"Leo could be a dog, for all we know," Madison offered.

"We should have read more."

"What if they started talking dirty?"

"Cringe," Ellie said.

"So gross."

"He's hiding something. He flat out told us that no one special was on his vacation. And now he's in dance lessons? That sounds special to me."

They both walked into the den and flopped on the sofa.

"What do we do now? If we ask him about her, he'll know we spied on him."

"That's exactly what we do. We spy on him. We find her by going to the dance lesson."

"He hasn't told us where they are," Madison pointed out. "If we start asking questions, he'll get suspicious."

"How hard can that be to find out? San Diego isn't that big of a city."

Turned out, San Diego was that big of a city.

There were at least a dozen dance studios. Not all had great websites and required phone calls to learn about their classes.

Thankfully, only one had just started a beginner class that took place on Tuesday nights.

Now all Ellie and Madison needed to do was wait until Tuesday.

And get one of their friends to drive them. Their father would recognize their cars a mile away.

And turn off their phones.

Not that he'd notice if he was flirting with a woman.

God, I hope he isn't having an affair.

Once Ellie's mind grabbed on to that possibility, nothing else made sense.

And Tuesday was a long time away.

~

"How are the dance lessons?"

Rain was in the forecast, so instead of having their Sunday meal on the terrace, they gathered around the dining room in Mari's apartments. On occasion, they would take up space in the restaurant's grotto, but the room had been reserved before the threat of rain hit the radar.

Mari sat at the head of her table, Luca on the other end.

And Chloe was asking questions about Mari's Tuesdays.

"I really enjoy them," Mari told her daughter.

"What about you, Rosa?" Salena asked.

"They're okay."

"That doesn't sound very convincing," Luca said.

I want to have dance lessons, Franny interjected completely in Italian.

Mari responded in Italian. *These are for adults.*

Leo sat in a high chair; his chubby hands playfully pounded on the tray.

"It would be better with a partner," Rosa said.

Mari shot her friend a look.

"How do they deal with that? Are there enough men in the class to even things out, or are you two dancing with each other?" Brooke asked.

"There are a few men in the class. And the instructor," Mari said. "It works out."

"I think it's great that the two of you are trying new things," Salena said.

"Mama needs more grandchildren to keep her busy," Luca said between bites.

Every eye at the table turned to look at him.

"I think Mama should keep busy with what she likes doing." Chloe glared at her brother.

"You like watching over Franny and Leo, right?"

"Of course, but—"

"You do know how sexist that sounds." Brooke placed her fork down to stare at her husband.

"*Cara*, you know that isn't how I meant that."

"No. I don't know that isn't what you meant," she said. "Babies keep a woman busy?"

"I'd say the same thing if Papa was still alive. Grandparents help with grandchildren. It's just how it's done."

The voices at the table started to elevate.

"Mama already raised her children. We're good." Chloe turned to Mari. "You take all the dance classes you want. You earned it."

Considering the only other man at the table was a toddler, Mari felt the need to come to her son's rescue. "Rest assured, Luca, my grandchildren will always come first."

"Mama! We can take care of our own kids," Chloe said.

Mari let her gaze drop to her daughter's waist. "Is there something you want to tell us?"

Chloe slapped a hand to her stomach. "No, no . . . not us, not yet. I just think it's time for you to live your life."

"What is it I've been doing if not living?"

Chloe looked at Salena. "Help me out here."

Salena picked up her wineglass and waved it toward Mari and Rosa. "I see two single, beautiful women who have dedicated their lives to caring for their families. Both of you did that alone."

"I wouldn't have changed a thing," Rosa said.

"Me either," Mari added.

"There is more to life than raising kids. Like cruises and dance classes." Salena looked at Chloe. "And romance."

James's image swam in her head. Mari did everything in her power to keep her face from exposing her thoughts.

A single laugh from the far end of the table interrupted the silence.

Brooke glared. "Do you have something to say?"

Luca dropped his smile and took the temperature of the room. "Yes, but I don't like sleeping on the couch."

"Why do you need to sleep on the couch?" Franny asked.

"Sometimes it's safer."

Rosa reached for the bottle of wine. "I want romance," she said, point-blank.

"Good for you," Salena said.

No one seemed to be shocked by that announcement.

"And another thing . . ."

Mari and Rosa looked at each other. For a moment, Mari thought for sure she was going to say something about James.

She didn't.

"I don't want a husband."

Cue the jaws dropping.

Mari might have been the only one that wasn't shocked to hear this.

But the energy at the table shifted off her, and for that, Mari was grateful.

"Go, Rosa," Salena teased.

"I never want that road again. I'm happy that you've all found your person. Wish you all the love for it. But I'm done."

"Your divorce is new, Rosa. Give it time," Luca said.

Considering Luca was the only one at the table that could relate to divorce, Mari felt his comment was sincere.

"But my marriage was long."

No one could deny her that.

"When are we booking our next trip?" Mari asked. Hoping the question cemented her support of her friend's decision.

"I'll let you know."

~

Cindy showed up at James's front door midafternoon on Monday.

"Hi," he said, a little confused about why she was there. "Is something wrong?"

"Maddie called me, asked me to meet her here after school. She didn't tell you?"

James moved aside and let Cindy in.

They walked into the kitchen. Cindy set her purse on a chair.

"No. What's going on?"

Cindy smiled. "Relax, James. She said there is an email from Caltech waiting to be opened. She didn't want to look at it until we were both with her. Then asked if I could leave work early."

A strange, heavy feeling pushed into James's heart. "Oh, wow."

"I know," Cindy said with a nervous laugh. "It's really happening."

"I'm sure she got in," he said.

"For her sake, I hope you're right." Cindy walked over to the refrigerator and opened it.

"Can I get you something?" James asked with a chuckle.

Without pause, Cindy grabbed a bottle of water and closed the door. "I got it."

"Make yourself at home."

She sat at the counter and twisted the cap off the water and pointed it at him. "Thanks."

Sometimes, being around Cindy was like conversing with a distant cousin you had a beef with as a child. Only you were adults now and still family. And you never had to tell your family to be comfortable in your space. "What was the price tag of Caltech again?"

"Sixty . . . ish."

James cringed. "Ouch."

"Let's hope Ellie pulls a scholarship."

James leaned against the counter, facing his ex-wife. "Makes me glad we didn't have more kids."

Cindy laughed. "You're not kidding."

"What do you think about Trevor?" he asked, changing the subject.

"He's a pretty good kid."

James moaned.

"Give him a chance, James. You just don't like the motorcycle."

"Do you?"

"No. But in a few months, we won't be able to stop her from riding on it."

It wasn't the motorcycle he was worried about her *riding*. That thought made him want to throw up a little in his mouth.

"Speaking of, I'll be taking her dress shopping next weekend. Be prepared to pony up some serious money."

"How serious?"

"Some of these dresses are over five hundred—"

"For a *prom* dress?" he shouted. "You didn't spend that on your wedding dress."

She started laughing. "You're going to need a second job to pay for that."

His shoulders fell. "How can I be worth so much and feel so broke?"

The sound of the front door being flung open interrupted their conversation.

Madison ran in, her backpack tossed on the floor, her feet skidding to a halt at the counter. She held her iPad in her trembling hands.

James's pulse doubled. His daughter's excitement fueling the air.

Please let her get in, he sent out to the universe.

"I am literally dying," she said. Her hands fumbled with the iPad to bring up her email.

Cindy and James moved to stand behind her.

"Do you want to wait for your sister?" Cindy asked.

Madison shook her head. "I forwarded her the email and told her not to tell me."

"And she didn't?" James was shocked.

"I haven't seen her since third period."

Cindy took Madison's hand and pulled her attention away. "No matter what this says, we both love you, and everything will work out."

"Okay, okay."

James glanced at Cindy. "She's not listening."

"Shhh!"

Madison pulled in a reassuring breath.

James found himself holding his.

Then she opened the email.

The only thing James saw were the words:

> Dear Madison Russell,
>
> It is with our greatest pleasure to inform you that you've been accepted . . .

Madison jumped back and started to scream.

Cindy opened her arms and folded them around their daughter.

"Hell yeah!" James yelled with his full chest.

Madison's arm strangled his neck with her joy.

"I'm going to Caltech! I'M GOING TO CALTECH!"

The hugs came again.

James looked over his shoulder to Cindy.

There were tears in her eyes.

Seeing them shot emotion down his throat.

Emotions he needed to breathe past.

Madison untangled from his hug and started to jump up and down.

That first jump caught his chin and made him bite his tongue. "Ouch."

"Sorry, sorry . . . I'm going to—"

The front door opened again and then slammed.

Ellie came in screaming.

Madison joined her.

Both of them hugging each other so hard they nearly fell to the floor.

"You're going to Caltech."

James placed a hand on Cindy's shoulder and whispered in her ear, "We did a good job."

Tears freely fell from Cindy's eyes. "We did."

CHAPTER TWENTY-ONE

James spun Mari around as they walked out of the studio and into the parking lot.

As he did, he caught her around the waist, not a move that they'd been officially taught yet, and pulled her close.

"A little ahead of yourself, don't you think?"

He buried his face in her hair. "Shhh, I'm counting here."

He loved the feel of her laughing in his arms.

Rosa walked out behind them, saying something in Italian.

Mari laughed harder.

"Do I want to know?" James asked.

"She said she's leaving in five minutes, with or without me."

"Then we should make the most of it," James said.

Mari lifted her chin, and James took advantage of the darkness. This time, he sunk in a little deeper, a little longer.

Her tongue met his, her hands explored a little more with each kiss.

When he broke away, her eyes were closed, and her breath was heated.

"My girls are with their mother this weekend. Let me take you away . . . even for one night."

James knew what he was asking.

The fact that she didn't deny him instantly was proof she wanted the same thing.

"We're two grown adults, Mari. I don't want to sneak around forever. I want to take you out and show you off."

Mari placed a finger over his lips and silenced him.

Her quiet made him squirm. Until she said three words that changed everything. "Friday, after work."

She said yes. Holy . . . He expected resistance.

"You're sure?" he asked.

"Do you want to talk me out of it?"

He placed both hands on her shoulders. "No. Friday night it is. One night or two?" he asked.

"I need to be home on Sunday. I'll tell my family about you then."

James started nodding and didn't stop. "This is good. Okay." He kissed her again, briefly.

"*Andiamo,*" Rosa called from the car.

Mari rolled her eyes. "I'm leaving her home next week."

"I can pick you up."

Mari lifted a finger in the air. "One hurdle at a time."

He could accept that. "This is good. So good."

Mari laughed at him. "You make me feel like I'm twenty again."

He could beat that—she made him feel alive.

The dome light on the car made him squint when he opened the door for Mari to get in. Once there, she said, "And congratulations again on Madison's acceptance. I'm happy for both of you."

James couldn't stop smiling. "I can't wait for you to meet them."

"Let it be just us until Sunday."

He could live with that.

Rosa leaned over Mari and looked up at him. "Ciao, James."

"Ciao," he found himself saying.

As Rosa pulled out of the parking lot, James all but floated to his car.

It was turning out to be an exceptional week.

~

With her decision made, Mari set the intention of getting away for the weekend. This time, she didn't use Rosa as the anchor. Instead, she told Luca and Brooke that she was going up to the mountains with someone she met through bunco. That they had a cabin and had invited her.

All of which was true.

Except that James didn't *have* a cabin, he had rented one.

Salena agreed to be on Saturday night, and they were fully staffed for Friday.

Mari had nothing else to do but pack.

She held the negligee Chloe had hidden in her suitcase for the cruise and contemplated exactly what it meant to pack it for this trip.

Rosa, who was quickly becoming someone Mari hardly recognized, had shown up with a gift bag the day after their dance lesson.

When Mari went to open it, Rosa stopped her and suggested they open it in her apartment.

One look inside explained why.

"Rosa Mancuso. What have you done?"

Mari pulled out three tubes of lubricating jelly.

Rosa watched with laughter. "There is plain, heated, and flavored."

"Flavored?" Mari had no idea they made cherry-tasting sex lube.

"You have options," Rosa said. "Besides, we're not young. You're going to need it."

"But flavored?"

Mari pulled out the next gift. A small box of condoms. "I can't get pregnant." She'd been postmenopausal for three years. One of life's blessings as far as she was concerned.

"Use them. Don't use them." Rosa shrugged.

Last was a pair of lace panties. Which Mari especially appreciated. "I needed these."

Rosa beamed. "I'm happy one of us does."

Now Mari stood over her small suitcase filled with sexual intention.

The last time she'd had sex was with Paulo. And that had been nearly a year before his death. Between the medications, chemo, and the overall extent of his diminishing health, the desire and ability at times made it impossible.

Mari couldn't help but look at the picture of her and Paulo that sat on the dresser in her bedroom.

She picked up the frame and ran a finger over his image. "This doesn't make me love you less," she said to the photograph.

Mari walked out of her bedroom and put his picture on the countertop that held multiple others. Wedding photos of her children. Pictures of Franny and Leo. The family celebrating Gio and Emma's first harvest. Loving images of her past and the family she loved. Paulo among them.

But if she was inviting another man into her bed, she needed to take Paulo out of her bedroom.

Mari took one last look at her late husband, turned, and went back to packing.

~

Ellie and Madison parked several blocks from the restaurant where the woman their father kissed in the parking lot lived.

At first, they thought they had it wrong.

That maybe Mari was just going out for a late dinner after leaving the dance studio.

But the woman who drove Mari had dropped her off in what looked a little like a back alley. Or back entrance of the restaurant.

Madison thought maybe she worked there.

Ellie wasn't convinced.

When they got home to their mother's house, they'd huddled over a computer and looked up the restaurant online.

The website boasted the longevity of the family-owned establishment, along with a picture.

Mari D'Angelo standing in front of the restaurant with a menu in her hand.

In the "About Us" section of the site, a short history told Madison and Ellie what they were looking for.

Paulo and Mari D'Angelo took over the business from the founder thirty years ago. Recipes from their Italian grandparents filled the menu with tastes of Tuscany. Luca D'Angelo was now the head chef, and sommelier Giovanni D'Angelo, along with his wife, Emma, now supplied the restaurant with wine from their vineyard in Temecula.

And that was it.

Madison and Ellie read all they needed to.

Their father was having an affair with a married woman.

And now, Ellie had convinced her sister to walk into the restaurant and see the woman with their own eyes.

"Maybe he told her about us," Ellie said. "And if she sees us, she'll know we know."

"And if he didn't tell her about us?"

"Then we tell him that we thought we saw the woman in the picture he showed us. It's Little Italy. We were hungry."

Madison, still high on her Caltech acceptance, wasn't as passionate about plunging into her father's love life.

Watching their father kiss someone had a cringe factor neither of them ever wanted to see again.

Get a room already.

"We need an excuse for being in the city," Madison told Ellie. "It isn't exactly on the way home from school."

"We'll figure that out later."

For now, Ellie practically dragged her sister into the restaurant and stood behind two other parties waiting to be seated.

Ellie craned her neck inside to try and find the woman.

For a Thursday night, Little Italy was busy. Instagram had put Little Italy on the map, and tourists were starting to descend on the city.

"*Buonasera,*" the hostess greeted them when it was their turn. "Two?" she asked.

"Yeah," Madison responded.

"Inside or out?"

"Inside," Ellie said.

The hostess led them to a booth that sat against a wall, giving them the perfect view of the inside.

After the hostess assured them that someone would be by to take care of them soon, she was off.

Ellie kept scanning the room.

Madison thrust a menu in her hands. "Oh my God, you're so obvious."

She picked up the menu and pretended to read it. Still, she scanned.

The bar sat in the center of the restaurant, there were booths like the one they sat in on the edges, with tables everywhere else.

The kitchen, which was obviously in the back, had a small window where you could occasionally see one of the chefs pass.

"You think that's the husband?" Ellie indicated the man behind the bar.

"The bartender?" Madison asked.

"Yeah. Seems to be the right age." Assuming this Paulo was close to their dad's age.

"He looks Italian."

As did many of the waiters and waitresses. The hostess was definitely Italian.

As the staff rushed by each other, they spoke in Italian, which Ellie thought sounded a little like Spanish. Only two years of that language in high school proved it wasn't.

Ellie kept her eyes glued to the hall that the waiters disappeared behind, only to return with plates of food.

A waitress approached the table and introduced herself.

They both ordered Coke, and she walked away.

"I don't see her."

"She may not be here," Madison said.

Ellie looked at the front door. "It's busy, and she owns the place. I bet she's around somewhere."

"We can't sit here and just drink Coke." Madison hit Ellie's menu with hers.

She set it down without looking. "I'll have the spaghetti."

"That isn't on here."

"It's an Italian restaurant, they have to have spaghetti."

"*Pepe e olio?*" Madison asked.

"Pepper and oil?"

"It says it's with spaghetti."

"Does it have tomatoes?" What kind of spaghetti was made with only pepper and oil?

"I don't know."

Ellie stopped searching for Mari and looked at the menu.

Yup, it was pepper, olive oil, and parmesan cheese. It sounded gross. And if it was, she could ask to talk to the manager . . . or owner.

Sometimes Ellie thought she'd make a great spy. If the big leagues didn't want her, maybe the FBI would.

The waitress returned with their Cokes and took their order. All the while tossing in a few words in Italian.

"Where is she?"

"Maybe we should have come on the weekend when it's busier," Madison suggested.

"The place is packed."

And only got more so.

While they waited for their food, Ellie made a trip to the bathroom to scope out the back of the place.

She lingered in the hall where the bathrooms lived, then glanced around a corner that said "Staff Only." There was an office door, but it was closed.

Footsteps made her double-time her return to her table.

Then the food came, which Ellie had every intention of sending back.

Only . . .

"That looks wrong," Madison said as she picked up her fork to dig into her ravioli.

Ellie slurped up a noodle. "It's really good."

"How?"

She pushed her plate in front of her sister and waited for her to take a bite.

Her face lit up.

"Weird," Ellie said, pulling her spaghetti back.

Convinced that Mari wasn't there, they ate their food, annoyed that it tasted so good.

They procrastinated with dessert, which was worthy of licking the plate.

That sucked, too.

"Why can't the food be bad?"

Neither of them wanted to like anything about this woman. They wanted their dad happy, not hooked up with the wrong woman.

Unable to stay longer without looking suspicious, they paid the bill and headed out the door.

Ellie hesitated in front of the bar.

"I have an idea," she said and stepped in front of one of the free barstools.

"What are you doing?" Madison asked between clenched teeth.

Ellie scowled.

The old dude on her left looked her up and down.

Cringe.

The bartender finally took notice of her and walked over. "We don't serve minors."

"I hope not. I just wanted to see if the manager was here, or owner?" Ellie waited for the man to say that it was him.

He didn't.

Instead, he waved his hand in the air and called out in Italian.

There was an exchange between him and a woman across the room.

The bartender left her and moved aside to take an order.

"What are you doing?" Madison hissed.

"He isn't the owner," she whispered.

"Oh." Finally, Madison understood.

A woman stepped up behind them and smiled. "Is everything okay? I'm Salena, the manager."

Tall, stunning, and belonging on a magazine cover and not in a restaurant. Ellie cleared her throat.

Damn it.

"I, ah . . . I just wanted to compliment the chef." Ellie shifted off one foot to the other. "I had the pepper and oil pasta. How do you make that so good? I thought all spaghetti had to have tomato sauce."

Salena smiled. "Italians have many ways of eating pasta. Almost like Americans eat potatoes. Baked, fried, smothered in cheese."

Ellie wasn't sure what to say next. This wasn't the person she was hoping to talk to.

"Well, I've never had it before. I guess that's one of the family recipes."

"Yes, it is."

Madison pleaded with her eyes to leave.

"My dad said to always compliment the chef," Ellie said.

Her sister squinted.

Their dad never said that.

Salena looked over Ellie's shoulder and pointed behind her. "You can do that yourself. Mari, these girls wanted to applaud your food."

Ellie's smile fell as she and her sister slowly turned around.

Mari stood behind the bar, wearing a chef uniform and a smile.

One that started to fall when she looked at them.

Madison grabbed Ellie's hand.

For several seconds, they all stood there staring at each other.

Dad is going to kill us.

This was a horrible idea.

Maybe they could just pretend like they didn't know who she was.

"Uhm . . ." Maddie muttered.

Ellie's palm grew damp.

“The food was good,” Ellie shot out so fast the words almost tripped on themselves.

Mari said nothing.

It was then Ellie realized the bartender and the manager stood close by, and no one was talking.

Mari let a deep breath go, and her full smile returned. “You must be Ellie,” she said directly to her. “And you’re Madison.”

Ellie’s mouth went dry.

“Congratulations on Caltech.”

Ellie looked at her sister to see the same shock in her eyes.

“Thank you,” Madison said.

“You know these girls?” Salena asked.

Mari looked to her right at the bartender, then to Salena, then back to them.

“I’m dating their father.”

Even with all the noise in the restaurant, the space around them fell completely silent.

CHAPTER TWENTY-TWO

Mari stood under the weight of her friend's and employee's surprised stare.

Sergio, their bartender and friend that went back two decades, could catch a fly in his gaping mouth.

Salena raised an eyebrow and smirked.

Mari wiped her hands on the towel she'd taken from the kitchen and set it down. "Tell Luca to take over. The girls and I need to become acquainted. Without interruption. I'll talk to my son later."

The twins were rigid, scared stiff.

Mari didn't have to guess if their father knew where they were, any more than she had to guess that Mari's entire family would know what had just been revealed within minutes.

She walked around the bar and motioned for the girls to follow her. "Let's take a walk."

Privacy was not going to happen on the patio of her restaurant. Instead, Mari led them out on the main street, past the other establishments, until they emptied into the piazza.

The lights strung between the buildings illuminated the space that was filled with tables and chairs. Weeknights that weren't in peak season meant they weren't at risk of being overheard.

Mari pulled out a chair. "Sit. Please."

Like puppets, the twins did as they were told.

The girls kept looking between each other.

"You have questions," Mari said.

Ellie was the one that nodded.

"Ask them."

Poor girl, her hands were shaking.

Mari tried to put her at ease. "As long as they are appropriate, I will answer them honestly." There was no reason to lie now.

"Are you married?"

That, Mari wasn't expecting.

The girls tracked her down thinking she was married? That she and James were, what . . . having an affair?

Mari leaned forward and placed a hand between them on the table. "No, sweetheart. My husband passed away ten years ago."

They both physically relaxed, if only for a second.

"You thought your father was having an affair?"

"He was keeping secrets," Ellie said as if that was proof of an extramarital affair.

"Does James know you're here?"

They both shook their heads.

"Then he isn't the only one keeping secrets," Mari chided.

Madison finally spoke. "We didn't want to say anything to him until we knew for sure."

"I commend that. Getting the facts straight is always the best approach." Mari paused. "Is that why you came here? To learn if I was married?"

They nodded in unison.

"I can see by the looks on your faces you still have questions."

Ellie was the bold one of the two. Something Mari realized by how James described her. "Why are you guys keeping it a secret?"

"Your father did that for me. I loved my late husband. I didn't think I would ever want to date again. Then your charming father snuck into my life." Mari placed a hand to her chest. "I wanted to make sure this wasn't some passing attraction."

"But you're taking dance classes together."

Mari tilted her head to the side. "I'll ask you how you know that in a second. But those classes are where your father and I have realized we'd like to be open about our relationship. He planned on telling you about us after the weekend."

"Oh," Madison said.

Ellie hung her head and sighed. "We shouldn't have come," she said just above a whisper.

Mari didn't agree or disagree . . . verbally.

"If you don't trust your father enough to ask him directly about me, maybe there is something I don't know about his character." The statement was meant to bait them. And it worked.

"Dad's great!" Madison said quickly.

"Everyone trusts him."

"Most dads and moms, when they're divorced, fight. Dad hangs out with Mom and Clayton all the time," Madison rattled on.

"We can talk to Dad about everything." Ellie stopped herself. "Almost everything."

Mari hid her smile.

"He doesn't have girlfriends. I mean, he hasn't dated anyone in a long time."

Ellie scooted forward in her chair. "Yeah, he's not a man-whore."

Mari clicked her tongue. "Young lady!"

"Sorry. I mean, f-boy or—"

"I know what you mean," Mari said. Sadly, she'd heard all the terms raising her own kids.

"He's not that guy. Did he tell you he owns his own business?"

"But he isn't married to it. He always has time for us."

The twins tripped over each other as they went on and on.

Mari let the girls boast on their father's behalf, selling him as boyfriend material.

By the time they exhausted their lists of attributes, Mari learned that James had more patience than their mother when they were learning how to drive. He loved animals, even though they didn't have any. He couldn't cook, but they never went hungry. He went to all Ellie's games, and all the science fairs. He liked to give gifts. And finally, he liked to dance, even though it embarrassed the both of them.

The girls were just as charming as their father.

One of Mari's neighbors walked past and hesitated. "Mari, *buonasera*. How are you?"

"*Va bene*. You?"

"Good, good." Her neighbor glanced at the girls, who Mari had no intention of introducing at that moment. "I won't interrupt. Let's have coffee soon. I want to hear about your trip."

Mari smiled. "I'll call."

"Ciao."

Mari turned back to the girls.

"You speak Italian?" Madison asked.

"I do."

"That's sick," Ellie said.

The piazza was clearing out. Even though it wasn't terribly late, weeknights had a way of turning in early.

"Isn't tonight a school night?" Mari asked.

The twins exchanged glances. "Yeah."

"We should go."

"Where are you parked?"

Ellie pointed. "A few blocks that way."

"How many blocks?"

"Four, maybe."

Mari stood, pushed her chair back. "Okay, let's go."

"We're okay. We can . . ."

"I know my neighborhood. Too far that way can be a problem." More like six blocks in the direction they indicated, but she wasn't going to take any chances. "In the future, if you can't find parking closer, use my lot behind the restaurant."

"We don't want to—"

"That wasn't a request, Ellie."

Ellie closed her mouth. "Oh."

As the three of them walked to where the girls were parked, Mari told them her intentions.

"You know I'll be calling your father."

"Yeah."

They sounded defeated.

"I did not come back to how you found out your father and I were in the dance class together, or how you knew to look for me here. And you should know that your father hasn't been here, so you couldn't possibly have followed him."

The girls stayed silent.

"I would suggest you're one hundred percent honest with James. Lies are like poo," she said. "The more they pile up, the smellier they get."

They crossed the street and kept going.

"What are you going to tell him?" Madison asked.

"That depends. What would you have done if I had been married?"

The only sound was a passing car.

"We didn't think that far," Ellie admitted.

"We wanted to protect him, you know?"

Mari chuckled. "Your father is capable of protecting himself. But that is what I will tell him. That despite your ill-advised intentions, they were executed with a kind heart."

"He's going to be pissed anyway," Ellie moaned.

"As you would be if he spied on you and Trevor."

"You know about Trevor?"

Madison slapped her sister's shoulder. "Of course she does. She knew about Caltech."

Four blocks turned into five.

"Where is your car?"

"One more."

Mari stopped and looked behind them. "There was plenty of parking closer."

"We didn't know if you knew what we drove," Ellie told her.

Mari wasn't amused. "Don't let me catch you parking this far away again. You may not be my children, but I have no issue with scolding you if it keeps you safe."

They didn't argue.

Two blocks shy of the part of town where crime and drugs were prevalent, Ellie's car came into view.

"Arguing on the phone when you're driving isn't safe. Tell me now if you want to talk to your father first. I'll give you that."

The tight jaws and wide eyes gave away their fear.

"Maybe you should . . ."

That would have been Mari's answer, too, if she was seventeen and having to confess her sins.

"Fine. Drive carefully," she told them.

With timid waves and quick goodbyes, Mari watched the girls drive away.

They were just as James described.

Ellie had a fire in her belly.

Madison was more reserved.

And lovely. Both of them.

The walk back home was likely the only quiet she was going to get for a while.

Like it or not, Mari knew her omission of the truth about James was a lie in itself. Which meant her personal pile of crap needed to be shoveled out.

~

"Hey," Chloe answered Salena's call with one hand and dug into her popcorn bowl with the other.

"Guess who has a boyfriend?"

For a second, Chloe didn't have a clue what Salena was talking about. But then the conversation they'd had for the past couple of weeks moved front and center in her brain.

Her mama. That's who had a boyfriend.

Chloe's hand stopped midway to her mouth and then dropped. "No."

"*Yes!* She just walked out with two teenage girls after telling me that they were the children of the man she's dating."

Chloe's feet fell off the coffee table and onto the floor.

Dante, who was sitting beside her, scrambled to keep the popcorn bowl from flying. "What is it?"

"Mama has a boyfriend," she practically yelled before talking into her phone. "Was the boyfriend there?"

"No, just his daughters. I don't think Mari had met them. It was all pretty tense."

Chloe pushed the bowl farther onto Dante's lap and stood. This was not news to sit on. It required pacing. "I knew it. I knew she was seeing someone."

"Seeing who?" Dante asked.

"Do we have a name?"

"No. Your mama only said she was dating someone. And then asked that I tell Luca to take over in the kitchen."

"Oh . . . shit. Did you tell him?" Chloe asked.

"I didn't have to. Word spread like wildfire. Once I picked my jaw off the floor, I went to the kitchen. Luca was already on the verge of spontaneous combustion."

Chloe paced. "Is she back yet?"

"No."

"Okay, okay. I'm calling Brooke. If anyone can calm Luca down, it's her."

"I already texted Ryan. He's calling Emma."

Good, that took care of her brothers.

Chloe couldn't stop smiling. Her happy dance looked a little like jogging in place. "I guess we know who has the cabin in the woods."

"Eeeekkk!" Salena squealed.

"My mama is sneaking away for a weekend rendezvous with a lover." That last word came out in a husky voice.

They both made noises fit for women half their age.

"Who is he?" Salena asked.

"Only one person would know."

"Rosa," Salena said.

"Rosa," Chloe replied at the same time.

Chloe waved at Dante. "Call your mama."

"Why?"

"Just call her." Chloe made a rolling gesture with her finger.

Dante paused the program they were watching and reached for his phone.

Rosa picked up on the first ring. "*Pronto.*"

Dante put her on speaker.

Chloe did the same with Salena.

"Cat's out of the bag, Mama Rosa. Who is my mama dating?" Chloe asked without preamble.

"Ah . . ."

"We know, so spill the tea."

"You should ask Mari."

"We can't, she's out talking to her boyfriend's daughters," Chloe told her.

"Madison and Ellie went to the restaurant?" Rosa asked.

"Yes."

"Without James?"

Chloe couldn't stand still. "James who?"

Dante, who seemed a bit disinterested in the beginning, was catching her excitement. "Is he a good man?" Dante asked.

"No. He's a three-time felon with a heroin addiction."

Chloe stopped moving.

Dante busted out in laughter.

"Of course he's a good man. Do you think I'd let my best friend see a piece of garbage?"

"Mama!" Dante scolded.

Rosa sighed. "His name is James Russell. He owns a crane company, or something like that. Has a home in La Jolla, two daughters. They met on the cruise. Anything else you have to know, get it from Mari. I've already said too much."

"You're the best," Chloe said.

"Why the big secret?" Dante asked.

Rosa snorted. "I'll give you two. Luca and Giovanni."

That sated Dante's question.

"I gotta go and make sure the gossip isn't halting everyone's work," Salena told them.

"If you need backup, call me," Chloe said.

She hung up one phone and turned her attention to Rosa on the other. "What's James like?"

Rosa was quiet for a minute. "What's he like? He makes your mama smile in a way I haven't seen since your papa. And you should know that Paulo never wanted your mama to be alone. You remind your brothers of that if they give Mari a hard time."

That was music to Chloe's ears. "I will. Dante and I are happy for her."

"We are?" Dante asked.

Chloe nudged her shoulder to his, shutting him up. "Thank you."

Once the line disconnected, Chloe resumed her happy dance. And then scrambled to look up James Russell on the internet while hitting Brooke's number on speed dial.

~

The weekend bag James packed sat inside his walk-in closet, ready to go. He'd filled up the tank on his car, took it through the wash, and had the address to the Airbnb, along with the phone number for the host. Oftentimes in spring, there was a slight chance of snow in the mountains, but the forecast only suggested a little rain.

He was walking out of his bedroom when his phone rang.

Mari's name showed up on his screen. In that second, he realized that after their families were told about them, he could change her name to a picture.

And what was better than a Pink Lady on a cruise?

He answered his phone with a smile.

"Hello, beautiful."

"You and your compliments."

"Don't even pretend you don't like them."

"I won't."

He laughed and glanced out the windows by the front door, didn't see Ellie's car, and continued to talk.

"The girls aren't here, so you have my undivided attention." Another positive, after the weekend, James wouldn't have to take a walk to his office or close his bedroom door for a private conversation when Mari called.

The list of perks was stacking up.

"They should be there in a half an hour, though I won't doubt if they take longer."

James laughed and then paused. "Wait, what?"

"I had some visitors tonight. Two, to be exact."

His smile fell. "The twins?"

"The twins," she confirmed.

How? Why? When did they find out? Who told them? So many questions listed in his head, he had a hard time asking one. "Wha . . . how . . . who?"

"Most of those questions I don't have an answer to."

James walked into his kitchen and put the call on speaker. "My girls were at your home?" He placed the phone on the counter and talked over it.

"They came to the restaurant, had dinner. Luca and I were in the kitchen. A rarity these days. I stepped out and found Ellie and Madison talking with Salena. I recognized them immediately, and there was no doubt they knew about me."

"How?" James braced his hand on the counter and gazed across the room into nothing while Mari's words processed.

"You'll have to ask them. My guess is they overheard a conversation, or maybe Summer said something to your ex-wife."

"If Cindy knew, she would have said something. She doesn't hold back like that."

"They knew about us, and the restaurant," Mari said.

"They didn't do anything stupid, did they?" He couldn't see his daughters making a scene, but who knew?

"Other than parking entirely too far away, no."

"What did you say to them? Were they rude?"

"Take a breath, James. Your daughters are lovely girls. Curious girls. Somehow, they got it in their heads that I was married and we were having an affair."

"What?" James cried out to the empty room.

"We can only blame ourselves for that. Out-of-character dance classes, late-night phone calls. They came here to find out for themselves, all in an effort to protect their father."

Mari's voice held so much kindness, James felt his blood simmer. "I'm sorry, Mari."

"Don't be ridiculous. Once I cleared up their misinformation, we had a nice chat. By the time they left, they were telling me how wonderful you are," Mari said. "I'm relieved, to be honest."

"This messed with your plans."

"By a few days."

The next question, he didn't want to ask. "Do you need to cancel this weekend to deal with this?"

"No." Her answer was swift. "It's better this way. You and I can disappear, and my adult children can discuss this among themselves."

That was a relief. “My nonadult children are grounded for life.”

“Oh, James. Be easy on them.”

“They invaded my privacy.”

“That’s laughable. When family is around, there is no privacy. I couldn’t use the bathroom for ten years without a hand pounding on the door. Then Franny was born, and it started all over again.”

She had a point.

Lights from a car pulling in the driveway illuminated the front room of the house. “The girls are home.”

Mari sighed. “You deal with your children. I’ll deal with mine.”

“Okay.”

“Tomorrow,” she started. “I’ll have you pick me up. I’ll introduce you to Luca.”

This was good, despite how it happened. “I look forward to it.”

“We’ll talk tomorrow,” he said.

With the call disconnected, James took a long, cleansing breath, folded his arms over his chest, and waited for his daughters to walk in the door.

CHAPTER TWENTY-THREE

By the time Mari got off the call to James, she had text messages from Chloe, Gio, Emma, Rosa, and Brooke.

Chloe: I can't wait to hear all about James.

Gio: I have questions.

Emma: Ignore your son. I'm happy for you. We both are.

That last bit was a fabrication.

Rosa: If I can help with anything, call me.

Brooke: Luca loves this family. Don't let his fear step on your happiness. He will come around.

Mari sent a group text, omitting Luca. She'd talk to him in person.

James and I met on the cruise. He was completely unexpected, and I needed time alone with this . . . relationship to see if it was what I wanted. Mari paused as she was typing. Chose her next words carefully. It is. We can talk on Sunday.

Mari hit "Send."

Downstairs, the restaurant had cleared out, the staff had cleaned and prepped what they needed for the next day.

Luca lingered in the kitchen, cleaning up for the night. A task that was often delegated to junior chefs.

Mari stood in the doorway and waited for her son to turn.

He knew she was in the room.

She waited out his silence, knowing he couldn't keep it forever.

Finally, Luca set the towel in his hand down. "Who is he?"

"His name is James," Mari said to her son's back.

Luca placed a hand to his forehead. "I don't know what to do with this, Mama. I thought you were happy."

She took a step forward. "I am happy."

He turned. "With this family. That we were enough."

"This family is more than enough and growing every year. I'm the happiest woman in the world."

Luca's eyes searched hers. "Then why him? Why this 'James'?"

"I've asked myself that question many times. Why James? Why now? My family is enough. I have more love in my life than my heart can handle."

"Then I don't understand," Luca raised his voice.

"I didn't either, which is why I didn't share it with you. Any of you. I wasn't expecting James. I have not once considered another man after your father. Paulo was my life, my anchor. Together, your father and I were the rock for you, this family. Learning to live without him was the most excruciating experience of my life. With him, I was a rock, without him, a pebble. I didn't swear off love because I feared that pain returning. I didn't think I had it in my heart to love anyone other than your father."

Luca's jaw dropped. "You love this man?"

Mari opened her mouth, then closed it. "I don't know yet. In keeping James from all of you, I haven't been able to be myself. It was just now that I met his daughters. Twins, by the way. Both of them are going to college this year. They wanted their father to go on the cruise to meet someone. Fearing to leave him alone as they started their lives."

"He was on the ship with a purpose, then."

Mari laughed. "James was hiding in his stateroom, working. Neither of us were looking, Luca. Yet here we are."

"But—"

"Were you searching when Brooke walked in this door?" Mari asked, knowing the answer. "I'm not saying James is my Brooke. But I owe it to your father to find out if he is."

"How can you say that? Papa wouldn't have—"

Mari stopped her son with a hand in the air. "Your father made me promise him that I'd try and love again." She placed her hand to her chest, the familiar ache that came on from time to time sat there bleeding. "I lied to him and told him I'd try. James has given me the opportunity to keep that promise."

Luca's words dried up.

The confusion on his face shifted slightly into understanding.

"James will pick me up tomorrow. I'd like you to meet him."

Luca started to shake his head.

"It would disappoint me if you refused." Mari knew when to play the guilt card. She dealt it now without remorse. Now that Luca knew about James, he would stew in his own misconceptions until he met the man.

The kitchen fell silent, only the hum of the refrigerators buzzed.

~

James met Mari at the back door of the restaurant, which doubled as the front door of her home. It was three in the afternoon, which had given him the morning to work, and the afternoon to stress over picking up his girlfriend and meeting her family.

The fluttering in his gut had less to do with the woman smiling at him from the back landing and more to do with what awaited him inside.

When was the last time he'd needed to measure up to another man in order to spend time with a woman?

That would have been college. And likely Cindy's father.

Yet here James was, reaching for Mari's hand, leaning in to touch his lips to hers, and stepping back with a smile. All the while anticipating his introduction to her oldest son.

Luca.

"You look lovely." And tired, if he was being honest.

"Thank you," she said, and then looked over her shoulder. "Are you ready for this?"

"Are you?" he asked instead of answering.

She shook her head, and they both laughed.

James hoped his laughter put her at ease. "Let's get this behind us so we can enjoy the weekend."

He placed his hand on the small of her back and encouraged her to lead the way.

The rich scent of tomatoes, herbs, and spices lofting out the door grew stronger as they entered the building.

A small hallway that led to a stairwell paved the path to the apartments above. Halfway in the hall was an open door.

"That's the back door to the restaurant. I'll show you around that when we get home."

"Has it been difficult to live where you work? It must be tough to walk away."

Mari shrugged as they made it to the stairs. "I've never known it to be any different. I've lived in this building nearly my entire life."

"Does that feel like stability or stagnation?" he asked.

She paused halfway up the first flight of stairs and glanced at him. "Both."

As they approached the open door to her son's home, James stood a little taller. First impressions were everything, and for Mari's sake, he wanted this to go well.

The open floor plan of the apartment had a good-size kitchen on one end, a dining table, and a complete living room with windows on three sides.

Luca and Brooke stood over the kitchen island in conversation as Mari led James inside.

The sound of them entering the room had the couple looking up.

Mari said something quickly in Italian, then quickly switched to English. "Luca, Brooke, this is James."

Brooke had an easy smile. One of warmth and welcome.

Luca stared James down, the expression on his face so very neutral he could be a poster child for Switzerland.

James stepped forward and extended a hand to Mari's son.

Luca's grip was hard, his eyes sharp. "It's nice to meet you."

James wouldn't bank on *nice* being Luca's first choice of words. But he appreciated it anyway.

"I've been looking forward to this since your mother and I met."

Thankfully, James didn't need to play tug-of-war with his hand. Brooke extended her hand next, this one much softer and quick. "It's a pleasure. Can I get you something to drink? Glass of water? Coffee?"

James took his cue from Mari.

"Water before we go would be nice," she said.

"Please, have a seat." Luca indicated a seat at the dining table. He brought a cup of what smelled like coffee with him.

The scuff of chairs shuffling along the floor as they all sat filled the room.

Brooke brought James and Mari glasses with ice water and took a seat beside her husband.

James thanked Brooke, and silence took over.

"I know this comes as a surprise," James said, addressing the elephant in the room.

"It does," Luca quickly replied.

The sound of a clock ticking amplified the quiet.

Mari cleared her throat.

Luca glanced at his mother, sighed, and turned his attention to James. "How did you meet?"

James felt warmth in his own smile at the memory. "The first time I spoke with your mother was in line at a bar. An older gentleman was hitting on her when all she was doing was being polite."

Mari laughed. "He was at least twenty years older. Rude, too."

"But the first time I noticed her was by the pool when we'd just boarded."

Mari clicked her tongue and rolled her eyes. "That boy was a child."

"What boy?" Brooke asked.

"The young man I told you about."

"A kid fresh off a divorce also took notice of Mari and offered to buy her a drink."

Luca looked at his mother. "What were you doing?"

"Nothing. We were gathered on the pool deck while we waited for our luggage to arrive in our staterooms. There were several singles groups, many of us had matching T-shirts. Once I realized the shirt was a target for attention, I didn't wear it again."

"And you were part of their group?" Luca asked.

James answered with a nod. "Yes, but I opted out of the shirt. I went on the cruise to appease my girls, not to announce I was single."

"The twins?" Brooke asked.

"Seventeen going on thirty," James offered.

"Exactly how I see Franny in a few more years," Mari said.

"I've heard a lot about your daughter. I look forward to meeting her," James said.

"We haven't told her about you." Luca's delivery was cold.

"Considering you just learned about me, that's probably for the best."

Again, the conversation stilled.

James placed both hands around the glass of water he had yet to drink from. "I imagine this is difficult for you."

"That my mother has been seeing a man for weeks and didn't say anything? Yes. It is."

Brooke moved closer to Luca's side and placed a hand over his.

"It wouldn't have mattered if you knew from the beginning, Luca. This still would have been difficult. I appreciate you accepting James and treating him with the kindness he deserves," Mari said.

"Deserves?" Luca's brow rose.

"That I will earn, if you give me a chance," James said.

Luca released a heavy sigh, sat back, and tossed both hands up in the air. "I will try."

"You will," Mari half growled.

It was James's turn to set his hand over Mari's. "I have no doubt that Luca promised Paulo that he'd watch over and take care of you. Turning a blind eye to a man that enters your life wouldn't be making good on that promise."

When James met Luca's gaze again, he found a hint of respect.

A hint that James could live with . . . for now.

Brooke cleared her throat. "We need to pick Franny up from school. And I'm sure you want to leave before traffic is horrible."

"Good idea," Mari said.

They all stood.

James extended his hand once again.

Luca accepted.

"You are just as your mother described."

"Stubborn and angry?" Luca asked.

"Strong and protective."

Luca relented and let James's hand go.

Mari moved to her son and hugged him, then moved to Brooke. "See you Sunday."

James let his shoulders relax once they left their apartment and walked to Mari's to collect her bag.

"That went better than I thought it would," he said once they were alone.

They walked into Mari's home, a duplicate of the above floor plan, the furnishings very different. Luca and Brooke had a flair for the modern, and it looked as if Mari had gathered a few family heirloom pieces brought over from Italy itself. Heavier wood pieces with plush white sofas, a dining table twice the size as the one in Luca's home. Family pictures everywhere.

"Luca could have been kinder." She left James by the door and crossed the room to a hallway.

"He's skeptical."

James walked over to a shelf filled with photographs.

"I'm his mother, he needs to trust me," she said from the other room.

He picked up a picture of Mari as a young mother, holding the hands of both her sons, her belly swelled with her daughter. As beautiful as she was then, James thought she was more so now.

His eyes settled on an even younger photograph. This one, she was in white, the candles of a church in the background.

And Paulo.

A handsome man who gave his features to his oldest son.

"I'm ready."

James turned to find Mari holding a coat and her purse, pulling a suitcase beside her.

He moved to her side and took her bag.

"Did you bring hiking shoes?" he asked.

"I live in the city. The best you're going to get are tennis shoes I use on my walks."

James nudged her toward the door. "That's easily fixed."

CHAPTER TWENTY-FOUR

The drive up to Lake Arrowhead took over three hours.

In those hours, James told Mari how he handled the twins when they'd walked in the door with their proverbial tail between their legs.

The overactive imagination of the girls provoked them to spy on James. From looking for pictures on his computer to clicking into his text messages.

Then following him to the studio and witnessing the two of them kissing.

"I made them hand over their cell phones and unlock them. Then scrolled through their messages between their friends while they watched in absolute horror," he told Mari.

"Did you learn anything?"

"Madison gossips more than I thought she did, and she's insanely jealous of her sister's prom date. And Ellie thinks Trevor might be 'the one.'"

"The one what? She's too young to be considering marriage." When James didn't elaborate, Mari caught on. "Oh, you think she and Trevor are going to sleep together."

James winced. "I spoke to Cindy this morning. She's surprised that they haven't. Trevor turned eighteen in December. The girls' birthday is in two weeks. Before prom."

"She's waiting until her birthday."

He nodded. "My brilliant plan of making the girls feel the pain of me invading their privacy, and all it did was backfire. I don't want to know what I now know."

Mari laughed. "Before Giovanni married and moved out, he used to 'entertain' women in the small apartment above Luca's. I pretended not to notice. The only thing you can do for your daughters is to make sure they're safe."

"I know that. But it sucks."

The cabin James had rented looked out over the lake.

It was everything a mountain cabin should be. Open log-beam ceilings, cozy furniture with fluffy blankets. A fireplace with plenty of wood to ward off the chill in the air.

"This is nice," Mari said as she crossed to the window overlooking the lake.

"I used to take the girls up here at least once a year. Eventually, playing cards and collecting pine cones on the trails couldn't compete with their friends."

Mari looked over her shoulder and smiled at him. "A strange thing happens when your children turn twenty-three or twenty-four . . . you become smarter and much more interesting to hang out with, and they come back."

James moved to her side and draped an arm over her shoulders. "Something tells me your children never doubted your IQ."

She laughed. "They did. I simply didn't give them an audience to voice it."

"How did you manage that?"

"Intimidation and guilt."

James fist-bumped the air. "Parenting for the win."

Mari turned to lean against the window and smiled up at him. "What is on our agenda?"

James wrapped his arms around her waist and stared her in the eyes. "There is a decent barbeque place in town that has a live band and dancing. And since we're practically professional dancers, I thought it might be a good idea to show everyone how it's done."

There was comfort in James holding her, feeling his arms and having the freedom to lean against him. "Two lessons make us experts?"

"I bet it's two more than most of the people in this town are used to."

Mari watched her hands that sat on his chest. "Do I need to change?"

He shook his head. "Grab a coat. As soon as that sun is down, it's going to get cold."

It had been a long time since Mari had been in a restaurant that had sawdust on the floor and more beer on tap than wine in bottles.

A potbelly stove sat in the corner of the establishment, emanating enough heat to keep the space warm and cozy. Individual tables and chairs peppered the dining room, and a band had set up residence on a small stage.

They were seated a couple of tables back from the dance floor. James ordered a beer, and Mari settled for a hard cider.

The energy in the place was already palpable. A few families sat on the perimeter, children ran around, much like Franny had most of her life. Several people roamed from table to table, talking to each other.

"This must be where the locals hang out," Mari leaned over and said to James.

James had pulled his chair close to her, making conversation a little easier over the volume of the music piped in through the speakers.

"It hasn't changed in years."

She ran her foot along the floor. "I hope this has changed." How this passed the health department, she never understood. But a lot of backroad country places used sawdust as part of the charm.

A bowl of shelled peanuts sat on the table, and the menus looked like sections of a newspaper, complete with headlines of some of the locals and what they were up to. A marriage, a new store that had opened up or closed down. It was charming.

Their drinks came, and they held off on ordering, opting instead to take their time.

The band had set up but hadn't started to play.

A combination of country music and pop that swayed to the country side of the fence played through the speakers.

"When the girls were kids, I'd bring them here to run off any energy they had left over from our day. There used to be a row of video games in the corner." He pointed to a wall that was now filled with merchandise. Sweatshirts, ball caps . . . mugs with the name of the place. "When the music started, they'd dance with each other until they were exhausted."

"How often did you come here?"

James sat back, tipped his beer to his lips. "At least once when it snowed. Sometimes again in the summer."

Mari rested her chin on her folded hands. "I bet they'll come here with their own families at some point."

"What about you? Where did you take your kids when they were growing up?"

"Nothing like this. We took them to Italy twice. There was one road trip to the sequoias."

James laughed. "That sounds like a lot more than a weekend in the mountains."

She shrugged. "Bigger trees."

James leaned forward, took her hands in his. "As much as I miss those days, I like where I am now."

Mari didn't have a moment to respond before the waiter returned and took their order.

When the band started to play, James pulled her onto the dance floor.

Thoughts of Luca, Gio, and Chloe were completely pushed aside. For a few hours, the restaurant disappeared. Life's responsibilities faded . . . it was almost as if nothing but that moment mattered.

They ate dinner between songs they liked. And laughed when they stepped on the other's toes.

A couple of hours in, the bar filled up with the younger crowd, and Mari and James called it a night.

The brisk wind outside snapped Mari's spine straight up.

They jumped into his car, shivering despite the heat they'd built up on the dance floor.

"I don't mind the cold, but I'd rather have it with snow," James said as he started the car and turned up the heat.

"The forecast suggested rain, not snow."

"It's not cold enough."

"I haven't seen snow in years," Mari confessed.

"Do you ski?"

She laughed. "Not even the bunny slope."

"I'll teach you," he said as he pulled the car out of the parking lot surrounded by pine trees.

Mari found herself staring at his profile as they drove to the cabin. Would he teach her? Was this . . . what they were, something that could last long enough for another season? Ski lessons and holidays?

That all felt so far away.

The restaurant was less than a mile from their rental, and walkable if not for the dark road they would have had to use to make their way back.

The car was still chilled when they pulled into the driveway.

The owner of the Airbnb had strung up white lights between the trees, creating a fairylike whimsy trail to the front door.

As James fiddled with the key to let them in, rain started to fall.

Mari shifted from one foot to the other as if that would keep her warm.

Finally, the door opened, and they both hurried in.

"It's freezing in here."

James tossed the keys on the kitchen counter. "I'll start a fire."

"I'll find a thermostat."

The light switches at the front door managed to turn on everything but the lights in the living room.

James switched on a single lamp and headed to the fireplace.

Mari followed his lead and went to the individual lamps to turn them on.

"I think I saw a thermostat in the hall," James told her.

There were only two bedrooms and a short hallway that housed the cabin's only bathroom.

Mari found the heating control, saw the temperature, and cringed. "It's fifty-eight in here."

"I should have turned it on before we left."

"It didn't feel that cold earlier."

She played with the dial until she heard the central heater turn on.

With that out of the way, she stepped into the restroom and closed the door behind her.

She turned on the hot water and waited for it to warm up. In the mirror, her reflection stared back. Hair damp from dancing and the rain. Her cheeks flush from the cold. And a strange sense of calm sat behind her eyes.

She was alone, with James. They didn't have a deadline on when to leave, at least for the night. And no family that could walk by and question what was happening.

And for the first time that night, Mari thought of what came next.

What she wanted to come next.

Yet those jitters and maybe fear hovered just beneath the surface.

It had been so long since she'd been in this very position. Paulo had been her only lover. Someone who had seen her grow ripe with their children and slowly age.

The sink started to steam.

Mari ran her hands under the warm water, heating them up.

This was no time to second-guess what she knew she wanted. James had seen her in a swimming suit, she'd seen him in only swim shorts. Neither one of them was in their twenties, and there was no room or need to be shy.

After taking a few minutes to use the restroom and refresh herself, Mari emerged from the bathroom and returned to the living room. She tossed her coat onto the back of a chair and walked to where James stood.

The fire was slowly catching along the bottom log, the crackle and pop was the only sound in the room.

"That's nice," she told him.

James stepped by her, his palm catching her waist. "I'll be right back."

As he disappeared, Mari kicked off her shoes and stood in front of the fire.

White-hot flames lapped up one side of the logs as tiny wisps of smoke traveled up the chimney. Every once in a while, the path would switch and catch a patch of bark before moving back. Back and forth, back and forth, until the entire section of wood became one fiery blaze.

It was mesmerizing to watch and just the distraction she needed to ignore the way her pulse had picked up in the minutes James wasn't by her side.

The flames had one goal. Heat.

But that wasn't right. The flames offered heat, but they also released a scent only burning wood emitted. It smelled like winter. It felt like a vacation. Probably because the only times Mari had felt the warmth of a fire was when she wasn't home. Living in an apartment meant she didn't have a fireplace to enjoy.

A fireplace that hypnotized her and pulled her away from any fear or anxiety she might be feeling.

The squeak of the floor behind her brought her attention to James walking back into the room. "Nice, isn't it?"

Mari smiled over her shoulder, then went back to staring at the flames. "There are only two drawbacks of living where I do. No fireplace and no yard."

James stood behind her and wrapped his arms around her waist.

Mari, captured, folded him close and leaned her back against his chest.

"What would you do with a yard?" he asked, his lips close to her ear.

"A garden," she said without thought. "I grow a few things in containers on our terrace, but I'd grow more if I had room. There is nothing compared to tomatoes off your own vine or garlic out of your own soil."

"Something tells me you'd create a culinary masterpiece with only tomatoes and garlic."

"I'm not sure about a masterpiece."

"I am." James dropped his lips to the side of her neck.

She closed her eyes and tilted her head, giving him more room.

He moved his lips and grazed his teeth over the lobe of her ear.

Shivers raced up her spine.

She felt him chuckle at her response.

"You taste like spring."

"I do?"

James trailed his attention down her neck. When her hair got in his way, he released her waist with one of his hands and swept it to the side.

Between the cold air and his warm breath, she felt her body responding again. A tightening in her belly and a wave of dizziness in her head.

James fanned the palm of his hand on her waist, his thumb edged the underside of one breast.

A simple yet so very intimate touch.

Her hand fell and grasped his thigh. All the while, James explored the column of her neck with soft, slow kisses.

"I want you more than I want my next breath, Mari. But if you need more—"

She stopped him by turning around and lifting her lips to his.

His kiss was fierce, a claiming.

Their mouths met with opened joy and a mix of tongues and teeth.

James held on to her hip and back.

Mari clenched onto his shoulder and waist.

She felt lost, blind and searching. And with every pull of her lips against his, her world started to ground. This . . . this with James was exactly right.

The feel of his hand wrapping around the globe of her butt and pulling her close made her gasp. The length of his desire pressed warm against her abdomen.

She made a noise that didn't sound like her at all. The kind fueled by want and desire.

James walked her a couple of steps, until the wall beside the fireplace met her back and she had no place to go. He pressed into her, from hip to shoulders. Their lips never parting.

Timid touches morphed into demand. Cool air touched her waist when James reached up her shirt to grasp her breast, his finger and thumb bringing one nipple to attention.

She couldn't breathe, broke their kiss. It had been so long, too many years of lying dormant. A rose frosted over in the snow, never feeling a spring thaw.

Mari pushed up on her tiptoes, her knee lifted until she felt the outline of his erection stretching in his clothing against hers.

One minute she was searching for more contact. The next, James lifted her off her feet, settling his hips between hers. "Hold on," he told her.

She did.

Arms wrapped around his neck, her legs circled his hips.

James pushed into her and kissed the cry from her lips.

Even clothed, she saw stars.

Her body woke up. Not a slow stretch of sun poking over the horizon, but a quick drawback of curtains that blasted a blistering sun that shot you out of bed.

Her hips pushed into the pleasure James was providing.

As he pulled her away from the wall, she started to slip.

James gripped harder and turned them toward the couch that was blanketed in the light of the fire. "Here or the bedroom?" he asked, giving her the choice.

Flickering heat and the way the light danced off his face made the decision for her. "Here."

He lifted a brow, his lips curled into a smile.

"It's cold in there," she added.

"I'll keep you warm, wherever we are."

"Promise?"

He let her slip out of his grasp, her feet touched the floor. "Lifetime guarantee," he said.

Mari allowed her hands to pull at the edges of his shirt and began to remove it from his shoulders.

When one of his arms pulled free, he worked on hers until they stood there, his bare chest against her in only a bra.

There wasn't time to wonder what he saw before James bent his head down and kissed the space between her breasts, his hands working to unclasp the hooks in the back.

As soon as her bra hit the floor, James's breath passed over one nipple. The shiver that racked her didn't come quietly. And it didn't come without her own want to touch and taste.

She wanted more, wanted to feel . . . more.

Mari inched her hand between their bodies, her fingers grazing the outline of the hard length of him through his jeans.

James stopped what he was doing and rested his forehead against her chest.

What he said didn't sound like a word she recognized. But she understood what he meant.

She started to pull her hand away.

James reached for it and put it back. "Please," he whispered.

The power in touching him and the way he responded was addictive. She cupped him fully and played with the button of his jeans with her free hand.

James helped her, pushing at his own clothing until the bare heat of him settled in her grip.

He was bigger than . . . well, larger. Or maybe she'd forgotten.

Mari touched him like she had the right to.

James tilted her chin and forced her to look into his eyes. A rawness stared back as his hips pushed him into her hand. Her fingers tightened, and James's eyes rolled back in his head.

A sultry laugh escaped her lips.

Was she ever this bold?

Yes. Always. Only she'd forgotten how wonderful this desire could be.

There must have been a button she pushed, because James started pulling at the remainder of her clothes.

Mari let him go to kick her pants aside, her panties along with them.

He kissed her again and lowered both of them onto the sofa. Mari was cognizant that a blanket had been draped over the back and pulled under them before they landed.

The deep couch had room for both of them. Just barely.

James stretched out beside her and rested his knee between her thighs.

"You're beautiful, Mari. Every inch of you." As he spoke, he traced a finger over her shoulder and down to her hip.

"I'm rusty at this."

That made him smile. "If this is rusty, I'm in trouble."

Laughter bubbled from her core.

His next kiss was tender, the kind that melted her from the inside.

"Tell me what brings you pleasure, stop me if it doesn't."

Their eyes locked.

She pulled her leg farther up his and opened herself slightly.

Understanding brightened in his eyes. James reached behind her for something on the table behind the sofa.

She looked to find lubricant in his hands.

He turned the bottle upside down and squeezed some onto his fingers.

Turned out she wasn't all that rusty after all. Without looking away, James reached between her legs.

She opened and waited.

And when he touched her for the first time, she wanted to weep. Her body had already responded to his touch, his kisses, but the extra slide of his fingers took care of any leftover edges that needed more. "Oh, James."

Mari closed her eyes and simply felt.

As James learned what it was she liked, Mari was reminded how much she enjoyed moments like this. Where she could only be a woman being loved by a man.

It wasn't long before fingers weren't enough.

She drew him down, forcing his body to lie on hers. The glorious weight of him, the way his lips possessed hers, this feeling would burn into her memory and keep her warm for weeks.

James pulled her underneath him. "I want to see your eyes when I bury myself in you."

The rawness of his request had every part of her body stretch closer to his.

Not looking away, James inched into her.

Her breath caught. The feel of him filling her, stretching her. It was almost too much.

She stilled, and he stopped.

One breath turned to the next, and her body relaxed once again.

"Okay?" he asked.

All she could do was nod.

And then he was there. Not a hair of space between them.

Slowly, he started to move. And all that heat that brought them to this point returned. The friction, the need . . . everything.

Her hands grasped him, guiding his hips, his pace. Her body reaching toward his until he found exactly what she needed. "Just like . . . yes."

And he did . . . just like that. Exactly like that. Not faster, not slower, until every nerve settled in the perfect place and rushed over the side.

James captured her release with his kiss. Only she couldn't think enough to kiss him back.

Only when her soul found its way back into her body did James change his angle, his grip. Mari uttered soft words in Italian as his orgasm gripped him and he repeated her cries.

While they both caught their breath, the only thing that could be heard was the crackle and spark from the fire that warmed the room.

CHAPTER TWENTY-FIVE

James reached out to find the space beside him empty.

The light seeping in from the window suggested the sun had yet to crest the horizon.

Stretching his legs in one direction, his arms in the other, James rolled out of bed to find Mari.

He paused in the hall when he found her.

She sat on the couch where he'd made love to her the night before. Curled up in a blanket with a cup of coffee in her hand, she stared out the window over the lake.

Lost in her thoughts and completely oblivious to the fact that he was watching her, James allowed himself to stare his fill.

She was so much more than he expected. He'd been prepared for a few ounces of doubt or maybe insecurities when they finally gave in to the mutual attraction that had been brewing for weeks. But that didn't happen. What she called rusty, he thought was unabashed. Learning what a new lover wanted and responded to took time. Yet that wasn't how the previous evening had gone. They'd rested on the sofa, Mari in the crook of his arm as they watched the fire burn. They spoke of how sex all by itself seemed to get better with age. James liked to think that was more about the partner than age.

They'd dozed on the couch before finally making it to bed.

Mari had stirred at least once during the night, waking him.

James pulled her close, silently laying claim. It had been a long time since he'd slept beside a woman, even longer for her. But they fell together like magnets, enjoying the safety of another person. Eventually, they succumbed to the abyss of dreams, and now James watched Mari taking her time to start her day.

"Good morning," he finally said, letting her know that he was in the room.

Mari smiled over her shoulder, their eyes catching. "*Buongiorno.*"

James reduced the space between them and leaned down. "I know that one," he said right before he pressed his lips to hers for a brief kiss.

"I made coffee."

"Thank you."

"It's not good."

He crossed to the kitchen and pulled a cup off the open rack. "As long as it does the job."

"That may be debatable."

He poured himself a cup. "How did you sleep?"

"Surprisingly well."

One sip and James knew what Mari was referring to. The coffee was stale. Not overly strong, just awful.

"Why surprising?"

"Outside of the occasional visit from Franny, I haven't slept in a bed with another person for ten years."

James sat on the other end of the couch. "Do you miss it? Sleeping beside someone?"

"It's going to take more than one night to answer that."

He took another sip of the awful coffee. "I volunteer as test subject."

A playful nudge of her foot against his thigh made him smile.

He placed a hand on her leg and left it there.

"I do miss this."

James raised his eyebrows in question.

"This," she repeated. "The quiet moments. The freedom of a morning kiss or sitting on the sofa in a bathrobe." She looked at his hand. "Touch."

He ran his hand along her leg. "Being around you and not touching is torture."

Her cheeks flushed, and Mari lowered her gaze. "We wouldn't want that."

James went to tip his cup to his lips and frowned. "This is awful . . . I can't."

Mari lowered her cup so he could see how little she'd drunk. "I gave up a half an hour ago."

He reached for her cup and put both of them down on the coffee table. "We can't have you uncaffeinated."

James pulled her to her feet.

"Why is that?"

He wrapped his hand around her waist and pulled her close. "Because I have plans for you. Plans that require you to be awake."

Watching a grown woman blush never got old.

~

It was one thing to have her family watching her with a hundred questions in their eyes. But quite another to have her employees avoid her with the same look.

Parts of Little Italy took a while to wake up on Sunday mornings. Many restaurants, like D'Angelo's, were open for only lunch and dinner. The popular breakfast places, the kind that trended on social media, were isolated in the piazza.

When James brought her home on Sunday, the opening staff members were there to watch them as James brought her luggage up to her apartment. But guests had yet to arrive for lunch.

Neither Luca nor Brooke made an appearance during James's brief visit when dropping her off. There was no telling if they'd even seen them drive up.

It was Sunday. Giovanni and Emma were due to drive down for dinner. Chloe and Dante were supposed to be out of town, but a text late the night before said they were coming to dinner. Then there was Rosa. Salena and Ryan . . . And of course, Luca, Brooke, and her grandchildren.

Everyone.

Mari knew this wasn't by accident.

With her head high, Mari made her rounds in the restaurant. The kitchen was fully staffed for the day. No one had called in for the waitstaff, bartender, or help in the back.

Not one employee asked about her weekend. Or about James.

But Mari wasn't born yesterday, and her dating anyone was news. With news came questions.

Up in her apartment, Mari settled in to prepare her family a meal.

With her hair back and apron on, she piled flour on her kitchen island and cracked the eggs inside the crater she'd created. While she mixed what would become the pasta dish for the night, she thought of the times she and Paulo would share this part of Sundays over that very island.

Paulo liked efficiency. Getting the job done. And Mari enjoyed the process. The kneading of the dough, the twist and turn. They didn't make the decision on the shape of the noodle or whether it would be ravioli until they looked at the ball of unformed dough and it told them what it wanted to be.

Linguini, she decided.

Next week, she'd shoot for ravioli.

Next week, when James and the girls were coming.

She'd field the questions about her relationship on her own, before her loud and passionate family got involved.

Mari was hanging up the pasta to dry when she heard the coos of her grandson.

Brooke peeked in through the open door of her apartment with Leo in her arms.

"I thought I heard you," Brooke said when she saw her.

Mari pulled the apron from her waist and reached for Leo. "Where's my boy?"

Leo all but lunged out of Brooke's arms and into hers. With a fist in his mouth and drool absolutely everywhere.

After pressing kisses all over Leo's cheeks and letting his wet hand smear over her face, Mari smiled at her daughter-in-law and motioned her toward the living room. "How are you?"

"Good. I think he's bringing in a new tooth. We're not getting a lot of sleep."

They both took a seat on the sofa, Mari bounced Leo on her knee.

"Maybe you need to sleep with Nonna tonight. Would you like that?" Mari asked in a high-pitched tone reserved for when an adult spoke to a child that didn't understand what was being said.

"That wasn't a hint," Brooke told her.

"The offer still stands."

"I'll let you know."

With one eye on Leo, the other on Brooke, Mari glanced toward the ceiling. "How is my son?"

Brooke sat back, took a deep breath. "It's been an interesting weekend."

"I can imagine."

"The phone hasn't stopped ringing. Luca gets off the phone with Gio, then Dante would report in with what he learned from Rosa. Then Chloe would call me or do a group chat with Emma. Salena has handled the employee gossip."

"What is being said?"

Brooke hesitated. "They're concerned."

"There is no need. James is a good man. And I'm not a young woman easily influenced for the wrong reasons."

"We've told them that. Chloe, Emma, and I. It might be a good idea to introduce him to the family sooner than later."

Leo scrambled to get off Mari's lap.

She set him down, and he headed straight to a basket filled with toys that lived in her home.

"He and the girls will be here next Sunday."

Brooke smiled. "Perfect."

"Luca should have put his brother at ease. Unless there was something that he didn't like when I introduced them before we left on Friday."

She could tell by Brooke's hesitation that there was something.

"Brooke?"

"What can I say? He's not Paulo. Luca told me more about his father in the last two days than I've heard since we met."

Mari glanced over to watch Leo pull a colorful plastic toy into his lap and start to pound on it with wet hands.

"I can't replace Paulo. James is not that."

Brooke sat forward and placed a hand on Mari's knee. "Luca and Gio will get used to this. The rest of us are already there. Chloe searched the internet to get information on him and as many pictures as she could."

"How much could she have possibly learned?"

Brooke tossed her head back and laughed. "If you were actively dating when you met him, you'd know how deep you can dig with a few strokes of a keyboard."

"What did you learn?"

Leo switched toys. This time, the sound of a train saying "Choo choo" filled the room.

"He has a successful business and doesn't seem to have made any enemies. He had his picture taken with the mayor two years ago at a tape-cutting ceremony when they started the airport renovation."

"James is a part of that?" Mari had no idea.

"Apparently. Chloe did a background check. No criminal record."

Mari clicked her tongue. "How did she . . . why . . ."

"After Eric?"

Brooke didn't have to say any more. Eric was the online match that ended up stalking and assaulting Chloe. "Oh."

"That was a topic of discussion for half a day. It took Rosa to calm that panic, or you might have had company on the mountain."

Mari leaned back, shook her head. "I can understand some of that concern. But James is a good man. An honorable man."

A small smile took form on Brooke's lips. "What's he like?"

Mari felt her cheeks warm. "He's thoughtful, considerate. Loves his girls. When I had to sleep in his cabin on the ship, he was a complete gentleman."

"You slept in his cabin?"

Oh, yeah, Mari hadn't shared that part of the cruise with the family. "Maybe the boys don't need to know about this quite yet."

"Good thing I'm not a boy," Brooke said.

"The staff on board the ship was concerned that Rosa's illness was contagious, so she isolated in our room. James had a suite with a separate bedroom and volunteered his space."

"I'm sure he did."

Mari made a slapping motion against Brooke's thigh as she laughed. "It wasn't like that."

Brooke questioned her with a raise of an eyebrow. "It was a little like that."

Mari covered her face with both hands and spoke into them. "Oh, Brooke. I didn't see him coming. I didn't think I wanted a man in my life."

The feel of Brooke's hands on hers, pulling them away from her face, had Mari looking up. "I think it's wonderful. You're too young to hang up the towel on romance."

"I had my romance."

"Is there a rule you can only have one? Aren't you enjoying the company? Because from what I'm seeing, you're happy."

"I was happy before."

"Yeah, but now . . ." Brooke screwed up her face. "Now it's deeper. Just talking about him lights up your face."

Mari placed her hands over Brooke's. "What if the boys don't accept him?"

"They will. If James is as good as you believe him to be, they have to. It's just going to take a little time. And you have us girls pushing them to get there faster."

Leo had pulled himself up on his feet, balancing beside the coffee table. He slapped his palm on the furniture. "Mama. No, no."

"Nonna," Mari corrected.

Leo kept repeating "No, no."

Nonno was Italian for *grandfather*. A thought that wasn't lost on Mari.

~

Mondays never ceased to be hectic.

The twins had been at their mother's for the weekend, with strict rules due to the fact that they were both grounded until they were twenty-five. No unsupervised time in James's home for the immediate future. Especially since Trevor "might be the one."

Even with a good night's sleep on Sunday, James met Monday feeling exhausted. It probably had to do with the late-night conversation with Mari after her weekly family dinner.

She spun her experience with dinner as her children having questions, but nothing she didn't expect.

That's what she said.

Her tone and enthusiasm said differently.

This was new for both of them. Mari had never dated since her husband's death. And the last time James tried to date someone, the girls were young, and so was the woman he'd seen a few times. As were that woman's children.

Adult children should be easier.

Shouldn't they?

Adults understood the desire for connection. So why did it feel like James would be battling Mari's children for space in her life?

These thoughts kept interrupting his morning as he worked his way through his schedule.

Just before noon, AJ knocked on his office door and let himself in.

"There's a Mr. D'Angelo here to see you. He doesn't have an appointment—"

James put his hand in the air and pushed his chair away from his desk. "He doesn't need one."

James followed AJ out to greet Luca . . . only it wasn't Luca.

Extending his hand, James said, "You must be Giovanni."

Giovanni shook his hand, his eyes locked, his grip firm. "Mr. Russell."

So that's how this was going to go.

James glanced at AJ. "Hold my calls."

James let Giovanni into his office and closed the door behind him. "I thought I'd have to wait until Sunday to meet you. This is a surprise."

Mari's youngest son studied James's office. "A complete surprise. For all of us."

"Is everything okay? Mari?"

"My mother is fine. I'm not here for her. I'm here for me."

James indicated the table that sat on one end of his office and went ahead and took a seat.

A couple of seconds passed before Giovanni followed his lead.

"All right, then. What can I do for you, Giovanni?"

"Gio, or Mr. D'Angelo."

James nearly laughed. "Is that really what you want me to call you?"

Gio didn't answer. Instead, he asked his own question. "My mother said you're divorced."

"I am."

"Why?"

"Excuse me?"

"Why are you divorced?"

James narrowed his gaze. "I'm not sure how that is any of your business."

"You're dating my mother. I can learn about your business, your education level, get a general idea of net worth from online sources, but

I can't do a Google search on your character. And since we don't know the same people, I'm going to ask you. Did you divorce because you married too young? You're a workaholic? Someone cheated?"

Getting Mari's boys to accept him was going to be a serious hurdle. "I understand that you want to protect Mari."

"I *will* protect her."

"Not from me. I won't give you a reason."

Gio stared, took a breath. "I don't like that you didn't insist on meeting us sooner. We're adults."

"As is Mari, and she wanted it this way. I'm sure she told you that."

"If you hurt her . . ."

"That's not my intention."

"Intention or not—"

"Gio, I understand what you're doing here. I applaud the fact that you and your brother are so fiercely protective of your mother. She warned me. I suppose I'm grateful that you came here to have this conversation in private instead of on Sunday in front of my daughters. I would appreciate it if we show each other mutual respect and give each other the benefit of the doubt about each other's character. Your mother dating anyone was bound to cause some . . . strife. I care for your mother."

Gio started to say something.

James cut him off.

"And I don't scare easy."

Gio pushed his chair back and stood. Either he had heard enough or realized he wasn't going to get any more out of James.

"My mother doesn't need to know I was here."

That did make James laugh. "Then you shouldn't have come. I won't set the foundation of my relationship with your mother on lies."

James couldn't tell if that last request was a test or not.

They stepped out of the office, and James walked Gio out.

CHAPTER TWENTY-SIX

Mari and James sat in his car in the parking lot of the dance studio, talking like teenagers that didn't have a home to go to.

Mari was fuming.

"He had no business confronting you."

"He did, and it's over."

"Over? What's over? My son acting as if I'm a child?"

James stretched across the seats and took her head in his hand, leaned over, and kissed her.

"That isn't helping," she said.

He kissed her again, this time when he pulled away, she was smiling. "Not even a little?" James asked.

"You fight dirty."

"Are we fighting?"

"Errr."

James lowered his forehead to hers. "They're going to have to get used to me. I'm not going anywhere."

~

"Keep me from killing my sons," Mari begged Rosa.

James and the girls were due to arrive anytime. Mari was stressed.

Normally, having her entire family two weeks in a row put joy so deep in her chest she bounced off the walls.

Normally, her sons were predictably kind and welcoming to any guests.

There was nothing normal about how her sons had been acting since they learned of James.

"I've already asked for Dante's help. He promised to step in if Gio and Luca cross the line."

"Does Dante know where the line is?" The boys had been tight since their school days. It wasn't often that they didn't have the same mindset.

"He does. Chloe is on top of it."

Mari looked over the dishes of the cold food, ready to go. Everything that needed to be hot sat in warmers or was in its last minutes of cooking.

The terrace table had been set, the heaters were on, and everyone except James and the twins was there.

"This is my family. I shouldn't be this nervous."

"When the boys start acting like themselves, you won't be." Rosa grabbed the charcuterie board. "*Andiamo.* A glass of wine is in order."

The volume on the terrace hit a frequency that Mari adored.

No less than four conversations were going on at the same time.

Luca and Gio stood a little too close and eyed Mari when she walked out.

Chloe and Brooke noticed them, kept their conversation going, and moved dishes around on the table to make room for the food.

Salena sat beside Emma, with Leo in her lap, while Ryan and Dante were wrestling one of the space heaters closer to the sitting area beyond the dining table.

"Gio," Mari called over to her son.

He looked up.

"Can you get Rosa and I a glass of wine?"

With a nod, Gio moved to do as she requested.

Franny bounced over. "Can I help?"

Mari touched her granddaughter's cheek and smiled. "Bring up the bread and oil."

Franny ran off while Gio walked over with two glasses.

Mari took the glass from him. "Best behavior," she warned.

"Have I ever let you down?"

"Yes," she said quickly. "Monday, when you did not present your best behavior."

Gio didn't even try to look ashamed.

He only smiled.

Which had her back teeth gritting.

The sip of wine helped.

"Look who I found!" Franny had a way of speaking so loudly, all conversation stopped.

Mari turned to find James standing beside Ellie and Madison.

Ellie had flowers in her hands.

Madison offered a tiny wave.

James looked directly at Mari and smiled.

She set her wine down to welcome them.

"Are those for me?" Mari asked Ellie.

"Ah, yeah."

"Grazia."

Keenly aware that everyone was watching, Mari stepped closer to James and lifted her chin.

He kissed her briefly.

"Thank you for coming."

"You couldn't have kept me away."

He said that now. Mari hoped he would be saying that in a few hours when dinner was finished.

"There are a few people here you haven't met." Mari turned to her family.

Chloe stepped close.

"Chloe, my daughter, and her husband, Dante."

Smiling ear to ear, Chloe moved right past a handshake and opened her arms for a hug. "I'm so happy to meet you."

Mari's heart melted.

Today, Chloe was Mari's favorite child.

"And you are?" Chloe asked, turning to the girls.

"I'm Ellie."

"I'm Madison."

Dante shook James's hand. "A pleasure."

Mari kept pointing. "Brooke."

Brooke opted for a handshake.

"That's Emma and Salena. My grandson, Leo."

The two of them waved from where they were seated.

Leo sucked on his fist.

"That's Ryan, and of course, you already know Luca and Gio," Mari said.

When Luca and Gio didn't move their feet, Mari shot daggers with her eyes.

They stepped forward and shook hands.

"Good to see you again," James said.

Rosa moved in when Luca and Gio stepped away. "Hi, James."

She hugged him, helping break the tension after the tight handshakes from Mari's sons.

Rosa approached the girls. "I've heard a lot about you."

Franny waved the twins over. "Do you want something to drink? There's a cooler . . ."

James looked around the terrace. "This is amazing."

"The closest we have to a yard."

"Do you drink wine?" Chloe asked James.

"Yes. I would have brought some, but I understand Gio is the expert," James said.

Chloe scoffed. "Don't tell him that or it will go to his head."

Mari reached for her glass while Chloe poured some for James.

"How was class on Tuesday?" Rosa asked.

"I don't know why you quit," James said. "Everyone was asking about you."

Mari felt her shoulders relaxing once the initial introductions were finished.

Rosa helped ease James into conversation with Dante and Ryan.

The twins made their way over to Emma and Salena, with Franny chatting away.

Brooke seemed to be saying something under her breath to Luca and Gio. Who had made the polite hello, but nothing else.

Mari felt the disconnect with her sons.

If James noticed, he didn't say a thing.

"He's handsome, Mama," Chloe whispered.

"Thank you for making him feel welcome."

Chloe rolled her eyes and called out to her brothers, "Luca, Gio. Let's get the food."

Mari watched her children disappear and hoped Chloe could talk some sense into her brothers.

~

James had never seen so much food on one table in his entire life. Including holidays.

Mari had said her family was loud.

She wasn't kidding.

Sitting beside her, with Luca and Gio at the far end of the table, was probably for the best. Even better, Ellie and Madison sat beside Franny, who was also at the other end of the table.

Every once in a while, he'd hear a snippet of their conversation.

While Gio and Luca didn't have much to say to him, they had no issue talking with the girls.

Probably in an attempt to learn something about James's character.

Chloe sat beside James and spoke under her breath. "Your girls are adorable."

"Ha. When they're not spying on you, they're great."

Salena laughed. "I heard they thought Mari was married."

James glanced over. Ellie was chatting away with Luca and Brooke. "They did."

"Did they really stake out the dance studio?" Chloe asked.

"Pretty impressive, if you ask me," Dante said.

"No one is asking you," Rosa chided.

Salena laughed.

Dante said something to Salena in Italian.

Salena pinched her fingers and waved them at Dante.

"Ignore them," Rosa told James. "These kids have known each other since grade school. It's like they're all siblings."

"Not all," Chloe corrected, winking at Dante.

"Well, if you don't give me grandbabies soon, I'll think you're living like siblings."

James caught Mari's smile out of the corner of his eye.

Under the table, he placed his hand on her knee.

For a moment, she fell into his gaze.

James brought another ravioli to his lips. "I'm never eating in another Italian restaurant again."

"I tried to tell you I made the best."

He loved the pride in her voice.

"Nonna?" Franny called from several seats away.

"Yes, *tesoro*?"

"Is James going to be my *nonno*?"

Nearly everyone at the table stopped talking.

Mari coughed on the wine she'd just sipped.

"What does *nonno* mean?" Ellie asked.

Madison pushed her sister with her shoulder. "Grandpa, dummy."

"Hey, I didn't know."

"Well?" Franny asked again.

"They're just dating," Luca answered.

James met Luca's eyes. Clearly, the oldest son didn't like the question.

Franny looked at her father. "You and Mama Brooke dated. And Zio Gio and Zia Emma. And—"

"Not everyone who dates gets married." It was Ellie who spoke up.

"Oh," Franny said, her voice disappointed.

"But that would be cool," Ellie said with a smile.

James heard at least two voices snicker.

"Would that make you my sisters?" Franny asked.

"No," Madison said. "We would be your dad's sisters and your aunts."

"But you're only seven years older than me."

"Age has nothing to do with it," Ellie said.

While the girls dominated the conversation about family connections once a couple went from dating to married, James leaned close to Mari. "Is she always this inquisitive?"

Mari nodded several times. "And her ears are always open. Be careful what you say around her. She picks up on everything."

Slowly, the conversation at the table started up again.

Forks hit plates, voices rose and lowered.

And James found himself staring at Mari. *Nonno* wasn't a title he'd even considered. But *husband* was starting to sound like something he wanted again.

~

"What was that?" On his feet, James shouted at the field or, more to the point, the referee calling the plays.

Ellie's softball game was a first for Mari. Sitting in the stands, with James's ex-wife, Cindy, on one side of her and Cindy's husband, Clayton, on the other side of James, Mari embraced the experience with both arms.

Cindy was lovely.

The way she and James interacted felt more like they'd had a teenage romance and had grown up to marry other people.

While James and Clayton discussed the game, Mari found herself in conversation with Cindy.

"I'm told you're quite the cook," Cindy waxed on. "I'd be jealous, but cooking isn't anything I've ever done for fun. More for necessity."

"Food is a part of my culture. It's much more important to sit around a table eating and talking with your family than falling asleep on the sofa watching the TV."

"I guess. The girls didn't learn a lot from me. If it came out of a box or can, I'm good." Cindy glanced over to James. "James isn't much better. Anything you want to show the girls will be appreciated."

Mari shrugged. "I've attempted to show my daughter around a kitchen since she was a child." She shook her head. "Nothing stuck."

Cindy smiled. "That makes me feel a little better."

Ellie's team was in the outfield, with Ellie covering third base.

They were in the bottom of the fourth, the score zero to one, for the opposing team. There was a runner on second, with two outs.

Mari had gone over the general rules of the game the night before. Maybe for the average person living in America, they'd know how the game was played. For Mari, whose children didn't play the game growing up, she wasn't exposed to it. Sure, she knew enough to understand there were nine innings in baseball but was surprised to learn that softball only went to seven.

Madison sat with a group of friends at the bottom of the bleachers and several rows over. Every once in a while, Mari would find her looking over.

The opposing team hit the ball, causing the spectators to gasp and the parents on the other side of the field to clap.

"It's okay, Ellie. C'mon," James yelled as if Ellie could actually hear him.

"Is he always like this?" Mari asked Cindy.

"Yeah. He was ecstatic when Ellie expressed interest in the sport. Without a son, he didn't think he'd get the chance to be the dad in the bleachers yelling at the field." Cindy looked up and laughed at her ex-husband.

With eyes on the game, James said, "Don't think I didn't hear that."

Mari's belly laugh was felt to her feet.

"Listen all you want. You know it's the truth."

Clayton leaned over. "He almost got us tossed out of the game twice last year."

"Me and three other dads." James smiled down at Mari. "The referee was blind. Literally, he retired at the end of the season."

The opposing team hit the ball straight to left field, everyone watched in suspended animation to witness the outfielder catch the ball and complete the inning.

James and Clayton clapped, and James sat down.

The teams switched places, offering them a chance to talk without the game being played.

"You're bringing Mari to the girls' birthday party, right?" Cindy asked James.

"We hadn't discussed it, but yeah." James placed his hand on Mari's thigh and gave it a squeeze. "A bunch of screaming girls . . ."

"And boys, James."

He narrowed his eyes. "Not for the sleepover part."

"Of course not. They'll have to wait for college to do that."

The pragmatic way Cindy said that was somewhat refreshing.

"Don't forget what I read in those text messages," James pointed out.

Cindy leaned over Mari and lowered her voice. "Now that we're onto that, it won't happen."

It being sex with Trevor, and after the eighteenth birthday being the timeline.

"It happens whether you like it or not," Mari told them.

Cindy sat up straight. "We're having some family and friends over for a potluck before the girls go off with their friends. A few will stay over."

"Let me know what I can bring," Mari offered.

"Careful, hon. Cindy's idea of a potluck is the plastic veggie trays from the supermarket."

Mari started to suggest James was exaggerating, but Clayton and Cindy sat there and shrugged.

"I will ask the girls what they want."

An hour and a half later, James and Mari were in his car headed to his home.

The twins went with their mother.

"Franny would have really enjoyed today."

"What was Luca's excuse for not letting her come?"

Mari knew her son's reason was just that . . . an excuse. "A family day. The zoo."

"Family days are important."

Mari didn't comment. Everyone in the family had come around.

Except her boys.

"I'll insist the next time. Franny should be exposed to things like this. Just because Luca wasn't into sports doesn't mean Franny shouldn't try something out."

James pulled off the freeway and started weaving his way through La Jolla traffic and potholes.

"After we drop off my things, I'd like to find a grocery store."

This was the first time Mari would see where James lived his life with his daughters, and the first time she was staying the night.

Another reason Luca was cold.

Not that Mari had any intention of having Franny over to James's home. But Luca refused anyway.

"I have food."

"Anything that comes in a box is a convenience, not food."

"I don't want you to feel like I'm putting you to work," James said. "We can go out."

Mari turned, looked at him. "How will I ever teach you what you can help me with if we're always sitting at a table having someone else serve us?"

"I burn water, honey."

Mari chuckled. "We're going to the store. I'm cooking. You can chop and clean."

James reached over, placed a hand on her leg. "I'm good at uncorking wine."

"Where would we be with wine that is corked?"

CHAPTER TWENTY-SEVEN

Chloe stood in the back of the restaurant, talking with Salena and watching her mother grow more comfortable in her new world.

The world of James.

He sat at the bar, talking with Sergio while having dinner before driving her mother to their swing class.

A thought that always made Chloe smile.

"How often is he here?" Chloe asked her best friend.

"Couple times a week. The regulars have stopped asking who he is."

"That's saying something."

Chloe heard Luca call out from the kitchen to one of the chefs.

"How is Luca handling it?" Chloe asked.

"You mean tolerating? Poorly." Salena glared over her shoulder. "It's starting to piss me off. I've heard him and Brooke get into it more than once after Mari and James leave."

Chloe lifted both hands in James's direction. "What's not to like? Decent man, employed, almost adult kids. Mama said he gets along with his ex. Luca can't say that about his ex." It helped that Antonia didn't live in America, but still.

Before Chloe and Salena could discuss it further, Mari walked around the corner.

Her hair was pulled back in a simple ponytail. She wore an outfit Chloe hadn't seen before. Loose pants and a short-sleeved top that hugged her frame and made her look . . . well, younger. Her mother wasn't one for a lot of makeup, but she was wearing a little more these days, and the few gray hairs that had a way of catching the light seemed to be less and less.

"You look nice, Mama."

Mari waved her off and lifted a bag she held in her hand. "The right clothes and the right shoes make all the difference."

"Eventually, we'll have to see these dance moves," Salena said.

Mari pointed a finger in Salena's face. "Our dancing doesn't involve a pole."

Chloe busted out laughing. Salena's pole-dancing studio had taken Mari some time to get used to.

"Dancing is dancing, Mama Mari."

Mari tilted her head. "Running a studio is a full-time job. I'm not sure why you're still working for me. When the day comes, make sure you hire a good replacement, okay?"

Chloe and Salena stood frozen in place.

"Ciao," Mari said as she walked away.

"Did she just say that?" Salena asked.

Chloe nudged Salena's shoulder with hers. "Yes, she did."

Mari approached James and slid onto the barstool beside him.

James leaned over and kissed her cheek.

Even from where Chloe stood, she saw her mother's face light up. "He makes her so happy."

Almost on cue, Luca shouted an order to one of his chefs from the kitchen.

"I'm not going to let either of my brothers screw this up," Chloe growled.

~

Mari pulled the SUV Luca and Brooke owned into the parking lot where the construction workers left their trucks.

James had told her that he'd be on the construction site with several of his crane operators to discuss the scope of a new project. One that had been brought up in conversation several times.

A contract with the city was a big deal and, according to James, if done right, would lead to more city projects around the community.

Mari wanted to celebrate.

She opened the back of the SUV and started to pull a folding table from the back.

A man she didn't know wearing a safety vest and a hard hat walked over. "Need help?"

"Please."

She pointed to the side of the car for him to set it up.

"Something smells good."

"Thank you. Do you happen to know where James is?"

"James?"

"Mr. Russell?"

"Yeah, he's on the other side of the jobsite with some brass."

Mari looked the man up and down. "Do I have to wear that to go over there?"

"Especially with the brass. Technically, you should have a hard hat on here."

Mari looked up, saw the building that was going to be remodeled from top to bottom. "I wouldn't want to get him into trouble."

The guy smiled. "From the smell coming from your car, I think you'll be forgiven. Want me to go get him for you?"

Mari had sent him a text when she left the restaurant, but he hadn't responded.

"That would be nice. Tell him lunch has arrived."

Without exchanging names, the man left, and Mari started removing her catering trays.

Ten minutes later, she saw James walking across the parking lot.

Orange vest, white plastic hat.

And a smile.

"This is a surprise," he said.

"I wanted to celebrate your new project."

He looked at her spread and shook his head. "What is all this?"

"Lunch," she said. "For you and your crew."

"Mari, sweetheart. I have one foreman and three operators."

She spread her arms out to the parking lot.

"Then who are all these people?"

"City engineers, inspectors, the primary contractor, and about half of his crew."

Mari reached for a bag filled with paper plates and utensils. "They have to eat, right?"

James just laughed. "You're incredible."

She waved him away with the back of her hand. "Go, tell them my food is getting cold."

James moved into her personal space, captured her head with his hands, and kissed her long enough for Mari to tune out the noise around them.

He ended their kiss, their eyes locked.

"Still getting cold," she teased.

James laughed and walked away.

Nothing made Mari happier than watching people enjoy her food.

Men in business suits and hard hats accompanied blue-jeans-wearing construction workers as they hung off truck tailgates and makeshift benches constructed of two-by-fours and buckets.

"You're spoiling me."

Mari leaned her head on James's shoulder. "It's food."

"It's more than that, and you know it."

Maybe.

Mari changed the subject. "Any more colleges respond?"

Madison had received a backup acceptance from a college on the East Coast. And Ellie had been accepted to San Diego State, which wasn't her first choice.

"Ellie is still waiting."

"That must be hard."

"Two of her friends applied to Arizona, and they haven't heard either way." James finished his last bite and pushed his paper plate off his lap. "Have you convinced Luca to come to the girls' birthday?"

"I'm trying."

James sighed. A sound Mari was starting to dread hearing. "And Giovanni?"

"Emma is finding it hard to sit on long drives."

James nodded a few times but said nothing.

"Chloe and Dante aren't leaving for their trip until after. They will be there."

"Where are they going again?"

"Positano," Mari said.

James's silence brought physical pain to Mari's chest. They'd talked about her sons enough to know he was feeling the sting of their rejection.

She placed her hand on his. "They'll come around."

The smile James gave her wasn't convincing. But he held her hand up to his lips, kissed it, and said, "You'll be there. That's what matters."

~

A giant downstairs rec room had been turned into a dormitory fit for six girls. At least for one night.

Ellie and Madison's eighteenth birthday had been epic.

Most of Ellie's softball team showed up, along with Madison's nerd friends and enough adults bringing cards filled with money to make the twins happy.

Now they were dressed in matching pajamas with four of their best friends spread out around the room.

Ashley and Taylor were both on Ellie's team. And Rachel and Jennifer were friends from their mother's neighborhood that they had known since elementary school.

Jennifer was the dramatic one of the group, and the only one that wasn't going away for college. She had her eye set on Hollywood. Two roles in their high school theater program, along with an Instagram account showing other teenagers how to put on mascara, and she was convinced she had what it took to make movies.

While Ellie supported her friend, she secretly thought it was stupid. It wasn't like Jennifer had a half a million followers or anything. More like five hundred.

Rachel wanted to be an accountant . . . or better yet, her father wanted her to be an accountant. She had been accepted to UC Irvine, her father's alma mater. If it was good enough for him, it was good enough for Rachel. Another stupid choice as far as Ellie was concerned since Rachel was wicked good at turning little black dots into art.

Ashley was leaving softball in high school and was headed toward getting a degree in physical therapy. Likely brought on by the torn meniscus she suffered in her junior year and subsequent PT by a guy she had a massive thing for. Ellie couldn't see a problem with her friend's choice.

And Taylor was like Ellie. Both of them were waiting on Arizona and were desperate to share a dorm together. Taylor was a solid outfielder with a decent batting average. And she was smart, which helped.

Upstairs, Ellie and Madison's mom and stepdad had already gone to bed, so Ellie, her sister, and the girls were trying to keep their giggles and gossip on the quiet side.

Not to mention, they were plotting.

"So . . ." Ellie was nothing but whispers. "I think we're doing it on Tuesday."

"Tuesday? That's random," Jennifer said.

"Our dad is out with his girlfriend on Tuesdays."

"Your dad is hot."

"Shut up, Taylor. That's gross," Madison chided.

"Why not on a weekend? Tuesday's a school night." Jennifer had her hand in a popcorn bowl while adding her suggestions to the conversation.

"Weekends are sus. Our dad still hasn't chilled since we spied on him. He's watching," Madison said.

"We already have a plan. And we need your help." Ellie looked directly at Taylor.

"You can't have sex with Trevor at my house."

"No. That's not what I mean. We have midterms, and the three of us need to study." Ellie waved between Madison, Taylor, and herself.

"We do?"

"Yeah, chemistry. Madison is going to agree to help us out." Ellie could see by the expression on Taylor's face, she wasn't understanding.

Ellie started over. "We're supposed to be here on Tuesdays. We're going to tell Mom that you and I are struggling with our chemistry midterm, and we're going to your house to study. Trevor will pick me up there."

"My mom isn't going to let Trevor take you on a date from my house," Taylor said.

"Your mom won't know. Madison will leave me at the gate, and you guys can hang out. I'll text you when I'm back."

Rachel spoke up. "Don't your parents track your phones?"

Ellie smiled. "I'm leaving my phone with Maddie. I'll use Trevor's phone when we get back."

Jennifer nodded. "That could work."

"Aren't you nervous?" Rachel asked.

"A little, I guess. But I think I'm ready. And if we wait until prom, that's all I'm going to be able to think about at prom."

Her logic seemed to work with her friends.

"There's nothing to worry about," Jennifer said. "It's not a big deal. I mean, it hurts the first time, but . . . it gets better."

Jennifer had a steady boyfriend the previous summer and into their senior year. Until she caught him cheating on her.

Now they all hated him.

"Are you in?" Ellie asked Taylor.

"Sure."

Ellie's heart raced in her chest. This was going to happen. None of her best friends were against it, and they all knew Trevor.

What could go wrong?

CHAPTER TWENTY-EIGHT

Chloe walked into her brother and Brooke's apartment after a sharp knock on the door followed by a quick "Come on in."

Luca and Franny sat at the dining room table, building what looked like a school project that required glue and glitter.

"Hey," Chloe said as she closed the door behind her.

Franny jumped off her chair, ran over, and threw her arms around Chloe's waist. "Hi."

After hugging her niece back, she asked, "What are you guys building?"

"It's a diorama."

The look of pain on Luca's face made Chloe grin.

As far as Chloe was concerned, her brother deserved some discomfort these days.

"They still do those?" Chloe asked.

"Sadly," Luca replied.

Franny climbed back on her chair and continued cutting whatever she'd been cutting before. "It's about the book we read. There's a girl that got lost in the woods, and this is where she finds a wolf."

Chloe pointed to the trees. "Was there glitter in the trees?"

"It's supposed to be rain," Franny told her.

"I can see that."

But looking at her niece's school project was not what she was there for.

"Is Brooke here?"

"She's at a mommy-and-me thing."

"Thing?" Chloe asked.

"Don't ask me. She read about it, so . . ." Luca finished wrapping twigs in thread and placed the bundle in a pile with others.

"Do you have this, Franny? I need to talk to your dad."

Luca lifted an eyebrow in question.

With her tongue sticking slightly out between her teeth, Franny nodded with an "Ah-huh."

"Great." Chloe pointed at her brother and crooked her finger, telling him to follow her.

"What is—"

Chloe kept walking . . . out his door and up the stairs to the terrace apartment.

With each step, she grew more determined to give her brother a much-deserved lecture.

"What's up?" he asked the second the door was closed.

Chloe swung on him, defiant arms on her hips. "What is wrong with you?"

"I'm sorry?"

"Dante and I just left the twins' birthday party."

"Okay."

"Why weren't you there?"

"Franny has a school project."

Chloe gasped. "That's a shit excuse, and you know it."

"Brooke has—"

Chloe shook her head. "No. I'm not buying that. School projects are given weeks in advance, and even if Brooke had something important to do, that doesn't stop you from showing up. Giovanni and Emma, they have a good excuse. You don't."

Luca had the good sense to look away. "I'm not trying to be difficult."

"Really, cuz you're acting 'difficult.' The girls asked about you guys. I heard them talking about my 'thirst trap' brothers and their 'lucky' wives to their friends."

"Thirst trap?" he asked, completely clueless about what that meant.

"Oh my God. 'Good-looking,' okay? They talked about Emma being pregnant with twins, and how Franny was a cool kid. And that they'd be great babysitters. And the whole time this discussion was going on, Mama just stood there smiling. Only not the proud, 'those are my children they're boasting about' smiling, but sad smiling."

Luca ran a hand through his thick hair.

Chloe kept going. "James is a good man. Yeah, he isn't Papa. He isn't Italian, hell, he isn't even Catholic, but he adores our mother. And the only thing getting in the way of Mama letting herself adore him just as much is you." She poked a finger into her brother's chest. "You and Gio."

"I'm not stopping her."

"Stop lying to yourself. This family is the only reason Mama got up and kept moving after Papa died." Chloe took a breath and tried to calm her shaking hands. "When you and Gio got all up in Dante's shit when you learned about us, I checked that off to big-brother love and worry because you knew all of Dante's secrets. Worried that I was just another doe-eyed conquest. And ten years ago, that may have been true. Mama and James are in their fifties, Luca. They're not kids playing around. They have families that would be involved if it didn't work out. And maybe it won't, but if it doesn't because you and Gio don't accept that Mama is capable of making this choice, then shame on you. How dare you deny our mother a chance at what we all have? Can you imagine going to bed at night without Brooke there?"

"Don't say that."

"Exactly." Chloe crossed her arms over her chest. "I can't be the only one accepting James and his family. Dante and I are leaving, and I need to know that you and Gio aren't going to screw this up for her."

Luca looked her in the eye.

"Promise me."

His jaw clenched.

Then he released a long-suffering sigh. "You're right."

Pressure eased from Chloe's frame.

For a moment, they were both silent.

"I miss him, too, you know. James doesn't erase Papa."

Luca held his head with one hand and pulled Chloe in for a hug with the other.

Chloe held on to her brother for longer than she had in years.

"I'll call James. Personally invite him for Sunday dinner."

"And talk to Gio," she insisted.

"And talk to Gio," Luca agreed.

Chloe pulled away from her brother's embrace. Then looked up.

"You have glitter in your hair."

They both laughed, and the love that was never far away when it came to her family swarmed in.

~

"Curfew is eleven."

Just hearing her mother recite the rules was enough to make Ellie's heart skip a beat.

"We're eighteen now," Madison shot off.

Clayton laughed from where he sat on the living room sofa watching TV.

"Okay, then, ten thirty."

Ellie's eyes widened.

"But—" Madison started.

"Shall we go ten?"

Check and checkmate.

"Fine. Eleven," Ellie said.

Their mom stood there smiling. Proud of her parenting skills if Ellie had to guess.

"Cramming for a test always backfires," Clayton said from his perch.

"Actually, there are lots of studies that say—"

Ellie tugged on her sister's arm to shut her up. "Save it for chemistry."

Tossing her backpack over her shoulder, Ellie started to turn around.

Their mother stopped her. "What's with the makeup?"

Oh, snap.

Ellie wasn't one to wear a lot of makeup, unless she was going on a date.

"Ah . . ."

"Duh, Mom. We've been experimenting for prom. Jennifer suggested a smoky eye."

Ellie could kiss her sister.

"Yeah. I don't know if I like it," Ellie said.

Their mom sighed. "It works. Maybe a little more eyeliner."

Ellie found herself bobbing her head like one of those dolls. "I'll try that."

Madison pushed her toward the door. "See ya."

They stumbled out of the house, passed the Ring camera, and jumped into Madison's car.

"That was close."

"Good thing Mom didn't notice you shaking."

Madison turned over the engine right as rain started to splatter on the windshield.

"Was it that obvious?" Ellie looked at her hands, then clenched her fists.

"To me."

They pulled away from the curb and started toward Taylor's.

"Thanks for having my back," Ellie said.

Maddie glanced over, then back to the road. "You sure about this?"

"What? Yeah." Her heart rate wasn't coming down. "I mean . . . aren't you curious?"

"Sure, but I don't know. Do you love him?"

Ellie knew the answer to that question should be yes, so that's what she said. "Of course. I wouldn't be doing this if I didn't."

She wasn't sure her sister believed her.

"It's not just because he asked you to prom?"

"No." Ellie took her phone out of her backpack and clicked on Trevor's picture. "We're eighteen. We're adults now."

Maddie scoffed. "I don't feel any different than I did last week."

"I do. Trevor's waited until now. No one can say I'm too young." *No longer jailbait* was how Trevor put it.

Ellie sent a message to Trevor. I'm on my way. Then placed a kissing heart emoji.

They were adults, and adults had sex. Maybe they could even make a long-distance relationship work. It happened in the movies. Ellie knew that was dumb to even think. One thing she did know was Trevor wouldn't stick around if they didn't do this. What college guy was going to avoid other girls if his girlfriend wasn't having sex with him?

And she wanted this.

She wanted this.

"Do you have condoms?" Maddie asked.

"He said he's bringing them."

"If he doesn't—"

"We're on the pill. I'm not going to get pregnant." Their mom had seen to that when they turned sixteen.

They'd both adamantly told her it wasn't needed, but their mom insisted. "You'll always know when your period is coming, and they won't be as heavy. Trust me."

And she'd been right.

But Ellie and Madison both knew it was more about teenagers making a lifetime mistake.

Right now, Ellie was applauding her mother's wisdom. "Do you think Mom ever snuck out like this when she was our age?" Ellie asked.

"Maybe."

"I bet that's why she put us on the pill. I wonder if she ever thought she was pregnant before us. When she was in school."

Madison turned up the speed on the windshield wipers. "I'm not sure about Mom, but I bet Dad did all those things."

"You think he got someone else pregnant?"

"No. But he is always saying that he was a teenage boy once, and you just know there was some girl."

"Yeah . . . probably."

Ellie's phone buzzed.

I'm already here, Trevor texted back.

Her stomach flipped.

They turned the corner to Taylor's street, and there he was.

With arms folded over his chest, Trevor leaned against his motorcycle with a hoodie thrown over his head.

Maddie pulled the car over and put it in park, but she kept the engine running.

Ellie sucked in the deepest breath she'd taken all month. "Okay." She looked at the phone in her hand, then shoved it in her backpack.

"Did he say where he was taking you?"

"His parents' yacht on the marina. That's romantic, right?"

"I guess."

Ellie leaned over and hugged her sister. "I'll text you when we're headed back."

Ellie reached for the door.

Madison stopped her. "What about your chemistry test?"

Ellie rolled her eyes. "Bruh, that was today. I did fine."

With that, Ellie pushed out of the car, bundled farther into her coat, and ran to Trevor.

~

Tuesdays had become Mari's second favorite day of the week. Sundays taking first place because of her family.

On occasion, James would arrive early and have dinner, then they'd have their dance lesson, and sometimes they'd go out with another couple to the equivalent of a dive bar that had live music and a dance floor.

And since their objective was to dance and not drink, the dive bar worked fine.

Being the oldest couple in the dance class, the younger ones often made fun of the music they liked. Which was comical since the dive bar played primarily classic rock from the '70s and '80s. Music Mari and James knew all the words to.

Nicoli and Levette were in their early thirties. They'd been married for three years and had no interest in having babies. Information Mari and James were hearing for the first time.

"We're too selfish," Nicoli said. "You need to give up your life when you have kids and hope you get it back when you're old."

They sat at a small bar-room table. Both Nicoli and Levette had drinks in front of them while Mari and James stuck with club soda.

"Kids add to your life," Mari argued. "You get so much more than you give up."

"Oh yeah . . . like what?" Levette asked.

"Love, laughter, joy . . . grandchildren."

"Babies are expensive," Nicoli said.

James scoffed. "Wait till they're in college."

Mari nudged him. "You're not helping."

"I love my girls. They're worth every penny."

That was better.

"And gray hair?" Nicoli asked.

James screwed up his face in an attempt to look offended.

All it did was make the rest of them laugh.

Mari leaned forward. "I dye mine."

Nicoli leaned forward as well, his elbows on the table. "Listen, all I'm saying is, kids aren't for everyone. The more parents that know that, the better off the children are."

"What are you going to do with all your time?" Mari asked.

Levette laughed. "Work, make money, travel . . . and hey, dance classes on Tuesday nights. All of our friends are starting families, and none of them have any time for themselves. We're planning our next trip. There's a salsa cruise in the fall. You guys should look into it."

"Since you're finally able to enjoy your life and you don't have to make decisions based on what your kids are doing," Nicoli finished for his wife.

"Most of the decisions that needed to be made were about work, keeping the restaurant going, not what my children were doing," Mari told them.

James nodded several times. "True."

"Okay, but . . . isn't the goal of having a business so that you have more time and not less? And did you work your whole life keeping the restaurant because you needed it to provide for your family? What really tied you down? Your business or your family?"

"Both," James said.

"Both," Mari said at the same time.

Nicoli shrugged. "We have one less tie."

The band faded one song out and started on another one.

Nicoli grabbed his wife's hand. "C'mon, let's burn some carbs."

The two of them swung onto the dance floor, leaving James and Mari alone.

"Did any of that make sense to you?" Mari asked. Life without her family would have been empty. Especially after Paulo.

James didn't immediately say no.

Mari turned and focused her whole attention on him.

"I wouldn't change Ellie and Madison for anything."

Thank God.

"They have a point, though. Society says you have to have a family to be whole. Sometimes a family can be two people."

Like she and Paulo before Luca came. Admittedly, there wasn't a lot of time being a family of two before they became three. And then, yes, ninety percent of the focus was on Luca . . . then Gio and then Chloe.

"Life would have been completely different if we didn't have kids. Empty," Mari said.

"Maybe." James nodded toward the dance floor. "For them, they only see the negative. We have parenting in the rearview mirror. Or in my case, almost."

"Is it ever behind us?" That was laughable.

"Not if they live with you," James said without pause.

Mari's eyes shot to his. "Luca and Brooke live in the apartment above me."

James hesitated and then seemed to pick his words carefully. "And did you tell them that you wouldn't be home tonight?"

Yes. Brooke. Mari had avoided Luca, and since the kitchen was slammed when they left, it was easy to do.

James took one of her hands in his. "I'm not saying it's a bad thing, hon. It's just, look how much of our time, together or apart, is spent on the worry of what our children would think."

"Your girls are fine with us."

"And Luca and Giovanni may never accept me. And if they don't, where does that leave us?" James stared right through her. The raw truth of his words hurt.

Air sucked at her lungs and made Mari want to hold her chest.

"I know they come first. I would never make you choose."

Would it come to that?

Mari felt moisture gather behind her eyes.

James placed his hand on her cheek.

She leaned into him. "They'll come around."

He smiled like he always did when she said those words. A smile that wasn't full, wasn't convinced. "I'll be here when they do. As long as you're falling for me as much as I'm falling in love with you."

Mari caught her breath, a gasp escaped.

The tempo of the music changed for a slow song.

James pulled her to her feet, and she followed numbly as they found their way to the dance floor.

Mari rested her head on James's chest, the two of them quiet in their own thoughts.

"Promise me you'll try and love again."

A single tear escaped Mari's eye.

She didn't have to try anymore. She was already there.

CHAPTER TWENTY-NINE

Trevor kissed her in the rain as Madison drove past.

"I thought you'd bring your parents' car," Ellie said as he handed her a helmet.

All that effort on curling her hair had been a complete waste of time.

"No way. They'd want to know every place I went and when I'd be back."

Ellie thought about her phone sitting in her backpack, all in an effort to ward off any questions from her mom and dad.

"Okay." The helmet went over her head, and cold fingers fiddled with the latch in an attempt at securing the thing.

Trevor placed a pair of sunglasses over her eyes and patted her butt when he was done.

His helmet had a shield that kept the rain off his face.

Ellie would have to duck behind his head to avoid the wet assault.

"I'll keep you warm," he told her.

Ellie hoped her laugh didn't sound forced.

And it was forced.

Not only was she breaking all the rules sneaking off with him, but riding on the back of his motorcycle, in the rain, was way down the list of "accepted behavior," according to her parents.

She swung one leg over the bike and scooted back.

Trevor hopped on and brought the bike to life.

Ellie took hold of his waist over his jacket and gripped him harder when he took off.

By the time they made it to the marina, Ellie was shaking so hard, her teeth were threatening to bite off her tongue.

Her hair was soaked, her jeans glued to her body.

Trevor used a code to open the gate that led them onto the dock.

Ellie hung tight to the railing to keep from slipping until the railing ended.

"I got you."

She smiled, liked it when Trevor did those little things. Holding her hand, putting his arm around her when people were watching.

Romantic.

The rain was coming down in sheets, and the dock was moving with the waves.

Ellie had never been on Trevor's parents' yacht.

When he stopped at a boat that wasn't a lot bigger than the kind you'd use to taxi to something moored in the middle of the bay, Ellie hesitated.

Trevor didn't notice.

He let her hand go and reached for the side of the boat and attempted to gain some balance before hoisting himself on board.

The sound of ropes slapping against the poles sticking out above the sailboats was something Ellie knew she'd remember from this night.

Trevor's parents owned a sailboat.

Not a yacht.

Trevor reached out a hand. "C'mon."

She didn't like this. One slip, and she'd be in the water between the boat and the dock.

"I won't let you fall in," he promised, reading her mind.

Against her better judgment, Ellie placed her freezing fingers in his gloved hand and squeezed tight.

Twice she started to lift herself onto the boat, chickened out, and pulled back.

The third time worked.

Even on board, she crouched low and held on to anything she could, following Trevor to where a small opening took them inside.

The narrow passage and even smaller door made her duck to get out of the rain.

Trevor let go of her hand and moved to a panel on the wall.

Ellie shut the door behind her and wrapped her arms around herself.

"This is . . . lit," she said, teeth chattering.

"Right?"

Trevor flipped a switch and pushed a button. Light filled the space that the fading sun outside didn't reach.

As suggested by the outside of the boat, the inside was small. A kitchen that looked no bigger than the half bath in the hallway of her house was squeezed into one side. A dining table for two filled the other side, the table itself was overloaded with books and papers.

But it wasn't the kitchen and table that caught Ellie's attention.

It was the bed.

On it was a brown blanket, and an orange pillow that looked like it had been left to weather a storm outside, then brought in by accident, sat at the foot.

Trevor grabbed the two life jackets that lay on the bed and pushed them off to the side.

Or the floor.

The six inches of floor between the bed and the wall.

"Sorry, I was going to try and come earlier and clean it up, but—"

"It's okay." She looked around. "Is there a heater?"

Trevor scrambled to the control panel. "I don't know if my dad got it working. It's not usually cold."

It sounded like something turned on after he hit another button. "There."

Trevor rolled his shoulders back and punched his chest out.

He turned and put a hand on each of her shoulders. "We should get you out of these wet clothes."

Her eyes looked at the bed, then him.

Swallowing hard, Ellie tugged at the edges of her coat to pull it past her cold, wet hands.

Trevor stood back and mimicked her actions.

His coat was off and added to the collection on the table before she'd pulled one arm out.

"Let me help."

She lifted an arm and turned for him to remove the coat.

Once it joined his, she felt a shiver run up her entire body.

Trevor choked out a laugh. "I know, right? It's cold."

She nodded a couple of times and looked at him.

Ellie opened her mouth to ask if there was a bathroom, but Trevor's cold lips pressed against hers.

Unlike any other time they'd kissed, this time felt hurried. Maybe he was as nervous as she was.

Either way, he pressed against her, his teeth hit her lips.

She pulled back.

"Sorry," he said as he leaned in again.

Ellie pressed a hand to his chest. "Uhm, is there a bathroom?"

"Oh." He took a step back. "Yeah."

A tiny door Chloe hardly noticed was at the very bottom of the stairs leading down into the boat.

Trevor pushed the door open.

"Thanks."

Ellie didn't know bathrooms could be smaller than on an airplane.

But apparently, they could.

One look in the mirror horrified her.

The rain had not only ruined any possibility of a hairstyle, but it also smudged the eyeliner her mother had suggested she needed more of.

Ellie turned the knob to the sink.

Nothing happened.

"There's no water," she called out.

"Hold on," Trevor yelled from the other side of the closed door.

She envisioned him back at the control panel, pushing another button.

Apparently, everything on this tiny boat required a button.

Water started to flow.

Cold water.

With a swab of toilet paper, Ellie tried to dab at the eyeliner to fix it. All she did was make it worse. With each pass, the black smeared more.

She wet a finger with soap, which worked, but it also got in her eye and had her tearing up. "Fuck."

"Is everything okay?" Trevor asked.

"Yeah."

She was taking forever.

After trying to run her fingers through her hair . . . to do what, she didn't know, Ellie glanced at the toilet. She didn't need to go, and honestly, the thought of baring her butt to the cold room was right up there with using a Porta Potty in the snow.

After one last look in the mirror, she told herself she was ready for this and opened the door.

Trevor had taken off his shoes and pulled off the hoodie he'd worn under his coat.

It looked as if he'd shaken the water from his hair as well, leaving a cute curl falling in his eyes.

He really was a good-looking guy.

"Better?" he asked.

"Yeah."

Then why was she still shaking even though the room did seem to have warmed up a degree or two?

Trevor reached for her again.

Before he tried to kiss her, Ellie asked, "Can I get some water?"

Trevor stopped. This time, a little huff escaped his lips. "Sure."

Under the table was a plastic-wrapped bundle of bottled waters. The kind you picked up from Costco.

He tugged one free and handed it to her.

She twisted off the cap and took a small sip, then a second.

Trevor stood there watching her.

She smiled and set the water on the tiny kitchen counter behind her.

They looked at each other. "Are you nervous, baby?"

"Yeah," she admitted. "A little."

He put his hand on her hip and backed up until his legs hit the mattress, bringing her along with him. "It's okay. I'll be careful."

What Ellie really wanted him to say was that they didn't have to. That if she wasn't ready, they could wait.

That's not what happened.

Trevor kissed her again. This time, his lips weren't as cold.

She closed her eyes and kissed him back.

She liked this. The kissing.

She tasted mint. Like he'd managed to pop a mint in while she'd been in the bathroom.

Trevor's hand that had been on her hip slipped under her shirt. Something she'd let him do before. Only now he didn't hesitate to cup her breast.

One minute they stood like that. The next, Trevor was pulling her down to sit next to him on the bed.

He broke their kiss long enough to adjust his position, then started kissing her again.

Ellie's heart was beating so fast she thought for sure he could feel it thumping under his hand. The hand that was right back under her shirt, until it fell to the top of her wet jeans.

He was going to undress her.

That's what happens, right?

You can't exactly have sex and do it with your clothes on.

Trevor leaned her back on the bed, one hand managed to undo the button on her jeans.

Then she felt him try and wedge his fingers between the wet fabric and her skin.

Ellie froze.

She turned her head to the side. "I can't."

Trevor kissed her neck like he didn't hear her.

"Stop. Trevor, stop."

He did.

Like a switch, he left his hand where it was, left his body pressing against hers, and opened his eyes.

"Fuck," he said as he pulled his frame away from hers.

"I'm sorry. I can't. I'm not ready."

The face that always smiled at her, the one that seemed to always have a look of understanding, didn't look so understanding now. "I knew this was going to happen."

She sat up, tugging her shirt down as she did.

"I'm sorry, Trevor."

He moved away from the bed and leaned against the tiny kitchen counter. "When are you going to be ready? You've been saying this for months."

Ellie was quick to button her pants. "I thought I was. I mean, it's cold, and I'm soaked."

Trevor waved a hand at the heater, which was working. "It's a boat, not the Ritz."

Ellie felt her throat clogging up. "This should be special. I don't even know if we'll see each other when we're at college. We never talk about that."

Trevor ran both of his hands through his hair. "What are you going on about? Who said anything about college?"

"Will I still be your girlfriend?"

"Fuck, I don't know."

She felt him slipping away. "Maybe by prom I'll be ready."

"What?" He screwed up his face. "Prom . . . You know what? No. Senior prom is supposed to have a happy ending. I just know you'll do this again."

This wasn't happening. "What are you saying?"

The face that stared back at her every time she turned on her phone glared at her now.

"I'd rather go to prom by myself than spend a bunch of money on something that isn't going to happen."

Ellie's jaw started to shake, and it had nothing to do with the cold.

The boat rocked, causing Trevor to lose his footing slightly.

Ellie didn't trust herself enough to stand.

One second, and he was tossing her jacket at her. The next, he was jabbing at all the buttons he'd pressed when they'd gotten on board.

She just sat there staring.

The second the lights went out in the cabin, Ellie realized how dark it had gotten outside.

"C'mon. I'm taking you back."

She slowly stood; tears fell down her face. This wasn't how this night was supposed to go.

Her wet coat drove home the reality of what had just happened.

Not only did Trevor just break up with her because she wouldn't have sex with him, but he was being a complete ass about it.

She didn't see that coming.

A big part of her wanted to start yelling at him. But instead, she felt her insides crumbling.

Her dad was right. Trevor was after one thing.

How could she be so stupid?

Before her jacket was even zipped up, Trevor was out the door.

Wind and rain hit her face the second she was on the deck of the tiny boat.

Yacht. It isn't a freaking yacht.

And how many other girls had he taken there?

Forgetting how slippery the deck was, Ellie nearly slid right off the side on the first step outside.

Trevor looked over her shoulder, said something she couldn't hear in the wind, then pushed behind her to close the door.

Just as rudely, he worked his way around her again and jumped off the boat and onto the dock.

Between the boat rocking and her tears, getting off the boat was even more difficult than getting on.

Trevor rolled his eyes and reached out a hand for her.

Eventually, she stood on the dock beside him. Both of them squaring off to each other.

"For the record, I didn't touch you once after you said to stop," he shouted at her.

Ellie started to feel her backbone showing up. "Okay."

"Just because you're eighteen doesn't stop a guy from being accused of something they didn't do."

"Do you want a sticker? Unlike you, I'm not going to be a little bitch." That felt good.

"Screw you."

He started to walk away.

Ellie's feet stayed grounded.

Well, as grounded as they could be on a rocking dock.

Trevor stopped when he realized she wasn't following him.

"C'mon."

She shook her head. "I don't want to ride on your motorcycle when you're this mad."

"I wouldn't be this mad if you . . ."

The tears felt like they were coming back.

She didn't want to show them. Gulping down her pride, she thrust her hand at him.

"What?"

"Your phone. I'll call Maddie to come get me."

He reached for his back pocket. "Whatever."

She took his phone from him.

The lock screen had a picture of both of them on the field after one of her games.

She wanted to cry all over again. Ellie shoved the phone back at him. "It's locked."

Trevor took it, cussed when the facial recognition didn't work, and then typed in his passcode.

Grasping the cold phone with freezing fingers, Ellie tried typing in the only phone number she'd memorized.

Only she kept pressing the wrong number. "Dammit."

"Jesus!" Trevor cussed.

"Stop yelling at me!" she shouted back.

Her teeth were chattering so hard, and she was having a hard time keeping her footing as the choppy sea slapped upside the dock.

Trevor reached for his phone.

She tried to hold on.

The next thing she knew, the phone was falling to the ground.

Trevor lunged for it.

Ellie stepped out of the way and watched as the phone slid right between the slats of the dock and into the sea.

Trevor caught himself before falling in after it. He came up sputtering. "Fucking, God damn . . . shit."

"You shouldn't have tried to grab it away."

"That was brand fucking new."

Ellie pointed at the ocean. "That wouldn't have happened if you weren't being such a dick."

Trevor stormed off the dock.

The locked door clapped back into place after he went through, leaving Ellie on the other side.

Opening doors for her was over.

It was all over.

In truth, she wanted to throw up.

Trevor shoved his helmet on and looked at her. "You coming or not?"

A clap of thunder was her answer.

She'd take her chances.

Ellie shook her head.

Trevor didn't say anything else. He turned over the bike, revved it twice, and sped away.

His back wheel skidding out as he did.

CHAPTER THIRTY

Ellie didn't know the area.

The building that looked to be a part of the marina was closed. And even though she'd driven by the location many times, she couldn't say for sure which way she should walk to find the nearest anything that had a phone.

In the freezing rain, a mile felt like ten.

Eventually, a gas station became a beacon.

The anger and bravado she'd felt for those fleeting moments when Trevor's phone was becoming one with the fish had passed, along with any dry portion of her body.

She didn't bother holding back her tears, and no one could hear her sobs.

The small convenience store attached to the gas station had a lone man behind the counter.

Feeling completely out of place and stupid for being in her current position, Ellie walked inside and approached the man.

She opened her mouth to talk, and emotion choked her up so much she couldn't get her words out.

"My phone . . . I, uhm . . . my . . ."

"Are you okay?"

She shook her head.

"Are you hurt?"

She shook her head.

"Are you homeless?"

Did she look that bad? Ellie looked down at herself, then back up at the fiftysomething-year-old man with a gray beard and brown skin.

She shook her head a third time and managed a tiny "No."

Ellie took a deep breath and swallowed hard. "Can I use your phone?"

He didn't answer, he just reached for a cordless landline and handed it to her.

She dialed Madison's number and heard it ring . . . and ring.

When her sister didn't answer, it dawned on Ellie that the call would look like spam.

The phone made a clicking noise and then announced that the mailbox was full.

Ellie's bottom lip started to quiver all over again.

She hung up and tried again.

This wasn't happening. "C'mon, Maddie, pick up."

The tears started fresh and hot.

"They didn't answer?"

Ellie couldn't talk. Who else could she call?

She racked her brain.

Why hadn't she memorized her friends' numbers?

Even her mom . . . dad. She didn't even care that they'd find out. She was cold, wet, and a little scared. It was too far to walk, too dark.

Mari. Her father was with Mari at the dance studio.

Only she couldn't remember the name of the place.

The clock on the wall behind the man at the counter said they wouldn't be there anyway.

The restaurant.

"Do you have a cell phone?" she asked the man.

She saw the skepticism on his face.

"Can you look up the phone number of a restaurant? My dad's girlfriend owns a restaurant."

That seemed to appease the stranger.

He grabbed his phone that was sitting on the counter behind him but didn't hand it over.

"It's called D'Angelo's. *D* with an apostrophe."

"A. N. G. E. . . ."

"L. O. S.," she finished for him.

He showed her the number, and she dialed it on the landline.

"D'Angelo's. How can I help you?" The pleasant voice belonged to a woman.

Tears were choking her up again. "Uhm . . . is Mari there?"

"I'm sorry, no, she's not tonight."

"What about Luca?"

"Yeah, he is. Did you want a reservation?"

"No. I need to . . . need to talk to Luca." Ellie's voice was breaking. "Please, it's really important."

"Okay. Who is calling?"

"I'm Ellie."

"Luca knows you?"

"Y-yes."

Instead of being put on hold, Ellie heard people talking and then the sound of dishes, laughter. "Luca. You have a call."

"Can you take a number?"

"No!" Ellie shouted into the phone, unsure if the person who answered could even hear her.

"The girl calling is crying. Said her name is Ellie."

Please, please, please.

The sound of the phone scratching something, sounding muffled, and then Ellie heard a familiar voice.

"Ellie?"

She couldn't stop the tears. "I didn't know. I didn't have any numbers. I can't—"

Luca's voice softened, and the noise in the background faded.

"What happened, *tesoro*?"

"I n-need a ride. He left me. I didn't want to get on . . . h-his motorcycle. I shouldn't have come."

"Where are you?"

"A-at a gas station."

"Okay." The sound of Luca shouting in Italian was followed by him coming back on the line, his voice soft. "Is there someone there with you? The person who works there?"

"Yes."

"Give them the phone."

Ellie offered the phone to the stranger. "Can you talk to him?"

The man put the phone to his ear. "Hello. Gas Mart a mile south of the marina . . . yeah, that's the one."

The attendant looked at her.

"I can't tell. She's pretty upset. No, no one. Of course. No problem."

The attendant handed her the phone again.

"Hello?"

"I'm ten minutes away. Fifteen tops. Don't go anywhere. Stay inside."

"O-okay."

Luca hung up the phone, and Ellie handed it back to the attendant. "Thank you."

"It's okay, honey. Why don't you wait over here?" He motioned to the side of the counter to a lone chair.

Her fingers started to tingle as feeling started to come back into them.

The man handed her a handful of paper towels that she used to remove a layer of rain from her hair and face. He offered something to drink, but she refused.

Thirteen minutes later, a car pulled in front of the glass doors, and Luca jumped out.

He walked in, calling her name. "Ellie?" A level of fear laced his voice.

She stepped from behind the counter and opened her arms.

He folded her in. "Shhh, it's okay. Jesus, you're freezing."

Luca thanked the attendant and opened the car door, tucked her into the passenger seat, and got behind the wheel.

He cranked the heat and then turned to her.

"Where do you want me to take you?"

Her dad was right.

Her mom was going to be pissed.

And all Ellie wanted to do was crawl into a tiny ball and wake up after graduation.

She shrugged and shook her head.

Luca put the car in drive and headed to Little Italy.

~

"When did nine thirty start to feel like midnight?" Mari asked from the passenger seat.

The windshield wipers clapped against the glass at a rapid speed.

"When did driving in bad weather become something you dread instead of a teenage adventure?" he asked in response.

They'd left their new friends behind and were en route to James's La Jolla home when Mari's phone started to ring.

She reached into her purse and looked at the screen. "It's Luca."

James tried to keep his face neutral. His first thought was her son wanted to interfere with their night. Mari spending Tuesdays with James was new and likely to get some pushback.

Mari lifted the phone to her ear. "*Pronto.*"

When Mari fell silent, James glanced over.

"*Cosa?* Okay, okay. No, we're in the car headed to . . . Okay." Mari placed a hand on James's arm. "Turn the car around. We need to go home."

"What's the matter?"

James could hear Luca's voice but not his words.

"Wait, James needs to hear this."

Mari held her phone between the both of them and put it on speaker.

"What's going on?" James asked.

"It's Ellie. I just picked her up from a gas station by the marina, soaking wet and crying."

James felt every muscle in his body tense. "What—"

"She's fine. Not hurt, anyway. I don't know all the details, but it sounds like she snuck out of the house to meet her boyfriend."

"What the hell did he do to my little girl?" James glanced over his shoulder and changed lanes.

"I'm not sure he did anything. Brooke is in with her now, getting her in dry clothes and talking to her."

"Why didn't she call me?" James pulled off the freeway, only to get in the lane to get right back on in the opposite direction.

"Her phone is with her sister. Ellie didn't want to be caught sneaking off. Didn't want for you to track her. And apparently, memorizing phone numbers isn't a priority, she didn't remember yours, so she called the restaurant."

James gripped the wheel. "If he hurt her, I'll kill him."

"Wait until we know what happened, okay?" Luca asked.

"We'll be there shortly," Mari said before hanging up.

James slammed his hand into the steering wheel. "I knew that kid wasn't any good."

Mari placed a reassuring hand on his arm as they sped their way to Mari's home.

"Do you want me to call Cindy?" Mari asked.

"Let's get some facts first." James wanted to stop his mind from reaching for the worst-case scenario, but it was damn hard to do. "She sneaks out to meet her boyfriend and ends up alone at night in the rain?"

"Don't let your mind go there, James. If Luca thinks she's fine, she probably is. Maybe Trevor was drinking, and she didn't want to get in his car. We don't know."

James didn't bother parking properly.

He pulled into the back lot, turned off the car, and ran toward the back door.

He made it to Luca and Brooke's apartment and was happy to see the door open.

Luca and Brooke sat at the dining table with mugs in their hands.

"Where is she?"

Luca and Brooke both stood up.

"In our room, resting," Brooke told him.

Mari held on to James's arm as they talked.

"Is she okay?" Mari asked.

"She is, Mama," Brooke said.

Luca indicated the chairs across from them.

James didn't want to sit, but he also wanted to know what was going on before seeing her.

"Did he hurt her?" As much as James wanted to consider a life with Mari, if he had to go to jail defending his daughter, he would.

"According to Ellie, no."

Mari pulled on his arm until they were both sitting.

"She made arrangements to see her boyfriend . . ." Brooke looked between James and Luca before setting her eyes back to James. "I know this is hard for dads to hear, so please hold off on any judgment."

James looked at Mari.

He knew exactly where this was going. "They had sex."

Brooke bit her lip. "They were going to. She got cold feet."

Thank God.

"And when she stopped him, he got angry. Broke up with her, called off prom. Said some shitty things. Ellie told me twice he didn't try and force her or manipulate her . . . well, maybe by holding prom over her head, but she didn't backtrack," Brooke told them. "He'd taken them to his parents' sailboat in the marina, and when they were leaving, she tried to call Madison, and his phone ended up falling into the ocean. He got even more pissed, and no, he didn't hit her. I asked," Brooke said.

"I never liked that kid."

"Ellie refused to get back on his motorcycle, so he left her there."

"At the marina?" James asked.

"Yes."

"At least she had the good sense to not get on that bike," Mari told him.

"He left her there at night by herself. Anything could have happened," James pointed out.

"My thoughts exactly," Luca said. "If she refused to get on the bike, he should have walked with her to find a phone."

James went back to his default solution. "I'm going to kill him."

Luca nodded a few times. "I think that's reasonable."

Mari glared at her son. "You're not helping."

"If it were Franny, I'd do the same thing."

"No one is killing anyone," Brooke interrupted both of them. "They're both teenagers making dumb mistakes."

"Mistakes that could have been worse," Mari said.

Slowly, James's nerves started to settle.

He reached for his phone and looked at the locator app to see both of his daughters over at Taylor's house.

"I need to call Cindy."

Mari offered an understanding smile as he stepped away from the table.

James walked into the outside hallway and dialed his ex-wife.

"Hello," she answered.

He released an exasperated sigh. "It's ten o'clock, do you know where your children are?"

After getting over the initial shock that Cindy had no idea where Ellie was, James was able to deliver the facts and ease her concern. And promise to make Ellie call if she decided to stay with him tonight.

For now, it was divide and conquer.

James walked back into Luca's apartment and pointed to the hall. "Which one is your room?"

Mari walked with him and stopped by the door.

"If you need me . . ."

James placed a hand on her shoulder, smiled, then reached for the door.

~

Mari sat at the table, waiting for James and Ellie to emerge.

"I'm so thankful she had the good sense to call here, to ask for you," Mari told Luca.

"I am, too. It's not like I've given her a reason to think she could."

His comment caught Mari off guard.

"What do you mean?"

"You know what I mean, Mama. I've met the girls once. Not that you haven't tried to make that happen again." Luca smiled at Brooke.

She smiled back.

"If something had happened because she didn't call here or felt like she couldn't . . . I don't think I could forgive myself."

"You don't know them well, no one could blame you."

Luca looked at the ceiling. "I would. And I would want Franny to call on James if she needed him. Clearly, the man is a good father. And he has excellent taste in women."

Mari gripped her cup.

Did Luca just say what she thought he said?

"What are you saying, Luca?"

Mari sent up a prayer, or a request, or whatever it was when she struggled to understand her children. *Please, Paulo, help me out here.*

"According to the women in my life," he said, looking at Brooke, "I haven't given James a fair chance. I'm going to change that. And since I'm the older brother, I'll bully Gio to follow my actions."

Mari's heart truly burst into a million tiny pieces. The sparkling kind and not the ones that hurt. She placed her palms together and looked up. "Thank you."

She pushed out of her chair, rounded the table, and put her arms around her son.

"I love you. Thank you."

Luca embraced her back. "I said I'd give him a fair chance; I didn't give him permission to marry you."

Mari pushed him away, teasing. "Like we'd need your permission."

Luca frowned.

"She's teasing," Brooke told him.

"We're not there yet." But having his blessing to even see if they could go there was more than Mari thought she'd get out of this day.

The door in the hallway opened, James stepped out.

Mari pulled away from her son. "How is she?"

"Remorseful," he said. "Embarrassed. Angry. Hurt."

"All the feelings," Brooke said.

James looked at Brooke. "She said her clothes are in the dryer."

"I'll get them."

As Brooke walked away, James moved close and extended his hand to Luca. "I cannot thank you enough for answering her call. I don't want to think about what could have happened if you didn't."

Mari stood back and watched her son and James genuinely connect.

"It's family," Luca said. "You never have to thank family for doing the right thing."

"It makes me very happy to hear you say that."

Mari had to bite her inner cheek to keep herself from tearing up.

Ellie and Brooke entered the living room. Hair still damp, but at least in dry clothes, Ellie had swollen eyes from shedding too many tears.

Mari crossed the room and wrapped her arms around the young woman. "It breaks my heart to see you sad."

"I feel so stupid."

Luca cleared his throat with a small laugh. "Everyone in this room has done something just as reckless."

Mari started to nod. "I haven't," she teased. "But they all have."

Ellie laughed, that beautiful smile finally lighting up her face.

They started for the door. Ellie hesitated by Luca and Brooke. "Thanks."

Luca stepped forward and ruffled her hair, just as he did Franny's. "Call anytime, *sorellina*, day or night."

Mari placed a hand to her chest, the pet name for "little sister" rolling off his tongue said more than anything he had before.

~

Mari relived the time when her children were navigating the end of their adolescence.

James sprung for a limousine to take the girls and three of their friends . . . girlfriends . . . to their senior prom.

The memory of James standing beside the limo, setting all the rules, would live in her heart forever. "Remember, don't add to the population, don't subtract from the population. Don't end up in the ER, the newspapers, or jail—"

"And if you end up in jail, establish dominance early!" the twins had finished.

"Everyone have their phones? All charged?" James asked.

The girls either nodded or rolled their eyes.

"Let them go, James," Cindy told him.

Mari leaned over, whispered in Cindy's ear. "He's going to bounce off the walls when they leave in the fall."

"Thank God he has you," she said.

And he did.

Having the blessing of her children had opened parts of Mari she didn't realize were closed.

For years, the restaurant had dominated her life. For her family, with them . . . because of them. Now if she spent any time in the kitchen, it was a rarity. The automated system put much of her work into the hands of a computer, again taking away hours that busied her up.

Salena had hired and was in the process of training her replacement.

And Mari spent about half of her nights miles away in a house with a yard. And a man who whispered beautiful things in her ear at night and woke her with a cup of coffee and a smile in the morning.

They'd even managed to have a Sunday dinner at James's home. The weekend after Ellie was accepted to the University of Arizona. Cementing exactly where she was going in the fall.

With Emma's due date just around the corner, the family made the trip to Gio and Emma's vineyard estate for their family dinner.

A long table stretched under a canopy of lights hanging off a trellis covered in bougainvillea.

Emma sat with her feet up on a chair while Chloe, Brooke, Salena, Rosa, and Mari set the table. Inside the house, dinner was in various stages of readiness. Not that anyone was overly famished since dinners at the vineyard were most often overnight events and there was never an absence of food.

The sound of the twins and Franny splashing in the pool was music to Mari's ears.

Leo was constantly entertained by the girls.

And watched over like the prize he was.

"What do you think they're talking about?" Salena asked, pointing to the men in the family that were walking outside of the wine cellar.

"I'm sure Gio is boring everyone with the process of smashing grapes," Emma teased. Both of her hands were perched on her belly . . . her impossibly large belly.

Mari could hardly wait to hold those babies.

"He's already done that," Chloe said. "Dante probably knows the process better than him at this point."

"Yeah, but James is a new audience, so let the learning begin."

"James loves all the attention. It means they're accepting him."

"They are, Mama," Chloe said.

Salena set the last of the cutlery on the table and took a seat. "So . . . when's the wedding?"

Mari snapped her gaze to Salena.

Everyone grew quiet.

"Who said anything about marriage?" Mari asked. She hadn't even thought about it . . . much.

Salena snorted.

"Maybe I need to invite James to church, Mama. Have a little sit-down with Jesus."

Considering Mari had done just that with all her children at least once after learning about a serious relationship, Chloe's suggestion shouldn't have come as a surprise.

"And when was the last time you were in church?" Mari asked.

"Leo's baptism. And you're missing the point."

"I'm avoiding your point," Mari told her daughter.

"You'd say yes, though, right? If he asked," Emma said.

"I suppose we'll have to wait and see."

"That means yes," Rosa announced.

"No one asked you," Mari told her friend.

"Oh, please, Mari. I'm the one willing to live in sin. You're not. Don't even pretend."

"Mama Rosa!" Chloe tried to act shocked.

No one at the table was.

"I didn't lose all this weight and get my confidence back just to blow it on *one* man."

Laughter broke out.

Emma held her stomach. "Don't make me laugh, it makes me have to pee."

That sent up another wave of mirth.

"And is there a man?" Salena asked.

"No." Rosa pointed at Salena. "But if you know of anyone single I would like, set me up."

"Most of the single men I know are young."

"And where is the problem with that?" Rosa asked, deadpan.

Emma doubled over. "Stop . . . oh, man. I need the bathroom." She dropped her feet from the chair.

"Poor baby," Mari cooed.

Brooke walked with Emma into the house, leaving the rest of them behind.

"I hope James doesn't wait too long to ask," Chloe said.

Rosa shrugged. "He won't."

"What makes you say that?" Mari asked.

Rosa plucked an olive out of a dish and popped it into her mouth. "He asked me to find out your ring size."

"What?" Mari snapped.

"Seriously?" Salena asked.

Chloe slapped at Rosa's arm. "And why did you tell Mama that?"

Never mind why, Mari was still reeling from the ring size question.

"Because unlike the first go at marriage, you want to think long and hard before going into that again. Men in this family like to make grand gestures when popping the question, and the last thing any woman wants is to say no in front of an audience. If Mari has any doubts, she should cut him off before it gets to that point."

"Then why didn't you tell me the day he asked about my size?"

Rosa looked away. "Because I know you're going to say yes. Am I wrong?"

Salena sat forward. "Wait, when did he ask?"

Another olive made it between Rosa's teeth. "A couple of weeks ago."

Mari turned then, to the direction the men were gathered and talking in.

And as spidey senses did, every one of them turned to look toward her.

Salena started laughing, slow and staccato.

~

"It really is amazing what you've built here," James told Gio.

They were inside the room where wine was processed. Most of what Gio said was completely over James's head. But in time, he'd learn.

"I'm living my dream," he said.

"Your dream was my nightmare," Ryan said.

Luca must have noticed the confusion on James's face. He pointed the glass in his hand at Ryan. "Ryan refused the family business model early on."

"Right. Your parents' vineyard is close by?"

Ryan nodded and lifted the glass in his hand, the amber liquid was in direct contrast to the rest of them holding wineglasses. "Which is why I like beer," Ryan said.

"Have you ever thought about starting a brewery?" James asked.

Dante nudged Ryan's shoulder. "That's not a bad idea."

"That sounds like a lot of work." Ryan took a drink.

"None of you strike me as lazy."

"I like passive income. That's why I have rental property. And my schedule doesn't interfere with Salena's."

James could understand that. Long workdays turned into long weeks, then months. And lately, all he wanted was to plan things like salsa cruises with Mari.

"You have a point there, young man," James said. "I've been thinking a lot about how my business can run without me there every day."

"Retiring early?" Luca asked.

"Not sure about retirement, but . . . less physical time at the office. I won't be saddling the girls with my business. Eventually, I need to figure out something."

"Bring on a partner or apprentice. Make them invest so they can't just walk away, retain control, and teach them what you know," Ryan suggested. "Then when you want to retire . . . poof, passive income."

A giant light bulb went off in James's head. "That sounds so easy."

"It doesn't have to be hard. That's the problem with a lot of things. We try to make it difficult when it isn't. We spend so much time spinning to make time. Just stop spinning and do the thing." Ryan pointed to Dante. "Buy the yachts, hire the crew, they do the daily work, you enjoy the paycheck." Ryan looked at Luca. "Hire and train the chefs, maybe open a sister restaurant catering to a different clientele. How many Italian restaurants are in Little Italy? All of them filled. Or tapas and wine tasting? My point is volume, but let it run without you. That's when you have freedom. I learned that from my old man, much as I hate to admit it. This life is short. I don't want to miss any of it."

"Damn, Ryan . . . that was deep," Dante teased.

"Fuck off."

They all laughed.

"You do have a point. Life is short." James looked between Luca and Gio. Now was as good a time as any. "I don't want to waste any time."

Stone rubbed against stone as James shifted off one foot and onto the other.

The five of them were silent for a moment.

Almost as if everyone knew what was coming next.

"Luca . . . Giovanni."

"Oh," Ryan muttered.

Dante stepped back.

Luca and Gio stared.

"I love your mother. She's the best thing that has happened in my life since my girls. I'm going to ask her to marry me. But I know I won't stand a chance if the two of you don't approve."

Faces that weren't identical, but definitely related, stared back at James.

"You sure it's not too soon?" Luca asked.

James shook his head. "No, it's not. All you guys, you have fifty years left, sixty. I'm staring down at thirty if I'm lucky. I want every one of those with Mari."

James held his breath.

The feeling of someone watching caught on the back of his neck.

He turned to where the women were sitting around the table and found Mari watching.

"Every last one," he said for good measure.

~

It was the perfect time of year.

It wasn't hot enough during the days to allow any biting bugs to hatch, but it was still warm enough that the evenings didn't nip at your skin.

The lights over the table illuminated the space, much like those on the terrace at the restaurant. Spring flowers were filling the air with jasmine and lavender.

Dinner had stuffed every belly, and everyone was talking, laughing . . . joking.

Franny sat between the twins, attempting to teach them words in Italian.

Mari couldn't be any happier.

"Since we're all here, we need to coordinate some schedules. Starting with the absolutes." Gio pointed at the twins. "When is your graduation?"

"May twenty-eighth," Ellie said.

Gio pulled out his phone and started typing into it.

"And do we know when you're moving yet?"

"End of August." James's chest clenched.

Mari patted his shoulder. "The airport is a few miles away."

He smiled. "I was thinking about tuition."

Madison tossed an olive pit at her father. "Thanks, Dad."

Laughter sparked among them.

Gio placed a hand on Emma's belly. "The babies are only cooking for another month. Which might keep us from your graduation."

"We get it," Ellie said.

"And if we're in labor during graduation . . ." Gio pointed at James. "We'll see you after. Mama, you too. You can only sit in the lobby and wait anyway."

It hadn't dawned on her that the twins' arrival could interfere with the girls' graduation.

"It's okay if you want to be at the hospital, we'll understand," Madison said.

James patted her hand.

"Graduations take a few hours. Labor is a lot longer," Mari said.

Emma moaned.

"Drugs, Emma. Trust me on that," Brooke said.

"Mama, you're here the first week after the twins arrive."

"Week? You're going to need more help than that," Mari argued.

"Emma's mom has the next week," Gio continued.

Mari looked at James. "I'm already in withdrawal, and the babies aren't even here yet."

"Don't worry, Mari. I'm not a martyr," Emma said.

"I want to babysit," Madison said.

"Me too," Franny added.

Rosa sat forward and glared at her son and Chloe. "Since I'm obviously not going to be a grandmother anytime soon, I want a turn."

"Ah, so much love," Mari cooed.

Gio threw both of his hands in the air. "You guys can figure everything out past week two. And when Emma and I need time alone with the babies, no one argues . . ."

That didn't sound reasonable at all. But Mari nodded anyway.

"Dante has a birthday in June, Brooke's is in July . . ." Gio looked up from his notes. "What am I missing?"

Luca pointed at his brother. "We need to squeeze a wedding in there somewhere."

"Oh, shit . . . that's right."

What?

"Who's getting married?" Franny asked.

No one is engaged.

It was in that moment that Mari realized every eye at the table was on her.

She literally jumped when she felt James moving beside her.

He pushed his chair back far enough to get on one knee.

Mari turned in her chair, numb.

James gathered her hands in his.

"Mari—"

Her heart was in her throat. She glanced up at her family.

Her family who watched with huge smiles and knowing nods.

He brought her hands to his lips, kissed the back of one. "I didn't realize how much I was missing in my life until you came along. One yes changed everything. One yes, and I got on that ship. There you were. God-awful shirt and beautiful smile. One yes, and we were on the dance floor and jumping into waterfalls. One yes, and I fell hopelessly in love. I need you to give me one more yes, Mari." James stared into her soul. "Will you marry me?"

"Oh, James . . ." She lowered her head to his, eyes locked and lips almost touching. "Yes."

James pressed his lips to hers and brought her with him as he stood and took that kiss deeper.

Mari was vaguely aware that her family was clapping, and someone was even knocking on the table.

The kiss ended, their bodies close. "I love you," she whispered.

"I love you."

"Where is the ring?" Rosa shouted above the applause.

Mari couldn't care less about a ring.

"Oh, yeah." James stood back and fished in his pockets.

He pulled out a black box, looked at it, and shook his head. "Not that one."

He went in again, pulled out a white box.

"You have two?" Chloe asked.

James placed the black box on the table and opened the white one.

A simple yet large round diamond on a band of gold in the shape of intertwining leaves with tiny diamonds spaced out between them. It looked like a flower in bloom. "It's beautiful."

Mari lifted her hand to him so he could slip the ring on her finger.

"I love it."

She kissed him again.

Ellie and Madison were the first to jump up, run around the table, and pull them into a hug. "Does this mean we can call you Mama Mari now?" Ellie asked.

"You can call me anything you want, *tesoro*."

Luca stepped up to James and put out his palm. Mari watched as a handshake turned into a hug. "Well done," Luca said.

"Thanks for your help."

Luca turned to her next, his embrace was long and loving. "I want you happy, Mama."

"I am. Thank you. Thank you for your blessing."

Gio stood by. "It's my turn," he said, pushing Luca away.

Gio rocked her side to side. "I thought I was the next one to add family to the table. You're showing me up, Mama."

Mari placed her head on his chest. "You'll catch up soon enough."

Chloe didn't hug. She grabbed Mari's hand and squealed. She kissed her cheek, then turned to James and did the same.

Eventually, the hugs and congratulations had done their rounds, and Mari slid up beside James. "What a perfect day."

"It will be hard to beat," he said.

"What's in the other box?" Rosa asked, her question muttered by several others.

James grinned.

Mari knew that smile. It said he was up to something.

"If she didn't like this one, I had a backup. Something I know she likes."

Mari glanced at the box, then him.

"Gonna be hard to take back, though, it was custom made," James said.

A question sat behind Mari's eyes.

"What?" he asked. "I told you my love language was gift giving."

"Open it, Mama," Chloe said.

"Yeah, Nonna, open it." Franny had practically climbed up on the table.

Mari looked at James again. "What did you do?"

He shrugged. "Open it."

She was scared.

The black velvet box had some weight to it.

Slowly, she eased back the lid and burst out in laughter. She snapped the lid closed before anyone had seen it.

"You're nuts."

"Hey, when a woman tells you she likes something, you listen."

Their laughter was contagious, everyone was laughing even though they weren't in on the joke.

"Mari . . . what's in the box?" Rosa asked.

Mari opened the box again, took a long look at it, and then showed it to her family.

Some of the laughter died.

Mari and James, on the other hand, couldn't stop laughing.

"It's awful," Madison blurted out.

"What the hell, Dad?" Ellie asked.

She pulled the ring out of the box and put it on her right hand. "I love it. I don't think I can wear it on the same hand, though."

James was doubled over.

"What are we missing?"

The diamond-encrusted skull ring wasn't nearly as god-awful as the ones in the storefront in the Caribbean, but it was pretty damn bad.

And Mari loved it.

Almost as much as she loved the man who bought it for her.

EPILOGUE

There was no best man.

No maid of honor.

Mari wore a three-quarter-length dress in white silk, a simple bouquet of white flowers in her hands.

James's all-white suit was missing a tie. A simple rose pinned to his lapel.

The flowers were the only distinction among those who attended their wedding.

Everyone was dressed in white.

The family members that had been at the proposal were the only ones on Dante and Chloe's yacht, watching James and Mari say yes for the final time. Including the brand-new set of perfectly identical twin boys.

They'd kicked around the idea of taking the yacht out to sea so Dante could perform the ceremony. Only after a little research, Mari and James learned that wasn't a thing. By the time that was figured out, everyone had gotten into the idea.

So even though Mari's faith suggested they should marry in the church, James wasn't a Catholic. Though he was willing.

"We'll ask for a blessing later," she told him once they made the decision to let Dante do the job.

"Ask for forgiveness and not permission?" he'd asked.

Oh, how she'd changed. James brought out the laughter in her. And a ton of snark. "We probably shouldn't use the skull ring with the priest, though."

There wasn't a moment that wasn't funny.

Mari did wear the ring.

Not all the time, and not at their actual wedding, but she did put it on.

There were so many questions.

Dante's half-serious, half-hysterical ceremony was perfectly executed.

"Do you, James, promise to smile in the face of Mari's temper, even if she starts yelling in Italian?

"And do you, Mari, promise to find humor in every horrible piece of jewelry James brings home?

"Do you both promise to dance in the rain like no one is watching and love each other so deeply that you glow when you walk into a room?"

Yes, yes, and yes . . .

When Dante announced them husband and wife, an entirely new page turned in her life.

"My God, Mama, you look ten years younger," Chloe said after the ceremony was over.

"I feel younger."

"That would be the sex," Rosa said without missing a beat.

Chloe gasped and then laughed.

Mari nodded a few times. "Definitely helps."

Chloe covered her face with her hands but laughed the whole time.

"Do I look ten years younger?" Rosa asked.

"Ahh . . ."

"Are you having . . . I mean, did you meet someone?" Mari asked.

"No. I haven't. Someone needs to find me a fountain of youth." Rosa lifted her champagne glass as she walked away.

"Is it me, or is she a whole different person these days?" Chloe asked.

"It's not you. Behind all that wit is a level of hurt. Sometimes when you're hurt, you make the wrong choices. You and Dante need to keep an eye on her. Let me know if you see something I don't."

"We will."

Music played in the background as the yacht floated in the bay.

James, along with most of the men, had already removed his suit coat.

"James? Mari?"

Mari looked up to see Ryan holding a bottle of champagne and an empty glass. Ellie and Madison stood at his side with hopeful expressions on their faces.

Mari glanced at James for his approval.

"Ahh . . ."

"They leave for college in a month."

James looked at Mari for an answer.

"You married an Italian, honey."

"Fine," James conceded. "But don't overdo it."

"I'll make sure they drink water along with it," Chloe said and then walked away.

Mari walked over to Emma, who was staring down at her boys, both sound asleep and curled into each other.

"How are they asleep?" she asked.

"Genetics. Giovanni slept through everything until he was ten."

The music rotating through a curated playlist changed songs, and Mari turned to find her husband.

James heard the beat, too, and started dancing her way.

They met in the middle and wasted zero time falling into step.

All those dance classes, and not once had they had an opportunity to show off to their family.

The bride and groom's first dance morphed into the second, and the third. Until Ellie pushed her way into her father's arms and asked him to show her what they were doing.

Luca took James's place, and eventually, others joined in.

The wedding and reception were everything Mari loved in life.

Family, food, wine, and laughter.

The words that were painted on the walls of the restaurant.

~

Mari stood in the center of the place she'd called home her entire life.

Nearly all of the furniture stayed.

And even some of the family photos.

The space itself wasn't going to be closed off to her or James, but it was in the process of getting a fresh coat of paint and a slightly new look.

It would now be used as a larger place for Gio and Emma to stay when they didn't want to make the drive home on those late Sunday nights. Or maybe even Mari and James if the wine had been poured a little heavy.

But it wouldn't be called home.

At least not day and night.

The one room that was being completely emptied out and started over was the primary bedroom.

Mari felt she owed that to James.

That was where she'd shared her life with Paulo.

The pictures of only the two of them stayed behind, too.

A few photographs of the children growing up would sit in albums that she could pull out on occasion, Paulo in them. But now was the time for new images, new memories.

James and Luca were carrying the last of the boxes Mari wanted moved across town down to Luca's SUV and James's car.

Mari walked over to the picture of her and Paulo.

An overwhelming sense of love washed through her. "Thank you," she said as if he was standing right there. "Thank you for wanting this for me. For giving us your blessing in your darkest hours. For making me promise that I'd try." Mari closed her eyes and slowly breathed in from her nose. The slightest whiff of his cologne lingered just out of reach. "And thank you for bringing James to me."

She opened her eyes and released anything left that tied her to the sorrow of her past.

Footsteps on the stairs announced James and Luca's return.

"Is that everything?" Luca asked.

"I think so."

"It's not like we can't come back, hon," James said.

The unmistakable sound of Franny running down the stairs announced she was coming.

In her hand was a backpack.

"I'm ready."

Mari looked at James.

"She wanted to spend the night with the girls before they left."

"Pop Pop said it was okay."

There was a very deep discussion on what James's "grandfather" name was going to be.

James couldn't wrap his head around *nonno*. "The last thing I want is to be known as the no-no guy. I like yes, yes."

Mari had tried to articulate *nonno* with the Italian accent. But in the end, it didn't matter.

Pop Pop it was.

"Okay, then. Let's go."

James followed Franny, then came Mari and Luca.

"Pop Pop said if we got a puppy, it could stay at your house since you have a yard."

"He did, did he?"

James looked over his shoulder.

Luca moaned.

"I love dogs," James said.

"See?" Franny said.

They spilled out into the back alley of the restaurant.

"How is it *your* dog if it lives at *our* house?" Mari asked.

"Didn't you warn him about the puppy question?" Luca asked.

"I didn't think I had to."

Franny grabbed James's hand and smiled.

The kind of smile that said she knew exactly what she was doing.

"Pop Pop said." She shrugged like it was already a done deal.

James smiled. "I'm the yes, yes man."

"Don't make me dislike you, James," Luca said.

James started walking away. "Too late, Luca. We're already married."

"*Cazzo!*" Luca whispered under his breath.

"What kind of puppy do you want?" James asked Franny.

Mari looked at her son. "It can stay with us *after* the puppy phase."

Luca cussed again.

Franny jumped into Luca's car.

Mari buckled up in James's.

James placed his hand on hers as they both looked up at the building.

"You ready?" he asked.

Mari released a tiny laugh. "It's too late to ask that question, James. We're already married."

It was his turn to laugh.

James pulled her head to his, kissed her softly. "Let's do this."

"I love you."

"I love you, too."

ACKNOWLEDGMENTS

A heartfelt thank you to Maria Gomez and Lindsey Faber. Sometimes when I'm writing, I ask myself, "Self? What would Lindsey say about this, and what would Maria suggest I do here?" And I try and do that shit before my work ever gets to you. And hot damn, it worked! Having you both on my editorial team is such a joy. I hope you know that.

And to my copy and line editors . . . You do a lot of heavy lifting, thank you!

Jane Dystel, my biggest cheerleader and forever friend. My heart is with you now more than ever. Thank you.

Thank you to the Village People . . . that cruise ship will never be the same after we left.

To Brandy and Kari, who remind me daily that I'm on deadline and shouldn't wait until the last minute to finish my book. After forty-five books, you'd think I'd learn my lesson.

Blink.

Blink.

And finally, to my readers. Those who encourage me to write books about other characters in a series who didn't get their HEA. I was reluctant, at first, to attempt Mari's story. But then I looked in the mirror and realized that I'm her age. And I'm single . . . and I'm not done. So why not Mari? I hope I've done her justice and that you enjoy her and James's story as much as I do.

Happy Reading,

Catherine

ABOUT THE AUTHOR

Photo Credit © Catherine Bybee

Catherine Bybee is the *New York Times*, *Wall Street Journal*, and *USA Today* bestselling author of forty-five novels that have collectively sold more than eleven million copies and have been translated into more than twenty languages. Raised in Washington state, Bybee moved to Southern California in the hope of becoming a movie star. After growing bored with waiting tables, she returned to school and became a registered nurse, spending most of her career in urban emergency rooms. She now writes full-time and has penned the Not Quite series, the Weekday Brides series, the Most Likely To series, the D'Angelos series, and the First Wives series, among others. For more information, visit www.catherinebybee.com.